# Knights Of The Wind

## *The Power of the Mage*

*R. B. Michaels*

ISBN: 978-1-95-163054-6

# About the Author

R. B. Michaels is a renowned fiction author who has recently published the book called *"The Knights of the Wind"* which focuses on an amazing story consisting of pre-historical creatures. The story about the knight and his battle against evil are one of its kind. R. B. Michaels has truly written a masterpiece, embedding his thoughts and imagination into his book and sharing it with the world.

# Preface

The world of *"The Knights of the Wind: The Power of the Mage"* is different as it has humans, elves, orcs, and dark creatures. This world is once again in danger, as it was a few centuries ago. A brave knight then beat the darkness, with the help of a great wizard. With the new evil on the rise, the world needs a new Knight of the Wind to defeat it. With the knight trial tournament taking place after four years, the king thinks he can unite the different cities with their separate Knight Orders.

However, what they are all missing is a wizard who has the acumen as Oracon the great; the famous wizard who defeated evil centuries ago. Can a boy who has barely turned into an adult keep a secret from his family, understand his mission, and still enjoy the pleasures of young love? You will learn these and other secrets and be ready to indulge in this fantastic series.

Although this story remains the journey of Jarrod as he goes through several tests and pressing situations, you need to keep an eye on Garren, Evie, and Leah as well. Don't forget to keep in mind how Dalimar operates, and you will have all the tidbits that you need to follow this engaging series that's all knights and mages. These are imaginary, but the setting of this series in the present, and you will not feel as if they are taking you to a time that you are not familiar with.

So, let's start reading this story where Jarrod is living with his brother Garren. He prefers to manage their family inn, instead of pursuing the illustrious career of a noble knight.

# Contents

About the Author................................................................*i*

Preface.............................................................................*ii*


Chapter 1 ............................................................................*1*

Chapter 2 .........................................................................*14*

Chapter 3 .........................................................................*22*

Chapter 4 .........................................................................*32*

Chapter 5 .........................................................................*42*

Chapter 6 .........................................................................*64*

Chapter 7 .........................................................................*82*

Chapter 8 .........................................................................*96*

Chapter 9 .......................................................................*125*

Chapter 10 .....................................................................*152*

Chapter 11 .....................................................................*174*

Chapter 12 .....................................................................*204*

Chapter 13 .....................................................................*248*

Chapter 14 .....................................................................*286*

Chapter 15 .....................................................................*314*

Chapter 16 .....................................................................*337*

Chapter 17 .....................................................................*368*

Chapter 18 .....................................................................*390*

Chapter 19 .....................................................................*418*

Chapter 20 .....................................................................*443*

Chapter 21 .....................................................................*468*

Chapter 22 .....................................................................*489*

Chapter 23 .....................................................................*515*

Chapter 24 .....................................................................*533*

Chapter 25 .....................................................................*553*

Page Left Blank Intentionally

# Chapter 1

Lankule Stromblade scanned the valley from a hill, overlooking the raging battle below. Next to him was his Silver dragon outfitted in his dragon chain mail. He watched as the legions of undead marched toward the knights, waiting to fight to the death for their homes and families. His eyes showed desperation, knowing they were hopelessly outnumbered, but he was also sure if he was going to die, then let it be like this. He proudly mounted up on the dragon and took the reins, as the dragon reared up on both legs let out a roar.

He spread his huge wings and leaped off the hillside moving fast toward the legions. Lankule could hear low rumble of cheers from the Knights of the realm as the Knight of the Wind was heading into battle rallying them to fight on. The dragon veered left and then shot straight down towards the enemy. Lankule yelled the knights' battle cry with his spear in hand and the dragon reins in the other. The cry was so loud that it hesitated the march of undead, who saw the fierce dragon heading their way.

They turned to face flames from the dragon that scorched column after column. The sheer power of his wings when he flew over caused the skeletal warriors to buckle apart. A Death Knight of Ovesgard and minion of Krometh appeared out of nowhere riding a Demon Dragon. The legendary dragon dwarfed Lankule's silver dragon and headed straight for them. Lankule sensed the danger and pulled the reins just as he was about to be snatched off the silver dragon.

He banked right then left and was clearly faster and more maneuverable than the giant beast. He moved up into the dark clouds, and the Death Knight screamed as they lost the dragon in the clouds. The silver dragon banked hard left and then straightened into a slow dive. This maneuver set them right behind the giant beast. Lankule readied his spear and thrust it into the Death knight just as the two collided together. The Death Knight yelled in agony as the blessed spear went through him and pierced the demon. Lankule struggled to hang on as their aerial dual caused them to tumble out of the sky, wings intertwined, claws slashed as the ground became ever closer, falling, falling...!

Jarrod awoke with a thud and a feared surprise, as he hit the floor with an *"Uhhg"*. His eyes snapped open as he realized he had fallen out of the bed. The dream caused him to feel like he was falling. He slowly raised up, trying to shake off the fear of falling out of the sky.

*"I have got to stop reading those Stromblade family history books. That dream seemed so real like I was there."*

He slowly got off the floor and got dressed thinking about the dream. He made his way to the parlor area of the old house and walked over to the window to gaze upon the sunrise.

Jarrod watched as the sun started to rise over the valley; glistening orange at first and then turning to a dull reddish orange. He was thinking of all the friends he had left behind recently at the school. He was not able to keep up with the physical tests of school, which were for the intense training for Knighthood, and every young man's dream of becoming one of the few *"Knights of the Wind"*. There had only been four in history to this point. These men were so brave and durable, they could command Dragons and call upon the great power of the wind at will. The Knight can summon forth a dragon from the Dragon Realm who would fight and die at his side.

*"Everyone's dream except mine"*, thought Jarrod to himself. *"I would be happy just running the Inn and having time to read and study history."*

He often thought of the magic of old and has been reading a lot about the magic arts since he left the training academy.

*"One day, I will travel to the ancient library located somewhere in the lands of the High Elves to see what other information I can find on a number of ancient topics."*

There have been tales that there is a secret city there that still harbored Elves, and in that city, there is the Library of Time. An ancient library with books stretching out time for over 2,000 years. Jarrod smiled at the thought of sitting in the great hall of the ancient library and reading about the days of old. Even better would be to see an Elf in person.

The Knights are the protectors of each city, and King Reordin lives in the capital Crystal City, which is on the Restenthor River about a three days ride to the North and East of Vallenwood. The city is not really made of crystal. Instead, the castle gleams from a rare stone used in the building of the castle. It makes it look like crystals are shimmering in the sun.

The order of the Crystal Knights has their own training academy and stronghold near the city. Many of their graduates go straight to the capital city to serve in the king's royal guard, as do the order of the White Knights right near the Cove, at the Greyborne Academy. While there is not much need for protection in the southern lands, the people fear what lies north and beyond the Black Gates of Talmiris.

This is where the Black Knights hail and owe their allegiance only to their black Lord, Valence, who is said to have magical powers and only lusts for gold and power. The lands beyond Idesport City are forbidden but are traveled sometimes by the fool-hearty, never to be seen again. There is talk sometimes in the tavern of evil spreading to South, but there have been no problems for decades, other than an occasional show of force from the North which happened around 15 years ago. A band of Orcs and Goblins attacked the city of Volshstein. A messenger was sent to the king, who leaped into action. King Reordin dispatched his Knights and sent them all running back to Drakenfur lands, and Volshstein was held.

*"What a story that was!"*

King Lantier was grateful, and now the Plains Knights from Volshstein participate every four years in the games. Lord Valence would not dare rise against King Reordin and the Knights, even without a Knight of the Wind.

Other strongholds in the land have their own leaders and even call themselves *"Kings of their lands"*. King Reordin holds the largest population and has the most potent military force including Knights, bowman, substantial infantry, and even a large band of Paladin Clerics which makes for a formidable army. The Realm also has a large fleet of military and supply ships to guard the Southern ports of entry.

The king believes all should have the choice of their own lands and heritage, even though he would like to unite all the strongholds under one king. He is always ready to help any city who asks for help. In this way, peace is kept in the land.

*"Thank goodness we have a good King, unlike Lord Valence who rules through force and tyranny."*

The village of Briar's Cove just outside Vallenwood is where Jarrod and his brother Garren Stromblade were both in training since they were five years old. They were twins but not identical. Garren is the bigger of the twins and stands nearly six and a half feet tall, weighing 240 lbs. of lean muscle.

He has long, dark brown hair and full features with dark eyes. Garren was the best in the school at all the physical tests. His big problem was his studies in which he often lacked interest, at best. Jarrod needs to help Garren all the time and motivate him to study. With only a few days before Garren's written tests and three full days of the trial games, Jarrod had a full plate. The inn duties and helping Garren with his studies took most of his time.

Jarrod was the best at studies and especially liked to study old magical themes. He read almost every night although he was very good with only one weapon, the bow and arrow. Jarrod just struggled with stamina because he was the smaller of the two brothers at merely 5'7" inches tall. He has sharp features with long blond hair and blue eyes, and he is a very handsome young man. He relished the idea of being better than his brother at something.

Jarrod enjoyed teasing his bigger brother about how bad he was with a bow. Realistically, Garren was pretty good with a bow, but Jarrod was that much better. He loved to read about the ancient times, the Great War, and the Knights of the Wind who saved the world. Back when there was a lot of magic, dragons, Elf-kind, and Dwarves; the entire world was united against one great evil. Now, there are only tales of Dwarves and Elf-kind from the occasional traveler who swears they saw one once.

He stood alone in the family room looking out the window, thinking to himself, *"What it must have been like to ride a dragon and stand beside an Elf."* He shook his head and shrugged off the thought, as he gazed into the back yard and down the path to the inn.

Jarrod thought more on his decision to leave school, he sat down and put his fists under his chin.

"*Am I really doing the right thing?*"

Master Olvin thought that he was not being rational. However, he loved the stories at the Traveler's Inn, owned and operated by his father, Hardin Stromblade. Now Jarrod runs the inn with the family's long-time friend, Ms. Frieda and her husband Riello. Hardin seemed proud to pass the Inn and tavern down to Jarrod because he had become quite good at the books and inventory.

Hardin knew he was getting old, but he was just as proud of Garren's accomplishments. Hardin was hoping that Garren makes it through the intense training to become a Knight just like his Uncle. Hardin was hurt by a runaway cart at an early age, so he always had a limp and could not compete for a chance to be a Knight. To see both his sons competing was quite a proud moment for Hardin. For him, it was now time for resting and fishing in the Vale River.

In fact, it was Jarrod, Ms. Frieda, and Riello who were running the whole inn and eatery. Jarrod was now just two months away from being out of school and still a full three weeks away from his 18th birthday. His father would still operate things a couple days a week and check on Jarrod's progress. Hardin would just go fishing and travel to nearby villages like High Bluff and Roxshun for supplies. It was mostly the locals who would frequent the Travelers Inn and tavern called Briar's Whiskey.

However, there was always the occasional traveler who wandered through the Cove. Ms. Frieda practically ran everything else anyway. She and her husband, Riello, were friends of the family for as long as Jarrod could remember. There were there ever since the twins' mother, Anidah, died when they were very young. Ms. Frieda would watch after them, and Riello would help as much as possible. They were like their grandparents. Ms. Frieda would run the tavern at night, while Jarrod worked in the kitchen and would correct the books in the office. Jarrod used this time as an excuse to study up on the history of the land.

If anyone got out of hand, Ms. Frieda would handle it most of the time but could call on Garren if needed. Garren was always there at night, talking and laughing with the folks. Even sneaking a drink every now and then. Garren loved to do that. His sheer size was enough to deter any bad things from happening. Plus, there was always a regular there that would step in to help if required.

This was a rare occurrence because other than an occasional traveler, everyone knew everyone there. Jarrod could not wait to get to the office tonight because it was Saturday night, and he would have even more time to read on Sunday. His father brought him a book from High Bluff titled The Swords of the Ancient Knights. He could not wait to read it tonight and the next day.

Vallenwood boasted the most exceptional training for the knights, the school of the White Knights was where the last Knight of the Wind came from and lived right here. Jarrod glanced at the massive picture of Lankule Stromblade, dressed in his Silver / White,

Knight of the Wind dragon scale plate mail, holding the reins of what appeared to be a White Dragon.

The broad sword above the mantle was the sword used in the Great War by Lankule Stromblade himself and had been used by every Stromblade Knight since. His father claimed that the sword was magic and was forged by the Elvin King Dersonyn I, using the mythical Sky Forge. Garren was so looking forward to getting the blade handed down to him when he graduated in a few weeks. Jarrod also hoped that his father would give the blade to Garren and smiled at the thought.

*"That is if he passes all the tests and wins the trial contest."*

Underneath the big picture were smaller sized pictures of all the Stromblades, who had become Knights including the last White Knight, Jarrod's Uncle Clayborn Stromblade. Uncle Clayborn died a few winters ago. The sword and main picture were given to Hardin by Clayborn's wife, Herrah. The pair had been handed down in the Stromblade family for nearly six hundred years. The picture still gave Jarrod chills as he met the gaze of Lankule's eyes and felt the pride of being a Stromblade.

Jarrod turned suddenly to the sword and stared at it. It seemed to gleam a bright light for a split second. Perhaps, it was the sun reflecting off the blade?

He shrugged, turned away, and started for the kitchen to make breakfast mumbling under his breath.

"*It is almost time to wake up Garren, you have a big day ahead of you*", as he smug snickered.

# Chapter 2

Jarrod started to make breakfast when he saw his father stagger out of the cold storage shed with an axe. He yelled out the window.

*"Father, you need some help?"* His father motioned his hand down and yelled back.

*"No, mind your business and make sure the books are right tonight, I will be checking them later. Going for some supplies!"* Jarrod looked perplexed and didn't understand why he was so angry.

*"I have not made a mistake so far."* Jarrod proudly announced to himself.

*"Sooooo, talking to your-self, are we, little brother?"* Startling Jarrod. Garren stomped in, chuckling to himself, and knowing it would bother his brother.

Jarrod scrunched his eyes and snapped back in a stern voice, *"I am not your little brother! I am the same age as you. You are just taller than me."*

*"I know, I know, I was just naggin at ya!"* Garren further added, *"What's wrong with father?"*

*"I don't know, I asked him if he needed help, and he said for me to mind my business."*

Exclaimed Jarrod with his hands in the air.

Garren laughed and said, *"Sounds like what I tell you all the time, Ahaaahaaa!"*

*"Very funny, Garren,"* Jarrod shook his head with disgust. *"Here, eat some breakfast!"*

Garren quickly grabbed the plate of food and with a smile to Jarrod, *"Thanks, little brother,"* chuckling under his breath as Jarrod walked to the other side of the room and turned with a sharp glance. Garren broke into a laugh and was pleased with himself. They finished breakfast and cleaned up, realizing that their father was not going to show up for breakfast.

*"Garren, I need you to fix the door to the tavern when you get a chance. It is about to come off the hinges."*

*"Okay, Jarrod. I will do it when I get back from school today. Are you going to help me with my tests?"* Garren begged as he asked the question.

Jarrod smiled a wry smile, *"I don't know! I am going to be really busy."*

*"OHhh, come On, Jarrod, don't be like that, you know I was just kidding you. You know I can't ..."* Jarrod shot a smile over to Garren who stopped in mid-sentence. They both paused and then laughed together.

Garren proclaimed, *"I knew you were just kidding me."*

They had their laugh together and then talked about the test strategy. Garren's big test was just one week away, and then it would be the trial games. Four grueling days of trial tests including, axe throwing, bow and arrow, the joust, hand to hand combat, sword fighting and the arrow defense. The inn will be filled for the games ceremony because this year, the winner will be picked to go straight to the King's guard. Garren gave a big pat on the back.

*"See you tonight, little brother!"* He said with a gleeful whisper, as he ran out the door laughing. Jarrod watched Garren get to the gate where he turned, and with a wave, he started off down the road. Jarrod continued to watch him head down the road, thinking at the same time.

"*One of these days!*" Then he went down to his secret room to read.

He stumbled on the secret room by accident a couple years earlier and spent some time, making it a small "*get away.*" The hole in the floor must have been a secret room many years ago, for what, he had no idea. He loved it because he could be alone. It was quiet, and he had trouble sleeping at night, anyway. The rest of the time, he spent studying or reading.

"*I cannot forget the time tonight.*" Jarrod thought to himself.

There had been more than one occasion that he had almost been late for work because he was so enthralled in his reading. He knew if he was late that his dad would never let him hear the end of that, and even worse, Garren! He rolled his eyes at the thought.

The room was small enough to be well lit by a few candles. The desk and chair he found down there made it a perfect sitting room. He even had a small cot where he could lie down if he wanted. The desk was clearly an antique and had all kinds of compartments and drawers. It was made of a dark wood he had never seen before, and the top was lined with books six feet across. The desk almost surrounded Jarrod when he sat down. He thought it would take both him and Garrett just to lift one side. However, the desk was very lite compared to the size. Jarrod had all the way till late afternoon before he had to be at the tavern, so he wanted to make the best of it. He sat down and opened a book and started to read aloud,

*"The swords of the knights in ancient times were made by……"*

Jarrod shifted his weight and moved to get more comfortable when he felt something with his knee under the desk.

*"What is this…?"*

There was a bump on the bottom side of the desk that was in the shape of a wooden toggle button.

*"I never noticed this before,"* Jarrod spoke softly to himself as he examined the button.

It didn't appear to be linked to anything at all. It was just there all by itself. He checked every compartment, and finally he had examined everything he could see.

*"I hope there is nothing bad going to happen,"* he thought aloud as he closed his eyes and pushed the button. Click! Jarrod's eyes blinked open, as it sounded like a door opening and sure enough, a hidden compartment opened in the desk. There before Jarrod, was the most beautiful book he had ever seen other than covered in dust. There were some ornate writings on the front in a language he could not read, and there was a scroll with it.

The book was made of leather and had a golden clasp on it. Jarrod was shaking with jubilance and could not for the life of him understand how he missed that button for the last two years. He lifted the book out of the compartment, and he blew the dust off. Jarrod laid the sealed scroll down on the desk and admired the wax seal made with some ancient crest with old crusty pressed wax.

It was in the shape of a shield with a massive tree in the middle and a sword above the crest. His gaze moved to the book and examined it. The clasp would not open no matter what he tried or how he tried to open it. The edges of the pages were hidden inside the book. The book was like a case hiding the pages within. He was careful not to break it. There is no telling how old or valuable the book was. The size of the book was massive, almost like a huge encyclopedia, but it weighed practically nothing. He estimated maybe the equivalent size to a 2,500-page volume. The ornate carvings on the front were duplicated in reverse on the back. Jarrod was indeed in awe at the book, and he stared at it for a half hour before he turned his attention to the scroll. Jarrod wondered should he break the seal and read the scroll or not? There was no way to know how old nor how long the scroll and the book had been inside that desk.

Jarrod sat over the scroll for a long time and finally concluded that he was not going to find out anything by starring at it. He picked the scroll up and gently broke the wax seal. It snapped and crumbled in his hands, and as soon as it snapped, a wind from seemingly nowhere blew out all the candles in the room. Jarrod felt an intense chill go over his body when seal broke to pieces, and he dropped to the ground in agony. His hands and legs hurt as he clutched his chest, his breath was taken from him. He could no longer breathe as the pain ran across him until he was about to pass out. He crumbled slowly to his knees and softly whispered to himself. *"This must be the end!"* Finally collapsing face first to the floor struggling to take one last breath. He slowly closed his eyes and faded into a deep coma-like sleep.

# Chapter 3

Dalimar awoke with a start and sat straight up from his sleep. A fierce and raging storm in the distance, throwing bolts of lightning and clashes of thunder that shook him to the bone.

*"What was that? I have not felt that shudder since seeing the face of Krometh."*

Dalimar shook his head as he slowly moved to the eating area.

*"No, it cannot be! He was banished, never to return. Is it possible he has found a way back to Yshanall?"*

Dalimar shook his head no and decided to meditate later. He had studied late into the night researching Oracon the Great, the greatest wizard to ever inhabit the land.

He was so powerful that during the Great War with the Knight of the Wind at his side, they were able to cast down the great evil one, Lord Krometh from this world, supposedly banished to another plane of existence never to return. Oracon's power consumed him, and he too was killed during the Great War, as he sacrificed his life to save the world. That area is now the Dead Lands beyond the great ice-capped mountains, north of Idesport City and into the ruins of Ovesgard. This is where Lord Krometh had his evil residence. It is said to be nothing but a barren wasteland where the very air is death to those who enter. Dalimar was always searching for a way to tap into Oracon's power. He whispered to himself, *"The Bracers of Power"*.

Oracon had the power to keep himself young and wielded great powers of magic, multiplied by the bracers. Dalimar quested to find the power of Oracon but had not succeeded to this point. Even the great, high Elvin king would not help Dalimar find the power. He told Dalimar that Oracon's power could not be controlled and would always lead to evil and destruction.

There were only three of his kind left, two being himself and Valence. There was also Tanin, who was Dalimar's student around 25 years ago. Tanin turned dark and tried to open the door to allow Krometh back into the world. Dalimar entrapped his body in a place where it would never be found. He shuttered at the thought of teaching him magic skills.

Tanin had found Krometh's book of death, and it is rumored that he found part of Oracon's power in the land of the Elves, which Dalimar thought to be ridiculous. The book rotted his soul into blackness and evil. Tanin left Dalimar with no choice.

*"I had to rid this land of Tanin because he had turned evil. It saddens me because Tanin was a good person in the beginning."*

Dalimar just shook his head in sadness, *"There is another worry in the land, and that is Valence. The leader of the black lands. I have been keeping an eye on him for years to make sure he does not get too powerful. So far, he has proven to be no match and only wields a small amount of magical power. He is a mere dabbler in the black arts,"* Dalimar smiled at this thought.

A more pressing issue rising in his mind was that Dalimar knew he would have to find his replacement and pass on his knowledge, so there would be another protector of the world.

*"I am getting too old for this work. Where do I begin to look? Who could possibly take my place? I will have to put my quest aside and find my replacement quite soon. Time marches on, and I hope this search does not bring me to the same result as the last time I searched for my replacement. Tanin was not a very good choice in the end, and I refuse to make the same mistake again."*

Mages have long lives because of their knowledge of time, which allows them to hibernate for years at a time. Dalimar goes into this state about every 10 years or so and has not been in hibernation for around 15 years since his own student tried to kill him. He shuttered at the thought of that because he woke from the last hibernation to find Tanin wanting to kill him. Dalimar himself is pushing the century mark although he barely looks 50 in any mirrors.

"If I could find Oracon's power, then I would be able to live as long as he did."

Oracon could make himself young again and was over three hundred years old when he died. There is a big difference in hibernation and being able to become young. Hibernation allows the mage to not age from the point that he hibernates, while Oracon could take years off his life at one time and become young again. He died before he could pass on his power to his student, Dremont, and then my teacher, Themous the White. Dalimar is tall, and a well built, man. He is 6'1" and has long grey hair and a long grey beard. He wears a grey cloak with a hood and carries a staff that has a claw grasping a clear stone at the top. This was handed down to him and was Oracon's staff. Some called him The Old Wandering Traveler! Dalimar thought the name was rather foolish but the folk of the land enjoyed the title, so he just let it stick.

Dalimar, being well known in the land as a seer and wanderer, knows that a Mage's life is not easy. Living alone in the keep of the Magi on the southern side of the ancient Dwarven City of Kall is a very solitary existence. The great Majestic Mountains to the East are the back-window view with the Majesty Lake in the front.

*"Ahh, the great Dwarven Stronghold. I will have to visit them one day, along with my Elvin friends,"* he

smiled with fond memories of his Dwarven and Elvish friends.

*"It has been 30 years since I visited the Dwarves and even longer since I visited my friend, the Elvin King. I wonder if King Wargton is still King of the Dwarven city, or if one of his nine children have taken the throne?"*

The dwarves also keep to themselves inside their great mountain home of Stoneforge Cavern, which is a vast underground labyrinth stronghold. Dalimar thought back of the great Dwarven halls with gold lined entryways and jeweled rooms. They feel that mankind is too greedy, and the Elves are too *"stuck up"* to deal with either of the races. Dalimar was amused at this thought, knowing the vast riches of the dwarven halls. Recently though, there have been some exciting trading between the outer sections near Volshstein, and they have even allowed a couple of dwarven families to start a forge there.

*"Things are looking up in this world."*

Dalimar lit his pipe after having something to eat and sat to contemplate the up and coming events. The new Knight's trials were going to be held this year at the White Knight's stronghold in the Vale.

*"Maybe it is time to make a visit this year to see what the competition is like."*

All the Knight classes will be represented, including the Black Knight's from the western Drakenfur lands. The Dark Knight Valence will try anyway to get the Black Knights into the King's guard. He would not risk open war, so he sends a representative batch of knights every four years to the next set of trials to graduate into Knighthood and try for the coveted prize into the royal guard.

There is always trouble when they show up. King Reordin allows this because he believes that one day, even the Black Knights will be a part of the world and prosper as part of his kingdom. The Black Knights' Lord must fend off a hoard of Orcs and Goblins from time to time. Lord Valence as he requires his minions to call him, even tries to control their feeble minds with his magic.

*"Hmmm, I wonder if that is what happened a few years ago when they marched on Volshstein?"*

Dalimar laughed at the idea even though Valence is strong-willed and could easily do this if he wished. There would have been an uprising if there was proof Valence had anything to do with it.

He blew a large smoke ring and then puffed a smaller one through the larger one. He smiled at the accomplishment. His thoughts moved from knights and the trials to the dream he had about Krometh. The Mage's vision as Dalimar calls it is not always accurate and can be from the past, present, or future. The wise mage scrutinizes each episode and then makes the correct determination. Krometh was not only a mighty Black Knight, but he was also a possessed Dark Wizard. He was always seeking a way to immortality and never-ending dominion over the world.

Krometh was so evil that he was possessed by a powerful demon that gave him immense power. He tried to be the supreme ruler but found out the power of Oracon the Great was even more than he could stand. Along with a Knight of the Wind, Krometh and his minions stood no chance. There have been a few who tried to follow him, but none have succeeded. Even in this time, there is Lord Valence who is ever seeking a way to bring Krometh back, but he lacks the power to do so. It would take the power of a dark lord and a dark mage to be able to open a door.

However, with the book of the evil mage, he might be able to do it. Dalimar convulsed at that thought.

*"Oh no, thought Dalimar!"*

Dalimar lowered his pipe and closed his eyes. The gift of future sight is the first power of a true Mage and something that his former student, Tanin, did not have. He had to use some kind of magic object to see the future, like a gem or an orb. A true Mage does not need to look in an object. Dalimar understood the power of sight that it is not always correct. It is the possible future and is never set in stone. It is just glimpses of what may happen and is tainted by reality.

A subject that Tanin could not understand. The key is to have the ability to separate the truth from the dream. He closed his eyes tighter as the dream came back to him. The evil Lord Krometh came to his thoughts, and he was torturing a young Elf girl. Suddenly, Dalimar remembered when he felt that startled awakening before. He snapped his eyes open and stood straight up. It was when Tanin found Krometh's book of the evil mage and tried to read it to open a gate and free Krometh upon the lands.

*"Who is this young, Elf girl?"*

Dalimar knew there were Elves still in the world, both High Elves and from the Woodland Realms. They keep to themselves away from the mankind world as the Dwarves.

*"I must meditate on this more! I cannot allow even the possibility of bringing Krometh's evil back to the world."*

Dalimar moved to his meditation room to gain more information about these happenings.

*"This could be the beginning of a new danger in the world, not only for all mankind but for all who share these lands. I must find my replacement and a new protector                                              soon.*

# Chapter 4

Jarrod stirred on the floor of the secret room in pitch black but said, *"what happened?"* as he got up and checked himself. Nothing was broken, no bruises, or scratches, he remembered the pain before he passed out.

*"What caused the pain?"*

He saw the scroll on the desk with the crumbled wax seal on the desk. Breaking the seal caused the pain. He wondered how long he had been passed out on the floor! Jarrod ran upstairs and opened the floor door into his room. The bright light of the day blinded him at first, but it did not take long to adjust at all. It was still sunshine outside but was getting cloudy out. He estimated that it was around 10am. Jarrod thought fearfully,

*"Still time to find out what happened and figure out how to read that book, or should I just put it back where I found it? No way, I must know what is in that book or at least the scroll. Perhaps the scroll will help me open it."*

He ran back down to the secret room and fumbled around in the dark to the desk and knocked the candle over on the desk spilling a bit of melted wax on the top of the desk. Jarrod set the candle upright, and as soon as he let go, the candle lit all by itself. He stopped with a surprised look on his face and slowly walked over to the next candle on the shelf. To his amazement, that one lit as soon as he reached for the candle.

*"Wow,"* he thought to himself. *"I wonder how I did that!"*

He walked to the last candle by the staircase and slowly reached for the candle, and again that one lit before he touched it. He starred at his hands and wondered if he had gained some evil power or was somehow touched with magic when he cracked the seal on the scroll. The thought caused fear to well up inside, as he walked over to the desk and took a seat with the scroll in front of him, seal broken and lying on the desk. Jarrod stared at the broken pieces of the seal, afraid to touch it again.

*"I cannot be afraid, I have to see what is on that scroll. It might hold the key to opening this book."*

Jarrod was building up his courage. He reached for the scroll and moved some of the broken seal pieces.

*"Hmmm, no pain this time."*

He slowly picked up the scroll and started to unwind it. He was astonished to see it was blank.

*"Seriously? Nothing on this scroll?"*

He turned it over and held it to the light, and nothing was there. Jarrod remembered tales of magical writing that could only be seen under specific circumstances or magic tomes like speaking an ancient elvish word or only under a particular moonlight can the words be seen.

*"Unreal, how am I going to figure this out?"*

Jarrod loved puzzles and riddles. He could always figure them out, but he knew this one was not going to be easy.

*"Let's try fire! I don't want to burn the entire scroll but let me see what happens if I burn the corner with the candle."*

He slowly moved the corner of the scroll over the candle, and it did not catch fire. He slowly moved the whole parchment over the fire, and it would not light. There was no damage to the scroll at all.

Jarrod exclaimed with excitement, *"I knew this was magical! Now, let's try water!"*

The water just rolled off the parchment and did not soak in.

*"Okay. How about the earth!"*

He gathered up some dirt and spread it on the scroll. Nothing happened! The dust just fell off the scroll. Jarrod thought what would happen if he ripped it. He tried to tear the parchment, and it would not rip.

*"Dammit!"* He cursed out loud.

There is a full moon the night after Garren's final exam. Maybe I can talk him into going out to the lake and see if the full moon will show something on the scroll. Jarrod rolled the scroll up and placed the book and the scroll back in the secret compartment of the desk.

But this world has two moons, and they are only full together in the night sky every odd year, and only one month out of the year in the hottest month. This will happen this year, so maybe that is the key to this book.

He turned his attention to his newly found power. He blew out the candle on the desk and was able to light it by moving his hand toward the candle.

He practiced different ways of lighting the candle and eventually got to the point where he could light the candle just by looking at it with a wave from his finger.

*"This must have been given to me when I opened the seal on the scroll. I wonder what else I can do."*

Jarrod had read about magical spells and items of magic and knew that spells required memorization of incantation and some object or property used to cast them. He wondered if this scroll had released some kind of energy into his body. Jarrod felt extremely tired and a bit weak for some reason, as he yawned and stretched. He was not sure why he was so tired but decided to take a nap. Jarrod laid on the cot and closed his eyes, drifting off to sleep.

He was squirming around as he dreamed many short dream episodes. He wanted to wake up but could not awaken from the dream-like state. When one finished another immediately started. He felt everything from anger, to fear and hate, to love, happiness, and sadness all at the same time.

*"So many emotions, I need to wake up!"*

Jarrod struggled to wake up and still could not. He dreamed of a girl who was being tortured by a man in black armor with a horned helmet and ornate carvings on the breastplate. The armor was so dark that it radiated a dark purple haze around the wearer. Jarrod wanted to kill him and was filled with hatred and anger, but also feared the masked being. The demon-like person looked at Jarrod with red glowing eyes and laughed as he shouted.

*"Now watch her die!"* in a low growling voice.

The masked figure raised his sword, and Jarrod screamed out.

"NOooo" and closed his eyes tight as the sword thrust downward toward the girl. Jarrod felt his eyes open and saw the girl gasp a last breath whispering something in a soft voice. He could not hear what she said, and the dream faded with evil laughter in the background.

The next dream started with Jarrod at the inn. Jarrod was breathing heavy from the last dream, and he looked around the room. He finally heard Ms. Frieda.

"*Jarrod...JARROD*" He was startled around to see her standing there, asking.

"*Are you okay, Son? Time to get busy! It's going to be a packed house tonight.*"

She turned and walked off as Jarrod nodded and then whispered.

"*Am I really here? This is so real.*"

Just then, the door slung open and broke off the hinges which startled him. It was Garren being his usual and boisterous self.

"*Hello, everyone.*" Garren shouted with a big wave.

He opened the door so hard that it fell off the hinges and landed on the floor with a loud thump. "*Oops,*" Garren said sarcastically laughing.

Ms. Frieda hollered at Garren and took to hitting him with a broom.

"*You clumsy OAF! Now get that door put back on the hinges. Don't you know how to enter without breaking everything in sight?*" Garren cowardly blocked the broom thumps with his arms and hands with a totally surprised look on his face.

"*Sorry, Ms. Frieda!*"

"*You should be sorry you big, loud walking tree! I will not stand for this, coming in here, breaking things I've worked hard to keep up.*" She muttered as she walked off to the kitchen, yelling back, "*I'll beat you to a stump, till you understand that you cannot break other peoples' things!*"

All Garren could do was pick up the door and start placing it back on the hinges. Whispering, "*Sorr-ryy, Geesh, I'm sorry. I'll fix it, I'll get it fixed!*"

"*I heard that, and you better fix it quickly, before the crowd starts to arrive!*"

She yelled back at Garren. Jarrod was now laughing hysterically at big ole Garren, cowering down to the little old woman like that. It was hilarious to watch him get humbled, as the dream faded off, and a new dream started.

This one was about a young dark-haired girl who had her back to him the entire dream. She told him that she had fallen in love with him, and he had these strong feelings for her as well. However, she knew he could not stay. Jarrod wanted the dream to continue.

*"Stay where? What does she look like?"* Jarrod reached to turn her around, and the dream faded into a new dream.

He was standing with Garren near the waters' edge of what looked like the river crossing near their house.

*"Garren?"*

Jarrod shouted. Just as a giant wolf-like creature attacked Garren, and he was helpless to help. Garren fended the creature off bashing it in the head with his fist. The animal ran off into the forest as Garren looked over to Jarrod, falling to the ground with a helpless look on his face. Jarrod tried to get to him, and the more he tried to get closer, the further away Garren was. The dream faded away as he felt the sadness of losing his brother.

Jarrod suddenly woke from his dream-like state. He sat up on the bed and grasped his chest as his heart was pounding.

*"Thank the gods, it was just a dream."*

He intensely thought about what had just happened. The dreams were vivid and were about things that he did not understand, people he did not know, and even creatures he had never heard of or seen before. All this was happening like he was a person watching the events unfold in front of him. The feelings were so intense that he thought he was there, while these things were happening.

"What time is it? I have to be at the inn by this afternoon to early evening."

Jarrod quickly went up to the first floor of the old house and saw that he was not too late. He looked out the window and saw Ms. Frieda heading to the inn. She always got there a couple of hours early, so he realized that nothing had been missed, and he was feeling pretty good. Even though the dreams he experienced were a bit disturbing, he shrugged them off as just strange, bad dreams and went to get ready for work duties at the inn.

# Chapter 5

Jarrod got ready and headed for the inn arriving a full hour early. He opened the door and walked in to find Ms. Frieda sitting at a table enjoying a sandwich. He scanned the room and went into deep thought about the dreams he had earlier today.

*"Jarrod...JARROD!"* Ms. Frieda barked at Jarrod.

He turned and said, *"Good afternoon,"* and half-heartedly smiled with a weak voice.

*"What's wrong hon? Are you feeling okay today?"* She said with concern.

Jarrod looked back and managed to say with some hesitation.

*"I'm not sure today, Ms. Frieda. Oh, I will be alright."*

She noticed his skin and hair had a different tint to it, and he strangely looked different to her. Ms. Frieda got a determined look on her face and scrunched her eyes as she stood and walked toward the back room of the Inn. She turned to Jarrod, who was still standing there.

*"Come with me, it is time for you to know the truth!"*

Jarrod looked puzzled back at her. *"About what?"*

She turned with a still and forced look, *"About who you are, come."*

She motioned him into the room while opening the door. Jarrod hesitantly moved forward, but the lure of knowledge was too much for him. He quickened his pace as he strode into the room. Ms. Frieda followed him into the room and shut the door.

She started by pouring him a glass of juice, *"Sit down, Jarrod. I have a story to tell you, and you must listen with an open mind and do not let your emotions take command over you."*

Jarrod questioning looked on. *"What is this all about?"*

As he sat down at the table. Ms. Frieda slapped the glass on the table.

*"This is serious about you, and I do not appreciate your sarcastic candor about it back at me. You have been feeling something recently, some changes, perhaps...Yes?"* Ms. Frieda asked inquisitively.

Jarrod nodded yes in confirmation as he got up from the table. *"I'm sorry for my unkind expression, but I was just curious, how did you know?"* Jarrod asked with hardened concern.

*"I have always known this day would come."* Ms. Frieda sadly whispered as Jarrod sat back down. He listened intently as she started to spin the tale.

*"Your mother had a special gift. She could find specific components for spellcasters and ingredients for alchemy, many clerics use in healing. She went on many collection quests to sell these ingredients with your father before your father was hurt on one of the quests."*

*"But I thought..."* Jarrod started to say.

Ms. Frieda snapped back, which stopped Jarrod in midsentence. *"Listen! Do not talk! This is hard enough for me. When I am finished, all your questions will be answered."*

*"Okay,"* Jarrod reluctantly stated.

*"You didn't really believe your father was hurt by a runaway horse cart, did you?"*

Jarrod only nodded another reluctant yes, fearing her wrath if he talked. She laughed at the thought as she turned serious again, and her voice became just a whisper.

"*Wrong, your father was hurt in a battle that killed your mother. She was my best friend, and I swore as she was lying on her death bed that I would bring you this message, which is what she wanted. Your father was against it all along and did not want to tell you. That is why he left this morning because he knew, I was going to tell you soon if the "change" started, and he did not want to be here when you found out the truth of things. It may impact the rest of your life.*"

Ms. Frieda looked back at Jarrod, "*You are not who you think you are. You are changing, look at your skin tone, your hair and eyes are changing. I know you already feel these things within.*" Jarrod clutched his chest and nodded yes again. He hung his head and looked up with his eyes to Ms. Frieda, "*Truthfully, I have always known I was different.*"

Ms. Frieda reached for his chin and lifted him up, "*You don't know the half of it, and I am about to tell you everything. Just remember, this is not your fault! Your father and mother love you, and always will.*"

The old woman started again, *"You are not a Stromblade by blood relation. You were adopted by your mother, Anida, and your father, Hardin. Your real mother told your adopting mother these things would happen around your 18th birthday. Your body would go through a change. Anida and I discussed how to tell you this many times. You are half Elf! Your mother was an Elvin Princess, and your real father was a man. We were not told who he was or where he was.*

*That will be for you to find out later if you wish. You were more human looking when young, but now you are almost 18 years old, and your body will start to change. It is happening now, and you will turn more Elf as the years pass. Hardin and Anida, along with one of the clerics from the outer realm, stumbled on a dying Elf woman with paternal twin babies. A girl and a boy, both were alive. They tried to save the Elvin woman.*

*In the end, she succumbed to her wounds but not before Anida promised to take you and raise you as her own because she already had a recent baby boy, Garren, and you could be easily explained as a twin. The cleric Erin took the baby girl, and they never saw*

*Erin or the little girl again. Hardin and Anida loved you as their own.*

*Again, NEVER forget that, Jarrod! I love you, too, just as if you were my own."* As she moved closer and put her hands on his shoulders, comforting him.

*"You will have some time before you fully change, and you will have to decide whether to leave on your own or stay here. There is no wrong decision for you. We all hope that you will stay, but we understand if you leave. Every man must find his own destiny, and yours is even grander than most.*

*Garren knows nothing of this as your changes are quite subtle right now. I would think about this and won't tell him until you have made your decision. Garren has a lot of things to worry about right now with his tests and then the trial games. I am here for you if you need anything, Jarrod."* She hugged him and started to cry.

*"Don't cry Ms. Frieda, I am grateful that you told me, and I thank you as well. I can now understand why I have always felt a bit different than everyone else."* As he hugged her back tightly. Jarrod was shocked at this

whole thing but was excited to find out more, and now the future for him was not set. He was strangely exhilarated by this, as they walked towards the door.

*"Wait,"* motioned Frieda, *"I have something for you here from your real mother. Her name was Sarahsasyl. In the three days Anida knew her, she called her Sarah, for short. She was originally from the land of the High Elves, making her way through the mountain passes of Tamreal with her two young ones when she was attacked by a band of Orcs. None of the beasts survived the battle with her, but she had been mortally wounded when Anida and Harden happened close by."* Frieda unlocked a closet door and then opened a hidden door that contained several items. She grabbed something from the closet and locked both doors.

*"Here Jarrod, this is for you from your real mother, Sarah. Anida wanted you to have it."* It was a journal and was sealed with a golden clasp.

*"I have never opened it, and I probably couldn't read it even if I did. I promised Anida you would have it. There may be some information about your real*

*father and your twin sister in there.*" Jarrod hesitated but took the book.

"*Thank you, Frieda. I will always remember you and your generosity.*"

"*You better!*" She sniffled and snapped a smile with a smack on the shoulder.

"*Put that thing up, and let's get ready for our crowd tonight. You will have plenty of time to digest and read it tomorrow.*"

Jarrod smiled, "*Yes, it's time to get ready. Should be a good night,*" as they walked and chatted together into the inn area.

Jarrod was busy, doing work, trying to keep his mind off everything he was told by Ms. Frieda. All the problems he had growing up from being smaller and a bit weaker than everyone else was all too clear now and made perfect sense to him. What he was struggling with, was the sudden shock of all this now.

"*Why now?*" he kept thinking to his self. "*Why did they not tell me, until now? I guess I cannot dwell on that as they were just trying to protect me from the knowledge.*"

Jarrod looked around and was thinking heavily about the journal and wanted to read it now, but he knew that he had to keep busy for tonight. He probably couldn't read the language anyway because he could not even understand the cover. People were starting to come into the eating and drinking hall now. This building had both an eating and drinking bar atmosphere, as well as about 20 full-sized rooms upstairs for the weary travelers. There were also about 20 more rooms attached to the same floor, but they were a bit smaller and cheaper in price. The entire hall could feed up to 150 people, and if you include the bar and outside table area, there was room for around 350 people, and that would be full capacity.

The turnover would be near 1,000 tonight flowing into the street. Local Knights, as well as the guard factions that patrol the areas for any who may have ideas of mischief. Harsh penalties for anyone caught stealing from others, fighting, or involved in more violent crimes. There really have not been any issues for years because of the harsh penalties and enforcement of any criminal activity. It is mainly just an old-fashioned good time with folks eating, drinking, and being merry. Tonight's menu by Ms. Frieda, Riello, and their helper, Darrin, who had been around this facility for years, included a beef stew with potatoes, carrots, and peas with a homemade light gravy. It was served with fresh bread baked in the stone ovens and plenty of locally brewed mead and wine to go around. Ms. Frieda even made her specialty blackberry wine that will quickly sell out. They only had this vast amount of people during the trial games week once every four years. This year, they were expecting the largest crowd ever because all eight Knight Factions will be here with around 200 to 300 people with each faction.

Not to mention all the people that come to watch, including the King's court this year. The small town of Vallenwood and Briar's Cove population will grow from a mere 700 people to close to 10000 because of all who come to watch the famous, trial games.

People will park their food and trinket carts and pitch their canvasses from Briar's Cove all the way to Vallenwood and beyond. There will be horses and equipment for sale to clothes, hats, and waving flags for all the factions. Last time, there were almost 5000 people at the games, and the stadium holds up to 10000 people. Many more can watch from the surrounding hills from afar. This year, it will be expected to swell to over-capacity and standing room only because of the King's Court being present. Any chance to see the King and Queen, and their court is a big draw for the area. This will bring monetary fortunes like no other for the people, and they are excited to be a part of this great time in the kingdom. Jarrod was looking around at how many were there already tonight, seeing faces he had never seen before in wonderment, as the crowd had already surpassed a typical crowded night.

When suddenly, Jarrod saw outside as if he were looking through a window, as Garren rode up and hopped off his horse. He threw the reins over the standstill pole and made his way to the front of the Inn. Garren flung open the door, and it flew off the hinges to the floor with a loud THUD, as dust flew into the air.

"*Hey, everybody...Ooops,*" said Garren, embarrassed at breaking the door.

The entire crowd went silent, as Garren quickly moved to pick up the door and saw Ms. Frieda heading his way with anger. Now the crowd was starting to laugh a bit as Ms. Frieda lit into Garren. She hollered at Garren and took to hitting him with a broom.

*"You clumsy OAF! Now get that door put back on the hinges. Don't you know how to enter, without breaking everything in sight?"* Garren was blocking the broom thumps with his arms and hands with a totally shocked look on his face.

*"Sorry, Ms. Frieda!"*

*"You should be sorry you big, loud walking tree! I will not stand for this, come in here breaking things I've worked hard to keep up. I'll beat you to a stump, till you understand that you cannot break other peoples' things!"* All Garren could do was pick up the door and start placing it back on the hinges. Whispering,

*"Sorr-ryy, Geesh, I'm sorry. I'll fix it, I'll get it fixed!"*

Jarrod looked in utter disbelief as he watched the whole thing unfold. The old woman hollered back, but no one could hear what she said because the crowd was cheering and roaring with laughter. Garren took it all in stride and put the door back on the hinges. No one else could have picked that giant door up by themselves. Garren just laughed with the crowd, and everyone was having a great time with Garren, as he had a knack for turning things into a great big joke. Not to mention that he loved all the attention too.

*"Exactly as I dreamed it!"*

Jarrod stood in amazement with an uneasy feeling of Deja-Vu. Jarrod flashed back to the rest of the vivid dreams, wondering if any of these were as real as this one, he lowered his head and turned toward the office area.

*"What is happening to me? Is this part of the change Ms. Frieda was talking about, or is this something else?"*

Jarrod adjourned to the office where he could think alone for a bit. He thought hard about all he had been told and sat in the dark room thinking, where he could just hear the laughter from the other room.

*"Ms. Frieda is right, I should not tell Garren about all this until after the games next week. What I can tell him is about the new book I found and show the secret compartment I found in the desk. I need to focus on his studies, so he can pass the written exams. Otherwise, he will not be able to compete in the games next week. I must quit feeling sorry for myself and help Garren!"*

Jarrod stood up with determination and walked back to the bar area. As he came into the room, *"There he is!"* announced Garren, as he hid the large mug of mead he had just downed.

"Hey, Jarrod, come over, and let's have a talk!"

Garren winked at some of the crowd standing nearby.

Jarrod smiled and sarcastically muttered.

*"You should be getting ready to study for your test and not out drinking again!"*

As he scrunched his eyes and looked serious at Jarrod, *"drinking again?" Jarrod asked.*

*"Huh, Who?"* Garren questioned.

The crowd broke into laughter again with cheers for Jarrod not falling for another one of Garren's tricks.

The crowd shouted… "*Ohhhhh, Busted*" and "*Who's the fool now? Haaaa, Haaa.*"

Garren realized he'd been caught and quickly put his finger to his lips.

"*Shhhhhh, you want Ms. Frieda to catch me? She'll skin me alive this time.*"

The crowd roared again as Jarrod motioned for Garren to follow him. He turned back to the crowd.

"*Well, I'll be back in a few guys, save me a round. Shhhhh!*"

Laughter rang out again as they chastised Garren.

"*Follow brother, puppy dog,*" "*Jarrod has the goods on you now, Garren.*" "*Hey Garren, got to go sweep the stable?*" "*Ahaaa, haaaaa!*" Everyone was having a good time.

They were throwing lines like that as Jarrod led the way to the office. Garren just looked back and shrugged back at them, then held his arms out like he was in a mummy in a trance and hissed "*Yesssss Massssterrrrr!*"

Walking crooked with his arms straight out, looking back at the crowd with a huge grin. Again, the crowd roared with delight. Garren lowered his arms and let out a huge laugh as he thoroughly enjoyed the last word again.

Once in the office, Jarrod turned with his arms folded, staring at Garren while he closed the door blowing his friends a sarcastic kiss, as they roared again. Garren turned around, still enjoying the laughter.

He saw Jarrod's stern looking face and threw his arms up.

*"What? You got to lighten up brother. It's all in fun, Geesh!"*

*"That's the problem, Garren! You play too much when there are other important things for you to be doing. I have found something important, and I wanted to tell you what I found."*

Garren looked back and moved over to the office desk and sat down.

*"Oooh, I am all ears, what did you find?"*

Jarrod moved to the other side and turned to look at Garren.

*"Well, what did you find?"*

Garren was poised with excitement.

Jarrod leaned forward and whispered, *"A book!"*

Garren leaned back and put his hands on his head, "*A what?*"

Jarrod repeated, "*A book!*" a little louder this time.

Garren burst into laughter, "*This is what you drug me in here for; to tell me you found a book? I should've known. That is all you do other than work in this place, you read books.*"

Garren turned half serious back to Jarrod and pointed at him, "*You got to get out of here for some fun. Once I get finished with next week, we are going fishing. You are about to lose your mind.*"

Jarrod looked back and sarcastically noted, "*Are you finished? So, I can explain this a bit to you?*"

Garren understood Jarrod's tone and reluctantly gave in, "*Alright, tell me about this book!*" Jarrod looked back, perplexed, "*That's what is wrong. I can't open it. It is locked with a golden clasp. I found it in a hidden compartment in that old desk. The book has some ancient writing on it, and it had a scroll with it. When I opened the scroll, it had no writing on it. I couldn't burn it, soak it, or rip it in half. Very strange! What do you think?*"

Garren immediately spoke up with a shrug, *"You are the scholar! How should I know? Perhaps it is just garbage, and nothing is there to be read anyway."*

Jarrod shook his head, *"Oh no, there is something very weird about this book. I was thinking about taking it to the elders and see if they know anything about it. Then I thought maybe it is some kind of ruin from ancient times and can only be read by moonlight? Do you want to check it out after your tests, and we can go fishing, too?"*

Garren raised up and said that he would like that very much.

*"A good relaxing night on the shore of the lake after all this nonsense is over would be good for us both."*

Jarrod smiled at that and noted with hand held out to Garren, *"Deal?"*

Garren shook his brother's hand and patted him on the back, *"Good then. Now that's settled, let's get back to the party."*

Jarrod gave him a sharp look and answered.

*"Oh no, no, it is time you went to the house and relaxed. We have a lot of studying to do tomorrow to get you ready for those tests."*

Garren dismissed Jarrod's comment as he hurried back to the bar with a wave, *"Okay, brother. Just one more drink, and I will end it for the night."*

Jarrod rolled his eyes, knowing that Garren was not going to quit. *"I'm waking you up early, Garren."*

*"Ok...Ok, I will get up, promise!"*

Jarrod went back to working with the inventory and helping with the cleanup, as it was starting to get late. He wondered if he should have said anything else about what happened then thought better of it. It would just be best not to worry Garren with anything right now. He continued into the night and noticed they were getting low on some supplies, especially mead and homebrew. He went down to the cellar and inventoried the supplies there and found that there would probably be enough supplies for a couple more days when his father would return.

Ms. Frieda told him that they were going to open for dinner tomorrow because of the big crowd tonight.

They usually closed on the 7<sup>th</sup> day because that is the stock up day, but after tonight's crowd and knowing that more will be coming here for the trials, it would just be crazy not to open. She did let Jarrod have the night off since they were just going to be open from dusk till about 10pm for dinner. Then back open the next day for breakfast, lunch, and dinner all week, and into the following weekend.

Jarrod went back into the bar area after cleanup and all his book and inventory work, to check on Garren. Garren was nowhere to be found.

"*Wow,*" Jarrod thought to himself impressed that Garren was gone. He really did leave. "*He is finally making the right decision.*"

Jarrod worked with old Darrin to stock up the bar and food for tomorrow night. Then he went and got his journal and some other items to take back to the house, waiting for the last of the drunks to leave for the night. Ms. Frieda was already sending them out the door, and it was pushing past 2 am. The night seemed to fly by working with Darrin and Ms. Frieda.

Riello was there helping with stocks, and he had one of the young Torbin boys to help as well. He was only 13 and also studying at the academy in the intermediate level of his training. They were finished with training till the next semester, and Jaylor would help till he goes back. Jarrod was glad to have his help, and he told him he had done an excellent job that night. Jarrod finished his office duties and was ready to head out when Ms. Frieda peeked in.

*"Goodnight Jarrod. You relax some tomorrow and don't worry about the inn. We got it, and I will see you on Monday when your father should be back from the supply run."*

Jarrod walked to the door with Ms. Frieda, *"Thanks, I have a lot of thinking to do, and I need to help Garren with his studies."*

She gave him a hug, *"So much on your plate right now. No need to worry about things, the right answer will come to you in time."*

Jarrod headed down the street to his house, thinking while walking how he was not even tired. Probably the long nap he had taken after, opening the scroll had helped. He thought about not really being a Stromblade, and how he should be sad about all of this. Strangely, he was not sad at all. He was the exact opposite, almost exhilarated about the thought of being part Elf. Jarrod chuckled a bit.

*"Well, I always wondered what it would be like to see an actual Elf! What kind of changes both physical and mental am I going to endure?"*

Jarrod looked up, and he was instinctively opening the door to the house.

*"First thing I am going to do is to check on Garren and try to read this journal."*

# Chapter 6

Jarrod moved quietly through the house, passing through the main hall and into the entryway, which led to the lower bedrooms. He crept past his room and to the next room that was Garren's and opened the door. Garren was sound asleep snoring as usual. Jarrod quietly laughed and then closed the door. He headed to the study and down the floor hatch into his secret room. He raised his hands, and all the candles lit in the room.

*"That was fun, I'm getting good at that."*

Jarrod was amused at his new ability and reeled with a new strange feeling, looking at the candles. This was not something he felt before and was not sure he liked it. The feeling was like being invincible and proud to be that. He shook off the feeling and pulled out the Journal. The cover was written in Elvin language, and he was astonished that he could not read it earlier, but now he could.

*"Wow, I can read this! I was thinking I would need to learn this language somehow, but I can read it just*

*like I was always able to.*" The top cover was ornately decorated and read.

"*The Journal of the Princess.*"

Jarrod sat down at the desk and opened his secret compartment. He retrieved the scroll and the book and set them all beside each other.

"*Figures, I still can't read or open this book. I will have to see about it later.*"

He pushed the scroll and the book aside and opened the journal clasp. Jarrod thumbed through the book and realized that there were over 100 years of journal entries providing a history of where she came from all the way to her death right at 17 years ago. It meant that Jarrod was approximately one year old when she went on this journey. Jarrod scrolled all the way to the back of the book, and there was one entry there with many pages left.

The entry read;

*I leave this to you, my son, but do not wear this ring until you have decided what direction life is taking you. Beware of this ring, as it will try to control your mind, and if your father is still alive, it will call to him, and he will come for it and you. The ring is part of a great magical power and will provide an easy path to darkness.*

*Good luck, my son. Love, your Mother.*

Jarrod looked up for a moment and thought out loud.

*"What Ring? What is she talking about?"*

He flipped the pages forward through the last passage, looking for traces or a clue of what she was talking about there. Toward the end of the journal, the pages were cut out in a perfect square and inside was a golden ring with ornate carvings. Jarrod's eyes widened as he lifted the ring out of the hidden pocket and gazed at the ring.

He kept staring at it and admired its beauty, as it changed from gold to a deep silver and purple color and back to gold. Jarrod opened one of his desk drawers and pulled out a small leather pouch and emptied its contents into the drawer. He slowly placed the ring in the pouch heading his mother's words.

"I should research this ring before I wear it."

He pulled the strings tight with determination and placed the pouch back in the book. He had to press it into place, but it fitted nice and snug. Jarrod flipped back to the beginning and started to read the entries:

### Month of Thane, Day 11 of Year 367

Today is my birthday at age 50 Elvin years. My father is now 402 years of life and will live to over 1000 years. His father was 1205 years old when he died and lived through the Great Wars. In fact, he was there at the battle of end times and reigned triumphantly.

There was a grand celebration today because I am also a twin. My brother and I went out to the forge today to witness the making of Elvin swords and armor. The new style of forging created by the forge masters was beautiful. My brother was outfitted today with his royal armor. He was very proud of the new armor and is waiting anxiously for his sword to be completed. We had a grand birthday celebration for us. We had a wonderful time today.

I will be honored to accept the new position as Princess Sarahasyl for all the lands. I take this honor for the people of the High Elves and of this great city, as "keeper of the relics and history." I started this journal today to keep a record of all my activities from this day forth, as I am now the second heir to the throne. One day, my two younger brothers will be of age, and they too will be in the line of succession.

My brother, Dersonyn the III, will now be Prince of the lands and was honored as Captain of the great High Elvin army. He is also the first heir to the throne and announced his engagement at the celebration today to the lovely Iirelyn. She is a wonderful Elvin woman and will make a great queen one day.

### Month of Thane, Day 12 of Year 367

Today, I went to the ancient library and researched the history of our lands. I spent most of the day there and happened to run into an old friend. My best friend from school. It was nice to see her again, and we spent some good time together.

I am receiving many requests from suiters to gain my attention and affections. Unfortunately for them, I am not interested in any of them. I have no plans to date or to be married anytime soon.

Jarrod read for what seemed like hours. The entries went like this up to a point where he really started to pay attention. Jarrod's mother was a high princess and second heir to the throne. The day of the solstice, a stranger came to the great Elvin city and sought an audience with his majesty and King of the High Elves, Sarahasyl's father, King Dersonyn II. The stranger was captured by the Elvin guard and was placed in the custody of the King's guard. He was a Human, and there had not been a Human in this land for many years. His name was Tanin, and he said he was a student of the great wizard Dalimar. Dalimar was a friend and ally to the King and was the last person to be allowed into the High Elf City, many years ago.

The King enjoyed Dalimar's company, and they shared many stories. He decided to hear the stranger in respect to Dalimar. The stranger assured him that he just wanted to use the ancient library as Dalimar did when he came. The king was amused at the young man's attempts to befriend him, and after a week of hearing his pleas, he was allowed access to the ancient library with his own room in the palace. Sarahasyl was assigned to be his guide to the city by King's orders. She was to watch over all he did and report to the King.

Sarahasyl obliged the King and kept a wary eye on the handsome stranger. At first, she was worried that the stranger had some other intentions, but after spending a week with him, she started to drop her guard and became captivated by him. The king was actually beginning to like the young fellow and was spending even more time, telling stories of old. The young Tanin listened intently and looked at the King as a mentor. He presented nothing but good manners and spoke highly of Dalimar, his teacher. The king became more and more trustworthy as time went on, and even Sarahasyl was becoming attracted to him, hoping to see him and even going out of her way to make sure she saw him.

He asked her to go for a walk down the river path to the ancient high waterfall, and she was excited to go with him. There, he told her that she was the most beautiful women he had ever seen, and he was falling for her. She was so enthralled by this, she melted in his arms, and they had their first kiss. It was so passionate that it took her breath away, and she realized she was falling madly in love with Tanin. She had been waiting for this and now understood that he was the love of her life. However, the King would never allow such a union.

It was not conducive to the royal family tradition and was also not a normal position for a student Mage because it was believed that love in this manner could not be controlled and was a path to evil. High Elves were strictly forbidden to marry outside the kinship of the Elves, although it had happened in the past but never to a royal family member.

They agreed to keep their love for each other a secret but knew that both were going to have to give up their lives for the other. She would never be allowed to stay in the King's court, and he would probably have to give up the idea of being a Mage even though he strangely seemed to gain in power every day. Days turned to weeks and weeks turned into months when she learned she was now with a child.

They had been successful in hiding their relationship from the King, Queen, and Sara's older brother. However, the younger brother caught them together and was sworn to silence. To his credit, he never let on that he knew. The time was getting close to where the child she was carrying would be known. Sarahasyl and Tanin were going to have to tell the King and Queen. However, Tanin told her to stay quiet because he had a plan that was going to reveal itself soon. He promised her they would be together and that he was going to find Oracon's power to stay young, so they could live a long life together. She naively obeyed Tanin, and she watched as his power grew. The King's trust grew so much in Tanin that one day the King let Tanin see the Ring of Power. The ring was part of Oracon's Bracers of the Magi. During the Great War with Krometh, Oracon unleashed such power that he destroyed Krometh and himself that left a scar on the land forever.

There was nothing left but the bracers. The bracers were forged by King Dersonyn I and Oracon together, at the Elvin sky forge to destroy Krometh during the time of evil. The ring and bracelet magically merge together to Oracon's hand, which multiplied the Mage's power by a hundredfold. Oracon's mind was quite powerful, and he was wise well beyond years, so controlling the ring and bracelet was easy for him. Dersonyn took the bracer apart and separated them, vowing never to allow this kind of power again to reign upon the land.

The ring he kept here at the Elvin Palace, the bracelet was given to the King of the Woodland Realm, and the Magical Chain that combined them together was given to the Knight of the Wind who rode to the Dragon Isles and hid it somewhere on the island. Then the bracers were stricken from the records. Not even Dalimar knew of the magical bracers, and this was the key to Oracon's great power.

Oracon created a magic book that gave the reader extra powers, benefits, and the secret to both the bracers and long life, but Krometh also created a book of power which was hidden by the Elvin elders. The book was so evil that it granted such a dark force that made the reader almost invincible.

Sarahasyl's father promised that one day he would tell Dalimar but since his student was here, why not inform him to let Dalimar know. It had been so long since Dalimar made the trip to see the King. The King was not very happy about that and longed for his excellent sense of humor and news of the other realms. Sarahasyl realized Tanin seized upon that and sensed the King's longing for outside news.

He eagerly provided all the information the King wanted, whether real or not. Tanin asked to see the ring every day and to let him wear it, even if just for a few moments. The King declined until one day he finally relented. That was the day everything changed, Tanin's heart and soul were being wrenched apart. Tanin wore the ring and felt the immense power the ring imbued to him.

He was more and more reluctant to give the ring back to the King every day. The King sensed this and refused to provide him with the ring, and Tanin had to be restrained by the guards. The King told them to release him as he was a friend, still wanting and needing an outside friend.

The ring had twisted his mind and will call to him because the ring wants to be worn, it wants to...*to kill.* If we keep him away from the ring, his mind will return, thought the king as he dismissed the angry behavior from Tanin. As the weeks went on, it became apparent to her that Tanin was losing reality. He was spending more and more time in the ancient library and found something in the old crypt of the ancients.

Tanin was hiding something from her. She later discovered it was a black book that Tanin kept close to him all the time. His mind was becoming even more twisted and wanted to leave, but the King cast a magic bind spell on Tanin keeping him within the city walls until the spell wore off, or the caster was killed. Sarahasyl began to mistrust Tanin and was heartbroken.

She went to her father and told him everything about her pregnancy, and what Tanin had promised her. The King was furious and ordered that Tanin be locked up and the keys to be thrown away. But she pleaded for the King to have mercy on him and just to send him away because she loved him.

She told the King that she will leave as soon as the baby was born, and therefore, was able to spare embarrassment to the royal family. Reluctantly, the king agreed and ordered Tanin to stay here to watch the birth of his child, but then he was to leave and be forever banished from the lands. She agreed to the

King's wishes and realized that she would have to leave as well before the child's first birthday.

Tanin angrily agreed as he really had no choice in the matter. For the final weeks of her pregnancy, Tanin read this book incessantly and told Sarahasyl he had no time for her and that he was leaving soon, alone. Tanin could not resist the call of the ring and was tormented even to Sarahasyl. He was blinded by the power, and her love no longer meant anything to him. She was now crying in sorrow every single day and wished he had never come to the city.

The day came for the birth of the child, and the mid-doctor and physician notified her that she was bearing twins. Tanin was forced to watch the birth of the children and was clearly disgusted as he was to remain here imprisoned for another year as she gained strength enough, and the children became healthy enough to travel.

He promised to use this time to increase his own power and to unleash it upon the King and the people of the land. She was now spying on Tanin and informing her father what Tanin was up to. The King did not trust his own daughter, and the months passed as her sadness deepened for all she was about to lose. Her family, her love, and all she held dear. The only happiness she got was from her younger brother and now her children, who she loved dearly. Sarahasyl knew she was to be banished by her father from the kingdom along with Tanin. She knew she had to stop Tanin from what he was about to do but also feared for her children's safety. The people were already rumoring that she had fallen ill or even died because she had been locked away in the palace for so long. Her other two brothers had nothing to do with her, and she was all alone to contemplate what was inevitable.

Sarahasyl came up with her own plan. She was going to steal the ring herself, put it in the journal and sneak away before Tanin could get it and unleash a magical rage upon this city and lands. Without the ring, Tanin was not strong enough to defeat the King of the Elves alone. Elvin magic is a very formidable ally when used in defense of the Elvin City, especially the King. Sarahasyl snuck to the Kings Chamber hall and used a potion, which made her invisible to the eyes of the guards. She went to the hidden wall and opened the door. There on the shelf was the golden box that held the ring.

She stole the golden ring, packed the twins Jarryden and Evesshyl, and went to the outskirt room where she met her younger brother. She asked her little brother who she was very close with, to help her sneak away. Her brother would not let her go alone with the children, as the journey would be long and dangerous. Isranyd was the youngest of the family, but he was very skilled with sword and bow, and so he would not take a "no" for an answer and traveled with her. He promised to journey back once she was safe, and their father would forgive him. Sarahasyl, on the other hand, knew she would never be forgiven.

They left late at night and a full week before her banishment was publicly announced in shame. Whatever happened to Tanin or her father, she wrote that she did not know. She can only assume the worst, and her twin brother is now King because he probably did not know of the ring. No one ever pursued her for the three weeks she was gone. Her younger brother was killed in the battle when they were attacked by a band of Orcs and Goblins, and she was mortally wounded as well. That is when she met Hardin and Anida who were so kind to her.

She missed and longed for that kindness after almost two years of mental torture and abandonment. She liked her new name, Sara, and wished that she had more time with them.

Note to my Son,

And I, Sarahasyl was honored to meet your new parents, as I was wounded too severely to live on. I am so thankful for them, and the woman who took your sister. Destiny is strange at times. You must not try to find your father, Tanin. I fear his mind was corrupted by the ring, and if he lives, he is too evil to be approached. Be warned that he will always be searching for the ring. Your sister, I left a journal just for her, and I only met her new mother once who seemed to be a very honorable woman.

Seek her out and reunite together, as she will seek you out when she reads her journal. Only together, you can hope to stand against Tanin if he lives. You children are the keys to a door that will unleash evil on the Elvin lands. You must stop it if your destiny is to take that path. The decision to live against the evil that awaits or to choose the life you were given with your new parents is up to you. Your destiny can only be written by you. Beware of the search, as they will do anything to obtain the ring from you. Stay hidden if you must, to survive. Goodbye, my son. I proudly await you in the afterlife.

Jarrod looked up and closed the journal. His eyes were wide open, and his mind was clear.

*"The ring must not be found, but I must find a way to use it,"* Jarrod thought.

*"If I could stop the evil from rising, then I will do it. I know that I have some power as my father was a Mage, and I am an Elf as well. So, there is some hidden power inside, and I will need to learn how to control it. I have a sister and a father out there somewhere to find. So many questions: What happened to my real father? What happened to the Elvin King? After Garren's trials, I will tell him who I am and let Hardin and Garren know that I am leaving to find who I am, and*

*what my destiny is. I will promise to return one day to see them.*"

Jarrod suddenly remembered that he had to get Garren up and help him study for his tests. He rushed up the secret hatch and into the back room, looking outside to see that it was still dark out. He looked at the timepiece, and it was only close to 4 am. He read and absorbed all of that reading in only a couple of hours and was still not tired. Jarrod went back to the room and set his journal on the desk. He put the book and scroll back in the compartment and shut the door.

His thoughts raced back to the ring again, and his mind wandered to the powers that might be achieved. He opened the journal and just stared at the ring, thinking about how it must have been to wield that power. He reached for the pouch that was still tucked into the journal cut out......!

# Chapter 7

Dalimar hurried to his meditation room, which was also connected to the hibernation chamber. He had been contemplating a hibernation for a couple of years but wanted to make sure things in the land were stable and that he had a new student in training for some time before he started his next hibernation. During his last hibernation, he sent his student Tanin on a journey to the ancient Elvin library to study. He awakened just in time to be able to face Tanin, who was ready to kill his master.

A Mage has a watcher that is created before hibernation or before he leaves for study or questing to protect the Mage, the grounds, or both. The creature is a servant to the creator only and can defend the Mage and his grounds to death. The spectral creature can be killed, but it would take specialized knowledge of the beast to do so. If the creature is killed, then the wizard cannot awaken without another wizard or cleric of immense power and will most likely die. Only the creature can wake the Mage from his slumber easily.

The meditation room was a special place in his castle and consisted of a large centerpiece that looked like a tall table with a hole in the center with four clawed hands out to about a foot above, facing inward. Out of the round area, there was a glowing light that had a large turning globe floating in mid-air, just above the outstretched clawed hands.

There were some sitting chairs that had ornately carved designs along with a desk, another flat decorative table, and some ancient wall hangings, sconces, and paintings. The room was dark, with only the soft light from the table illuminating the room. Dalimar sat back in the chair, facing the orb and closed his eyes. It had been a long time since he used this room and meditation method. He mainly used his mage dream powers to see things.

He drifted into a deep state of meditation and started to see some very concerning images right off. As he drifted deeper into the meditative state, he saw a ring of power, Tanin, an Elf Princess, King Dersonyn, and Sarahasyl. I know this woman and met her in the High Elf court. She is in pain and heartache. King Dersonyn, my friend, is in sorrow and agony. The betrayal of Tanin caused the young Elvin girl came to him vividly again. She was killed by some evil looking person dressed in Krometh's armor. This is not Krometh but is someone who has his armor. This cannot be Valence, as I do not recognize this place. Then Valence came to his mind, ordering the black armored being to find the boy.

*"What boy? Who is this black Krometh armored individual that has amassed so much power?"* Then an image of the Hunter Dorgs, evil wolf-like creatures who can imitate other beings and can transform themselves into any living creature. These creatures have not been seen since the time of Oracon and Krometh.

They serve a master and hunt their prey endlessly, using their abilities to trap and kill their prey. They are also used to serve whatever their master wants. Then an image of magical bracers. Oracon the great had magical bracers that gave him extreme powers. They are the key to Oracon's power. Back to King Dersonyn, but this was not the king he knew, and there was Oracon the Great by his side.

They were forging the bracers in the great magical Elvin forges while casting magical spells into the bracers. The images faded into the current King Dersonyn, and this time, it was the familiar face that he knew. It was his friend and ally. *"Murdered? I just watched King Dersonyn II murdered by a now black cloaked person and the King's children, murdered, by who?"*

Dalimar's heart sank as he saw who killed them, *"Tanin!"* Dalimar whispered out loud as he saw Tanin with an evil smile on his face when he killed the Elvin family. Seeking them out one at a time and snuffing out their lives. He shook in anger as Tanin turned with his piercing eyes, *"And you are next, Old Man."*

Then he saw Tanin angered, as he could not find what he was looking for.

*"The ring, where is it?"*

He cursed as he realized who took it. The image faded with Tanin swearing to kill the woman thief.

*"The ring is mine, and I shall have it."*

The next images were of Sarahasyl, in a panic as she snatched up a child and then went to another child and was carrying two children out of the palace through a secret tunnel to her waiting brother and a carriage. She turned with tears of sorrow, as the image faded with the carriage heading out the hidden gates.

The next image was of a young boy playing by a river with a dog and another child. They were wrestling around and playing as young children do. A man was fishing on the bank as they frolicked in the grass, giving the boys a great big smile as the larger of them rolled into the river with a huge splash while the other laughed uncontrollably.

*"I know this man, thought Dalimar. Hardin Stromblade, kin to the last Knight of the Wind! He owns an inn down near Vallenwood. I visited there many years ago before these children were born, and Hardin was much younger. In fact, Hardin was in training in the academy when I visited there."*

The image faded with Dalimar seeing the smaller of the two clearly with his blond hair flowing in the wind. He waved at someone on the river, and Dalimar's eyes slowly moved to a figure standing in the middle of the river. It was shimmering in and out over the water. This was a strange ethereal character in the shape of a woman. His eyes met the eyes of the being, and the figure turned to, "*Sarahasyl.*" She waved with a smile back at the boy on the river bank and faded into a mist and was gone. Dalimar turned quickly to see the boy again, but the trance already moved to a new scape.

This one was of Sarahasyl in childbirth with Tanin standing in the room with her, but off to the side with guards on either side of him. Instead of participating, he was loathing at the woman in pain. Dalimar could see his thoughts.

"*I have to get the ring and leave this place.*"

First was a baby boy and then a baby girl, and the dreamlike picture faded into mist.

"This was why she left in such a hurry. They were in danger, and she knew it."

The next shadowed state was long in developing through Dalimar's mind but burst into the sight of a young knight in training. He was strong and fast, as he defeated trainee after trainee. Another young man much smaller but quick-witted came into view, and the two were studying as if the smaller was the teacher, and the larger was the student. Dalimar heard them refer to each other as, brothers. They were laughing and enjoying their time together. The one with blond hair turned to face Dalimar, and he recognized them both. They were the two young boys on the bank of the river. The blond-haired young man raised his head, then his hair turned color, and his eyes became a dark red. A deep, evil grin came over him, and his face changed to, *"Tanin,"* again Dalimar was shaken to his soul at the sight he had just seen.

The image faded, and a new focused dream came to him. This one was of an evil looking man reading a book and practicing dark arts, casting into a swirling purple haze in a wall. Dalimar saw that it was Valence on one knee, head down, with one hand raised. He spoke in a familiar voice.

*"I know the secret, my dark prince. I have her in the dungeon, ready for your sacrifice, my lord. I shall turn her to darkness, or she will die!"*

The haze spoke with an evil low grumble that shook the very floor.

"*You must find the boy, only when they both are turned to darkness or dead, will you have the power to open this gate and release me to my destiny. You shall be well rewarded, my servant!*" The man spoke again to the shifting haze.

"*It shall be done as you command. My armored mage is searching for the boy right now.*"

The voice answered, "*Bring the boy to me, alive! And you,*" the dark voice from the haze growled! The black-clad servant jumped to his feet and drew a sword as he looked at Dalimar. A clawed pointed finger came through the purple swirling mist, as he hissed.

"*Stay out of this, Old Wandering Fool, or you too shall meet your fate!*"

A blinding flash which caused Dalimar to flinch in his meditative state. For the first time in a long time, Dalimar felt the sensation of fear! Not for him but for the world because he knew who that was, "*Krometh!*"

Dalimar's eyes snapped open, as he forced himself out of the deep shady trance. This is how the images come during meditation. They come in streams and are mixed with past, the present, and future events. Once the mage is deep in the meditation, the explanations for each event come through as well. Scrutiny must be given to these "visions" because only past events seen can be verified as absolute truth. The rest are present and future events, which may or may not be accurate. Dalimar felt it was his responsibility as protector of the lands, to make sure that evil would not pass into this world.

"*I have to find out what is going on. These images were disturbing, to say the least. How have they evaded me for so many years?*" Dalimar thought deep into his dreamlike state.

"*There must be some great and dark power behind the scenes to keep this from me. How has Krometh partially entered this world? Ahh, the dark mage Valence was talking about it. Or it could be that in time, these things are revealed when there is a need for action. I must hide my thoughts from the evil lurking from the dark world.*"

Dalimar stood up with defiance and headed to his study.

*"I will get to the bottom of this and quickly, the young boy is the key to this. I must get to those children before Valence, or that dark mage finds him."*

Dalimar decided to do some research in his library, call Light-Shadow, his trusty steed, create the watcher, and take a good rest before preparations to leave were made. He knew it was at least a full three days ride to the Vallenwood area, and then he had to pinpoint where the young boys were without letting anyone know about his intentions. Even with his trusty friend, Light-Shadow, the quickest and most magnificent horse in all the land, it was a long journey.

*"Once I find the young man, I will try to convince him to come along with me to the Elders, and let them decide the proper course of action for the danger that is all too near. That too will take some convincing."*

Dalimar made it to the study and started looking for books on the Great War, books about Krometh and even some ancient ones he had on Elvin magic and the Sky Forges of the Elvin Realm. Dalimar read the ancient codices of the Elvin royal seals. These were given to him by King Dersonyn II, many years ago.

Although he had scrolled through them, he never sat down and studied their contents in detail.

Dalimar found a section in one of the manuals that talked about Oracon the Great and had a very good picture of him, as he was about to battle one on one with Krometh. The picture showed the familiar black armor-clad Krometh and Oracon standing with his staff in one hand and his other hand raised in the air, unleashing mighty power from the sky. Off in the distance was the Knight of the Wind riding a dragon, fighting legions of evil creatures on the ground from above, including trolls, goblins, orcs, and hunter dorgs.

There were even pictures of undead skeletons and skeletal warriors, as well as Krometh's minions, the Death Knights of Ovesgard. These were the three kings of the upper lands that swore allegiance to Krometh in life and serve him still in death. They are mighty beings, and Dalimar found out that these undead kings were banished when Krometh was defeated. This means that their power was linked to him. Dalimar's attention turned back to Oracon's picture and his outstretched hands.

*"There it is,"* The Bracers of Power magically attached to his right hand which made Oracon's hand look almost like an entity itself.

*"The bracers are alive, with an energy-like force. I can see it in Oracon's eyes. Why is there no mention of these in any of the books or even the codices? Wait a minute, there are some lines here that have been magically hidden. I can feel the presence of magic on these lines."*

Dalimar closed his eyes and began to speak in the magical tongue. The lines and pages reappeared as Dalimar removed the cursed rune placed on the codex. Dalimar sighed as he opened his eyes wide and started to read.

*"There is much more here."*

He went to the beginning of the codex and started to read. The book was over half again the size as when he began to read. He went through the other codices and found that all twelve books were set upon by a cursed rune. Dalimar looked up from his reading with a heavy heart.

*"Things are even graver than I originally thought by reading what is here. I must hurry and make my preparations, as I have awakened from my own darkness."*

He was angered at the thought of these things being kept from him and wanted to know why. This made him feel like he had been asleep to the real world.

*"Curse my own naivety! I will never be in the dark again, what a fool I have been!"*

Dalimar made his preparations, went to the grand courtyard of the castle and called forth Light-Shadow, his trusty steed who immediately came to his side. He was a large white horse with a long mane. He reached forward to pet the horse along his neck and muscled shoulders.

*"We have a long journey, my friend, and I need your strength once again."* The horse raised up on two legs and let out the horses wail as if to say, *"I am ready!"*

*"Easy, easy Light-Shadow. We will be on the road after a good night's sleep."*

Dalimar calmed the horse and then proceeded to pack with some rations and a couple of his spell books, some magic potions, weapons, and packed one codex from the Elvin sky forges. He also cast some protection spells on his own self, so that his activities could not be seen by dark forces.

His final preparation was to call to the underworld to bring his *"Watcher"* back to existence, to keep an eye on the castle while he was gone. Dalimar finished his preparations and laid down to rest from a long busy day before his journey begins on the morrow.

# Chapter 8

Jarrod reached for the pouch with the ring inside. Just as he was about to grab the ring, he closed his eyes.

*"No, I am not ready to make this step. I have my life here at the inn. I have Garren and my family to consider before I make this decision."*

He closed the book and stood up, pacing back and forth in the room, thinking about all that had transpired in a short amount of time. He had so many questions. Trying to formulate a plan to move forward in his life was undoubtedly challenging. While thinking, he postulated that this was too big for him at this point in his life. He liked his life, where he was, and thought hard about how to tell Garren.

He kept asking questions to himself. What would happen when Hardin got home? He thought about the inn and all the people he knew and grew up with, in the town of Briar's Cove. How could he just walk away? The world doesn't need me to save it from itself, does it? I am such a small part of this, why should I jump in with both feet? Do I owe the world some penance because my real father did not do what was right? So many questions to answer! He was wearing a path in the lower floor, pacing back and forth from his desk to the wall and back. My father is Hardin, and he is the only father I have known. My real sister, is she even alive? What are these new powers I have, and how should I use them?

After much consideration and no answers, Jarrod decided that he would just continue with life here, and let "*fate*" decide what he was to do. Right now, he had to help Garren with his tests and trial games that were upcoming, starting tomorrow.

Jarrod put up his journal on one of the bookshelves that have now developed into an extensive library of books and articles that he had collected or found over the years. Some were given as gifts as well from family and friends, all knowing his love for reading. He made his way up to the kitchen area and started to make some breakfast, wondering all the while why he was not tired or feeling sleepy.

"*I must be in information overload right now.*"

He started to make some bacon and fresh eggs and was beginning to cut some fruit for the table when in busted Garren.

*"Smells good, Jarrod! How did you sleep?"*

Jarrod looked back with a surprised look on his face, *"I didn't, couldn't sleep, I mean."*

*"Why not, I thought you were getting tired last night? You feeling alright? You look a bit pale."* Jarrod turned, and half laughed with some sarcasm.

*"Thanks a lot, Garren, but I'm fine, don't worry about it."*

*"Oh, you're welcome. Glad to help you out, Ah Hah!"*

*"Real funny, Garren. You ready to study today?"* Garren reluctantly sighed.

*"Yeah, I guess so. Since we can't go fishing, can't go work out in the stadium, or go for a horseback ride!"* Garren was using his best pleading voice.

Jarrod brought a couple of plates and said, *"No, we are studying today. If you don't pass these written tests, you will not be able to compete in the trials next week."*

*"I know, I know."*

Garren held his head down, then popped up with a smile.

*"But let's eat, this smells really good, my brother. Can't study on an empty stomach."*

Jarrod smiled and sat down with his brother, while thoughts of all the fun times they had together growing up ran through his mind. After they ate and cleaned up, they went right to the study and hit the books. Jarrod poured over mathematics, science, the common language, history, geography, the courts and politics, social works and humanities, with the Yshanall order of the world. All morning long, they studied with Jarrod creating mock tests, flashcards, oral, and written answers. Jarrod was impressed that Garren was doing so well.

*"I think we should take a break."*

Jarrod noticed that his brother was getting a bit overwhelmed.

*"Thank the gods!"*

Garren said with his head sluggishly moving back and forth, letting Jarrod know his brain was fried.

Jarrod allowed Garren to take a two-hour break and then hit the books again until supper time.

*"I think we will stop here, you are ready Garren. I'm impressed how well you have done today."* Garren proudly looked up.

*"Well, thank you. I must admit I am nervous about the tests tomorrow. I want to do well enough to be picked for the trials."*

Jarrod put his hand on Garren's shoulder.

*"I have complete confidence in you, and I think you are going to do very well. Just try not to think too hard about the questions. Close your eyes, take a deep breath, and let your answers flow out just like you did today. I will be there with you all the way."*

*"Thanks, Jarrod, you are the best. You know, I couldn't ask for a better brother."*

Jarrod raised one eyebrow, *"OhhhhhKayy, you are making me uncomfortable now."* The two looked at each other, and both laughed hysterically. As they finished their laughter, Jarrod chimed in.

*"You should get a good night's sleep tonight. Don't even go to the inn tonight, please Garren!"* Garren looked back and said in a defiant voice.

*"You are right! I will not even go there tonight."*

Jarrod started to say something back but thought better of it because he was so surprised at his response.

*"Hmmm, Garren is finally growing up, I think."*

He has a full day of testing and then a day of picks from the elders for all the games and a practice day should he be picked for the trials. Lastly, there will be three days of trial games where all the best young knights will compete to see who is granted the King's grand guard prize.

The winner being chosen to join the White Knight guard for two years of training to become a Paladin Knight and a chance to be selected as a *"Knight of the Wind"* once the Paladin training is complete. There has been no Knight who has risen to that title since the Great War, and Lankule Stromblade was selected as the last one.

They filled the rest of the day with helping at the inn, restocking, and talking with friends as the town was already starting to see people arrive early for the games. Even the side of the road was beginning to fill up. Ms. Frieda was in a particularly good mood this day because the inn, stables, and eatery were overflowing with people. Garren did as he was asked, dismissed himself and waived to Jarrod goodnight, thanking him for all his help today.

*"Good luck, Garren."*

Garren kept walking and waived as he was heading to the house. Jarrod smiled and shook his head. He talked to Ms. Frieda, who told him to go on home tonight and come back in the morning. We will be ready for the end of the week and the trial games. Hardin will be in tomorrow with a carriage of supplies, and we will be busy for the rest of the week. Ms. Frieda told Jarrod to make sure he goes to watch Garren in the trials and noted that he would need all the support he can get. Jarrod was happy she said that because he really wanted to go watch the trial games and be there for Garren.

He left the inn about an hour after Garren and hurried to his secret room, to learn more from what he had found. He wanted to rest but did not feel tired at all. He was worried he would just fall out soon, so he was going to try and force some rest. After reading for a while, Jarrod laid down on the bed, cleared his mind, and closed his eyes.

Garren woke up to Jarrod walking into the room. It was early, and he was already feeling the tension of the test day.

*"Good morning, Garren. Are you ready for the test day?"*

Garren looked back as he was getting ready.

*"I suppose I am ready, I can't wait for this to be over. I want to get to the physical tests. I am definitely ready for those."*

*"That's why it's essential to score well on these tests. So, you will make it to the physical tests."* Jarrod chimed in.

*"Good point Jarrod, as usual!"* Garren agreed.

Jarrod moved out to the kitchen while Garren finished packing for the day. Jarrod made him a good lunch and wished him luck, as he headed with his pack to his horse for the ride into Vallenwood. Jarrod walked with him to the stable.

*"I will be at the inn and wait on father to get here with resupplies. Good luck today, Garren and try not to worry, just take,"* Garren interrupted,

*"I know, I know, take a deep breath and relax."* Jarrod smiled back and watched as Garren headed to the Academy.

Garren arrived early at the academy to see the practice field busy with knights from across the lands.

*"Hmmm, a good time to watch some of the competition before testing today."*

He looked on and saw the order of the Paladin Knights, already marking areas in the main arena for each of the orders. Ten factions were participating here this year which made it quite full, and he thought this was really going to be a challenge this year.

While there were Knights that graduate every year from the academies, these games were only held once every four years, so there are knights here from ages 18 to 22 years old, depending on when they turned 18 and graduated from their perspective orders. Garren would not be able to compete again until he was 22 since he is only just turning 18 in a couple of weeks and is probably the youngest of the competitors. If he doesn't make it through the testing, he would have two more tries at age 22 and then 26. After that, he cannot compete, and would either be assigned guard duty on one of the outposts or become one of the city guards for four years.

*"Yuk, I don't want that to happen."*

He tried to shake off that feeling and realized he had just put more pressure on himself. He glared on at the individual factions. Garren had an intense intuitive sight that allowed him to quickly view an opponents' actions and then determine a weakness in his fighting style. He watched the practice and went through the knight factions' list in his mind that were present and arriving. The Silver Knights from Thane City, The Bronze Knights from Lushayl and Lukome, the Copper Knights from Ayster Hall, The Knights of the Moon from Roark's City, The Plains Knights from Volshstein, The Knights of the Sun from Caspian and Osgillian, and last but certainly not least, the Black Knights from Idesport City. There were five selected from each faction order, and he was watching them practice with each other. Garren spoke out loud, as he watched from the fenced area leaning on a post,

*"That Bronze Knight over there looks like he is pretty tough."* His eyes shifted to the Black Knight area and noticed one that was moving with a sword very fast. He was sparring and parrying with another Black Knight when all of a sudden, the knight blocked a sword thrust and quickly spun around to smash the other on the shoulder with the flat of his sword. When the attacker bent down, he kicked him to the ground where he threw his hands up in defeat. The black-clad figure stopped and moved off to practice some more moves.

*"Wow, he is another one to watch closely."*

A soft but firm voice startled Garren from behind,

*"Gauging the competition?"*

Garren turned, surprised by the woman's voice.

*"That is my brother, Mathis."*

Garren's jaw dropped as he looked upon a young woman dressed in an ebony colored woman's breastplate that spread across her shoulders to points with a set of black armbands stretched down her arms to a fitted ebony skirt to her knees with leg bracers to her ebony boots. The center of the breastplate had an ornate design that was a shield with crossed swords with an eye in the center. Garren's eyes went over her with complete surprise because he had never seen a woman dressed in complete ebony body armor. She was the most beautiful woman he had ever seen. *"Cat got your tongue?"* She chuckled and threw a tease at him.

Garren turned away, finally managing to speak, *"Na...No, you just startled me is all."*

Garren tried to play off what he had just done like he wasn't even interested, but she pressed on.

*"You didn't answer my question. Are you checking out the competition?"*

Garren nodded and spoke back softly, as he looked across the field, hoping she didn't notice he had just eyed her whole body and was uneasy.

He didn't falter as he spoke gently to her.

*"It's good to study your opponents? Don't you think?"* As he turned back to her.

She turned her head and said, *"Yes, it is! Especially if you think it will gain you an advantage. What is your name?"*

Garren turned and faced her, realizing how small and frail looking she was compared to his size. She was barely tall enough to reach his chest, but there was something about her. She exhumed confidence, and with her ebony made sword sheath on her side, she looked as though she could handle herself well. Garren was captivated by her, and he answered back.

*"I am the one who is going to win this trial tournament. My name is Garren, and what is your name?"*

She glared back at Garren straight into his eyes, and he almost buckled with the look but held himself up as he was determined to stare back into her eyes. She backed off a bit.

*"That's a brazenly bold statement, considering the company you are going to be around in this*

*tournament. Why are you not practicing? Are you so good that you do not need to practice?"* Garren realized this was not going well, and in an instant, he changed his tactics. He noticed her weakness right away. She did not like someone who thought they were better than her. He stepped a bit forward.

"I hope you have not entered this tourney. I would hate to need you to come to my aid or worse, it would be quite embarrassing to be defeated by a woman. However, I would sure raise your hand in victory, and be damned proud to do so!"

She wheeled a quick smile with soft eyes looking back at him, surprised by Garren's sympathetic answer about the power of a woman.

*"Thank you for that,"* as she lowered her eyes, *"But I am not a participant in the tourney. Father would never allow me to enter. My brother is in it though, and be warned, he is very good, and he knows it. Sometimes he is a bit ruthless, though."*

Garren smiled at her and nodded, *"Well, that is not right. I think you would do very well, judging by the way you confidently carry yourself."*

She grinned and laughed a bit as she continued.

"*My name is Evie. I am part of the Black Knight faction and here to support my brother and the Black Knight Order.*"

Garren thought for a minute brushing off what she had just said, and then asked.

"*What are you doing later? I have a test to take but should be finished later this afternoon. You want to go for a walk, or just talk maybe?*"

She happily answered, "*Yes, that would be great. I was hoping you would ask.*"

She looked back quickly across the field, "*Oh, I have to go,*" and she stood up on her tippy toes and kissed Garren on the cheek. Quickly turning to walk away before he could do anything. He managed to utter, "*Okay, see you here at around five?*"

She turned, as she skip-walked backward, "*It's a date!*"

With another smile and a wave, she almost dropped him where he stood. Garren watched her walk away, still stunned and amazed by her. He turned and headed up to the academy for part one of his written tests. As he walked toward the great hall, all he could feel was the anticipation to see her again.

"*Concentrate, focus, Garren,*" Jarrod came to mind scolding him, "*You have tests to take as he slapped his face. Damn girl,*" he stated with a smirk look, then whispered, "*can't wait to see you later, Evie!*"

Garren entered the great hall and saw all the test applicants. Some of the Elders were walking around just as a loud voice boomed across the hall.

"*All who are taking the exams, please enter the study area, so the testing can begin.*"

He headed into the study where there were long tables set up with the tests all laid out. He looked around and saw his classmates and a couple others he knew, mouthing "*good luck*" to each other. The announcement and rules were read by one of the Elders, who was also the test proctor. He sat at the large desk located in the front of the room that over-looked all the tables and called out the names of all who called "*Present*" when their names were announced.

"This is a timed test. We will break for lunch, or you can continue until you finish the test, or time reaches 5 pm. At that time, all tests must be turned in, and no more work will be allowed. If you finish early, turn in your test here, and you will be excused until this time tomorrow for part two. Open your test books, sign your name at the top line, and begin!"

Garren started reading through questions, sighed loudly, and began his test. He went on slowly as he tried to stay focused on the questions and his answers. He couldn't help daydreaming every now and then about his encounter with the beautiful young girl. He would gather himself together and get back to the test each time.

Later in the morning, he noticed some were already finishing their tests. One of his friends looked back at Garren with a scowl and indifference on his face, turning his test in. Then promptly left the building. Garren was not sure how he could have finished so quickly, and then back to his test, dismissing it altogether. Garren took a break at lunch and quickly ate and drank with a bathroom break, and he went right back to the test room. Time started to fly by, as he became more aware of how many more questions he had left. The pressure was building while more and more were turning their tests in. Garren was now finished with the test, and there were only three left in the test room that was filled with around fifty earlier. He was also fully aware that only five would be chosen. There were about twenty minutes left before time was up, he got up and turned his test in. The Elder looked at him as he turned it in with grateful confidence.

Garren walked out into the hall and was greeted by his friends. The one who turned it in early told him that the test was too hard, and he totally bombed it. The others were all worried about how well they did. He agreed that it was a hard test, but he thought he might have at least passed it. If it was good enough to get through to the next part, he wasn't sure. He anxiously said farewell as he would see them on the morrow.

He came out of the building and looked down the path to the fenced practice area, where lo and behold! It was Evie waiting for him at the exact same spot, they had met earlier in the day. He smiled and waved at her as he walked toward her noticing her apparel. She had changed into a leather outfit with a tight shirt that had leather drawstrings she was about to bust out of, showing off her breasts that were perfectly proportioned to her body size. He noticed how her straight blonde hair was set to both sides with the front neatly braided back into a ponytail.

*"Fancy seeing you here?"*

Garren shouted with a great big smile on his face.

She didn't even hesitate an answer,

*"I see your pace quickened when you saw me. Did you think I wouldn't be here?"* Evie smiled back at him with a witty answer.

Garren thought for a second,

*"Well honestly, I wasn't sure but was hopeful."*

He grinned as he walked up to her and stopped. She gave him a great big hug and then said.

*"Well, now, you know! C'mon, let's go for a walk because I cannot stay out late."*

She reached for his hand, and he looked at her, giving his hand to her. They strolled together, holding hands, talking, and laughing together. She let go of his hand, wrapped her arm around his, while holding the same arm with her hand, walking closer where their bodies rubbed gently together with each step.

"*How did you do on your test?*" Evie asked as they stopped by the river walk.

"*Okay, I guess. I was thinking about you all day, so I was distracted.*"

They both laughed at that. Garren moved to sit on the fence and Evie backed into him and leaned with her head on his chest, as she let him wrap his big arms around her upper waist while she held his forearms. She looked up with a strange look on her face, Garren was again enamored by her beauty. She whispered softly to him,

"*I don't know what it is about you, but you make me feel....*" She stopped and looked back down.

"*Feel what?*" Garren asked with extreme curiosity.

This time she hesitated and choked out, "*Safe!*"

She pulled away from Garren and sadly announced with a faltering voice, "*I, I have to go.*"

Then she started to walk off, and Garren said with concern.

"*Wait, what's wrong?*"

She turned and was now quietly crying with tears slowly falling down her cheek.

*"Hold on, Come here."*

She stopped and waited for Garren. He wiped her tears away with his thumb and wrapped her up with a soft hug, kissed her on the cheek, and whispered back to her.

*"I can't let you leave like this, can we see each other tomorrow?"*

She pushed him away and sadly replied,

*"I will try to get free, promise. I will find you."*

She backed away looking at Garren, giving her a big wink, as she smiled and turned back toward the encampments. He stood and watched her till she was out of site. He reluctantly turned back toward the stables kicking the ground, walking slowly, and thinking about Evie. He had plenty of girlfriends in the past, but none had the effect she had on him in such a short amount of time, already longing to see her again. He pulled his horse out of the stable area and started by walking beside the horse and then hopped up with a slow trot back to the inn.

\*\*\*

Jarrod was thinking about Garren and how he was doing while working at the inn. Hardin came in the early afternoon, full of supplies. He met his father, who was trying to keep a strong face knowing that Ms. Frieda had her talk with Jarrod. Hardin knew Jarrod would want to talk, and after they unloaded all the supplies, Jarrod, Ms. Frieda and Hardin went into the office area. *"I suppose you want to talk about what happened to your family, and why we never told you the truth?"*

Jarrod thought for a minute,

*"No, I was thinking about how wonderful it was that you took me in and gave me a wonderful life."* Hardin gave Jarrod a big hug and told him that he was his son no matter what he decided to do and that he wanted Jarrod to stay on here at the inn. But, Hardin would support whatever decision he made. Whether to go off and pursue who he was or if he decided to stay in this town, Jarrod was a Stromblade, and no one could ever take that away.

They also discussed Garren, and how they were not going to tell him till after the testing and trials were finished. Then together, all of them would let Jarrod make his decision. They all hugged again and left it there. Jarrod stayed at the inn preparing the supplies and the books while Hardin walked back to the house. He was going again in the morning for more supplies.

Garren rode up to the inn, and it was already alive. Jarrod saw his brother heading toward the inn and made him a good plate of dinner and had it at the table when he walked in. The crowd cheered for Garren, as he waived to all in the entryway. He got pats on the back and hopes of good luck for the next test.

Jarrod looked his way.

*"Let's hear it! Tell me how grand you did today."*

Garren held his eyes down and shrugged,

*"I am not sure, brother, but at least I finished the test with a few minutes to spare. I guess we will see tomorrow."*

Jarrod boasted with confidence,

*"I am sure you did well. Now you should eat and head back to get some rest tonight."*

"*Yeah, I will definitely do that,*" Garren answered.

Jarrod raised one eyebrow. He quickly thought something was up with Garren and said,

"*That was unusual, I wonder what's bugging you? What's wrong, Garren? You have never agreed with me that fast before.*"

Garren looked up from his food and laughed,

"*You almost have a woman's intuition about you Jarrod, and that's pretty scary, just saying!*" They both laughed again and then Garren mentioned out of nowhere,

"*I met a beautiful girl today, and we went for a walk after the tests.*"

"*Really? Oh, for crying out loud, Garren, you must stay focused. You cannot be thinking about some girl you met with this test coming up. What's her name? Did you even get a name this time?*" Jarrod chuckled at his statement.

Garren looked up with solemn eyes,

"*Yes, her name is Eve. I think I really like her.*"

Jarrod knew this was different immediately,

*"Okay, Garren. Just try to stay focused on your tests."*

*"I know, and I will."*

Jarrod was now curious about this girl.

*"Where is she from?"*

Garren suddenly became all quiet and whispered almost weirdly,

*"She is from Idesport City, the land of the Black Knights."*

Jarrod shot him a concerned glance, and Garren looked up with pleading eyes to Jarrod, who was now sober as well.

*"She is not evil, Jarrod. I can feel how kind she is and wants to be, but something has a hold on her."* Garren defended.

*"Okay, Garren,"* Jarrod was talking calmly,

*"A hold? What does that mean?"*

Garren shrugged and told Jarrod he wasn't sure, but it may be nothing as they had just met.

Jarrod put his hand on his shoulder as he stood over Garren,

*"I will help you after the trials if I can."*

Garren looked up and smiled,

*"I know you would, but this one I will have to do on my own. I am going to bed brother, I will see you tomorrow."*

*"Alright, sleep well, and don't worry, it's going to be just fine."*

Jarrod watched as his brother headed to the house. He thought this might be the spark that makes Garren focus on these tests.

*"I will have to meet this one."*

Jarrod smiled at that and went back to work, finished, and went home.

*"I have got to get some sleep tonight if I can."*

He went straight to his room and tossed around for about an hour. He decided to go down to his reading room and see if that would make him tired. Jarrod sat down at the big desk and opened his journal to read. He closed his eyes and thought about some of the passages, and a vivid image appeared showing a huge wolf, growling and snarling in an attack stance. Just as the creature jumped, he opened his eyes.

He closed his eyes again, and this time, he saw a picture of a woman chained to a wall. She was slumped over, and though he tried to see her face, he could not. He only saw a glowing wall with a strange, dark armored hand exiting and pointing to the girl.

The picture faded, and the next image came to him. It was the site of a battlefield, no one was alive as he walked through an endless sea of the dead. Overhead was a creature flying toward him in the distance with a spectral-looking rider, who spoke to him as it was getting closer and closer.

*"Give us the ring!"*

Closer, closer, so close he could see the outstretched talons of the flying demon. Jarrod turned to run, looking behind him to see the creature about to snatch him off the ground. His eyes popped open so fast, it startled himself.

*"Okay, that was scary. This ring I have is a part of this whole thing. Why am I seeing such images? Are they real? I have got to try and understand this."*

He kept reading and heard a thud off in the distance in the house.

*"I wonder if that was Garren getting up. I hope he is going to focus on his final test today, instead of some cute girl he met. Humph, I think he would be more interested in her than getting his tests completed."*

He had a nice little howl about that and put his book down.

*"And no sleep again, how do I manage that? I am not even tired. Perhaps these are the changes that the journal talked about and what Ms. Frieda told me. I will have to research more about Elves at the academy and may even talk to one of the Elders."*

Jarrod came up early from the secret room after reading and seeing those insane visions all night. Still not understanding anything, only to find his brother gone already.

*"I thought I heard him get up and leave. He is finally doing something with all his strength, which is what I have been trying to teach him. He has done it on his own. Good luck today, brother,"* as he looked toward the academy.

Maybe I can help father get ready to go for supplies this morning, he thought to himself. Jarrod walked out to the stable area to find the carriage gone already.

*"Imagine that, as he threw his arms up. I am behind everyone this morning."*

Jarrod was amused at this for a minute because he is usually the one that had to get everyone motivated for the day, and here he was, the last one up and out. But then, he was kind of disgusted because it was as if he was already alone.

*"I have not even made up my mind yet on what I am going to do, and I am standing here all by myself!"*

He shrugged, oh well, back to reading for a bit and off to the inn. Tonight, is going to be another busy night.

# Chapter 9

Garren rode up quickly to the Academy and was a full three hours early, to see if he could talk with Evie in the morning. To his disappointment, she was not there.

*"Well, crap! I guess she didn't like me at all. I was so looking forward to seeing her again. Maybe she couldn't get away this morning. We don't even really know each other yet, so I should not worry about it."*

He started to pace back and forth from the river walk, which leads down to the Greyborne Lake all the way back to the horse stables.

*"I can't say I am not worrying about it now,"* as he laughed out loud.

*"I am wearing a trail in the ground from the stables to the river pathway."*

Garren gathered himself and went on up to the academy hall. Once inside, he found the same crowd there like yesterday. They hung out talking lightly and joking around until Elder Hansen came out to corral them all into the testing room.

*"When your name is called, please exit through the main hall. This means you did not make the final round of testing because your scores were too low."*

Master Hansen started calling names, and Garren was not expecting this. He held his fingers crossed and hoped for the best. Only the top twenty will continue to the next test. As he scanned the room and heard a couple of his friend's names called, he was sure after every name that he was next. There were no jeers or catcalls, and the only voice heard was of Master Hansen. The next name, and the next name, then the next and next. Garren was gaining some confidence.

Finally, Master Hansen announced that the next name would be the last, and the name was called after what seemed to Garren at least half an hour. But it wasn't, it was only a couple of minutes when the name was called. He made it to the final round of testing. He leaned back and put his hands on his head with a massive sigh of relief. Master Hansen scanned across the room,

*"Congratulations to all of you, and good luck on this next round. Remember, only the top five combined*

*scores in both the preliminaries held last week in the trials and the two rounds of testing will move on to the final trials, starting on this 4th day of Luna, which is four days away and will continue for three days. There will be two alternates selected, who will be the 6th and 7th selections from today's results. There are twenty-four of you left. Unfortunately, we will see the rest of you in four more years. The Grand Winner will be selected to the King's Guard, and training will begin to join the coveted Paladin Knight order and have the possibility to become a 'Knight of the Wind'".*

The ones that were left, all let out cheers and whistles for this opportunity. Elder Hansen continued after he raised his hands called for silence.

*"Settle down, quiet please, we will also pick a runner up this year at the King's request, who will immediately join the Crystal Nights of the Realm. The King has requested to have this, and we agreed. From now on, there will be two winners from the final trials. You have until 5 pm this day to finish this test, and the results will be announced tomorrow morning at 9 am. Everyone, be here at that time. The next day will be a*

*day of practice for the final five and two alternates if you choose to use that time. The trials will begin at 9:00 am the following day and go until we are down to the final 4 contestants. The final four will trial on the 6th day of Luna and will go until we have a clear winner and a runner up selection. There will be ten Knight Orders here, who have all already completed their testing with five competing in the trials from each faction. All this said you may now begin your test. Good luck, and may the gods be with you on your next journey into destiny."*

Master Hansen sat down, and all the test takers began the arduous tasks in these performance trials.

Again, time seemed to fly by as Garren continued his testing. He was clearly sweating with this test, focusing to the point of almost physical pain. He looked up, finishing the last question on his test and had time to go over answers before he turned the test in. He thought at first, he had missed a section because he finished with an hour still left on the time clock. He realized he had skipped lunch, which accounted for at least 30 minutes of the hour. He got up and turned his test in, and there were only about five or six students still taking the test. Master Hansen nodded to him as he took the test and put it on the completed pile. He hurried out of the hall and down toward the stable with a huge grin on his face because he was so happy this was over. His gaze came back to the stable and was stopped in his tracks. His heart jumped into his throat as standing there with one leg propped up on the side wall with her arms folded into her midsection was Evie. He started to move again toward her while she brandished a huge smile and moved forward to meet him.

*"Hey Garren, I was thinking about you all day today."*

She practically jumped into his arms and stopped him in the moment while planting her face to his. He picked her up and twirled her around as they hugged and passionately kissed. Garren gently set her down.

*"I thought you didn't like me when I got here this morning, and I didn't see you. I waited here for three hours, and when I didn't see you, I basically gave up."*

Her jaw dropped, *"What do you mean, gave up?"*

Garren stuttered and back peddled, "*I didn't mean it like that.*"

"*Okay, Garren. Well, I just thought you didn't need the distraction before your test, and perhaps you would concentrate harder.*"

Evie softened her gaze,

"*Sorry Garren, I wanted to be here, but I just couldn't get away. My brother knows something is up, and he was drilling me with questions. We cannot let this be known. If you can understand that, then only can we continue our relationship.*"

Evie turned her back to Garren,

"*If you cannot understand that we need to keep our relationship a secret for a while at least till these trials are completed, then I can leave now, and you can forget about me.*"

Garren gently took her arm and turned her back toward him, staring straight into her eyes.

"*I understand, and I agree. I promise to keep our secret safe with us. Promise on my honor!*"

As he put his hand over his heart and put up the three fingers of Knight Honor, which she completely understood.

She smiled at Garren, and again they sealed it with a kiss,

*"You want to go get some dinner? I made us a picnic dinner, and I thought we could go down by the water, sit together, talk, and have something to eat."*

Garren bowed, *"Well, Madam Evie, I think that is a grand idea,"* while he raised back up and held his arm out for her to take. They locked arm in arm,

*"Lead on, my lady."* As they walked together arm in arm heading for her horse, where she had a blanket and packed a dinner.

Together, with Garren carrying the picnic, they headed down the river walk to the Greyborne Lake. The lake splits Vallenwood and the Greyborne academy, but there are plenty of quiet, exclusive areas where the two could have some privacy and enjoy the lake. They arrived at a sweet, quiet spot on the lake and were getting to know each other. Garren had plenty of questions.

*"So, tell me about you. I want to hear about where you are from."*

Evie started by letting him know that the Black Knights are an honorable Knight Order. They believe in law and order. Most think the Black Knights are bad or evil, but that is not true. There is only one order that is evil, and that is the order of the Black Rose. We Black Knights get a bad reputation because some people move to that order from the Black Knights. In fact, there are only a handful of Black Rose Knights. However, Evie shared that her brother is moving in that direction. Ever since the *"Black Mage"* showed up a few months ago, both my father and my brother have changed. They keep trying to change me as well, and I refuse. Garren scrunched his eyes as he listened intently.

*"Black Mage? Sounds sort of ominous. Is he evil?"*

Evie quieted her voice as though she was looking into a dream,

*"Yes, he is evil, and I fear he is trying to turn my father and my brother to evil too, and there is nothing I can do about it. Everyone is afraid of him, and if he is*

*successful, our entire city will fall under his evil hands."*

She looked around to see that no one was coming, leaning in toward Garren and whispered.

*"There are several of us that have sworn to leave the city if he turns my father to evil. My father is second in line only to Valence because he is his brother. Valence rules with tyranny and fear using us, the Black Knights at every turn to uphold his law. Unfortunately, Valence is also the leader of the Black Rose faction, so our own leader is evil. My father was the only one left to hold him at bay, but if he turns too, Idesport City is finished, and I am out of there."*

Garren quickly interjected,

*"Well, you could always come live with us here in Briar's Cove."*

He realized what he said, *"Umm, I mean the town, the town is great, and all the folk would accept you as you are."*

Evie smiled back, *"I appreciate the offer, and I will certainly consider it, but I have got to stop this if I can. If I don't try, I will feel like I failed all my friends and the people of Idesport City. You understand now why we must keep our relationship a secret?"*

Garren didn't hesitate and said instantly, *"Yes!"* He quickly turned and jumped to his feet.

Evie exclaimed, *"What is it?"*

*"Horses!"* said Garren back, *"They are heading this way."*

She stood up, *"Oh no,"* as three Black Knight riders came around the corner, raised the horses up to a stop.

*"Evie, get over here now!"*

Evie moved forward and spoke in loud defiance,

*"You don't own me, Mathis! Go back to the camp, and I will be back shortly."*

The big knight flipped one leg over the horse, and jumped to the ground, removed his helmet, and placed it on the horses' handhold. Then turned quickly and charged at Garren who was ready. He instinctively reacted, catching the knight's arm and flipped him to the ground.

The other two jumped to the ground and drew their swords.

"*Stop,*" shouted Mathis, "*He's mine,*" as he quickly got back to his feet.

Garren moved in front of Evie to protect her, holding her at bay with one arm. She sidestepped him and moved to an attack stance on Mathis drawing her hidden dagger.

"*So, you are going to fight me because of him?*"

Mathis spat out to Evie while laughing at her.

She shouted back, "*If I must!*"

Mathis pointed at Garren who was still in a defensive posture, watching all three, and said, "*I will see you soon. And you Eve, come back to the camp with us. Now!*"

The riders got back on their horses, slow trotted, and stopped at the corner.

"*C'mon, Evie!*"

Mathis shouted to her from the ridge just a few yards away.

"*I'm sorry Garren, I have to go. Will I see you tomorrow?*"

She questioned with pleading eyes.

Garren took her hands, nodded, and whispered back, *"Of course, my lady. I wouldn't miss it even if my life depended on it."*

She slowly walked backward away as their hands came apart, looking at him with sad, longing eyes. Then turned and walked swiftly to Mathis, who held his hand out, never losing his angry stare at Garren. She took hold, and he pulled her to the back of his horse as she jumped on the back with her arms around his chest. Mathis glared a wry smile back to Garren and jerked the horse around, the horse raised up on two legs with a cry and a snort. They whirled around and left in a gallop while Evie turned and looked back at Garren till he was out of sight around the ridge.

Garren watched as they went out of his sight and finally relaxed with a relieved sigh standing back up.

*"What the hell was that all about? Geesh, I can't even get two hours with her. This really sucks. Hmmm, so much for our big secret! You will surely see me sooner than you think, Mathis! And, you might get more than you bargained for!"*

He snatched up all the picnic settings and put everything away, feeling angry at their interruption. Garren slowly walked to his horse, keeping a close ear and eyes all around. His senses were still on high alert, wondering if they would try to attack him again.

He couldn't help but think what Evie was going through back at their campsite,

*"I hope they are not too hard on her."*

Garren pulled up to the house but didn't go to the inn. All he could think about was what had just happened.

*"Should I tell Jarrod, or should I honor my promise? Naaa, the family doesn't count. I will tell Jarrod tomorrow and see what he thinks."*

He got ready for bed as he was exhausted from the days' activities. Testing all day long, worrying about the results, then having to deal with Evie's brother at the lake, and now, terribly missing her already.

*"Why is she so in my head? I have never felt this before with any other girl, and we still do not really know each other much. However, I sure want to know her better than ever. Maybe it is because she is so*

*intriguing. Her life, where she is from, what she has been through and going through, her warm voice, her soft body, she is a great kisser, and finally, she is just so damn cute!"*

Garren smiled warmly thinking about her, but the warmness left quickly as he was still worried about her safety, until he faded off to sleep.

Garren's eyes snapped open, and he jumped out of bed, thinking he was late but discovered that it was still dark outside and was only about 5 am.

*"The sun is not up yet, I have plenty of time to get there early this morning. I am not sure what I'm thinking about more, the test results or Evie? Let's see, is there any more pressure I can put on myself? I wonder where Jarrod is hiding. I have not seen him in a whole day, which is unusual. He is normally all about what I am doing."* Garren laughed again,

*"Man, I'm getting good at busting on him when he's not around. I think he understands the pressure I am under and is giving me space."*

He looked around for Jarrod but could not find him in the house. He crept down to their secret room, and he was not there either.

*"I wonder where he is. I've got to head out soon, but I will talk to him later. He's probably stocking up the eatery this morning."*

Garren gathered his armor and his trial sword, in case he made the cut. He stashed his bow and practice arrows in his pack and strapped it to his favorite horse.

*"You ready my friend?"*

As he gently stroked the horse's neck. The horse reacted as he always did, raising his head up and back down as if to tell Garren he was ready. Garren gave him a fresh carrot from the garden and then the horse's favorite oat feed while he finished packing for the day.

*"Still, no Jarrod! No choice now, I need to head up to the Academy."*

It was close to 7 am now. He wanted to get there early enough to see if Evie was there. He rode quickly this morning, hurrying to see his new girlfriend. He arrived at the academy stables and walked the horse into the corral marked with his name. There, he saw a note tacked to his horse's stall. He gently pulled the note off the tack, and then put his horse up. The note was written, *"Garren, with Love, Evie."*

*"Uh ohhh, should I even read this? Looks like a "Dear Garren" letter."*

Remembering the letter that Jarrod received from his former love. Garren sat on the bench just outside the stable, and stared at the letter, mustering the courage to open it.

*"Oh, the heck with it!"*

He unfolded the letter with a flash from his hand and slowly pulled the letter up to read;

"Dearest Garren,

I snuck away last night after I wrote this, so you would get it before you went to the academy. I wanted you to know I am just fine, and I already miss you. I have a plan that will include leaving my city sometime in the near future, and I want to tell you all about it later. Since I met you, I have never felt more like having a purpose in life. My allegiance to my brother and the Black Knights has changed dramatically, which I cannot explain.

I am tired of trying to figure it out, and I want to go with it. I will be at our spot at lunch time if you can get free, so we can discuss all these issues, feelings, and future plans. Good luck today, and I hope you make the trials, as I know how important it is to you. I am cheering with all my heart for your success! Watch out for Mathis. He is on a mission to destroy you, even if you do not make the trials."

Forever and Truly Yours,

Evie"

He folded up the letter and put it in his pocket. He stared off in the distance, thinking deeply about what he had just read, trying to determine what it meant and what hidden message was there. He felt helpless for the first time in his life.

*"I wish Jarrod was here. He would know exactly what this letter meant."*

Garren thought about the different meanings and was trying to read between the lines.

*"First of all, I am not worried about Mathis but does this letter mean goodbye, and she will end it this afternoon? Does it mean she is leaving her city in the*

*near future, which means she is going back to Idesport City? Is she saying that she loves me or likes me like a family member? Ahhh crap! I don't have time for this. It is too much to think about.*" And with that, he headed up to the academy to find out who is going to the trials.

He gathered all his strength and was never nervous or fearful, but this girl brought all those feelings to the foreground, and he did not like it one bit. He was even worried about the academy results, which he thought wouldn't bother him in the least. But, for some unknown reason, he wanted this more than ever now.

Garren reached the academy and was greeted by a big crowd of friends and family, all cheering as he walked up to the great hall entrance. He raised his hand and acknowledged the crowd to their delight. There was Hardin, and Ms. Frieda, Jarrod was standing there giving him the "raised fist" sign that had always been their sign of triumph. There was Riello, old toothless Darrin, and all his friends from the Inn as well as his friends who did not make the second round.

As he rounded the corner to walk up the steps and off to the right, Evie was standing there with that sexy smile that almost buckled him to the ground. Garren pointed at her, clearly excited and exhilarated to see her. He pulled the letter out and waved it to her. She immediately knew the meaning and slyly blew him a kiss, as he winked at her and gave her a huge grin stuffing the letter back in his pocket. Now he found himself extremely nervous because he did not want to let any of them down.

*"Wow, I did not expect this at all. No wonder I couldn't find anyone this morning. They were already here to support me, whether I made it or not."*

He turned before he walked into the hall, smiled, looking directly at Evie and waved at everyone, with loud whistles and cheers. No one even noticed his gaze at the young woman standing off to the side, except Jarrod. Jarrod knew immediately who she was.

*"Ah, you must be Evie?"* Jarrod silently spoke to himself and started to slowly make his way to her through the crowd as Garren disappeared into the hall.

Garren made himself proudly walk into the hall as some others came in right behind, making it through the gauntlet of people outside cheering and waving flags. There were all five Elders of the Greystone Academy. Master Hansen, Master Olffius, Master Alvure, Master Brevaleer, and finally, Grand Master Chun-Dracko, the leader of the Academy. Garren was awed by seeing the Grand Master who rarely made an appearance. Chun-Dracko stepped forward and started to speak,

*"Welcome to the final round, and I want to congratulate you all on your successful journey to Knighthood. While some of you will not make it to the trials, all of you should be proud of your accomplishments. When I call your name, please step forward, and face your classmates for your honored trip to the trials and their congratulations. I wish the rest of you great success and look forward to you continuing to increase your skill sets for the next trials in four years. Other Knight orders participating here already have five Knights competing in the trials. They are represented behind you in the gated stands above."*

All the White Knights turned to see them, and glaring an angry look at Garren, was Mathis.

*"Each faction's representatives, please stand to receive your honors.*

- *The Silver Knights from Thane City.*
- *The Bronze Knights from Lushayl and Lukome cities.*
- *The Copper Knights from Ayster Hall.*
- *The Knights of the Moon from Roarks City.*
- *The HartStone Knights from Brandstone.*
- *The Black Knights from Idesport City.*
- *The Plains Knights from Volshstein City.*
- *The Knights of the Rose from Rynah.*
- *The Knights of the Sun from Lavilia."*

All the Knight representatives stood one by one and received well-deserved respect, claps, and cheers from all, except the Black Knight, who sat in defiance with his arms crossed until his faction was called, where he so graciously waved and accepted his accolades.

Chun-Dracko continued,

*"Thank you all for making your long journeys and participation in the greatest trial events ever. You all shall be tested on the field of honor, and the winner shall be granted into the halls of glory and continue training into the elite faction of Paladin Knighthood. And now the five participants and two alternates from our faction, The White Knights of the Realm!"* All the White Knights cheered and threw up the gesture for the Knights of Honor to each other, with a loud battle roar seeing respectful standing and hearing claps from above. Except for Mathis, who just scowled at Garren.

*"First Place goes to: Lucus Gallenstar; from Caspian Township.*

*Second Place goes to: Marhtin Regal; from Restin Township.*

*Third Place goes to: Borrishnal Everfast; from Osgillian Township."*

Mathis stood up from above and hollered.

*"That big goof is not even going to make the cut."*

He laughed loudly annoying everyone around him while others scoffed at his disrespectfulness.

Master Chun-Dracko spoke with precise definition.

*"Silence and respect within these walls, Sir Knight!"*

He realized everyone was staring at him, and he quietly sat back down. Garren never acknowledged him and stood steadfast, with his eyes fixed straight ahead with his head held high. Chun-Dracko continued,

*"Fourth Place goes to: Demmeal Ezram; from Vallenwood Township."*

Garren's friend Kinnail sneaked up on the platform that overlooked the study, he relayed information back down to the crowd. The announcement of the last candidate came, and he shook his head no to Garren's friends. With every declaration, a resounding *"Ohhhhhh"* was heard amongst cheers for their selected candidate. Jarrod was near Evie and had been talking to her the whole time. She was clearly nervous for Garren, but Jarrod was intrigued with her. Both were anxious for Garren with the hope he was chosen, but it was not looking good. The Master continued with,

*"And now for the final selection of the White Knights representing the Realm is,*

*Fifth Place, Garren Stromblade from Briar's Cove Township."*

Garren finally let out a breath and proudly moved forward to take his place next to Demmeal and received his trophy. Mathis stormed out the back door, bumping into everyone and cursing the whole way, to the back courtyard, leaving before the announcement of the alternates. The White Knights erupted with glee inside and Kinnail, who watched and listened from the outside ledge, threw his arms, fists first in the air and jumped up and down.

*"He got it!! He got it! He made it through!!"* The crowd outside now erupted with screams of joy. Evie screamed out an excited *"Yes"* and hugged Jarrod, *"Oh, I am so happy for him."*

Evie joyously gleamed into his eyes with tears of joy. Jarrod laughed as they jumped up and down together laughing in synch.

*"So am I, I'm so proud of him!"*

Hardin just smiled with his head held high, as Riello and Frieda hugged him from both sides with Darrin in the back, and now joined by Jarrod and Evie who had now met Garren's entire family.

*"First Alternate goes to: Joeseph Arnah; from Roxshun Township.*

*Second Alternate goes to: Frayden Klisko; from High Bluff Township.*

*Congratulations to you seven, and we thank you for your hard work and commitment to the Knighthood practices."*

The seven bowed to the Elders then turned with their silver, white, and gold lined plate trophies held high. They headed outside with the younger students lined up in a row on either side of the path with swords drawn and held high in the air. All down to the central courtyard where everyone was now standing to get a glimpse at their perspective White Knights.

Master Chun-Dracko came out first and announced, *"Here are your new White Knights of the Realm."*

Drums started beating, horns blew, and cheers raised, as the seven started to emerge with the slow walk down the steps. The cheers started out low but then grew to a deafening level, as they held their honored trophies high for all to see.

Hardin and Jarrod were the first to meet Garren, then Frieda and Riello, Darrin tagging along, and even Kinnail was there. Garren was met with *"Congratulations, and good work son, pats on the back and so proud of you,"* all with thanks and smiles from Garren.

He grabbed Jarrod.

*"Thank you so much, I would have never gotten here without you,"* as he hugged him tightly!

Jarrod pulled away and pointed at him, *"and don't you ever forget it!!"*

They laughed loudly and then Garren started to look around preoccupied.

*"Are you looking for someone?"*

Jarrod questioned, moving his head to stay in front of Garren's eyes.

*"Yes, as a matter of fact...!"* Jarrod stepped aside, and there was Evie. He smiled at her but was thoroughly confused.

*"How, in the....? What are...?"*

Both Jarrod and Evie started laughing at his stuttering confusion.

*"Oh, we have been talking all morning, my brother,"* Jarrod boasted.

Evie rushed into Garren's arms and face planted right on his lips, as he just about dropped his trophy when he caught her and picked her up easily.

*"Hey, sunshine!"*

Garren whispered to her as Jarrod snatched the trophy, and they continued.

*"Get a room!"*

Jarrod smoothly spoke out just loud enough for them to hear.

They looked back at Jarrod and back at each other and kissed again with her arms wrapped around Garren's neck.

*"Okay, okay, break it up. There are youngsters around!"*

Jarrod ghastly announced as the family headed down the path followed closely now by Evie and Garren arm in arm.

# Chapter 10

Garren and Evie enjoyed the whole afternoon together with family and friends. They even rode to the inn together, with her hanging on to Garren the entire way home. Evie helped Ms. Frieda, Garren and Jarrod, helped Riello move supplies, and Harden had the youngster helping inside, who was in awe of Garren now. The inn was open, and business was booming already into the mid-afternoon.

Garren talked to Jarrod prodding for information on his and Evie's talk. Jarrod told him that he thought she was a lovely girl and better looking than any he has ever gone out with. She is smart and articulate, and she makes her point quickly and decisively. He told Garren they talked about her family, and I told her stories of when we were young. They had a good talk about how hard you worked for this, and how well you did in the preliminary trial contests. Jarrod informed her how ready Garren is for these finals. Jarrod stopped and just let that sink in, then started again. Evie told him about the worries in her land, her father, and her brother. It sounded like both are heading down the wrong paths. Jarrod started again,

*"How bad things are in her family is quite disturbing. I think we need to really look into this when you win this tourney."*

Garren said with a humbled voice,

*"You mean IF I win this tourney. Did she say she was leaving?"*

Jarrod looked up and shook his head yes,

*"But not till the tourney was over. She said she was going to have a talk with you later this afternoon. That is all she said about that. The more worrisome thing is the evil that is spreading through that city, and I fear it will be their downfall. I think we should talk with the Elders and get some advice, but I will leave that up to you and her. I will support whatever you two decide."*

Garren nodded in agreement,

*"Thanks, Jarrod. I will talk to her now and see. Tomorrow is the practice day, and I will do a light workout and focus on the contest. I have to defeat her brother, if he gets into the Knighthood, it will be their foothold into our lands."*

Jarrod looked back at Garren with concern,

*"Exactly right, so make sure you defeat him. I am sure that you will win anyway. You are the stronger, more prepared, and you're a Stromblade!!"*

Garren smiled at that with pride,

*"I appreciate your confidence in my abilities, but I am not so sure. That testing humbled me a little bit."*

Jarrod started laughing at him,

*"That is what those tests were supposed to do. Don't doubt your ability, Garren. You are going to win."*

"Thanks, brother. I will talk with you later. I am going to find Evie and get ready to take her back to the camp." Garren added in haste.

*"Be careful, Garren, I have an uneasy feeling about all this."* Jarrod was visibly worried.

Garren looked back,

*"Sure, and I will."*

Jarrod watched as he went back toward the back entrance of the tavern where Evieand Hardin were.

*"Garren, wait!"*

Jarrod ran up to him,

*"I almost forgot, she really likes you a lot, and you should not take that for granted. You were right, she is a good girl!"*

Garren nodded and showed a hint of a smile as he went on in. Jarrod went back to grab some more stocks into the inn. He came in through the back room and saw Evie talking with Hardin and Frieda. Garren stopped and just watched her talk to them as if they had known each other their whole life. They were laughing together with Evie sitting on a table. She had quite a crowd around her.

*"That is the effect she had on me as well. What is it about her? Everyone loves her, and so do I."*

Garren made his way in and was immediately seen by all who started with the cheering again.

*"Garren, great job! There he is, the man of the hour, Cheers to the Stromblades, Oy...Ohy...HURAYYYY!"*

He made his way toward his father, shaking hands and greeting everyone. He saw Evie with a great big smile on her face with a drink in her hand. He could tell she was having the best time of her life.

He walked up to Hardin who stood and hugged him again,

*"I am the proudest man in the land, Garren. I have a gift for you."*

Ms. Frieda ran to the back and brought out a long and ornately designed leather box,

*"Quiet down everyone, QUIET."* yelled Ms. Frieda as she handed the box to Hardin. No one would stand against her in the inn, and you could now hear a pin drop in the room. Even the new folk from other towns went silent.

He turned with the box and gave it to Garren,

*"I was going to wait to give this to you when the trials were over, but I don't see how I can be any prouder of you than I am now."*

Jarrod came in through the back and was enjoying the scene from a distance.

*"That said and without further ado, this is yours, my son."* Garren took the box and said, *"Thank you, father, for the kind words. What is it?"*

*"Well, open it and see."*

Ms. Frieda jumped in.

*"Uhh, yeah right, good idea."*

Garren placed the box on the bar counter and flipped the 3 latches and opened the beautiful case. His mouth opened with complete surprise when he saw lying in the felt lined case was the most incredible sword he had ever seen. He slowly picked up the long sword and admired the engravings.

*"This was the sword of my grandfather handed down to him for generations to him and then to me. Now it is yours. Lankule's Knight of the Wind sword!"* Garren turned and raised it in the air, as the crowd burst into Ooohs, Yays, Yeas and then loud cheers with chants of Garren, Garren, Garren!

Ms. Frieda held up her hand and Shhhh'd the crowd once again, as Garren placed the sword back in the box and gently closed it. *"Thank you so much, father, it is a fantastic gift, and I will be using it, and his voice raised to everyone, In This Tourney!!"*

As he raised his hand to all. Again, the roar of the crowd rose to shouts of encouragement, confidence, and congratulatory rants.

Garren turned to his father and gave him a huge hug whispering in his ear,

*"I will never let you down, Father!"*

Hardin grasped him by his arms and nodded as he shook with loving pride,

*"I know, I Know."*

Hardin was tearing up and so was Evie, as she put her hands over her mouth in utter awe at the family love and friendship she had never witnessed before. Ms. Frieda went over and hugged Evie who was trying to choke back the tears.

*"Twill be alright, love."*

Ms. Frieda consoled her as Garren finally made it to her side.

He gently touched her on the shoulder,

*"You Okay?"*

She made a soft whimper and could no longer hold the tears as she took him and gave him a kiss which turned into another. The crowd now could not be held back this time, as they burst with, "Yayyyyyy, Garren, Garren, Garren!"

The chants continued for a few minutes.

They stood and looked at the crowd, and Garren waved saying thank you and good night to all as they looked at each other, smiled to one another, and headed out the door with his gift in one hand and Evie hanging off his other arm.

Garren and Evie could hear the chants of the crowd, even as they got to the stable to get on Garren's horse,

*"My, you sure are the hero of the day. I love your family and friends."*

She softly spoke while climbing onto the back of the horse behind the already seated Garren. She pulled her breasts tightly against his back with her head resting sideways between his shoulders as they started off down the path back toward Vallenwood.

*"Hey, I don't want to go back,"* she boldly announced. *"I have never experienced such closeness in one town with family and friends, and I have never felt so warm and welcomed in my life."*

Garren stopped the horse and stayed looking straight ahead,

*"I told you they would love your...."*

He stopped in mid-sentence, lowering his head to the side toward her,

"*And so do I!*"

She let go of him startled by the response with an inward shocked sigh. She pulled him back to her even tighter than before raising up to kiss him on the back of his neck, whispering in a soft, sexy wind like voice,

"*We could go to your house instead of Vallenwood.*"

Garren sighed loudly, "*uhhgg*" and rolled his eyes.

Without hesitation, he whirled the horse around and "*Hahhh!*" burst from his voice, which set the horse to a gallop toward the house as she joyously laughed with him. They rode up to the house laughing together, and Garren jumped off the horse quickly throwing the reigns around the post. He walked back to Evie who was teasing him with a seductive look, still on the horse that made Garren want her so badly that his body ached. He reached up and snatched her off the horse as she let out a little *"Ohhhh"* in a high-pitched voice.

She was laughing, teasing him, and then kissed him passionately with her hands going through his hair and her squirming in his cradled grasp with a burning desire, moaning softly, and making quiet "mmmm" noises. He carried her toward the house up the stairs with her arms wrapped tightly around his neck. He awkwardly reached for the door and slung it open with a slam making her laugh again, not even bothering to close it as they were breathing heavily.

*"I want you so bad,"* she stuttered to Garren as they eagerly kissed each other again. She now relaxed in his arms while still kissing knowing deep inside that he was all hers now, they headed awkwardly to his room. Once inside the house, they left a trail of clothes leading to the bedroom.

***

Jarrod thought about all he was told and tried to correlate anything he knew about the past evil times to now. He was frustrated that he had no answers, but he was eager to find out. He felt in his soul that something was happening and that somehow, he was to play an important part in the events unfolding before him.

*"Is this the destiny I was told about? Still too many questions for my liking."*

He finished his work at the inn and walked back with Hardin to the house. Hardin put his arm around Jarrod who gladly accepted the gesture,

*"You understand that I am proud to have you as my son and very proud of all you have done as well. Garren was right, you know, he would have never got here without your help."*

*"Thanks, Father. I am proud to be a Stromblade,"* Jarrod replied.

Hardin stopped.

*"That is why I am so proud of you. After all, you have been told and been through, it is great to hear that. I wish now we would have told you sooner."*

They nodded together and walked back to the house, chatting quietly about Evie.

*"She is a fine girl, I really like her. I think she is good for Garren."*

Jarrod agreed and left it at that, as they approached the house and saw Garren's horse tied on the post and the door wide open.

*"Hmmm, I wonder...."*

They both saw the trail of clothes and looked at each other and quietly laughed together, as they knew exactly what happened. Jarrod picked up the clothes and put them by Garren's closed door. Hardin gently closed the front door and gave Jarrod a pat on the shoulder with a happy sigh.

*"What a great day!"* and he went to bed.

Jarrod couldn't help himself and stopped to listen for a minute at Garren's door. Hearing soft laughter and quiet talk and then noises he didn't want to be listening to.

*"Yikes, that's dis-concerning, but bed him well, my lady."*

Jarrod put his hand over his mouth with a laugh and silently tip-toed to his secret room.

***

Garren woke up early the next morning to feel Evie snuggled up next to him. He gently moved her as she softly moaned in her sleep. He chuckled at her, as he slowly climbed out of bed, trying not to wake her. He went to the shower and cleaned up to go for his practice day, leaving all her clothes at the end of his bed.

He was dressed now, grabbed his new sword, sheath, armor, and other weapons, packed his horse, and quietly snuck back in the house to his room. All weapons in the contest had to be entered at the tourney by noon to be outfitted with safety. Swords had the ends tipped with a rubber compound and edges were set with aged leather, so there would be no cuts. Only practice arrows could be used, lances had to be breakable with soft, rounded tips. Even this could hurt someone if there was an accident, but it was rare.

He stared at Evie for a moment watching her sleep and found himself holding his breath.

*"Breathe, dammit, breeeathe!"*

He walked to the bed, bent to her head, moved her hair to the side, and kissed her gently. She made a soft, high-pitched noise and snuggled deeper into the pillow as Garren smiled and left her there sleeping.

Evie woke up and reached across the bed to find that Garren was not there. She quickly sat straight up in the bed, thinking about the events from yesterday.

She warmly smiled, *"mmmmmmmm,"* slowly laid on her back while pulling the sheets up to her neck and wondering if Garren had left already. She waited a few minutes and heard some clinking and clanking in the kitchen area.

*"I guess he is in the kitchen."*

She got up and saw her clothes there but then got a sly thought. She went to the closet and pulled out one of Garren's button shirts. It swallowed her to just above the knees as she left it unbuttoned at the top to just below her breast line. She rolled the sleeves up and looked in the mirror, turning sideways and front ways, to make sure she was sexy looking but not trashy while admiring her newly created nightgown. She brushed her hair and headed to the door, still thinking he was in the kitchen.

Evie turned the corner and waltzed into the kitchen to see Jarrod with his back to her.

*"Whoa, Ooops, with a slight giggle."* She stopped and tried to collect herself before he turned around, but he didn't turn around.

He continued to pour the tea and cut bread,

*"Good morning, Evie. You want some hot tea and freshly made cinnamon fruit bread? Ms. Frieda made it this morning, dropped it off, and it is delicious."*

He turned to see her surprised look and then he almost dropped the cup of tea,

*"Uhhh!"*

She gathered herself quickly, and casually stepped, barefoot and all to the table acting, like it was no big deal dressed in nothing but a shirt.

*"Sure,"* she chuckled as Jarrod's eyes followed her to the table and watched her sit down. She put her feet in the chair with her knees to her chest completely covered with Garren's shirt so that only her toes stuck out the bottom. Jarrod shook his head fast as if to snap out of a trance and brought the teacup, filled with hot tea to her.

*"Thank you, Jarrod. Sorry about startling you. I thought you were Garren in here."*

*"No, no it's okay, we are just not used to having a woman in the house. There has not been a woman here my whole life except a lady years ago that dad was*

*dating. She eventually left as well, so Garren, Father, and I have been here alone for years."*

Evie took a sip of tea and Jarrod brought her a plate with a nice sized portion of the fruit bread. She picked it up, not bothering to use a fork and started to dig in as Jarrod watched in amazement. *"Mmmmm, you're right, this is good. The tea goes well with it,"* as she took another sip.

*"So, Garren has had no other girls stay over before?"*

She asked as though she were not interested, but Jarrod could clearly tell she was.

Jarrod laughed out loud, *"Actually, you are the first girl he has ever brought home."*

She smiled at that news and was seemingly happy. She continued to eat and drink her tea. Jarrod offered another cup, which she gladly accepted. They sat together and talked about the family and Garren, and she did the same. Jarrod told her the story of when they went horse-back riding, and they were racing to the river bank.

*"Garren's horse stopped suddenly, and he rolled over face first into the mud and slid all the way down the bank and into the water. He was so angry that he tried to jump up to run at me, and his feet went right out from under him and back first into the water again. I was laughing so hard that I fell and rolled down the bank too, right beside him in the water. And there, we were all covered in mud together."*

She was laughing so hard she was crying. They talked there for about an hour before she thanked Jarrod for the talk, tea, and breakfast, then excused herself to get appropriately dressed.

*"Make yourself at home, there's a shower and clean up area, fresh towels in the bathroom. Whatever you need, just help yourself. Wait for a second, I have a question for you."*

Evie stopped, folded her arms, crossed her legs, and stood with an inquisitive look on her face while listening intently.

*"Garren really likes you, in fact, it is not just infatuation. He cares for you, and we already care about you as well. You are a really good person, and*

*with Garren, you have brought out something new in him. I have never seen him so driven or in focus before, and it is you that has brought him to that level.*

*They say it was me that got him here, but I already know it was not, it was YOU. I know you have issues with your life back home, but are you planning to try and tackle this yourself? I do not have a good feeling about this at all. I feel there is something big on the horizon. I am just going to say it, I fear you cannot handle what's coming all alone. You're going to need some help...,"*

His voice cracked louder,

*"A lot of help! And I don't want to see Garren, or you get hurt or even killed. Because he has such a strong attachment to you, he will not let you go alone, and he would rather die than see you get hurt, so please think about what you are going to do."*

Evie lowered her head and thought for a moment, then answered while raising her eyes back to him,

*"Thanks, Jarrod, I will give it a lot of thought. To be honest, I have no idea what I am going to do. All I know for sure is that I have fallen head over heels in love*

*with Garren, and I think I want to spend every day with him for the rest of my life. I have never felt so safe, so secure. Garren, you, and your family have given me the best gift I have ever received. A warm and happy feeling in my heart. And I don't want to lose that. However, I have friends and family members in Idesport City that I must save if I can. If it requires me to sacrifice my life, then I must do it. Wouldn't you sacrifice your life for your family?"*

She pleaded with Jarrod, who closed his eyes in deep concentrative thought with a sigh. He opened his eyes back to her,

*"Yes, I would. So be it then! We are going with you because I know Garren, he would never let you go alone."*

Evie looked back with a loving smile and ran to Jarrod and gave him a hug and as she released him to walk away,

*"I knew in my heart that you would say that. Somehow, I feel as though I have known you forever."*

Jarrod sighed again and with a steady voice, *"Me too. I feel like we are connected in this somehow together. But not in a kinky or weird kind of way, you are like my,"*

Jarrod's eyes got wide as though he had figured something out in his mind.

Evie noticed right away and questioned, *"Like my what?"*

Jarrod turned from her, still concentrating with his head down and leaning on the counter, *"Nothing, never mind, it was nothing."*

Evie brushed off the comment and continued with her thought,

*"Though I appreciate the offer and setting aside my feelings for Garren, I could never ask that of you nor him. This is my task, and I have to do it alone."*

Jarrod jerked around and put his hands out, pleading.

*"Think about it Eve, please, there is way more here than you know, and even I have to figure it all out. You think all of this was just a coincidence? Nothing happens by chance anymore! You here, me, Garren, my father?"* he stopped there.

Evie smiled and conceded to his pleas,

*"Okay, Jarrod, I will think about it and let you know."*

*"Good! I will not say anything to Garren and will leave that for you to tell him. But I know what his answer will be."*

Again, she smiled back with admiration,

*"Thank you, Jarrod. I will see you later this afternoon when Garren gets back."*

*"Yeah, Okay. I will see you then, Evie."*

She could see Jarrod was struggling with his thoughts when he glanced back to her.

*"Help yourself to anything in the house, and if you need something, just give a shout."*

She nodded and went on back, leaving Jarrod standing in the kitchen in deep thought.

As Jarrod tried to collect his thoughts, he delved deeper into a standing trance where a vision faded into view. He clutched the counter tighter to hold himself steady, hearing Evie walking away from him as the vision came to life. It was a man leaving a huge courtyard on a horse, a huge white stallion. The path was lined with gigantic trees on both sides as the rider, and horse sped to full gallop.

He watched the rider from above as if Jarrod was a bird looking down on him. He saw a shape of the bearded man who was now passing through these Ivory gates with a castle in the background. The horse was moving faster and faster till the man's long hair and beard were flailing behind him. The picture slowly zoomed to a determined face of the man leaning forward on the horse, who he did not recognize, nor could he make out any details other than the scowl of determination on his face.

The horse sped up again to a speed that he could no longer hear, hooves thudding the ground, and it was like the horse was now gliding on air just off the ground. The vision faded in a haze, and Jarrod opened his eyes in wonderment.

*"Where did that come from? Who was that? Another question of reality, but these visions are getting stronger. I am starting to wonder if I will ever fit any of this together."*

He thought for another minute out, loud looking in the direction of Evie's exit from the room.

*"But I may have figured out this piece."*

He put everything in the sink, cleaned up, and went to his secret room.

# Chapter 11

Garren got on his horse and started with a slow walk then a slight kick to a trot toward Vallenwood, a path he had taken every single day since he was a boy. He passed the old dead tree that was still standing, crossed the creek and the standing stones on the side that he and Jarrod made years ago, all as if his whole life was passing before him, leading him to this moment in his life.

He thought about Evie and how he had fallen for her so quickly. He wondered about her home and how he was going to help her after the games. Garren wondered how well he was going to do in the trials starting tomorrow with all the competition that had arrived.

He knew this field of Knights were very talented but was also confident that while some were good in specific parts, he was pretty good in all of them. He passed the caravans setting up trinket shops on the roadside and starting to cook food for the crowds of people who will be here in the next two days. Garren rode up to the twin forks where to the left you headed toward High Bluff and to the right was the old broken road towards Restin.

Off the road and all on their horses were the rest of the White Knights waiting on Garren. He was all smiles riding up to each, congratulating them on their selection to the team.

Lucas met Garren with a strong gaze, *"I might have finished first, but we all know we had no chance to win this contest without you, Garren. We all voted, and we want you to lead us to victory as our Captain!"*

Garren looked at them all, and they all six acknowledged with a nod to Garren their agreement with Lucas. Garren spoke with defiant leadership and one hand raised, *"and so, it is done, we shall win, men of the White Knights, Win Together! I accept this honor!"*

They let out a simultaneous yell, *"Hell, Yeah!"* They turned with Garren in the lead and trotted together with heads held high in confidence the rest of the way to Graystone.

As they passed the entrance to the field, and the crowd started to cheer, Garren yelled back to his group,

*"Prance!"*

All seven of the white knights pranced their horses in unison to the roar and delight of the crowd to the stables. The knight factions who were already there clapped for them. Except for Mathis who was jeering and pointing thumbs down as he laughed and shouted obscenities toward the group, while the other Black Knights joined in with laughter. They turned in their weapons at the stables and got ready for practice.

The group had not practiced long when five of the black knights walked over to their location in the field. Garren noticed them heading over.

*"Hey guys, look at this!"*

They all stopped and made a semi-circle with Garren in front. Mathis spoke as he walked forward of the others,

*"You should just go home now before you get hurt, and where is Evie?"*

Garren glared at Mathis and calmly answered,

*"I have already thrown you to the ground once. The next time, I won't be so nice."*

Mathis lunged forward, but his guards grabbed him.

*"Not now, Mathis, Later! He will get his!"*

Garren held his guys back, shushing them as they pointed,

*"C'mon, let's do this right now!"*

A crowd of other factions was starting to move toward them. Garren calmly spoke again to his men, holding them back and then to Mathis.

*"Maybe your boys should let you go, so you can better express yourself."*

Mathis was enraged, and it took all four of them to hold him at bay. He turned and headed back across the field,

*"Let go of me,"* as Mathis slung away from the guys holding him.

*"Take it easy, Mathis. He will get his due!"*

The entire crowd around the white knights were laughing and shaking hands with Garren. He forwardly announced,

*"Okay guys, back to practice. The show is over, and there is a big day ahead. Good luck to everyone."*

They waived and passed pleasantries as they all went back to practicing for the big event.

After practice, Garren gathered his men together and held a meeting.

*"Let me start by saying that Mathis knight is scary! He is going to end up hurting someone just to get to me. Watch your backs tonight, and during the tourney, watch each other. Tomorrow is our day, it all starts here. Right here! Have confidence in this, if we work together, we will make it through until the finals. I want to see us all in the finals because then we will be declared winners as no faction can contest with each other. If we all win tomorrow, then it is just a pick from the team who competes. I will choose the best knight for each event, and the two alternates be ready at a moments' notice in case one of us is hurt. Sleep well, my friends, and tomorrow, we shall be victorious."*

They all shook hands and held smiles in agreement as they parted ways for a good night's rest.

It was still early afternoon and plenty of time to get home, spend some time with Evie and the family, and get some good rest. He thought about that for a moment and was amused thinking with Evie there, he might not get any rest, wanting to be with her as much as possible before she breaks his heart about leaving.

"*I hope she decides to stay here. I am not sure I can live without her. Wait, what am I thinking?*"

Garren shook the thought out of his head while getting on his horse to head back to Briar's Cove. He wanted to get home quickly but didn't want to waste his steed because of the trials tomorrow. He thought about the events while walking the horse through the gauntlet of make-shift shops and food stops along the roadway.

The eight events are as follows and will take all day long and probably go into the night: Axe throwing, Bow and arrow, Horse handling, Sword acrobatics, Sword combat, Hand to hand no weapons, Jousting, and finally, the main event called The Arrow Dance. He thought about Jarrod's words,

"*Think each event through. See yourself winning the event, and that is the way it will happen.*"

He gleamed at that thought while getting on his horse, realizing he was past everyone now and could probably fast trot the horse the rest of the way home. He pushed his horse, affectionately named Horizon, to a fast trot and rounded the last curve, the last two miles from home.

Suddenly out of nowhere, a giant log came flying toward him, which caught him in the mid-chest. Garren let out a loud *"Uhhhhg,"* as it took him off Horizon's back to the ground with a thud, and the horse ran off down the path. Garren's breath was gone, and he was trying to gather his strength on his hands and knees as a familiar voice rang out.

*"Not so smart mouthed now, are you? You bastard!"*

Garren looked up to see Mathis striding toward him. He managed to move his hands up and raised up on his knees as Mathis tried to kick him and he blocked the shot. But then got kicked from the side. The five surrounded him, kicking him and beating him with sticks till Garren was almost unconscious.

He still was able to think and was trying to get out of there as they stopped beating him. He couldn't hear, and his eyesight was fading in and out, while they were jeering each other on, poking and prodding at him. Garren made it to his hands and knees again and shook his head as blood ran into his eyes. All five were closing a circle on him again when suddenly, Garren pulled all his strength and lunged to his feet, kicking Mathis right in the chest, sending him flailing to the ground. At the same time, he side-stepped and punched the second one square in the head and down he went out cold. He swung his leg and caught the third awkwardly but enough to knock him off balance while throwing a spinning punch at the fourth catching him right on the chin with the back of his fist knocking him down and crawling away fast. The last one ran off. Mathis rose to his feet,

*"C'mon fellas, let's get going. We don't have time to finish him off. That will be tomorrow. Help Thax over there. Besides, he is done! We will be victorious tomorrow, and we can't afford for any of us to miss the events. He's not worth it!"*

Garren sort of watched leaning back and forth as they rode off first, placing his hands on his knees and then crashing to the ground face first. Garren faded from light to darkness and went unconscious. He awoke in the middle of the roadway, still hazy, to Horizon pawing at the ground in front of him flipping dirt on him. The well-trained horse kneeled low enough for Garren to take hold of the neck reigns and then the horse stood up, which helped Garren stand and steady himself to get on his back. Garren grunted in pain, "*Ahhhh*" as he was finally able to get on the horse. He leaned all the way forward patting Horizon on the neck,

*"Good boy. Take me home, my friend."*

The horse instinctively knew exactly where to go as Garren went limp forward with his arm wrapped around the horses' reins.

Jarrod looked out down the path as it was almost time to head to the inn to help out Ms. Frieda when he saw Horizon heading down the stretch in a slow trot.

"*Where is Garren?*" Then he saw the slumped figure on the horse.

"*Evie, Father!*" He yelled.

Evie and Hardin came out the front door and saw Jarrod racing toward the horse as Garren finally just slowly slumped off his horse to the ground.

Evie screamed,

"*Garren!!*"

She raced over there, making it there almost the same time Jarrod did even with a head start while Harden limped as fast as he could.

*"Evie, go get Riello and Ms. Frieda."*

She was almost hysterical and crying,

*"Oh, no, my Garren."*

She ran off only to see Ms. Frieda and Riello already running to her with two more friends from the inn.

Ms. Frieda got there, *"OMG, what happened to him?"*

Jarrod looked back with concern wiping the blood from Garren's face,

*"I don't know!"*

Looking over at Evie with a reassuring look for her. She understood immediately that Jarrod knew exactly who did this as she stood in horror with her hand over her mouth.

*"Let's get him to the house."*

Ms. Frieda already ran to get the physician. They got him into the house and to the spare room just as the physician came through the front door. They got some hot water and bandages.

*"Okay, I got this. Please let me work on him, and I will be back out in a few minutes. Ms. Frieda, I will need your help only,"* announced the physician.

Hardin hugged Evie and with his arm around her helped her out to the living area and sat her down as she was choking back tears. They were in there for what seemed hours but only 40 minutes had passed.

Riello left to go open the inn while Jarrod, Eve, and Harden patiently waited. Then the door opened to the room, and Ms. Frieda walked out. She was wiping her hands off with a towel as she came for Evie. All three were now standing in anticipation when she put her hand on Eve's shoulder and looked at all.

*"He is going to be alright. He was beaten pretty good, bruised up but nothing broken. Perhaps a mild head concussion, but he is alright. Who is Mathis? I never heard that name before. He said he was attacked by Mathis and his goons. He still has his sense of humor. Evidently, it was five or six against one. He is a strong kid. The doc will be out in a minute, and you all can go see him."*

*"Wow, thanks, Ms. Frieda."*

Hardin hugged her as she announced she was going to open the inn.

*"Hope that's it. I've had enough excitement for one day."*

They all laughed a bit at that one. Jarrod hugged Evie, and the three hugged each other.

*"It's my fault. It's my fault!"* Evie sniffled with tears flowing again.

Jarrod consoled her, and she put her head on his shoulder with another cry out. Jarrod reassured her.

*"No, it is not your fault. You have no control over Mathis."*

Just then, the doctor came out, and Evie moved forward.

*"Ms. Frieda, tell you?"*

They all nodded, yes.

*"Okay then, well he is going to be just fine. With good rest, he should be up in a couple of days. Here give him a teaspoon of this, every couple of hours for the pain."*

They all looked at each other, knowing the contest was going to start tomorrow. Hardin was crushed at the thought feeling like Garren might not handle this well.

"*You can go in and see him now. He has a pretty good knock on the head and some bruised ribs but should be fine.*" The physician informed them with assurance.

Evie rushed back there and was first to open the door. Garren turned his head to her and held out his hand. She rushed to his side and sat on the bed, holding his hand with tears in her eyes.

"*Oh, Garren, I am so sorry.*" Evie was emotional.

Garren grinned, "*Aren't you a ray of sunshine. Give me a kiss, I really need one. Don't worry, it takes more than a couple of goons to knock me out.*"

She leaned down and kissed him on the check, and then on his hand, as Jarrod and Hardin walked in.

"*Jarrod, Dad, good to see you. Oooh! That hurts as he settled back down.*"

Hardin said, "*Take it easy, son.*"

Jarrod stood behind Evie, "*Well, you look like you got run over by a heard of cows.*"

Garren laughed, *"Ooh, Owe, don't make me laugh, it hurts. I will be good tomorrow. Got a big day."*

Evie looked at Hardin and then Jarrod with pleading eyes. Neither of them said a word, but she saw in their eyes that, no he wouldn't. Instead, Jarrod answered back while looking at Evie.

*"You just get some rest and don't worry about that. We need to get you healthy quick."* Hardin spoke with a jovial agreement.

*"Yes, well, I am going to the inn to help out tonight. You kids, gonna be alright?"* They all nodded.

*"Rest well, son, and I will see you in the morning."*

Garren raised up, *"Ouch that hurts. Okay father, I will see you at the contest in the morning."*

Hardin sadly looked back but said nothing.

*"I am going to leave you two alone."*

Jarrod reached down and squeezed both their hands, looking at Evie and then Garren.

*"Take it easy and no wrestling each other in bed tonight you two, you need to rest."*

Garren laughed with Jarrod, complaining about the pain again while leaving the room, closing the door behind him.

*"Don't mind him, he is just being himself. Worrying is his job!"* They both laughed as she kissed him on the side of his mouth. *"That hurt?"* She asked with glowing eyes, and Garren shook his head no.

*"What about here?"* Planting a kiss right on his neck with a giggle.

*"No, actually that felt pretty good."* Garren snatched her onto his chest, taking a large intake of air and letting her go.

*"Yep, that one hurt!!"* He laughed, and so did she.

*"Quit playing, you are going to hurt yourself. Are you hungry? Can I get you anything?"*

*"How about some ice water? I can use a drink."*

*"Sure, be right back!"* Evie left the room.

Garren, put one hand up behind the back of his head as she quickly left the room. *"I could get used to this. Haha, ooooh, that smarts,"* rubbing his lower ribs.

Evie came back in with the water, and she held the glass for him as he drank and spilled some on her. She wiped it off, but it had already started to soak through a bit. Garren stared at her breast with a silly grin on his face.

She rolled her eyes, *"Yeah, you're feeling better already."*

He lifted both hands behind his head,

*"What?"*

She also brought in an ice pack and placed it on his head and held it there, watching him.

*"Mathis did this to you, didn't he?"*

Garren whispered back,

*"No, I did this to me. He caught me with my britches down after I warned everyone to watch their backs. No need for revenge or getting mad at him. Actually, your brother taught me a valuable lesson. It won't happen again."*

She pulled back the ice pack,

*"So you are telling me you are not mad at him? Well, I am, I am pissed."*

Garren eased his voice,

*"We are taught to learn from our mistakes. Anger and hatred lead to mistakes, darkness, and ultimately,*

*evil. Next time I will be ready, and he will rue the day he met me. I wouldn't go that far to say I am not mad at him, but I am mostly angry at myself."*

Evie was astonished, *"You are an amazing man Garren Stromblade, and I am so glad I met you. You are in my heart, and I love that about you as I love you."*

She leaned down and kissed him again.

*"Here, the Dr. said to drink this. It will ease the pain, and let you sleep."*

Garren took a big swig of the drink. He choked a bit and gasped.

*"Oh, that is awful!"*

*"Now get some sleep, and I will be right outside if you need something."*

Garren smiled and whispered, *"I love you too, Evie,"* as he slowly closed his eyes.

Evie heard that and looked back at him with sadness, knowing what she had to tell him sooner or later.

Jarrod went outside and ran to the stable, untied his horse, *"I need you tonight, old friend."*

He was determined to find something to help Garren. He read in one of his books that there was a healing potion that healed bruising, aches and pain overnight, and one of the healers from the Crystal City was already here.

"*I don't know if it will work, but I have to try,*" and off he rode toward the Academy.

It is about a 40-minute trot to the academy, but Jarrod was in a full gallop riding as fast as his horse would travel. He rode straight past the shops and shoppers all along the road, staying in the middle. Yelling,

"*Out of the way, out of the way.*" Parting the crowds to get through as fast as he could.

He was obviously an accomplished rider, avoiding people in the rode, jumping obstacles, and leaning forward like he was in a race. He rode all the way up the path with the same determined look as the rider in his vision.

"*I wonder if that was really me. Without the beard and long grey hair, of course.*"

He laughed at the thought and continued like a mad man on a mission. He tore through the streets and right up to the academy, slowing just enough to jump off in a full run up the steps and into the hall, startling Master Olvin.

He turned.

*"Here, here, Jarrod. What are you doing?"*

Jarrod stopped breathing hard, but he couldn't speak trying to take a breath.

*"Easy, son, eeeasy. Calm down and tell me why you are striving to see me."*

*"Sorry, Master, but I am not here to see you, I am here to see the Cleric Rosalind who I heard was here already from the men at my father's inn. Is she here?"*

Olvin looked at him strangely unprepared for that answer.

*"Yes, but why?"*

*"Garren was attacked on the road, and he is alright, but if I do not get him this medicine, he will not be able to compete tomorrow."*

*"Wait, hold on son. Attacked by what? An animal?"*

*"No not an animal, a group of ...well it doesn't matter. What matters is that I talk to Rosalind."*

*"A group of what, Jarrod? We need to know."*

*"Okay, okay! It was Mathis and his black knights. They ambushed him on the road to Briar's Cove."*

*"We will ban them from the contest in the morning!"*

*"No sir, there is no need for that. Garren would not want that, and the King wanted them to compete."*

*"You are right Jarrod. You are wiser than an old fool sometimes. I applaud you and Garren for that. Well, follow me, and we will see what she has."*

*"Thank you, Master,"* as Jarrod followed him to the guest's quarters.

They arrived at Rosalind's door, and the Master knocked. The door creaked open, and there was an old woman clad in a blue-robed dress with a shawl on her head.

*"Yes?"*

Came from under the shawl.

Master bowed to her.

*"Pardon our intrusion madam, but we are in much need of your assistance."*

She opened the door wider.

*"Come in master and young fella, what can I do for you?"*

Master Olvin told her that one of the knights competing was hurt and needed medical treatment to heal him fast so he would be able to compete.

*"Attacked by some other knights, was he?"*

Olvin and Jarrod looked at each other in a state of confusion and wonderment. Jarrod whispered to Olvin.

*"How did she know that?"*

*"Yes, and this is Jarrod, his brother."*

Jarrod bowed, in bewilderment by her spoken words.

The woman laughed and patted Jarrod on the shoulder.

*"Jarrod, Brother is it? You have a destiny about your oval face, my friend. There is much for you to learn in such a short amount of time. For one, seeking the forbidden spherical knowledge at such a young age is extraordinary."*

She moved to a cupboard, opened the door, and looked inside.

*"Ah yes, here we go."*

The old woman reached in and grasped a small vial of liquid.

*"Give him this, and he will feel much better. This still may not heal him enough to compete, but if you look hard enough into your rounded soul, it will surely work."*

She winked at him and held the vial out. Jarrod looked at her like she was insanely crazy not understanding a word of that but accepted the vial.

*"Thank you so much for your help,"* as he tucked it away in his pocket.

*"You are very welcome, young man. Hurry now, so you can circumnavigate the universe. Off you go, and best wishes to you, son."*

She started to laugh, uncontrollably.

They both said thank you and walked out, astonished at her, uh, wisdom?

They walked together to the door, and Olvin took Jarrod by both shoulders,

*"Hurry now, and what happened will remain here. I shall have his teammates notified of these events and that he will be here to compete!"*

He let go and smiled graciously.

"*Thank you, Master Olvin. I hope this works.*"

"*I am confident that you will find a way.*"

He waved at the Master as he hopped back on his horse and galloped away.

*****

Evie slowly opened the door to check on Garren, and he was still asleep. The medicine given by the doc must have been pretty good because he was out cold. She went in and pulled the chair up to his bed and was watching him sleep. She checked his bandages and looked at his head wound.

She hissed at the gash on his head and wiped it clean. She noticed the bruising had deepened, and his eye was starting to blacken. The swelling was still bad.

"*Sssssisk, this is going to be good shiner and a really nasty headache in the morning.*"

She thought about Mathis and what he had turned into, longing for the younger days when they were children running to the big lake and playing together. It made her sick to her stomach that he had so much evil in his heart. She felt that if she could get him away from the evil, she would be able to save him from himself.

She hoped it was not too late to help him, but she was ready to leave him there if she had to. Evie knew it was going to be really hard to forgive him for what he had done to Garren, but Garren's attitude toward what happened had turned her heart. Still, she couldn't help but think this was very much her fault. She teared up thinking what happened on the road and vowed to confront Mathis for this atrocious act of barbarism.

*"Five or six against one? That is a little more than an attack. That is a motive to take someone out for good."*

She thought about who was going to tell Garren that he couldn't compete tomorrow, or he will probably figure it out on his own.

*"Uh Ughhh, he is too proud. He will go anyway and probably get himself killed."*

She thought of something hilarious.

*"I know, we can always tie him down."*

She chuckled to herself and dozed off to sleep in the chair with her feet tucked under her in the seat.

***

Jarrod came to the curve where the attack happened, and there, off the road was the log they used still wrapped in rope. He slowed the horse to a walk and closed his eyes as a familiar feeling was coming over him. He felt the vision growing from within and saw the black knights hiding in the woods where they tied a large log to both sides and released it as Garren was coming by. He saw Garren get smashed in the chest, but he caught the log and went with the motion which prevented the log from breaking all his ribs.

Then he saw Garren being beaten on the ground, helpless to fight back, as they hit him over and over. He saw him gather all his remaining strength to fight back, fending them off, with them having to carry one of them back.

The vision faded, and another came of the eerie laughing old woman cleric. Her laughing face and the words she spoke.

*"Oval face...., forbidden spherical knowledge...., the rounded soul...., circumnavigate the universe?"*

The second vision faded, and his eyes snapped open, he was totally stopped in the road. He thought for a moment and then had an epiphany.

*"I know what to do!"*

Jarrod looked around as the sun was starting to set and he kicked the horse's flanks, *"Hhup,"* which jumped started him into a gallop all the way home.

Jarrod stopped the horse, leaped off in a full run, up the steps and flung the door open. Evie heard the commotion and opened Garren's door to see Jarrod running down the hall.

*"What's wrong?"*

*"Wake him up and get a glass of water, I will be right back. Go, hurry,"* as he ran right by her.

She didn't question him and went to get a glass of water and then ran back to Garren's room. By the time she woke Garren up, Jarrod came strolling in. Garren looked over, still groggy.

*"Hey, brother, what's up? You have that look on your face."*

*"Shut up, Garren, no time for jokes,"* emptying the vial into the water.

The water boiled up a bit and started to steam out of the glass.

*"Here, drink this!"*

Garren started, *"But...."*

*"Drink It!"*

Jarrod pulled the ring from his pocket and slid it on while closing his eyes. He suddenly felt a welling of energy from deep within, and he started to speak, low at first, gaining in strength until he was yelling the words but with no real effort or strain. His voice was almost deafening. He heard a squeal from Evie as she covered her ears, but Jarrod did not open his eyes. He felt his temperature start to rise, and he kept speaking the ancient words.

While speaking, he saw a black armored man who quickly turned to him and spoke in a dark, guttural whisper.

*"Bring it to me, or all that you know will Die. I See You!"*

Jarrod saw he was holding a rope connected to three evil snarling wolf-like creatures. He released them with, *"Bring him to me!"*

Jarrod concentrated and continued the words while the vision faded. As suddenly as the words started, he finished just when Garren finished the water, dropped the glass falling limp on the bed. Evie was aghast, *"What did you do to him? Garren, Garren!"*

Jarrod felt weak and was barely able to hold himself up while Evie shook Garren, trying to wake him. Jarrod just turned to stagger out of the room.

"I'm exhausted, Evie. He is sleeping now."

Jarrod held himself with one hand on the wall as he walked. Evie cautiously followed him to the kitchen while he took the ring off and put it back into his pocket.

*"What the hell was that, Jarrod?"* Evie stomped in, demanding answers. *"Did you see what happened to you?"*

Jarrod shook his head no while he drank some water.

*"You started to glow, your hand turned so bright I had to turn my face and your voice? Was that magic, Jarrod?"*

Jarrod looked at her with utmost concern, *"Yes, it was my first attempt. How did I do?"*

She looked at him closer now that the glass was down, *"Jarrod, look at your face! It has changed."*

He coughed a smile, *"Is it that bad?"*

She shook her head no in utter awe, *"Um, no. It's beautiful."*

Jarrod looked back with surprise, *"Really?"*

*"Wait there,"* Evie exclaimed swiftly moving down the hall.

*"Okay, I'm not going anywhere. Trust me,"* Jarrod spoke weakly while filling his glass with water again.

Evie ran to Garren's room and grabbed the mirror that she used often. She ran in with Jarrod taking the last swallow from another glass.

*"Here, look at yourself!"*

Jarrod reluctantly took it and looked at himself. His eyes opened wide with shock noticing his features had sharpened, his eyes were bright colored, his face was shimmering with a golden tan tint, and his ears had raised almost to a sharp point.

*"Hmm, well that is interesting, isn't it?"*

He handed the mirror back to Evie with no concern at all. She snatched the mirror back.

*"Jarrod, I have seen someone like you when I was quite young. I have a memory of her and how beautiful she was. She was an Elf."*

Jarrod shook his head, yes.

*"I know, and now you know that I am an Elf too, half Elf anyway. My real mother was an Elf, and my real father was a man. I was adopted by Hardin and his wife. Garren doesn't know, and I do not want to tell him yet."*

He left it there, not wanting to divulge what else he knew.

*"Why are you looking at me so strangely?"*

Jarrod moved his eyes away and turned to the counter, *"Promise me, Evie, like I am ....!"*

He hesitated, *"that you will not tell Garren what I am, or what happened in there tonight. In time you will come to know what I already know but now is not the time."*

Evie started to tear up again and choked out, *"I promise, I will not say a word!"*

"Good and thank you" He walked toward her gently placing a hand on her shoulder, she didn't move, hypnotized by his magnificent eyes, face, and beautiful smile. Jarrod hugged her and kissed her on the cheek. She hugged him back and accepted it with elegance and grace.

*"I have not slept in days, and I'm exhausted,"* patting her on the shoulder on the way by.

*"Good night Evie, and tomorrow if I am not at the contest, will you let Garren know that I am sick but am with him in spirit?"*

She shook her head, yes, *"Of course, Jarrod, and good night."*

Jarrod slowly walked to the secret room and went to his cot. He laid down and closed his eyes and fell immediately into a deep sleep.

# Chapter 12

Garren awoke after about four hours to see Evie asleep in the chair beside him. He moved, holding his breath, expecting to feel agonizing pain as before. He felt no pain moving the covers to check his bandages. His chest was still tightly wrapped in gauze as was his head. He removed the bandages from his head and felt around and again, no pain at all. He looked at his bandages and saw the splotches of blood still there but had no cuts, no bruising, and he started to get up.

A familiar voice sounded from the chair.

*"And just where do you think you are going?"*

Evie got up and went over to him and touched his head.

*"Oh my, there is no bump there anymore."*

Garren spoke with surprise.

*"What happened? I feel fine. Where is Jarrod?"*

Garren flung the covers off and got up like he was never hurt.

*"I bet I know where he is."*

He strode to the door in nothing but his drawers. Evie rushed in front of him, blocking the door with both hands outstretched flat to the left and right with her back against the door!

*"You can't, Jarrod is....is SICK. Uhh yeah, he is sick."*

She pointed at Garren, *"You get back in bed Mister!! You need to rest. Jarrod made me promise I would not let you out of here till morning."*

Garren crossed his arms and sighed, turned and crawled back in bed. As he pulled the covers up, turning on his side, he propped his head up with his elbow on the bed and his hand on his head.

*"Evie, you know something?"*

She relaxed and looked back with a puzzled expression.

*"What?"*

With a sarcastic voice and expression.

*"You are not a very good liar."*

Her jaw dropped, and she put her hand on her hip with the other in a fist, shaking it at Garren, *"Oh, you little,"* she rushed over to pop him but held back as

Garren ducked. He reached out and pulled her in bed sideways while she screamed a laugh.

*"You are supposed to be resting!"*

Garren leaned closer to her on her side as she snuggled in, and he kissed her on the neck.

*"Uh, huh, I am resting."*

She rolled over to face him while he pulled her closer, lying on his back. Her leg was over his with her hand, caressing his chest.

*"Does this hurt?"*

Garren pulled her closer.

*"No, not at all,"* as he looked into her eyes.

She leaned in, and they kissed and kissed and kissed again. She laid her head on his chest with her hand now caressing his neck and face, closed her eyes.

*"I thought I lost you, Garren!"*

With a surprised *"What?"* He assured her he would never leave her.

She raised up and kissed him on the cheek, then on the eye, and then took a deep inner sigh, and kissed with a passion that he had never felt before with their tongues intertwining together and their breathing increasing together.

"*Stop, stop Garren,*" Evie pushed him, then relaxed back in his arms.

"*You need your sleep, baby. We are going to have plenty of time together.*"

Garren relaxed his fire and told her she was right about that. They chuckled together and then closed their eyes, snuggling in bed together.

Jarrod awoke in the early evening thinking about what he was going to do. He got up and was wondering what time it was. He raised his hand, waved, and all the candles in the room lit. He was feeling much better, although he had no idea how long he slept. He sat back down on the cot with his face in his hands, rubbing his cheeks to the back of his neck.

He suddenly realized he didn't feel the points of his ears or the sharpness of his face anymore. He jumped up and quietly opened the secret door and came into the back study. He made his way quietly to the shower room and went straight to the mirror, closing his eyes just before he got there. He stood in front of the mirror and slowly opened his eyes. He gasped with exuberance, as he moved his head side to side and pulled his hair back to look at his ears and saw his face.

*"I'm back, for goodness sake, I am back! Oh, thank the gods. I had no idea how I was going to hide my features, much less explain them. I wonder if that is how I am going to look or was it just the power of the ring? I wonder how Garren is doing!"*

Jarrod went to the spare room where he last saw Garren, realizing it was only around midnight. He slowly opened the door to see both Garren and Evie snuggled together in the bed sound asleep. He quietly closed the door back with a slight click.

*"They really do care for each other. Sleep well, brother. That was a weird thought, and my sister?"* He shook off the strange feeling and continued.

Jarrod contemplated while walking back to his room.

*"Wow, it looks like the little vial worked. I don't think that little old lady was insane at all. She was right, and I think she knew I would figure out her little play on words, guiding me to the ring."*

Before he knew it, he was back in his secret room and had the ring in his hand.

*"That is not good. I do not remember pulling that out of my pocket."*

He placed it back in his pocket and started to run over the events.

*"Dark guy again, who is that evil looking figure? I keep seeing him, but this time he spoke to me saying something about bring him the ring, or all I know will die. Oh, and he also said that he saw me. However, he saw me as an Elf and not like this."*

Jarrod was pacing back and forth now. He looked down, and he saw he was twirling the ring in his hand and cursed quietly to himself.

*"Dammit!"*

He took the ring back to the pouch on the desk and put it back in the journal and closed it. Jarrod started to pace again in deep thought about the evil one. He remembered the girl chained to the wall, and as soon as he thought it, the image came to him again.

This time, the girl slowly lifted her head. He cringed, seeing the blood run down her face.

*"Oh, my god, noooo, it cannot be, Eeeevie."*

Evie spoke softly and then slumped back down in the chains. *"Run Jarrod, my true brother, do not come for me. It's too late!"*

Jarrod forced his eyes back open almost to tears.

*"My sister. I am sure of it now. Evie is my blood sister!! She does not show any signs and does not know yet. I will tell her when the time is right. With Garren at her side, she will be safe."*

Evie and Garren woke up together early, hearing shuffling noises from the kitchen. They both got dressed and walked into the kitchen. Garren walked in first to see Jarrod over at the stove, making breakfast. He had already showered and was ready to go.

Evie hesitated with a worried expression.

*"Good morning, brother,"* Jarrod said, turning around to face them.

Evie took in a deep sighed breath, still thinking he looked like an Elf and when he didn't, Evie exclaimed.

*"Jarrod, your face? I mean, you are awake."*

Jarrod and Garren both busted out laughing.

"*Yes, I am awake. Thank you very much,*" laughing at her awkwardness.

Garren walked up to him and bear-hugged him.

"*I don't know what was in that mixture you gave me, but it sure helped. I feel better than ever, and I am ready for today. I thought you were not feeling well.*"

Jarrod started and glanced at Evie, who had her lips puckered in a whistle look, with her hands behind her back looking at the ceiling.

"*Umm, yeah. I was a little under the weather, but I am good now.*"

Garren gladly boasted out, "*Great, then I will see you at the contest?*"

"*Of course, I wouldn't miss it.*"

While Evie snuck by and sat at the table.

"*Evie, are you feeling better now, too?*" Jarrod questioned, she quickly shook her head yes, "*Mmm hmm,*" was all she could manage after seeing Jarrod last night.

Jarrod continued.

"*Good, how about some breakfast? I made us some sausage and eggs, cooked up some potatoes, toast, and Evie's favorite, tea.*"

Garren sat down beside Evie, "*Sounds good brother, I am starving.*"

Evie and Jarrod started to laugh, "*Yep, he is feeling better.*"

"*What?*" Looking like he had been left out of the joke.

They ate, and Evie cleaned up everything as Jarrod watched stunned. He was the one that always cleaned up. It was refreshing for him. They were chatting about last night and events happening today when suddenly there was loud, raucous outside. They all jumped up to see all the other White Knights on Garren's team, riding up.

Garren stepped out, "*What's this?*"

Lucas jumped down while the others unhorsed.

"*We heard what happened and came to check on you before we went back. You okay?*"

Garren looked confused, *"How did you know? Yes, I feel great, thanks to my brother. He fetched me some healing from the cleric at the academy."*

All the guys were relieved.

*"We all received hand-delivered messages last night from Master Olvin."*

Garren looked back at Jarrod, who had a sly expression on his face, *"Well then, let's go kick some Black Knight ass today."* They all raised their hands in triumph, *"Yeaaaah,"* they yelled together. Evie stormed back into the house.

*"Too much manliness for me!"*

They all roared with laughter at her. Garren embarrassingly brushed to the side.

*"Uh hmm, excuse me guys, be right back."*

They all were rolling with chortles at Garren. He got in the house and saw Evie with an angry look on her face, tapping her foot.

*"He is my brother, you know. Try not to hurt him."* Evie pleaded.

Garren said, *"Trust me, I will make sure he is not hurt, promise!"*

She ran up and hugged him and gave him a kiss.

*"I trust you, you be careful, too, and I will see you up there. I will go with your dad and Jarrod."*

*"Okay, can't wait to see you."*

He kissed her again, got ready, gave one more hug and kiss with a stern nod of gratitude to Jarrod, who nodded back.

*"See you there, brother,"* and he ran out the door to get Horizon, and they were off.

Evie looked at Jarrod after they were out of sight, and he grinned at her walking back to the kitchen to clean up.

"You did well!"

Evie followed closely and was amazed.

*"What happened? How did you turn back? I feel like I am lying to Garren, and I don't like it."*

Jarrod laughed, *"Well, don't worry too much about it because you are not a very good liar."*

Her mouth opened, and she rolled her eyes whispering under her breath. *"That's what he said."*

Jarrod turned sharply, *"What was that?"*

No hesitation from Evie, "*Nothing.*" She turned and walked out.

Jarrod yelled back, "*Let me know when you're ready to go.*"

"*OK,*" came an answer back from the shower room.

Garren and his team arrived at the stables, and they went straight to the armory to put on armor and pick up their weapons for the beginning of the contests. They passed by some of the other factions on the way and saw them whispering and pointing, as Garren rode by with his head held high. He was hoping to see the Black Knights, but they had not arrived yet. He thought to himself that they had avoided some drama for the moment, but he was so wanting to show them that they had not won and would indeed face his wrath on this day.

The other team members were ready and waiting for Garren when the Black Knights team arrived on the other side of the arena. Looks of anger and the thrill of the fight were passed through, as each faction prodded the other for the inevitable clash. Garren walked out dressed in his White Knight armor with silver helmet in hand, sword sheathed at his side. He looked impressive, to say the least.

Garren pointed at Mathis across the field as to say, "*It's on*" with a determined and fierce look on his face! Mathis looked back across the field in disbelief, realizing they had stopped nothing.

He shook his head yes with the same look of hatred he had at the river, as he donned his helmet. Mathis looked menacing, clenching his fists. Even from across the practice field, Garren could see him breathing, as they stared at each other.

Garren slammed his helm on his head and turned to his team, who watched Garren's every move.

"White Knights, this is our day. This is our time."

They did not answer, only listened to Garren, as he walked around in the center of the circle the team made surrounding him, looking at each of his team members.

"*Those knights tried to stop us, they attacked without provocation, they are not honorable, but we will not stoop to their level. We will fight with honor in this field. Respect your rivals today gentleman, and even if a battle is lost, lose with honor and respect, and we shall win the day. There is time for nice, and there is time for respect, but this day, it is time to show them what we are made of, the strength of heart, the strength of sheer will, and the strength of The White Knights!"*

Garren pulled his sword, *"Mount up men, and let's show them what true Knights are made of this day."*

There was no cheering and no hurray, the men all donned their helmets, nodded yes to Garren, and mounted their horses. They walked their horses to the warm-up field to wait to line up for the team introductions. The crowd was already gathering in the arena anxiously awaiting the King's arrival. There were different sections around the arena for the fans to go, each cheering together for their perspective factions. Even the Black Knights had a pretty good crowd although they were coming from the furthest city. They were not the only Knights here who wanted to exact revenge on one of the knight factions.

The Knights of the Moon and the Bronze Knights were also bitter rivals and had their own inner battles with each other. The rival factions were separated to keep the crowds in check and allies were set beside each other. The Black Knight fans, only having one ally and that being the Knights of the Moon were set beside each other on the opposite left side of the arena. The White Knight fans were on the far right side of the field if you were looking from the grandstands where the Elders and the King will be sitting in the middle section of the arena. The Knights of the Rose fans from Rynah were selected to sit right under the King's section. The crowd was whispering rumors that this was a political move by the King to try to entice Rynah City to join his allegiance, but that was only the rumor mill and made for good city gossip. Any of the other city leaders who have arrived were also seated with King Reordin of the Crystal City.

This was a political excuse for Reordin to get as many of the factions together to strengthen allies and try to get more cities to recognize him as the supreme leader. While allies are noted, strengthened, and new alliances are formed, the results are always the same. Each city wants its own king and wants to own their surrounding lands.

The factions think King Reordin just wants to increase his power to instill Crystal City beliefs and order upon them. The reverse is true, though. Reordin thinks that together and united, they can better prosper as an entire kingdom with one king but can have city leaders for each area. The trumpets were starting to sound and drums beating, as other leaders were beginning to file into the arena's royal sitting area amongst cheers, jeers, and whistles from the fans. Then the Paladin Order with the King's personal guards came into the arena and moved to the Royal sections. Garren watched as the King passed through each of the Knight factions with a couple of personal guards, stopping at each and wishing them good luck and well wishes. The King was coming through the middle section, so they did not get to see him but from afar.

The whole place erupted for the King as his presence was announced, and he and the queen made their way to the Royal seats. He turned and waved at all as he seated the queen and then shook hands and welcomed each of the other faction leaders, chatting quietly with each as he passed by. It was a great turn out, and there were five other faction leaders present today with two more on the way for the finals.

Jarrod, Hardin, and Evie arrived to see the magnificence of the arena. As they walked into the arena, Evie pulled the hood of her shirt over her head to cover her as much as possible. She did not want to be recognized by her faction. There had been a lot of work done on the arena, and this being Eve's first visit inside, she was amazed at how nice it was. They even incorporated a smart announcing system that amplified the voice of the arena sergeant, who would announce the King's arrival, the participating knight factions, and the individuals who are set against each other. Evie turned to Jarrod sitting next to her.

*"This place is amazing. Where are all the Knights?"*

She scanned the walking area around the entire arena filled with people and a fence to keep them and the Knights inside. Each section has an inside waiting area where the horses are stored for each faction and can hold up to 15 factions in this arena. They have their own waiting areas and even an area where they can watch their teammates compete.

There is a medical area and a weapons storage as well as a hot shower area. Jarrod showed her the three sections, the Knights would be out of and then began to tell her how the events worked with different contests, and how they were scored. She listened intently, curious about the games, and could see the fans from her faction on the far left with flags waving. She was feeling a bit like an outsider and a traitor right now because of their known rivalry with the White Knights in the first place. And then, the fact that her brother was competing in the events against her White Knight boyfriend, which was the antithesis of betrayal to the Black Knights. She shook her head in disappointment, knowing she would never be forgiven. She brushed the thought off, remembering how mad she was at Mathis. His words at their last meeting after the lake event had hurt her deeply.

Jarrod noticed her despair and asked.

"What's wrong, Evie?"

She faced him and started.

"I am…." She stopped and put her head down, "now is not the time, we will talk later. Let's just try to enjoy the day, ok?"

Jarrod nodded in agreement, thinking he understood her bit of despair knowing she was from the White Knight rivals and that her brother was over there. He agreed that this was not the right time because he was not ready to tell her that Mathis was not her brother and that he was her real brother.

He turned back continuing with contest explanations, pointing out key areas and score locations while Evie was extremely interested in all the aspects of the contest. It was like she was wanting to know all the ins and outs of the whole process, trying to formulate if there was a hidden way for some faction to gain some tactical advantage. Although she had been trained to fight, she was not allowed to train as a Knight and so, had no idea how this all worked.

The entire trials last three days with the Prelims on day 1. The semi-finals on day 2 and the finals on day 3, where they will fight down to the last two Knights remaining to settle a winner. The expected outcome this year is the Bronze Knights.

They have won the previous two times and have placed three Bronze Knights into the Paladin order, which is the highest and strongest order of all the Knights in the land. They will be hungry for three wins in a row. The brackets are set up in teams for the prelims. Each team selects their best knight for each event. The Knight that is eliminated is removed from the event, although he can stay with his side if he wants.

Evie interrupted.

*"Are there significant injuries? What happens if a winner cannot continue either?"*

Jarrod was reluctant to answer, but he did.

*"Yes, there will, unfortunately, be someone who gets injured, although it is rare for one to be killed from the contest, it has happened, especially in the Joust event. The lances are breakable but sometimes will splinter and penetrate the armor. What happened once, a lance splintered and penetrated the eye of an opponent who later died."*

*"Ooh,"* exclaimed Evie as Jarrod continued.

*"If the winner of an event cannot continue, then he is eliminated, and an alternate on the team can take his place. The semi-finals have each knight remaining, compete in the top three events. Again, the losers of these events are eliminated. The finals have two sections to it, random single events and a randomly picked final event. The events are chosen in random as are the contestants, and each pitted against the other until only two remain. If there are two from the same faction remaining the trial is over, and their faction is declared the winner. The last time, the Bronze Knights had three of their Knights at the end, who destroyed all the competition. Of course, the previous two contests had only five and six factions present. This year there are ten factions, so the competition will be fierce.*

*Each event has its own scoring system. For example, the horse handling competition is scored on style, the difficulty of stunts, and how well the horse is trained by the rider, while the joust is scored by three hits no matter how they are done. The first to three hits is the winner. A single hit is scored 1 if the lance is broken on*

226

*a shield or torso to arms, scored 2 if a lance hits the helmet and is scored winner if the rider is unhorsed by a lance hit. If there is a tie, the contest continues or is settled by weapon choice and hand to hand combat. The prelims have eight events, and there are only five Knights for each faction, so some Knights will have to compete twice today or maybe even three times. The field dwindles fast the first day because each event will have multiple Knights competing in the same event.*

*For instance, there are ten factions, and the bow and arrow contest is running, there will be ten Knights on the field competing at the same time with one winner which means seven Knights will be eliminated in that one event. First, second, and third place will get to continue. Same for the Axe Throwing contest, they are announced first, and as each ends another event begins. Other events are judged by the referee, only consulting the judges if needed, like the Sword Combat event. There will be a referee for every two contestants battling. There may be six battles going on at once. It gets very crazy during the prelims.*

*I just watch for our Knight faction and don't try to keep up with them all. The judges are seated in the middle on the bottom row in those large chairs. There are eight judges, and each is an expert in at least one event although the crowd does play a big part in the scoring, the end is based on their final judgment with the referee. There are referees for each event, and if rules are broken, the referee can remove points, call for a rematch or recommend disqualification, if the rule broken is severe enough. They can call the event, keep order by stopping an event, and will even end an event if a Knight is in extreme danger or concedes.*

*I have seen a referee get hurt just trying to stop a Knight from hurting another one. He will grab the knight or step in and wave the contest over. Some Knights cannot control their emotions and will not stop until their concentration is broken by the referee, and that is understood by all. There is no issue with wanting to win. If a disqualification is recommended, the crowd, along with the judges determine if the person is disqualified. That's about it."*

Evie looked excited as there was an electric atmosphere in the arena.

*"Here we go, see the announcer heading out to the standing tower in the center? He will climb up there and start announcing the factions."*

The crowd settled down some as the announcer was heading to the tower.

He got up to the top of the tower and turned toward the King.

*"Ladies and gentlemen, here in attendance today; introducing The Crystal City and King of these lands, King Reordin!"*

The King stood up and waved to the crowd, with cheers and confetti ribbons thrown, speaking to the crowd.

*"Welcome to all the faction leaders present today, and I look forward to having conversations and dinner tonight with you at the academy. I want to wish everyone good luck, and please have a great time today with family and friends. Let the contest BEGIN!"*

The king seated and gave the announcer a nod.

*"And now I will announce the Knights in attendance today. Starting with, The Knights of the Rose, from Rynah."*

The five came out together with cheers and standing ovations from their fans, as they walked in unison to the center of the arena and turned to face King Reordin waving to the crowd, their fans, and then bowing in unison on their horses to the King who acknowledges with a wave.

*"The Black Knights, from Idesport City."* They trotted to their positions waving to their fans and pretty much ignoring everyone else.

*"The Bronze and Copper Knights,"* each from opposite ends of the arena. All came out in similar fashion, waving to their fans and allies, ending with a turn to the King showing some-kind of respectful gratitude to him.

Next was out of the middle section, *"The Knights of the Sun."*

The next was *"The Knights of the Plains."*

Both out of the center section and paying their respects. The last four from the ends of the arena and since the White Knights are the home team, they are announcing them with the last two.

*"The Knights of Hart and The Knights of the Moon."* Each came out in a trot and took their places.

*"And finally, The Silver Knights and The White Knights of the Realm."*

They came out each end and the Silver Knights trotted, while Garren prance-trotted their horses first to the left and then to the right, all five in unison to their spots waving to the delight and cheers of the home crowd. Garren was calling orders out from the middle and pulled their horses to front and center facing the King, all five horses knelt with their riders on top and bow from the riders. King Reordin thoroughly enjoyed it and stood for them with a wave. They had their horses all at the same time raise up on 2 legs and wail. Each coming down one at a time and running to their position. The King was clapping with all smiles, as was everybody else in the stadium.

Evie, looked at Jarrod with bright eyes and standing with excitement.

*"Wow, He is really good."*

Jarrod responded, *"Oh, you haven't seen anything yet. This is just the announcements. Wait till you see him in real action."*

Evie laughed at Jarrod, *"I am so excited to see the events, and I hope he does well. I hope he is not too nervous because I am."*

Jarrod chuckled.

*"He doesn't get nervous. Well, except when he is talking about you."*

As he glanced over to Eve, she grinned ear to ear and embarrassingly bumped him with her shoulder. They laughed together and started to watch the events. Jarrod talked her through what was going on, pointing and explaining as the contest was beginning.

The announcer continued and headed the Knights all back to get ready.

*"The contest will now begin with the bow and arrow and axe throwing events."*

Runners came out from all directions and set up the targets for both. Next came out the Knights, one from each faction. Each contestant had to make two shots. The first one was a short-distance shot, and the second one was a long-distance shot, with each keeping the best out of three attempts for each shooting for the bow and arrow. The axe throw was three attempts as well for the axe, and three attempts for the knife throw.

*"Where is Garren?"*

Evie asked as she looked around for him in both groups. Jarrod told her that Garren was Captain of the team, and it was up to him to pick who competes in each event.

*"He will pick from his team the best at each event during the prelims. Everyone competes in the semis and then who is left in the finals. That is Lucas with the bow and arrow event. He is our best bowman on the team. The axe and knife throw contestant is Borrishnal. He is the best thrower I have ever seen."*

Evie secretly wanted Jarrod to know what events her brother was best at and blurted it out.

*"Mathis is best at the sword combat and the Joust, although he is very good with the bow and hand to hand combat as well."*

Jarrod looked over as if to say thanks for telling me now, as she was watching the arrows fly to the targets and then quickly moved to the axe throwers. Both Borrishnal and Lucas continues with Lucas finishing third and Borrishnal winning his event.

Now the next group came out with the runners setting up the horse handling and sword acrobatics. The horse handling was beautiful as Marhtin came out with his horse on the fly performing flips and drops to the ground and back to the horse. Then stand walking his horse up on two legs, to prancing and side walking the horse. He finished 2nd and so far, the White Knights had no one removed.

Next was the sword acrobatics. This one was Demmeal who flipped and twirled his sword. He almost looked like he was a master baton twirler. And then he dropped his sword. "*Ohhhhh,*" came from the crowd as he flipped it up in the air with his foot and caught it, spun, then performed a side flip and grabbed the sword again, all to the crowd's delight. However, the drop was a significant points deduction, he finished 4th and was eliminated.

Jarrod was upset.

"*Well, there is one down!*"

Next was the sword combat. The setup fellas ran out to erect the circles for the sword combat. Out walked Mathis, slowly and with arrogance, his sword in hand paired against the Knight of the Plains. Garren came out to cheers from the fans, and he acknowledged them with a wave. He was matched at the opposite circle against the knight from the Silver Knights. There were also four more with two in each circle. The battle began, and all eight were battling in the make-shift rings each with their own referees. Garren looked magnificent, blocking and pairing, and mixing with attack spins and swings.

The silver knight was clearly outmatched by Garren, who ended the match by a sword attack that knocked the sword out of the silver knight's hand and caught by Garren. He held the swords crossed at the Knight's neck. The referee quickly stepped in and called the match, holding Garren's hand up. Evie clapped with glee and grabbed hold of Jarrod, shaking him. Garren sheathed his sword and flipped the sword handle forward to give back to the Siler Knight. He took the sword from Garren, and they nodded in approval at each other.

"*Good match, White Knight.*" Came from the Silver Knight.

They shook hands, and Garren trotted back to his area, as Mathis had his hands full with the Knight of the Plains. When he suddenly spun and hit the knight with his hand and then with the sword to knock him off balance. Mathis pounced on him with several savage two-handed strikes that caused the referee to stop the fight. Mathis gallantly raised his own hands and sword in the air, walking slowly as if he was the king of the world, leaving the Plains Knight there on the ground. The referee helped him up, and two of his teammates helped him limp off the field. It was now intermission for lunch, and there were only three events left, Hand to Hand combat, the Joust, and the Arrow Dodge.

Jarrod and Evie went to lunch, and Hardin went back home to ready his cart to get supplies for the inn. He mentioned he was going to miss the semi-finals but would return for the finals if Garren makes it.

Jarrod explained to Evie.

*"By the end of the day, the field of fifty Knights will be down to just fourteen, and by the end of the semi-final round, there will be just four knights left. It will start to get interesting tomorrow."*

Evie said this was already so interesting, and she was glad Garren made it this far. The White Knights are the only ones left with 4 knights still around. No one has been eliminated entirely yet.

*"I am surprised that Garren came out in the sword combat. I wonder if he is going to do the hand to hand or the Joust? Marhtin is also very good with the joust, so I bet Garren will do the hand to hand. Marhtin is the only Knight to beat Garren once in the joust. By this afternoon, we will know who is left because Borrrishnal will probably do the arrow dodge, which is my favorite event to watch."*

*"What is involved in the Arrow Dodge?"* Evie curiously asked.

Jarrod told her that there were two parts to this event. In the finals, they are reversed if selected.

*"First, there is a close shot where a bowman fires an arrow at the contestant who must catch or block the*

*arrow with his arm. The second part is the most fun to watch because a contestant is set up in front of a giant wall and 25 bowmen shoot at him from long distance. The contestant must successfully block, pair, catch or break every arrow with his hand, arm or sword. If one is missed or if he gets hit by any 1 arrow, he is eliminated. By far, the most exciting and difficult event."*

Evie gasped.

*"Exciting? Sounds dangerous to let someone shoot an arrow at you."*

Jarrod laughed, *"They are blunt arrows, so they just bounce off them."*

Evie felt stupid, *"Oh!"* She left it there to avoid any more embarrassment.

The afternoon started with more excitement right off, as Mathis was paired with Marhtin in the Joust. Garren was so upset he didn't pick himself for this one, longing to be face to face with Mathis finally. There would be two jousts going at the same time in the field. There was enough room for four contestants at a time.

The first run started with a wave of the flag. Marhtin and Mathis charged each other, lowered their lances. *"BaBAM,"* Marhtin nailed Mathis on the shield on the first attempt, Mathis missed completely, and the crowd of fans went into a frenzy. Evie pressed her hands to her mouth as Mathis took the shot. She looked down visibly not happy but back with fierceness.

*"If he gets beat, he deserves it."*

Jarrod glanced over, totally surprised by that comment. They lined up for the second run, flag down and both raised their horses on two legs and charged. Lances lowered and this time *"Kah Keerrash"*, the lances crashed together, and both were hit. Both got points, and the score was 2 to 1 in favor of the White Knight. They lined up for a third run as Mathis glared down at Marhtin with hatred in his eyes, slamming his helmet down over his face and snatching the next lance.

The flag dropped, and they charged each other again. Evie watched as if it was in slow motion, the crowd was silent, and all that could be heard was the sound of the hooves pounding as they reached each other. Mathis screamed *"Ahhhhh,"* as he lunged the lance forward

"*PRACSHCrash*", as the blow flipped Marhtin backward off his horse and toward the ground hitting his head on the railing on the way down. The crowd gasped in horror, and Evie put her hand over her gasps as she watched petrified.

Mathis sped by and stopped his momentum, pumped his broken lance in the air screaming, "*Yeah*".

He tossed the busted lance to the side and glanced back at the limp and nonmoving Knight on the ground. Jumped off his horse, raised his hands in triumph, and walked away. Garren made it to Marhtin and lifted his limp body and realized he was gone. Marhtin broke his neck in the fall. Garren looked up just in time to see Mathis turn and smile at him.

"If he dies, he dies, and you're next!" as he pointed at Garren, laughed and turned away.

Garren jumped up in a rage, and the others held him back. The crowd silenced in horror with whispers of contempt at the Black Knight. Garren scanned the crowd and saw Jarrod. Jarrod stood with a raised hand into a fist, Garren, Garren, GARREN! The crowd started to chant his name, starting low and growing around the whole stadium as he stood there in defiance, watching Mathis walk off, meeting his team with smiles and pats on the back. Garren watched in angered sadness, as they removed Marhtin from the field on a stretcher. There was a short intermission, and the joust continued.

*"The games must go on!"* Jarrod sat back next to Evie with sarcasm.

Evie was visibly upset and on the verge of tears sitting there, with one hand over her mouth. Jarrod put his arm around her and consoled her.

*"This is not normally what happens here. This is supposed to be fun and exciting, but accidents do happen."*

He choked out the next, knowing it was not valid in this case.

*"I am sure Mathis did not mean to hurt him."*

She snapped her head up to Jarrod in anger, *"Yes, he did! He wanted to hurt him. I saw it in his eyes."*

Jarrod just looked back to the field while they set up for the hand to hand combat.

Garren went to the remaining teammates.

*"This will not be our end. Instead, turn the rage into honor for our friend!"*

He asked which one wanted to do the arrow dodge. They agreed that Borrishnal was the best at the Arrow Dodge, and Garren was going into the hand to hand combat.

*"Don't let this incident get in your heads. We must finish this for Marhtin."*

The men all agreed. Garren changed into his leather light armor and walked onto the field with his soft hand gloves on, for the hand to hand combat. He was paired with The Knight of the Rose. There were five circles set up with two at each end and one in the center. Garren won his match and was again not really challenged defeating the challenger in three minutes of the first round by submission. He wrapped the knight up and took him down in a backward choke. The knight submitted. Garren didn't even brush off the dust, as he walked back to the team amid cheers from his fans.

He heard one familiar voice and turned to see, Evie screaming at him, *"GARREN."* She raised her hand, blew him a kiss. He managed a smile, waved to her, and continued off.

The next event was the Arrow Dodge, and this event was not a one on one event. It was an event for hand and eye coordination, to the extreme. Just the knight versus the arrows. One Knight from each of the ten factions would face the arrows this day. There is only a winner if they beat the challenge.

The ones who do not overcome the challenge are eliminated. The rest will be back for the semi-finals to be held the next day. Based on how many were left would be how many random events and random factions will face each other. The semi-finals are brutal. They set up for the arrow dodge with the first contestant, a Bronze Knight who made it through. Then there was a couple who didn't until finally, came Borrishinal's turn. He was dressed in his armor in front of the wall. The bowman pulled back, and *"RELEASE"* was heard. Borrishnal quickly turned and snatched the arrow from midair and held it up. He caught the arrow, Jarrod clapped in amazement as did Evie and everyone else. Next came the long distance, 25 arrows at once.

He pulled out his short sword and was ready. *"RELEASE,"* and all 25 arrows were headed toward him, He parried, sliced, and moved quick as lightning and then "Clink" an arrow hit him just as he sliced the last arrow. He was hit though and was eliminated. Garren sighed in despair as he watched Boris come toward him.

*"It's okay, Boris. You did good,"* with a pat on the shoulder.

By 4 pm, the events were finished, and they were awaiting the final announcements for the end of the preliminary events. This was the last event, and the announcement came with a factions list of who was in the Semi-Finals. Everyone was starting to file out of the stadium when their factions were called.

The Bronze Knights with 2

The Black Knights with 2

The Knights of the Rose with 2

The White Knights with 2

The Copper Knights with 1

The Silver Knights with 1

The Knights of the Moon with 1

The Knights of the Sun with 1

The Knights of the Hart with 1

The Knights of the Plains with 1

"*Good night, everyone, and we will see you back here tomorrow.*"

Garren sat in their locker room with his teammates.

"*We lost a good friend today, and I know we are not supposed to exact revenge and hatred upon others, but this one, I will make an exception. We will not let this be our depression, but instead our determination.*"

He looked up, squeezing his knife in his hand, pulled it through cutting his hand.

"*I swear on my own blood that we will not rest until Mathis pays dearly for this.*"

All his team together, "*here, here!*"

"*Lucas, it is you and me tomorrow. Go get some rest, and I will be here in the morning.*"

Lucas looked back.

"*I am staying here tonight to guard our things.*" Three others, including the two alternates chimed in, "*and we are staying here too for them.*"

Garren stood.

*"Good idea, Lucas, if you are here then I will stay as well."*

*"No, no Garren, our families could not come. Marhtin's family will be notified, and his body returned home to be laid to rest. You have family here, so go spend some time, and we will see you in the morning."* Garren nodded.

*"Thank you, friends. I will see you in the morning."*

Garren got cleaned up and went out to the stables, to see Jarrod and Evie waiting for him. She ran up to him and stopped, as Garren spoke while looking down.

"It's my fault, he is gone. I should have picked myself for the joust, instead of Marhtin."

He looked back, choking back tears. Both Evie and Jarrod grabbed him in a hug, and neither said anything as Garren started to sob. The only sound was Evie's soft voice. *"Shhhh, shhh,"* as she lovingly stroked his back. He looked up and wiped the tears, and they solemnly walked together with their horses in tow.

It was still early evening when they arrived at the house, and Jarrod went to shower up for work at the inn. Evie was with Garren in the kitchen and sat saying nothing. She was scared he would tell her to leave because of what Mathis did, so she kept quiet as not to upset him. She got up and made some dinner sandwiches and put together an excellent fruit dish along with some fruit juice and tea.

She set the table when Jarrod walked in and said.

*"What's this? Thank you, Evie. Looks good,"* and he dug in.

She announced, *"My turn!"* and walked out of the room. Garren barely looked up as she left. Jarrod waited for her to leave, slammed his sandwich down.

*"Alright Garren, it is one thing to mourn your friend, but sitting there feeling sorry for yourself is totally different."*

Garren raised his eyes in shock and then relaxed with a sigh,

*"You are right, of course, Jarrod. I just wish I would not have picked him. I was so confident and cocky that we were going to win everything. I was a fool."*

Jarrod picked his sandwich back up, *"Go back out there tomorrow and just do your thing and bust their asses. Don't worry about those goons. It was an accident, even though his behavior after what happened was apprehensible and not becoming of a Knight. You won both your events easily today. I loved Marhtin to, and we all will miss him. This is not your fault. He made a mistake when he turned into the lance.*

*He knew the risks in the tourney, as we all did, and he would not want you to quit because of him. Tomorrow you will face someone with confidence, as they have won some events. They will be confident, use that to your advantage. Take your strength and anger deep in your soul and apply it against them. Get your confidence back, and by the way, you should give Evie a break. She is torn between you and her brother, rivals in more ways than one.*

*She risks being banished from her home for you, so you could be a bit nicer to her. She loves you, and if you can't see that, then you are not only blind but just plain stupid!"*

Garren sat back,

*"Wow, Jarrod. I have never seen you so fired up before. Right, I'm sorry, it wasn't my intention to ignore her."*

Jarrod pointed at him, *"It's not me you should apologize to, it's her."*

Garren slammed his hand on the table, *"Okay, OK, I will, Jarrod, and thanks for the pep talk, but I think I can handle things."*

Jarrod blinked unamused, *"Well, it's about time you grew a pair."*

They both busted in laughter, just as Evie walked back in smiling when she saw them laughing together.

*"What did I miss? Hmmm?"* as she chomped on a sandwich.

Garren and Jarrod looked at each other and started laughing again while Evie shrugged it off. They sat together for an hour chatting together when Jarrod got up to leave for the inn.

*"Get some rest Garren, and I will see you tomorrow."*

Garren nodded and watched Jarrod leave. He was just out of sight when Evie raised up and kissed Garren on the cheek whispering.

*"Race you to the bed!"*

Garren quickly reached to grab her, she squealed and bolted to the back. Garren lunged forward racing just behind her, but there was no way to catch her, with Evie laughing, "*I win, I win,*" the whole way there.

# Chapter 13

Garren arrived at the stables early for the start of the semi-final rounds. His men were already there, and they started their warmups when a Knight walked in.

*"The King wishes a word."*

Garren and the others immediately got on one knee and bowed their heads. The King came in behind them, while other Knights stood at the door in escort. King Reordin walked up to Garren who was still kneeling and pulled on Garren's shoulder.

*"Rise, rise my friends."*

Garren stood up as did the others, *"Your majesty graces us with his presence."*

Reordin chuckled out loud.

*"Oh, stop that, Garren. Today we are just friends. Walk with me, Garren."*

They moved side by side slowly walking out the back of the stables and into the field with four Paladin Knights not far behind.

*"You are even bigger in person than I saw you on the field. I wanted to personally stop by to let you know*

*that we have sent a messenger to Marhtin's home. We have already prepared his body to be sent back tomorrow. We will send a grand escort to lay him to rest along with a loyalty payment for his service. You and your Knights should be commended for your valor not only on the field yesterday, but after what happened to your friend."*

Garren looked back at the king.

*"Thank you, your majesty. You're too kind."*

Reordin shook his head, no, *"No, it's true. The extraordinary courage, honor, and restraint your knights showed in the face of humility were exactly what a Knight of the Realm should show. I don't want to go against your Knight honor, so I won't ask you to exact revenge, however, and I say this with a heavy heart, I want you to beat them into the ground today and should one make it to the finals, do it again tomorrow. That Black Knight's behavior was despicable, and I am considering whether we will ever invite them again."*

Garren smiled at the King.

*"Thank you, Highness. I will make every attempt to do just that not only for us but now, for the honor of the kingdom."*

The king put his hand on Garren's shoulder and stared directly into his eyes.

*"Good luck today and tomorrow. Remember son, honor above all else. That is a Knight's oath and duty."*

He smacked his shoulder and walked off.

*"I will be watching your career with great interest my young friend, and I expect to see you very soon."*

Garren got in line behind the King's escorts and walked back to the stables. Lucas ran up to Garren with the others close behind.

*"What did he say?"*

Garren starred at them with determination in his eyes.

*"He sent his sincere apologies to us for the loss of our friend and a messenger to his family along with a payment for his loyal services to the kingdom."*

The others and Lucas stood with pride.

*"That is really good of our King. Was there anything else?"*

Garren snatched his sword up with anger. *"Yes, he said to go out there with honor today and kick their asses!"*

Lucas resounded while he pulled his sword and touched it to Garren's, *"Right, let us make them wish they had never come to this field."*

They nodded to each other and headed to the waiting area.

Jarrod and Evie arrived at the academy stadium to get to their seats a little early. They were walking together through the entrance gates when one the Black Knights who had been eliminated saw her and rushed over from the other side of the street. It was Kalluke who was Mathis' best friend. Evie saw him walking over with purpose and stopped Jarrod, as she faced the broad-shouldered young man.

*"Kal, what are you doing here, shouldn't you be up Mathis' butt as usual?"*

Kal grabbed her by the arm and yanked her.

Jarrod snatched Kal's arm off.

*"Hey, let go of her, I wouldn't go there if I were you."*

Jarrod glared at Kal with disgust as his arm slung off Evie. Kal was surprised by Jarrod's strength.

*"Oh, what you got here, Evie?"*

Kal turned to Jarrod with a sarcastic expression.

*"Another little protector?"*

He pointed at Jarrod who had moved in front of Evie still starring at Kal.

*"You stay out of this before I crush your head like a grape."*

He moved sideways to see Evie better.

*"I am starting to think your brother was right, you're just a little whore. To think I defended your absence. You make me sick, and your father will meet us halfway back, and I promise he will not be happy."*

Just then, a guard walked up and said.

*"Okay, folks, move it along. No need for trouble here."*

Kal started to walk away and pointed back to Evie.

*"We will deal with you later, and you,"* wheeling towards Jarrod. *"You better mind your own business."*

Jarrod and Evie watched him walk down the street and out of sight. She walked beside Jarrod. *"Sorry about that, Jarrod. He is just jealous because I didn't want anything to do with him."*

Jarrod raised an eyebrow back at her.

*"You don't say? I thought he was just wanting a casual talk over a cup of tea."*

Evie started laughing, *"My, that was sarcastic."*

Jarrod answered back, emphatically.

*"It's what I do. In all seriousness, though, I am even surer now than ever that you should not go back with them."*

Evie shallow breathed to answer, *"I don't think my own family would do anything to hurt me. They have been consumed by dark promises, and once confronted with the truth of things, they will come around."*

Jarrod pleaded, *"Okay then, I see your point but let us go with you."*

Evie concernedly shook her head no.

*"No way Jarrod, that would make it so much worse. Don't worry, I will be fine. I can handle myself. Mathis is more bark than bite, especially when it comes to me. We were very close growing up, and now he is worried about losing me from our home. Besides, I haven't*

*decided what I am going to do yet. You act like I am gone already. Relax, we will figure it out after the trials are over, promise. C'mon let's get to our seats. I want to see Garren compete and have a fun day."*

Jarrod reluctantly accepted her explanation even though he felt like she was being too cavalier about the whole thing, not understanding that there is something else happening. He kept quiet, restraining himself again because he still was not sure what was going on. He just had a feeling that there was something not right with all this.

They got to their seats just in time to see the first matches which had two factions set up for the arrow accuracy shots. It was Lucas vs. Arion, one of the Black Knights. Garren was matched against one of the Copper Knights at the next target sequence. Evie spoke out as she spied Mathis on the other side of the field lining up for his shot.

*"At least they are separated, for now."*

Jarrod managed an *"Uh huh."*

Lucas walked over and behind the Black Knight, who was up first. He raised his bow and shot,

FfffffffftTT, the arrow lodged almost dead center of the target, leaving very little room for a second arrow. Arion motioned to Lucas with his arm as if to say step right up, your turn, with a wicked crooked smile on his face. Lucas walked right by without even acknowledging Arion, stepped up to the line, aimed and THRUNG the arrow released. FFFFfffffffffutTTt! The crowd roared as the arrow hit dead center of the target. Lucas glared with pleasure at Arion who turned with hatred and walked off.

Arion was eliminated while Garren had just eliminated the last Copper Knight. Mathis defeated the last Knight of the Hart, and The Bronze Knights were both victorious, defeating the last Knight of the Moon and the last Silver Knight remaining. The Knights of the Sun were victorious over Plains Knights. They took a slight intermission with two Bronze Knights left, two White Knights left, one Black Knight, one Knight of the Rose and finally, one Knight of the Sun.

Jarrod explained the next events to Evie.

*"Semis are almost done already. It looks like the next event is going to decide who is going to the finals*

*tomorrow. They will add up the scores and wins so far to determine the next events. There are seven left, and the top four will go to the finals which will be the Arrow Dodge, and The Joust tomorrow. The judges are tallying the scores, and one will be picked to go to the finals tomorrow automatically."*

*"Garren has had three events, Lucas three events so we will see. Probably either one of the Bronze Knights or the remaining Knight of the Rose because they have each competed in four events."*

Evie asked with inquisitive curiosity.

*"Who will Garren fight next?"*

Jarrod answered.

*"I don't know, they are randomly selected. First, we have to get through who is going to the finals without another match. Here he comes, we are about to find out."*

*"Ladies and gentlemen, the judges have selected the Knight who is automatically selected to go to the finals."*

He hesitated as everyone waited in excitement.

*"The Bronze Knight Endar has been selected to the finals. He has a score of 98.2 with four wins."*

The Bronze Knight stepped forward from his area and waved to the crowd who responded with claps and cheers. *"This will be the last event of the day and decide the final three going to the finals. Good Luck, and may the gods be with you. The last event is the hand to hand combat. The matchups will be announced next. Please step to the center of the field when called."*

Bronze Knight vs. Black Knight

White Knight (Lucas) vs. Knight of the Rose

White Knight (Garren) vs. Knight of the Sun

Garren walked up and didn't even look at Mathis, who was glaring at him with hatred.

*"Avoided me again, Stromblade! Don't worry, your time is near,"* Mathis venomously spat.

Garren balled his fist and resisted, fighting the temptation to look over, knowing deep down that he would not be able to stop himself if he did. He did not even hear the crowd cheers as the two walked to their areas. Lucas pounded Garren's shoulders with his fist, and Garren did the same to Lucas.

*"You ready?"* Lucas nodded with a fierce battle face.

*"Okay, it's time. Let's take them out."*

They both got into their light combat gear with no weapons and went to their positions for warm up.

In the semis, the last event is done individually like the finals, so the crowd can enjoy the competition. The other Knights must wait for their perspective bouts. First up, was the Bronze and Black Knight.

Bronze Knight walked into the circle, and Mathis walked over to his side. They slowly started to circle each other, closing in for the inevitable clash, while patiently waiting for the sound to begin. The sound came *"Begin,"* and both rushed the other, throwing punches, to start with, each dodging the other. Mathis did a spin maneuver that took the Bronze Knight by surprise, but his reflexes kicked in, being well trained, and he blocked, took hold of his arm and flipped him to the ground.

Mathis flipped over back to his feet and attacked with a forward kick, ducked by the Bronze who executed a leg sweep that took Mathis down again. This time, Mathis jumped from his back straight to his feet and stepped back to gather himself. The Bronze rushed forward first with swings all blocked by Mathis who caught the second swing, turned his arm and struck him in the face. The first real strike that found its mark in the bout. It was strong enough to give a cut above the Bronze's eye even with soft gloves on.

Mathis took advantage of the staggering Knight and seized the opportunity to try another front kick, but the bronze knight dodged the kick and rolled forward delivering a side kick from the ground that stunned Mathis backward then forward. He leaped on top, and they wrestled on the ground whirling and twisting with the crowd in a frenzy.

*"Get him, Mathis,"* Kal shouted from the side.

They managed to wrestle up to their feet where Mathis maneuvered around behind Braxess.

The Bronze raised his arm and gave a backward punch with his elbow, which caused Mathis to release with a grunt. Braxess went to one knee and flipped Mathis over the top to his back, and then he was on top readying a strike. Mathis kneed Braxess that pushed him to the side, and now Mathis had him in an upper armbar. The Bronze Knight screamed in agony. SNAP!

The crowd gasped, *"Ohhhh"* was heard all over the stadium. Mathis broke his arm and released him as his arm went limp. The referee was ready to stop the fight but did not because Mathis released him. Mathis circled the flailing Knight who was trying to stand up with one arm limp and dangling.

*"Submit or feel my wrath!"* Yelled Mathis.

The Bronze shook his head no, *"Never,"* as he raised one arm in a defensive posture. Mathis attacked again this time kicking him in the side while he tried to block, but the force sent him to the ground. Mathis saw blood now with hatred black eyes, jumped on the defenseless knight and struck.

The referee had seen enough and tried to step in, as Mathis was pounding him. He slammed the referee aside and started to attack again. Garren rushed over, seeing enough and grabbed Mathis and threw him off to the ground just as the Bronze teammates arrived.

Mathis leaped to his feet, *"C'mon, you and me right now."*

The rest of the Knights around kept them at bay, as they helped the referee up. Mathis was declared the winner, and the referee reluctantly raised his hand.

*"That's right, I am in the finals now,"* defiantly shaking his head, yes, walking to the sidelines where he was met by Kal with water and a pat on the back.

He turned, spat out water on the ground, and glared at Garren. The other Bronze knights helped their fallen teammate back to the side, as Garren didn't say a word but backed up slowly then turned to his area. The handlers set up for the next bout, Lucas vs. the Rose Knight. Lucas walked out to the circle and met the eyes of the Rose Knight. They bowed their heads to each other and stood staring into each other's eyes, waiting for the referee to start the match. The referee walked over, *"Begin!"* Both moved like cats attacking prey, each with different blocks and strikes with no hits that amounted to anything.

They backed off ready again, and the Rose moved into a wrestling attack and flipped Lucas over his hip. He tried to come down on top of Lucas, but he rolled out of the way and back to his feet. The fight went on with each not being able to gain an advantage until the Rose Knight was finally able to score a good hit to the leather breastplate with his forearm and then an uppercut punch to the chin. Lucas sprawled to his back, and the Rose Knight pounced on top, holding his arms with his knees while punching straight down to his face.

Lucas made one desperate attempt raising up with his legs throwing the Rose Knight forward and off him. The Rose Knight rolled straight to his feet and attacked again. Lucas was done, no strength left and got cold cocked in the temple, which knocked him out. He went limp, and the Rose Knight jumped to attack but stopped realizing he was out cold, as Garren was on his way.

The Rose Knight moved to the side with the referee on the other side trying to revive Lucas, just as Garren came up, Lucas woke up. The Rose Knight helped Lucas up and patted him on the back. The referee raised the hand of the Rose Knight, turning him in a slow circle. Garren took Lucas by the arm over his shoulder and helped him to the waiting area, looking back at the salute given by the Rose Knight.

Next up was Garren versus the Knight of the Sun. They walked out and shook hands and waited for the start. Garren was so much bigger than the Knight of the Sun, but that didn't mean much because the Sun Knight would probably be much faster than him. They waited, and then the referee yelled, *"Begin."* Sure enough, the Sun knight was very agile, starting off with some kicks at Garren to keep him from getting ahold. Then Garren tried to throw some punches but all missed. His opponent attacked from the side, and Garren started to watch him and just fended him off from all directions. He was studying his tactics and looking for a weak point. Only then he realized that the Knight had no weak point, but his strong point was his legs. He was fast and agile. Garren set him up, so he would throw a side kick. He fell for the bait, and Garren caught his leg and wrapped it up with one arm.

He threw three quick punches to the leg and then twirled him with another blow to the thigh. While the Knight tried to catch his balance from the stings on one leg, Garren delivered a straight side kick that sent the Sun Knight straight to the ground. Garren leaped on the sun Knight and attacked his other leg throwing two vicious punches, and a knee shot to the other leg. He moved off him and stepped aside, watching the Knight. The Sun Knight slowly got up and limped a hop to steady himself. Garren did not attack but let him walk it off a bit.

The Sun Knight moved toward Garren and then attacked again, throwing a desperate arm and fist attack to only be caught by the White Knight, who twisted his arm and flipped him to the ground. The Knight slowly got up again, but this time, he waved off Garren and walked to him, put his hand on his shoulder, "*I am done, Sir Knight.*"

He turned and raised Garren's arm in victory, all to the crowd's pleasure. The two knights gave a quick hug and manly pat, and the Sun Knight slowly limped off the field, met by his teammates. The referee nodded at Garren and raised his hand to make it official. The crowd cheered with delight, as Garren walked off the field to joyously meet his team.

Evie, was up in the stands with Jarrod ecstatically laughing, cheering, and jumping up and down. Garren glanced a wave in their direction as Evie hugged Jarrod again.

The loud announcer started, and the fans quieted down.

*"Here, we are with the results. Your Knights for the finals, tomorrow night. They will step forward when called."*

The Bronze Knight – Endar

The Black Knight – Mathis

The Knight of the Rose – Anthan

The White Knight – Garren

The crowd booed and hissed, cheered and screamed at each, depending on which faction was being called as they filed out of the stadium. Evie and Jarrod met Garren at the stables with smiles and congratulatory comments as they readied for the trip home. Garren hopped on his horse and held his hand out to Eve. She took his hand and jumped up with glee, her arms around him while Jarrod started off.

They caught up to Jarrod easily, as Evie was kissing Garren on the back of his neck. They made it to the house, and Garren and Evie excused themselves quickly to his room while Jarrod went down to read for the night. The next day came fast and furious, and Garren was already at the stadium's waiting area with Lucas and the other White Knights.

The tension and electricity were already present because this was the final day. There were only two events today, and Garren was ready while thinking for a moment of being with Evie last night. She was so radiant and beautiful that she took his breath away. He thought for a moment again.

*"I face the dangers of these trials, but she glances at me, and I buckle. Ha, some kind-of Knight I am."*

He laughed to himself and then started to concentrate on breathing and relaxation exercises, still a little sore from yesterday. Nothing would stop him from finishing this day and was so looking forward to finishing it with Mathis. He concentrated on the two events of the day. The arrow dodge, how he was going to move, parry, and catch all the arrows.

Then his mind went to the joust. Raising the lance and using his strength to move the lance around. He practiced with a heavy lance moving it up and down, so the contest lance would feel like a feather compared to this one. His muscled arms and cut abs were shown in full. He swung it, stopped it in one place, raised it to the top over his head, and brought it back down to parallel to the ground. He held it out straight as-long-as he could with one arm not letting the tip hit the ground then the other arm until he could hold it no longer. No one else could do that with the heavy lance. He was ready, as the crowd was now filling in for the final events. The crowd was even bigger now than any of the other events packed to almost full capacity as the arrow dodge was set up. The order was set and placed on the big boards with the Black Knight first, followed by the Knight of the Rose. Then Garren followed last, by the Bronze Knight.

Mathis strut out with his helm in his hand dressed in his traditional black armor. The crowd was filled with booooos and whistles with only cheers from his section. He defiantly flashed a wave off to everyone, then turned to his section and held a fist in the air with gritted teeth showing. This did not have the reaction he expected, as people were throwing things at him. He slammed his helmet on and stood there, daring anything to hit him.

The announcer came on, *"That's enough, settle down or be escorted out."*

The crowd obeyed as the archers were ready. The crowd became silent as the word, *"Ready"* came. The archers pulled there bows to aim, *"Release!"* And the arrows were away.

Mathis waited and then fought them all off with blocks from his arms, hand, and his sword. He raised his arms and walked back, successfully fending off every arrow with screams and cheers from his section. Even Garren thought it was an impressive parry. He was now ready for the single arrow. He paced back and forth, waiting for the ready command, concentrating on the single arrow.

He heard the ready command and turned to face the single archer, who was already in the pulled position. *"Release!"* The arrow was away, and with one hand, Mathis reached up and snatched the arrow out of the air, making it look easy as he broke the arrow across his knee and threw it to the ground.

The crowd clapped at the display of skill but booed his behavior, as he jeered and laughed at the crowd saying, *"I am the best, get used to it!"*

Throwing his arms up and down to the crowd and laughing.

Next was the Knight of the Rose who had already taken his position, watching the spectacle of the Black Knight in disgust. He turned and was waiting for the ready command. *"Ready?" "Release!"* The arrows flew toward the Knight who started blocking and parrying, then tripped and fell, missing several arrows. He received *"Oooohs"* from the crowd. He got up and kicked the dirt, looking over at the commotion on the sides and seeing Mathis mocking and laughing at him.

He walked passed Garren who patted him on the shoulder on the way by. Garren moved to take his turn at the arrows. He waved to the crowd as the roar from the stadium grew to a loud cheer and drowned out the boos from the black knight fans.

Garren stood at the ready waiting for the command. *"Ready?" "Release."* Jarrod jumped up to watch, and it was if it was in slow motion, one arrow slapped with his hand, then an entire bunch with a swing of his sword and hand together. Jarrod thought Garren was moving like poetry in motion. He swatted and slashed and then dove for the last arrow as it was a bit to his left, and he caught it. Stood up and raised the arrow in triumph to the delights of the crowd, and especially Jarrod and Eve, who were excited and hugging again.

Garren readied himself for the single arrow attack. He put his helm on and stood with his legs shoulder-length apart and his sword sheathed, both hands outstretched in full concentration. *"Ready? Release!"* Shuuuuffffff and catch! Garren never moved an inch except for his hands and caught the arrow right at his chest. The crowd erupted as he removed his helmet, raised it to the crowd, glancing a sly smile over to Mathis. It was his turn for cursing and kicking the dirt.

Garren nodded at him with clenched teeth.

*"The time for honoring yourself is near an end."*

Garren stomped off to his waiting area, passing the Bronze Knight Endar, who stopped him and exchanged words. Endar nodded his head and kept going with Garren, watching him walk to the ready position.

Garren got back to meet Lucas, *"What did he say, Garren?"*

Garren looked back across the field at the Bronze Knight.

*"He thanked me for my actions on the field for his friend and walked off."*

They both watched on.

The Bronze Knight was ready and waiting for his command. *"Ready? Release!"*

Endar sprang into action moving faster than the wind, spreading out his arms and sword, knocking all the arrows. There was nothing clumsy in his fashion. Like a ballet artist and master martial artist combined in one, he jumped through the air while spinning with arms stretched out, blocking every arrow and catching the last one spinning to a stop. Garren had seen nothing like that before.

He was indeed the best at this event Garren had ever seen. The crowd roared with delight and to the highest level yet, as Endar threw the arrow to the ground and glared over to Mathis. He walked over and circled his area, then walked halfway to where his faction was seated, and all were quiet as the leader of the faction stood and raised one hand. The Bronze Knight nodded, and that section erupted again with cheers. Endar made it to his ready position and waited for his command, standing straight with his head held back, and arms slightly bent to almost straight out. *"Ready,"* Garren saw Endar lower his head in complete concentration to face his single shooter, *"Release!"* The arrow flew straight and true, Shhhuuuuu CRACK. *"OOOOhhhhhs"* from the crowd as the arrow bounced off the Bronze Knights' chest, who never moved a muscle. Garren jumped out of the waiting area as he watched the Bronze Knight just stand there. Then rushed to him as he slowly walked off the field.

*"Why did you....?"* Garren stopped when Endar removed his helmet.

*"The dishonor they have shown on this field can only be exacted by the honor you have shown. This was for the honor you showed my friend and my faction. Go make it right and earn this!"*

Garren looked over to their leader who saluted him. Garren rose his hand and saluted the faction leader with clenched teeth. The crowd exploded as the Bronze Knight held up Garren's arm in victory. The crowd of White Knights ran on to the field and raised Garren up and carried him off the field to their area, as the crowd cheered to a level that reverberated the halls of Graystone Academy.

It was an intermission, and the last event was to be set up.

*"How appropriate! The Black Knight versus the White Knight, never seen that happen before."*

Jarrod proposed to Evie, who was sitting there quietly and then looked at Jarrod.

*"I am not sure I can watch this. I think Garren might have to kill my brother because if he doesn't, Mathis will kill him."*

She turned serious, more like a worried stare. Jarrod knew and understood exactly what she was saying.

Garren was ready for the final meeting and was pacing in the waiting area. Lucas was with his horse and had him outfitted with the White Knight overlay and armor.

Garren leaped up on his horse with one jump and settled the horse, patting him on the neck. He slowly walked out of the tunnel on his horse to see Mathis already walking to the other end of the joust runway. Garren stopped his horse by the lance station, raising the ready hand to the flagbearer.

Mathis did the same but added, *"Time for you to pay for your insolence, Knight. You have embarrassed my family and me for the last time. And Evie will be going back, you can count on that!"*

The crowd was cheering them on as the announcer came up.

*"You will be the one who pays dearly, Mathis, and Evie has her own mind."*

Mathis laughed at him as he donned his helmet and snatched a lance. Garren did the same.

*"Good luck Knights, and may the best be shown here today."*

They were ready to start. *"Flagbearer referee, at your will."* The flagbearer lowered the flag, and the two knights charged at each other, lowering lances. KkkkraaackKRASh! As the two met, both struck the other on their shields. Trotting back to their original spots for another lance, passing each other with stares.

They readied, and the flag was lowered again. This time raising their horses on two legs and launching forward to full gallop, lowering their lances. Kkk-kRASHHH….as the lances connected again, but Garren's lance hit Mathis in the chest glancing off to the left while Mathis' lance hit Garren above the shield and glanced off his shoulder.

They passed again, *"This time you are going down,"* Mathis spewed at Garren.

Garren just huffed a laugh at him, *"We'll see about that."*

They readied again with a tie score, and the flag was lowered. Again, the horses raised with a loud *"Whinny"* and launched forward, as they sped toward each other again. The lances crashed again both lunging their lances forward to the other. Mathis knocked Garren backward, but he hung on as the lance splintered and shattered, raising back up in the saddle to a full seat. Mathis got knocked to the side with Garren's lance shattering in an explosion almost unhorsing him with the blow, but somehow, Mathis hung on and resituated on the saddle.

They passed each other again this time with no exchange of words because Mathis could barely breathe but did not want Garren to know how bad that one hurt.

They readied themselves at the starting lines as the referee announced.

*"The match is a draw. This will be settled by sword combat!"*

Lucas ran out with Garren's sword while another black Knight ran out with Mathis' sword. The setup runners moved the joust poles, and the two moved forward with helmets down. The crowd was going crazy at this point, and Evie could not bear to watch.

She ran off with Jarrod yelling her name.

*"Evie, wait!"*

Garren did not know what was happening up there, but Jarrod was trying to catch up to her when *"Begin"* sounded and the two started the clashing of swords. Garren twirled around, and Mathis dodged a midsection swipe while throwing an overhand strike. Blocked by

Garren! The swords were smashing back and forth neither gaining an advantage.

Garren backed off and circled Mathis as he watched. He ran in with two more attacks and a kick that were blocked by Mathis who stepped right and threw a backhand sword swipe that found its mark on Garren's arm. Garren immediately countered and hit his mark in the side of Mathis who flinched in pain at the blow.

Garren backed off again and watched what Mathis was going to do next. He came at him with a series of up and down mixed with side to side strikes and the last knocked the sword out the hand of Garren because one of the strikes hit his hands and numbed him for an instant.

Now Garren had no sword as Mathis laughed. *"Surrender, Knight!"*

Garren yelled, *"No, I'd rather die first."*

Mathis looked back at him and nodded.

*"Okay, die you shall then."*

Garren watched him closing in, circling his prey. Garren knelt on one knee, looking at Mathis as he charged forward. Garren stood just as his sword blow was coming down, caught Mathis' sword hand, turned his wrist over and threw Mathis to the ground taking his own sword away from him. Garren pointed the sword at Mathis, who was just getting back up from the throw, and he tossed the blade aside.

"*I will beat you with my hands,*" Garren shouted.

"*C'mon, lets end this here and now,*" spat back Mathis.

They charged each other with kicks holding each other arms from striking, neither gaining an advantage. Garren had a good hold and moved backward, quickly falling on his back and pushing Mathis in the air with his legs, over the top, and on his back. He rolled over and was now on top when Garren felt a sting in his arm. He rolled off to see Mathis had pulled a knife and had stabbed him.

Garren clutched his arm, both rose as blood was running down the arm of Garren. The crowd gasped in horror just when Mathis attacked with the knife sweeping back and forth. Garren dodged and pushed his knife hand out of the way. Mathis recovered quickly and returned with an overhand knife strike, which

Garren stopped in the downward thrust in midair. But the momentum was too much, and Garren went to the ground still holding the knife hand with Mathis pushing it closer and closer to Garren's chest as he was weakening. The referee jumped on Mathis's back and tried to pull him off, but Mathis elbowed the Ref in the face, which sent him sprawling. Mathis pushed the knife closer as Garren held him with the point inches from his chest.

The crowd was all on their feet, and suddenly, a voice came from nowhere.

*"MATHIS, STOP!!!!"*

It was Evie running across the field. Garren felt Mathis weaken as he turned his head towards the voice. Garren realized his opportunity and with all his strength, shoved Mathis' hand to the side, striking him so hard in the face that it stunned him enough to roll. When Garren rolled, he took the knife with him and was now on top of the gasping and nose bleeding Mathis. Garren short punched him in the face, and Mathis went almost limp. He held the knife to his throat, then stood up staggering, and screamed from the top of his lungs, Ahhhhhhhhhhhh, and threw the knife to the side.

*"You are not a knight, you have no honor!"*

Pointing down at Mathis, who was breathing hard and struggled to maintain conscience, slowly closed his eyes.

*"But I am!"* He turned just in time to catch Evie in his arms, and she kissed him.

*"Oh, Garren. I love you."* And they kissed again.

The crowd rose to their feet with a roar!

*"You are bleeding!"* Evie ripped part of her shirt and quickly wrapped his arm.

Garren told her it was just a scratch. The crowd was going absolutely nuts. The referee raised Garren's hand as he proudly looked up to the King, who was standing in applause.

Evie lowered down to Mathis.

*"Mathis, wake up,"* and she started to cry.

Garren bent down beside her when suddenly Mathis' eyes snapped open, and he sat up.

*"Get away from me!"* Mathis loathed seeing Evie and Garren close to him and tried to force them away.

Evie got up and moved off with Garren looking over her shoulder at Mathis, spitting blood and wiping his mouth. The other Black Knights helped him up, and he shook his head *"no"* at Evie who was still crying all the while he tried to wipe the blood from his face.

Jarrod ran up and hugged Garren and then Eve, Lucas, and the other White Knights met them with, *"Victory!!"* Garren was still clutching his arm holding the blood-soaked rag tight against his arm. The crowd started chanting, Garren, GARREN, GARREN!! Garren yelled over the crowd.

*"Where is Dad, Jarrod?"*

Jarrod shrugged, *"I guess he got stuck getting supplies."*

The announcement came, *"Garren Stromblade, the winner of the Graystone Academy Trials."*

The other factions and crowd cheered with Evie and Jarrod at his side along with all the White Knights. Master Chun-Dracko personally delivered his trophy.

*"Garren has already been accepted into the coveted training program for the Paladin Knights."* He shook Garren's hand, *"Congratulations, son. Your training*

*begins in three months right here, so enjoy some well-deserved off time with family and friends and report back here then."*

Chun-Dracko raised Garren's arm and turned him to the crowd, *"Your winner and White Knight of the Realm, Garren!"*

Master Chun released Garren, then announced.

*"There were two here this year, who showed unbelievable courage, strength, and honor."*

He turned to the Bronze Knights.

*"Endar, please step forward."*

The Bronze Knight pointed to himself as if to say, me? He came forward and stood beside Garren. He whispered to his new friend.

*"You deserved this Endar, and I am honored to serve with you."*

He and Endar shook hands as Master Chun continued.

*"Because of your bravery and honor on this field and the disqualification of the Black Knight, you have also been selected to join Garren in the Paladin Knighthood training."*

He accepted his honor and shook hands with Master Chun, who gave him the trophy. Garren grabbed Endar's arm and raised it with his, they walked together around the field, waving to the crowd in acknowledgment. The crowd chanted both names over and over again, amongst happiness and smiles around.

Garren got back to where Jarrod and Evie were standing.

*"How about a big round at the Inn tonight?"*

*"Sounds great, brother. Let's go home."*

Evie laughed and stood in between Garren and Jarrod, arm in arm.

*"I second that motion."*

They went to the stables and said goodbyes to the other Knights. They figured out when they were going to Marhtin's funeral and would see them all there. They left and headed home because finally, the trials were over.

Jarrod noticed a figure standing alone on the far side of the stables in the shadows. He saw the man was wearing a hood and was holding a walking stick. He squinted a second look to see who the man was, glaring at him but could not make out a face. He brushed it off when the man turned and walked slowly toward the academy.

They took their time going home, talking about the events of the day, and how great Garren performed. Evie's extraordinary courage to save Garren was the main topic along with many thanks from Garren to Jarrod who helped him all along. They discussed their father who missed the finals and were a bit worried.

However, they knew how things could get tied up when negotiating for supplies, so they didn't dwell too much on it. They knew he would have been there if he could have. They arrived home, and the carriage cart that Hardin drove for supplies was not there yet. They decided to give him till tomorrow and then go looking for him.

Garren cleaned up and Evie re-bandaged his arm.

*"Just a scratch, that is a deep cut! You're lucky, you don't need stitches."*

Garren told her not to worry. He has had cuts worse than that. He put his hand gently on her face.

*"Evie, you saved my life out there. If you hadn't screamed at Mathis, he surely would have killed me."*

He pulled her in for a gentle kiss.

*"Thank you,"* touching his head to hers and stroking her hair.

*"Garren,"* Evie started then stopped.

*"Yeah?"* he questioned, looking her in the eyes?

*"Never mind, we will talk later. Let's go have some fun at the inn tonight. I'm going to clean up too, be back in a few minutes."*

Evie went to the shower as Garren watched her leave, *"I love the way she walks, hmmm...hmmm!"*

He barely finished the sentence when Jarrod walked in from his clean up downstairs, *"Where's she off to?"*

Garren growled back with a sandwich, mouthful, *"Shower!"*

Jarrod left for the door, *"Okay, see you at the inn. We all have to talk sometime tonight. Okay?"*

Garren nodded in agreement.

*"Yeah, see you at the inn, and maybe we can get out of there early. I am tired."*

*"Sure, Garren. See you there."*

# KNIGHTS OF THE WIND

# Chapter 14

Evie came into the kitchen dressed, with her hair up in a towel and sat at the table with Garren to finish her sandwich and drink.

*"They chatted lightly, you ready to have some fun tonight? It will be crazy there tonight. All of them making a big fuss over me winning today."*

Evie smiled.

*"You should just let them have their fun and be yourself. You deserve it because your performance surprised even me."*

Garren's expression turned to shock, *"What do you mean by that? You didn't expect me to perform well?"*

Evie snapped back.

*"Now you know I didn't mean it like that. I just meant I wasn't expecting that your skills were so good. Way better than anyone else there."*

Garren just stared at her and changed the subject altogether.

*"Damn, you are so beautiful standing there with your hair up like that."*

Her face glowed with favorability.

*"You are just prejudiced."* While she took the towel down, *"What about now?"*

Garren licked his chops and stared at her, intently, *"Even more!"*

She came and sat on his lap, leaned in with her arms around his neck, and whispered, as she kissed him deeply.

*"You ole softy, what you say just melts me sometimes. I think I love you!"*

They laughed and played together in the kitchen, while her hair dried for some 30 minutes to head over to the inn. It was starting to get dark now, and they could hear the howls from the large crowd gathered as they walked up the steps.

Garren opened the door to *"hurrahs"* and pats on the back while someone handed them both pints of mead.

Three cheers rang out, and Garren leaned down to Evie.

*"See, I told ya!"*

She just grinned back.

*"Like you don't love the attention."*

He burst out laughing while chugging a pint and getting another one handed to him immediately. Ms. Frieda walked out and slapped him on the back.

*"I knew you had it in ya, boy. We are all so proud of your accomplishment, and we look forward to having another Paladin Knight in the ranks from little Briar's Cove, CHEERS."*

She drank, and so did everyone, *"Speech, Speech, SPEEECH, SPEEEEECH."* Chants for him to speak, rang out.

He stepped forward to Yays, and Oys, Ms. Frieda yelled out.

*"Quiet, let him talk!"*

The crowd stopped chanting and listened as Garren started to talk.

*"Dearest friends, no, I mean family! Cause that is what all of you are to me. I just want to say thank you for all your support and help. Most of all, for making me who I am today. I am proud and honored to know you all and to be from this town where lies the best family, a person can have. So, I toast not to me but to*

*all of you, My Family, My Brother, My Dad, and the Woman of my dreams, who saved my life today in every way, Evie! I love you all, and I promise to defend and protect these lands in your honor! Cheers!"*

The crowd hesitated as if they were shocked that those mature and humble words came from Garren, then *"Yayyyyyyy, Hoooray!"* Cheers and more pats on the back as Garren took a big swig. Evie came over and kissed him on the cheek with a sniffle.

*"That is the most wonderful thing anyone has ever said about me."*

Garren clarified by calmly saying.

*"Well, if it is true then it's true!"*

More yea's, cheers, and Evie chants erupted throughout the room as the music started. They brought in a couple of musicians to sing and make merry melody this night. People were dancing arm in arm, and Evie and Garren were dancing and drinking.

They were breathing hard from the dance escapades when she pulled Garren off the floor kissing him to the table, all through more cheers from the crowd.

*"I am having such a good time here with your friends and family. These people are so proud of you, and so am I."*

Garren blushed.

*"I am glad and still hoping that you decide to stay here with us."*

He looked at her with earnest contemplation.

*"Evie, I have never been more certain about anything in my life. I want you to stay here!"*

Evie turned away and quickly leaned back in.

*"Kiss me, and we will talk about it later. Can we just thoroughly enjoy this night?"*

Garren leaned forward and kissed her.

*"Yes!"*

They were stopped by *"Oh's"* from the crowd watching their bit of intimacy. Evie now blushed at everyone's sarcasm of the event. The crowd roared with laughter at her, and the festivities continued. Later as Evie and Garren's romance grew more and more bolder, they sneaked outside and back to the house as Jarrod came in again and confronted Ms. Frieda.

*"Where's Garren and Evie?"*

Ms. Frieda turned and pointed to the now empty table.

*"Uhhh, they were just there, I don't know now."*

Jarrod's frustrated expression was apparent because he knew exactly where they went.

*"Damn!"*

Ms. Frieda questioned

*"What's wrong, Jarrod?"*

*"Oh, nothing really, I just wanted to talk to them, but it will have to wait till morning now,"* Jarrod replied.

Ms. Frieda didn't say anything to Jarrod, as she was feeling a bit tipsy now.

*"Whoa, more music,"* she fared as *"Yes"* from the crowd. The music started, and the liquid sprits flowed again. It was getting close to 2 am, and Ms. Frieda was shooing people out the door.

*"We will be open tomorrow night and then closed for a couple of days."*

Jarrod finished up by 2:30 am and headed to the house, leaving Ms. Frieda to lock up. Jarrod thought Evie and Garren left shortly before midnight. Maybe they were still up, hopefully, finished frolicking around in the bed. He laughed to himself, probably not, although Garren had drunk more than he had ever seen before. He may have passed out on her. Jarrod got to the door and went in, trying to be quiet in case they were sleeping. He went to the kitchen and made himself a cup of tea. He thought about Evie and what she was going to do. He knew she was going to leave, and then he got an idea. He snuck past their room, listening as he went by and hearing nothing but sleeping noises went down to his secret place.

He grabbed the journal and opened it to where the ring was and put the leather pouch in his pocket. Closed the book and with the book in hand went back to the kitchen and sat quietly in the dark with the book in front of him, sipping his tea. It wasn't long, and he heard Garren's door creak open, quiet little steps through the door and then quietly shut. Evie crept into the hallway with her pack and shoes in hand so as not to wake up Garren. She came into the kitchen.

*"You're leaving, aren't you?"* Jarrod startled her, and she let out high pitched little *"Oh!"*

She whispered, *"Jarrod, you scared me to death! Yes, you know I am leaving. But I will be back in a few weeks. I left Garren a note right here and am glad you can deliver it to him. At least I can tell you goodbye. Please tell him goodbye for me, and I promise to be back soon!"*

She put her stuff on the table and gave him a hug which he just patted her on the back as she sat down with him at the table.

*"Eve, this will break his heart, and I am not sure what he will do. But I understand why you are leaving, so I am not going to try and stop you. However, take this book and promise me you will read it when you have time. It will explain a lot."* She looked at it.

*"But Jarrod, I cannot read the language it is in. How am I going to read it?"*

Jarrod turned cold, and his eyes changed to a dark color that scared Evie, and she backed up slowly in her chair.

*"You will, soon enough."*

He backed up quickly becoming normal again.

*"How can you be so sure that I will be able to read it?"*

Jarrod stood up and walked to the tea and poured her a cup. He set it down in front of her.

*"Because inside my family there is Elvin blood, my mother had it, I have it...."* He turned and glared back to Eve, *"and my Sister has it too, my blood twin sister!"*

Evie sarcastically answered back.

*"Are you suggesting that I am your sister?"*

Jarrod calmly looked back.

*"No, I am not suggesting anything, I am 100% positive that you are my sister."*

Evie took in a deep quick breath with a slight noise. Jarrod walked to her and took her hand as she looked at him in fear.

*"Eve, don't be afraid of me. You have seen what I can do."*

Evie nodded.

*"Okay, do this for me. Try to read this book, and if you can read it, then you will know that what I am saying is true. Be careful on your journey and just*

*remember, if you change your mind, you are most welcome here, and that would really make us all happy. I am leaving soon as well to find out who I am and what this mysterious power is, so I can use it for good. If it turns out that you cannot ever read this book, then I was wrong, just keep it safe for me until I return for it. OK?"* Jarrod assured her.

Evie nodded in agreement.

*"Sure, Jarrod. I will keep it safe for you. I will go try to save as many of my friends as I can, and then I am coming back here. I love Garren, and I don't want to be away from him, but I have no choice right now. I just don't want to put you or Garren in any danger."*

Jarrod let go of her hand, realizing there was no talking her out of it. She stood up and hugged him tightly, and he reciprocated this time kissing her on the cheek.

*"Please try to read this book every day for me."*

She nodded again.

*"Goodbye, Jarrod, and please stop Garren from following me. It will only make things worse. I promise I will return."*

Jarrod just stared at her but did not confirm anything, and Evie left the house with Jarrod looking down at the table, shaking his head, *"No!"*

Garren woke up the next morning hearing the roll of the horse-cart at the back of the old stable house. He got dressed smiling at the spot where Evie laid next to him, thinking she was probably in the kitchen. Garren walked into the kitchen to see Jarrod sitting quietly.

*"Good morning, Jarrod. How are you feeling this morning?"*

Jarrod didn't answer.

*"What are you thinking?" Garren asked quietly.*

Jarrod got up as Garren sat down with a worried look on his face, got a glass of juice, and went to sit back down.

*"Evie!"* Garren shuttered.

He got up and ran back hollering for her.

*"Evie?"*

He slowly walked back into the kitchen.

*"She's gone, isn't she? Damn, she didn't even say goodbye."*

Jarrod slammed his fist on the table.

*"Yes, she did. You were just too infatuated to listen. Sit down, Garren! I caught her leaving last night and talked to her. She left you a note. She thinks you are going to run off and try to stop her, and we can't do that. We must let her do what she thinks is right. She loves you, and if you love her, you will let her do this and come back, which is what she said she wants to do. Here is the note she wrote for you. Read it!"*

Garren opened the note and read it aloud to Jarrod.

*"Garren, I am so torn right now, but I must try to help my family and friends get out of that cursed city. I thought about taking you with me but feared that would make things worse. I hope you understand why I must do this. But also, know that I love you with all my heart, and I long for the day I can be in your arms again.*

*The time I have spent with you has been the best days of my life. I love your family and friends and can't wait to be here with you and the welcoming love that surrounds this little town. Thank you for giving me your heart as I will keep it safe within me. I love you, Garren, and I promise, I will be back in less than a month. Take care, I love you with all my heart, Evie!"*

Garren folded the note up with a purpose, shoved the note in his pocket, and put his head in his hands.

*"I will let her do it, Jarrod, even though my heart tells me to go and snatch her back. But you are right, if I did that she would hate me, and either way, I lose."*

Jarrod laid his hand on his shoulder.

*"Listen, if what I think is happening there is true, she will not be gone for long anyway and will come running back here to be with you and us. Believe me, I fear for her safety as much as you do, but she has her own life to figure out, and we have ours. For now, let's try to help dad with the supplies. I heard him come in early this morning. And, you have a funeral to go to in Restin. If you leave in about an hour, meet the Knights, go to the funeral, you can be back later tonight, and we can have some fun. We can count the days off together till Evie's return."*

Garren looked up with some gratification.

*"But I am not sure I can make it that long without her. She is in my soul!"*

Jarrod answered with sarcasm.

*"Oh, c'mon you love sick, Knight. That is what happens when you fall for an Elf...I mean girl,"* catching himself right away.

Garren's head quickly snapped around.

*"What did you say?"*

Jarrod started laughing, *"I was thinking about the book I read yesterday, Sorry, I misspoke!"*

Garren's face turned serious.

*"That was not funny, Jarrod!"* Then they both started laughing, although Jarrod's was a bit fake as if to say *"Phewww, almost busted myself on that one."* Jarrod thought to himself as they walked together to the stable.

*"He will learn the truth one day and will remember this lie. I am sure of that."*

Just as they got to the stables, the other White Knight competitors rode up to pick up Garren for the funeral.

*"Go ahead, Garren. I will help dad out, and you just be back here tonight."*

Garren nodded while pulling out his other horse and rode up to the house to grab a few things, including his armor and sword so they could adequately dress for the funeral.

*"See you later tonight, Jarrod!"*

Jarrod waved and watched them head down the old path, which was known to the boys as the short cut to Restin.

He was determined to find out why his father had not made it back for the finals. Was it because of cart troubles? Was it due to problems in picking up supplies? He just didn't know because neither of them had seen their father since he left the stadium. He made it to the back side of the stable and into the area where the cart was usually parked. The cart was full of supplies, but his father was nowhere to be seen.

*"Now, that is odd. He normally backs the cart in and immediately unloads everything to the proper storage locations."*

He checked the cart, and all looked good. He noticed something on the ground by the driver's side and took a closer look. It was blood drops and just wet areas from the drivers' box all the way out the back door. He looked back and noted the cart was not backed in, it was pulled straight into the barn, and the two horses had not been unhooked from the cart. They were a bit restless and looked exhausted. Jarrod unhooked the horses and stored their bridles, he led the horses to the holding pen, and they went straight to the water and feed troughs.

*"This is not like father to leave things like this. He loved these horses, and he loved going for supplies and doing his part to help up at the inn."*

Jarrod started to unload the cart, smelling a foul odor. He searched the cart and found nothing unusual other than some more blood up and around the cart. He was beginning to wonder if Hardin was hurt, but it could be blood from carrying the meat that sometimes spills on the way to the cold house storage area. Maybe he was just too tired and went to bed for a nap after that. Jarrod got busy, thinking he would finish unloading and go check on him later.

While unloading, his thoughts meandered around all the events and landed right back to thinking about Evie. He wondered how things went with her brother, and whether she tried to read the journal yet. He closed his eyes tight at some point, thinking hard about her, and all he could see was haze.

*"Wow, when I want to see something, I see nothing. I am sure I will see some sign very soon, at least I hope so."*

He continued working till the cart was empty and then went back up to the house. It was not even midday yet, so he went to check on Hardin. He got to the house, checked his room, walked all through the house, and Hardin was not there.

*"Now that is just too strange."*

He decided to go read some until the inn opened late this afternoon.

*"I have an idea."*

Jarrod hurried to the secret room.

\*\*\*

Evie rode up to the camp outside and west of Vallenwood to see the Knights busy packing camp, except Mathis who was not anywhere in sight. The men were glaring at her and throwing insults her way like, *"Whore," "Traitor,"* and *"Slut,"* as she rode with her head held high through the camp, not even looking their way.

Almost daring them to try anything, she got off her horse to find her tent taken down and packed already. All her stuff was neatly packed in the bags she brought and loaded on the wagon. Seeing this, she went to look for Mathis. His tent was still not packed, and she could see two guards outside the entrance. They stopped her for a second crossing their pikes at the entrance, so she could not get in.

*"Mathis, you want to call off your goons, so I can see you?"*

A voice came from within that chilled her to the bones as both guards grabbed her by the arms.

*"Bring her to meeee,"* the voice hissed.

The guards opened the tent forcing her in the held open doors, to see Mathis standing to the side of an orb inside a mount, sitting on a table with black glowing mist swirling inside. On the other side was her father, bound and held by guards on either side, holding his arms.

*"Father?"* She stopped as the voice from the Orb spoke.

*"Silence, Girl!"*

Her father shook his head no with his face saying, do not say anything.

*"Bind her hands."*

The guards obeyed while she looked at Mathis, who was staring at her with almost an evil glee in his eyes.

*"Mathis, you have to stop this!"*

Mathis walked to her and slapped her in the face to the delight of everyone, except her father, who tried to shake free. He hit her so hard she went to the ground as laughter rang out from the orb. Her father tried to get to her, but the guards smashed him and held him fast, stabbing him with the sharp ends of their axe pikes. She put her bound hands to her face rubbing the sting away, while Mathis walked back to the orb.

*"You were disgraced on the field, but your loyalty to this cause is well taken, Mathis. You shall be rewarded, unlike some here in our presence."*

Mathis looked at his father with disgust and then to Evie with hatred. Evie struggled to get up, and the guards picked her up and set her on her feet as the orb spoke again.

*"Bind her good and bring her to the city. Kill the father on the way and leave him for the carrion birds to feast on his carcass. Your defiance girl shall be punished and so will your white knight boyfriend. I have big plans for you both!"*

Again, laughter burst from the orb while her feet and legs were bound.

*"No, Mathis, you can't do this, wake up,"* as she struggled, but the guards overpowered her.

She and her father were thrown into a caged cart with a top over it. One of the guards grabbed her pack off her horse, threw it in the carriage with her, and locked the cage door. A big canvass cover was put over the cage so that no one could see in or out. She listened outside while they continued to pack up, hearing bits and pieces of things like the New Dark City, the new leader, the new order will lead the world.

Her eyes grew accustomed to the dark cage that was now her home, and she saw her father lying next to her unconscious. Evidently, they had beaten him to near death while dragging him to the cage. She was devastated, but there was nothing she could do now. She felt herself starting to panic with fear, hearing Jarrod's pleas for her not to go, and how she wished now that she had listened. She began to sob, thinking her dire situation would not get any better and realizing she might never see Garren again.

The cart started to move, it rolled over bumps and holes that caused her father to awaken, moaning a bit in pain, *"Evie?"*

She moved so she could see him, *"Father....?"*

She stopped as he started to speak.

*"I am so sorry, I tried to protect you from this. I saw what was happening in the city, and I rode day and night to get here to take you and Mathis away. I was too late. Mathis is under the spell of the evil wizard, and so is Valence. Soon, the city will be under the control of the evil wizard. I wish I had left sooner."*

Evie tried to soothe her father.

*"Shhh, Shhh, father. You need to rest. I will see if I can wake Mathis up from this spell."*

Her father groaned, then spoke.

*"It is too late for him and me, I am near death now anyway, Evie; but you should know that I love you very much."*

Raising his eyes to meet hers. Evie softened her eyes, *"Aww daddy, I know."*

He managed to take a labored breath.

*"I am not your real father, although I always wanted to be, and you always made me feel like I was."*

Evie was crying now, seeing her father labor for every breath. *"Wha, What, daddy?"* Crying through the talk, as she was thoroughly startled.

*"It is true honey, and I should have told you sooner. I adopted you from a dying cleric woman when you were not even two years old. I couldn't leave you there, so I took you as my loving daughter. And, you always were...."*

He started to fade as Evie tried to get to him. He forced his head up to see her eyes.

*"Forgive me child for not being able to save..."*

His head slumped to the ground as he released his last breath.

*"No, no, dad, Daddy?"* She put her head down and started to cry uncontrollably.

The cart rolled to a stop finally after about an hour, and Evie heard them coming toward the back. The canvass flew up, and there were two guards there with Mathis. Evie flew into a rage kicking at the ground, as they opened the door and dragged out the old man.

*"Mathis, how could you! He was our father."*

She breathed heavily because of her efforts.

*"Well, he is dead now. Saved me the trouble of offing him here as ordered."* Mathis casually remarked.

*"You are so evil, Mathis."*

Evie had managed to get to her feet and glared at Mathis with hatred now.

*"Ooh you are scaring me, Eve, Stop it! Ha, hah, ha!"*

Then he got serious and glared with anger.

*"Shut the hell up! You, traitorous slut! You deserve to die too, and if it were up to me, you would already be dead. You are no kin to me."*

She flopped to a sitting position with her head down, and hair flopped over her eyes.

*"Untie her and lock the cage, give her some water and food. We must keep her alive for the master. She can't go anywhere in this cage."*

The two guards jumped up into the cart, forced her back on her feet, threw a bag of food in and untied her hands, legs, and feet. She rubbed her wrists and blew her hair out of her face with a massive blast of air from her lungs and then charged the gate, screaming in anger. The guards managed to close the gate just as she got there, and she bounced off the cage on to her back with the momentum throwing her bent knees up while they locked it. Mathis laughed at her uncontrollably as she rolled to her stomach and clutched her head.

*"See, she won't be able to get through this gate. Let her be guys, and let's move on to the New Dark City."*

The canvass was pulled back down, tied, and they were off again. Evie rolled to a sitting position and looked around. There was the bag of food, and she rushed to it and saw there was fruit, bread, jerked meat and a big water flask in the bag.

*"Well, at least I'm not gonna starve."*

She chuckled at her wit and then scanned the cart again. She eyed her pack that was thrown in, and she rushed to that.

*"My knife,"* she thought while pulling the strings in a frenzy. She found the small dagger and sheath and slid it in her boot, *"This may come in handy, with a week ride to the New Dark City,"* she blurted with extreme sarcasm contorting her face as she said it.

Evie rummaged around some more in her pack with a couple changes of clothes, a washcloth, and a towel. Then she pulled out the journal.

*"Hmmm, I forgot about this."*

She looked at the writing on the front and could not read it. She pulled the clasp, and the journal opened. She perused through the pages looking for some hint but could not understand it at all. She slammed the book shut and threw it on the floor of the cart.

*"Worthless. I have to get out of here."*

She scanned around again but was getting very tired, realizing that if she didn't try to sleep, she would not have the energy to escape. She put all the stuff back into the pack and propped it as a pillow. They had a couple of old blankets in the cart, so she made a bed and curled up. Her last thought before going to sleep was longing to be in the comfort of Garren's safe arms.

Evie fell into a deep sleep which started with a vivid dream of playing around with Garren in the kitchen, laughing at the inn, and listening to stories from Jarrod that had her rolling on the floor with laughter. The fun times with Ms. Frieda, Riello, Hardin, and the old toothless Darrin reliving the memories in the dream and wanting never to wake up. Suddenly her dream turned to Jarrod, a blinding light and him smiling at her, making her feel that everything was alright. She snapped awake and could see that it was light through the canvass. She felt fully rested and stretched a yawn. She had no idea what time it was, as her eyes became accustomed to the dark and light areas.

She tried to peak outside and could see glimpses of the sun, so it must be past midday, which meant she probably slept for 6 to 10 hours because it was still dark when they dragged her father out and threw him on the side of the road. She was disgusted by this thought but could remember the dreams she had while she slept and sighed at the happy moments.

Something caught her eye where she lay, using her pack as a pillow. She looked closer, and the pack was pulsating a slight glow on and off.

*"What the...."*

She opened the pack and pulled the journal out, and now she could suddenly read it. She saw the cover writing was glowing slightly.

*"The Journal of Sarahasyl. Oh, my g...?"*

She opened the journal just as the carts all stopped and heard someone shout.

*"Make camp here, take six hours of rest, and then back on the road."*

She heard someone coming, and she scrambled to put the book up just as...Bang, Bang...BANG! On the side of the cage.

*"You alive in there?"* Mathis beat on the cage and yelled at her.

Evie hollered back, *"Shut up, Mathis! You make me sick."*

Mathis laughed loudly, *"We got a live one here, boys. For now!"*

As all the others joined in the laugh.

She realized they were not even going to lift the canvass. She pulled the book out, sat with her legs crossed, and started to read. By the time the Knights were moving around and gathering up things to leave, she closed the book in complete and utter amazement.

*"Jarrod was right, I am his real sister. Forgive my ignorance, brother."*

Evie lowered her head, realizing now she had made a terrible mistake. She wished that she had listened to Jarrod and just stayed with them. Evie looked at the clasp and then the cover of the book, seeing that she no longer could read it. She closed the clasp and put the book in her pack, thinking she would be able to read it again later.

*"I wonder where my journal is. Sarahasyl said she left me one too. I wonder if it is hidden in with Father's things back in the city?"*

She went back to thinking about Jarrod and what he had told her. She started to pace the cart back and forth.

***

Jarrod raised his head from deep concentration taking in a massive breath into his lungs and releasing. He opened his eyes, smiling ear to ear while staring straight ahead. Jarrod looked down at his hand, removed the ring, and placed it back in the pouch.

*"She knows now!"*

Jarrod started to think about Evie some more, pacing the secret room back and forth, unknowingly, twirling the ring in his hand.

# Chapter 15

Jarrod finished reading, put the ring back in the pouch, and in his pocket once again, wondering why he didn't remember taking it out again. It was quite odd because he usually remembered everything, so these memory lapses were puzzling to him.

He went upstairs after getting ready to go to the inn, seeing Hardin walking around the horse pen trying to corral one of the horses. He went outside to see if he could help and maybe talk to him. He looked fine from a distance.

Jarrod yelled from the back porch, *"You need some help?"*

A resounding *"No"* came back which caught Jarrod by surprise.

He watched as Hardin finally had the harness on the horse and was walking it back to the stable with his head down. The horse was restless, to say the least. Jarrod went back in to grab some of his things for the inn tonight and headed back out the front door. Just in time to see Hardin race off down the road.

*"Where in the world is he going this time of day? On a single horse, too. Now that is not usual. Father never goes anywhere on horseback. He seemed in a hurry too."*

Jarrod thought about where his father could possibly be going, on his way to the inn. He reached the inn to find Ms. Frieda already there. They passed pleasantries, and he learned she was going to bring some things in from both dry and cold storage areas. Jarrod asked if she needed help, and she said no.

She would get old Darrin to bring in a couple of mead kegs, and she would handle the dry storage. Something was smelling very good, and Jarrod couldn't help but see she was making her famous ginger cinnamon cakes. He walked by one of the freshly baked cakes and looked around, seeing no one, snatched one, and took a big bite just as Ms. Frieda walked in.

*"Go ahead,"* she said, *"just help yourself."*

Jarrod gulped a swallow, *"Sorry, I couldn't help it."*

She started laughing, *"I know, I know,"* just as he slammed the last of the cake in his mouth.

*"Mm, Ms. Frieda, these are so good!"* Jarrod continued.

She smiled at him and continued working. Jarrod went on to the back and pulled the books out to settle the receipts of the night before. As he was working, he heard a loud commotion outside with a faint scream, *"Jarrod," "Riello."*

He jumped up, realizing that was Ms. Frieda. Jarrod ran outside to see Riello consoling Frieda, who was sitting on the ground with her hands in her face.

He ran up, *"What happened?"*

Riello's look was grave, pointing to the cold storage room.

*"Take a look."*

Jarrod moved slowly over to the cold storage room and opened the door. He immediately shut the door back and looked at Riello, who was bent down with Ms. Frieda still blubbering with tears.

*"Who is it, and what do you think happened to him?"*

Riello picked up Ms. Frieda as a couple of others showed up.

Riello said in a low voice.

*"I think its old Darrin. Can you get Jonette who is at the old church to come and get him out of there?"*

Jarrod nodded, *"I will take care of it Riello, you look after Ms. Frieda, and I will be back with him and the carriage."*

Riello was walking Ms. Frieda back into the inn while he went back to the storage room and opened the door. A foul odor hit him that he recognized at the cart early this morning. He looked at the person who had been savagely torn apart by something. Jarrod looked for footprints and saw nothing out of the ordinary that would tell him if it was a wolf or a bear that had surprised Darrin. No struggle, no defensive wounds, just total devastation of a body. Jarrod looked up to see Jonette had just arrived already hearing of someone dying.

He pulled Jarrod aside and told him he would take care of this and to help them get ready for guests tonight. Jarrod gave him thanks and offered to help but was told by Jon he would take care of Darrin. Jarrod was saddened by the loss of old Darrin. He had been around this area his whole life and was a kind and generous man. He was a simple man living a simple life and for his life to be snuffed out that way weighed heavy on Jarrod's heart.

Jarrod thought back a few years ago when a lady was attacked by a bear on her back porch. So, it does happen, but what was so odd about this was that it happened this time inside the cold storage room, and there were no bear tracks, no rummaging around. How did a beast even get in there? He didn't smash his way into the room. The door is always shut, barred with a heavy wooden slide bar, and then at night, it is locked. He helped Ms. Frieda finish up and then told her if she wanted to take a rest, he would take care of the Inn tonight. She wouldn't have anything to do with that. The inn was her life, and if she couldn't be there, then she would just have to retire.

*"We must show that this will not stop us."* She was defiant in her words, and Jarrod admired her for that.

Darkness fell, and the enormous crowds of the past week were thinned out. The residents and regulars were in full force, especially after what happened to Darrin today. Rumors of evil creatures abounded in the inn tonight. There was a fear in the air in the customers, even though they were starting to relax. Jarrod looked around and was beginning to see some small talk and smiles again. It's incredible how a few glasses of brew can heal people's thoughts and make the tales taller.

The night carried on with some stories of the past week how Garren defeated five at a time at the trials, and he was a "shoe in" as another Lankule Stromblade.

Jarrod thought, *"Speaking of tall tales,"* he laughed and shook his head no while he carried some plates and glasses back to be washed by the new, young helper that Riello hired. He was doing a great job in place of Darrin. Just as Jarrod got back around the corner, the door opened and in walked Garren.

*"Hey everybody."*

The crowd was becoming more and more cheery as Garren came in. They were calling him the new Lankule, Garren Lankule Stromblade! One of his friends whispered in his ear.

*"You hear what happened earlier?"*

Garren took a drink and saw his friend had become serious.

*"No, what's going on?"* Garren inquired.

*"Well, Darrin was killed by a giant bear today."*

Garren looked horrified, *"What? Really? Where did this happen?"*

Jarrod walked up and interrupted. He took Garren to the back and told him what had happened, and Garren was shocked the same as Jarrod with no footprints, no damage to the door, or the entire area.

*"What are we dealing with here, Jarrod?"* Garren's unknowing expression was apparent.

*"I do not know, but one thing is for certain. It was not a normal animal attack. Let's finish up with the guests tonight, and we will discuss it more tomorrow. How was Marhtin's family today?"*

Jarrod abruptly changed the subject as they headed back to the crowded bar. Garren started to tell how the royal guard showed up to the funeral, and it was a grand procession in Restin. How the family was honored by the funeral activities, and how hurried they were in getting ready because everything was starting when they got there.

Suddenly the bar's large door swung open, and all the light sconces went out, flickered, and came back on. Everyone turned and stopped talking, as a hooded man was in the doorway. He slowly entered and shut the door, as all watched, including Garren and Jarrod. Jarrod was trying to see into the hood, but the man kept his eyes down using a walking stick about 6 feet long, to slowly move to the bar. He flung his hood back as Ms. Frieda walked in to the silent room. Everyone was watching the stranger who now turned and looked at Ms. Frieda.

He smiled at her, and she exclaimed, *"Dalimar?"*

She moved quickly with her arms out and received a laugh with a great hug. His voice was deep and said.

*"How are you, Ms. Frieda?"* As he released her.

She was glowing.

*"I am fine, other than poor Darrin died today. He was killed by a bear, we think."*

Dalimar reacted, *"I am sorry, Ms. Frieda."*

She led him to a table while he sat down.

*"How about a heated-up glass of wine?"*

He smiled and nodded at her. The crowd immediately went back to their drinking and laughing as if nothing had happened. One of the older patrons came over.

*"How about a good tale like you used to tell us, Old Wanderer?"*

Dalimar looked up to them while they were gathering around, saying.

*"Yeah, another good story. Yeah, it's been a long time."*

Dalimar brushed the water off his chest as it had started to rain.

*"Okay, okay, I will give it a try."*

The crowd cheered in anticipation, just as Ms. Frieda set a nice sized glass of warm honey wine in front of him. He gratefully took a swig from it and started.

*"It was long ago in the time of the dark age when the men of the world were besieged by an evil so great and powerful that none could stand against it. The darkness flowed from the north, Ovesgard, and dreadful dark storms swooped south, east, and west*

*through the Gates of Talmiris. The brave Knights of the southern realm moved to face the hoard of evil beings, marching to destroy everything."*

He stopped as all were listening, including Jarrod. He took another small drink as you could hear a pin drop until he started talking again.

*"The knights marched forth and set up to face their horrible fate. Knowing they were outnumbered in every way, but if they didn't stop this evil, it would surely be the end of the world with all being forced into slavery under the boot of Krometh and his evil minions. The king at the time played his hand well and dispatched archers and knights on the ridge, looking into the valley. He set up a defensive barrier to the east of 500 Knights of the Realm. He did the same thing to the west in hopes it would create a funnel to the awaiting archers from the ridge. But when the enemy first came over the furthest ridge, the Kings' hopes were dashed because out in front were the three skeletal knights of old and behind them were 10,000 skeletal warriors. Coming from the western hills, he could already hear the screams of battle, as they were attacked by*

*thousands of orcs and goblins, all under the spell of Krometh. To the east was another column of evil knights over 1000 strong, who were already engaging the Knights of the Realm stationed there. He had miscalculated the strength of Krometh's army.*

*The army of skeletons was urged forward by their knight leaders, and the king ordered the first barrage of arrows with which column after column of skeletons fell. They fired and fired, their arrows keeping the evil soldiers at bay as any who made it up the ridge were quickly dispatched. This went on for four hours, and it was looking like the battle was turning in the king's favor when Krometh appeared on the second ridged. He fired huge bolts of lightning into the archers and knights on the ridge which dispatched many. The king, knowing they could not take another barrage like that decided to charge his knights forward. The darkness was thick, as they charged forward for their last effort. The knights formed an expansive circle as they were surrounded from all sides. The men were falling 10 and 20 at a time until he was down to his last 50 men. Krometh halted the attack so he could savor killing all*

*50 of the Knights that were left, and he would be unchallenged to rule the world in darkness. Krometh hissed at the king to surrender the field and join him. The king yelled back, "Never Krometh, we will fight to the last man. Knights of the Realm, charge forward men."*

*Krometh did not yield.*

*"Then you shall die!"*

*He raised his hands and called forth a power of light from the sky. Suddenly, there were loud, high-pitched horns sounding from the east. The weary knights looked and saw the Elvin Knights from both the woodland and high elf lands. Their long bows showered arrows down on the hoard."*

The crowd cheered at the inn.

*"From the west, a low bass sound that made your chest vibrate, came the dwarven stone knights, and as they stormed down the ridge, they attacked the western front of evil knights with the Knights of the Realm."*

Another hooray from the bar as they were clapping now.

*"From overhead came a sound that sent orcs and goblins running for the hills. A dragon swooped in with Lankule Stromblade riding with anger outset in his eyes. He called forth the wind which knocked the entire northern front of skeletons down as the king had now re-engaged. The dragon swooped again laying waste to evil with a fire breath attack on one pass and cold attack on the next with Lankule swatting them down like flies."*

The crowd at the bar roared with cheers as the wanderer spun the tale as if he was there as a willing participant.

*"And then, with the sound of thunder, Oracon the Great arrived and dispatched a way straight to Krometh with a line of flames so intense that it scorched a track in the ground. He held his staff in one hand and with a raised hand, he sent forth an energy that knocked Krometh back ten feet through the air. He yelled at Krometh.*

*"Your days here are over, dark one. Krometh laughed at him."*

*"Now, you shall feel the real power of darkness. Prepare to die, old man."*

*Krometh unleashed a power straight into Oracon who held his staff out which placed a protection ball of energy around him, the attack hit the energy and moved to the sides and over the top. They fought each other all the way to the second ridge where Ovesgard could be seen.*

*Lankule was fighting one of the skeletal knights when Oracon unleashed a power so great that everything in front of him was destroyed except Krometh, who was now lying on the ground and trying to get up. Oracon raised his hand and staff high, there was a massive explosion that knocked all down, as the ground shook and Ovesgard started to crumble. They could see mountains rise up to the sky, north of Ovesgard, and the land was cracking all around. All the remaining knights, elves, and dwarves retreated as the ground opened, and a gaping fire was released all around.*

*They watched from a distance as the entire skeletal army disintegrated before them, and all the orcs and goblins headed for the mountains to the east. Lankule flew overhead in triumph as all remembered the fallen. The war was over and at a price not understood until modern times, but the world was saved."*

The crowd was on their feet at the story. Garren was clapping, and so was Jarrod. It was the best story he had ever heard. They started to sing in the bar. Dalimar sat back, satisfied with his story, and drank the rest of his drink. Jarrod walked over to the table and sat down with Dalimar.

*"Hello there, young man. You have a deep destiny in your eyes."*

Jarrod's face took a turn as he leaned in with one arm on the table.

*"You're the second person to tell me that in the last couple of days. Why are you here?"*

The old man sat back.

*"I am here because of you. Is there somewhere we can go talk, alone?"*

Jarrod stood up with a sigh.

*"Somehow, I knew you were going to say that. Follow me."*

Jarrod recognized him as the man on the white horse in one of his visions. The two got up from the table and went back to his office room. The old man sat down and waited not saying anything, so Jarrod started.

*"I am Jarrod and...."*

The old man interrupted.

*"No, you're not, you mean you were Jarrod."*

*"I am still Jarrod!"* Jarrod insisted.

Dalimar laughed.

*"Okay, I will give you that, but you have discovered something. Why don't you start there and just fill me in?"*

Jarrod remained undecided.

*"How can I know to trust you? I don't even know who you are, although I saw you at the trials. Didn't I?"*

He nodded, yes.

*"I was at the stables watching you and Garren who performed admirably by the way. How can I prove to you that I am trustworthy? I have known Ms. Frieda since she was a girl and I knew your father Hardin and your uncle Clayborne."*

Jarrod's expression changed to surprised.

*"How is it that we never met?"*

*"Because I am 103 years old and I knew your father before you came along."* The wizard replied.

Jarrod's eyes opened wide.

*"Are you a wizard?"*

Dalimar laughed.

*"Well, some say that. I am sort-of, well say, a combination, Druid, Cleric, and Wizard, and a protector of the lands. Now tell me, Jarrod, what have you discovered? My thoughts have been clouded, and I need to know."*

Jarrod pulled the ring from his pocket and set it on the table. Dalimar reached for the ring and stopped as a vision of the "Dark Mage" came to him.

*"Put that back in your pocket. Have you worn it, yet?"*

Jarrod looked at him and nodded. Dalimar stood up and sighed heavily.

*"The ring is evil, Jarrod. It will twist your mind. The ring wants to be found so that it can be returned to Krometh. You are tied to this ring now, and you must*

*learn to control it, only then can you truly have its power. Tell me more so that we can piece this puzzle together."*

Dalimar sat back down and listened as Jarrod told him about the visions, the journal, using the ring twice, Evie and Garren, and what he knew about Tanin, his real father. When he was finished, Dalimar sat quietly, then reacted.

*"Jarrod, I know you have been chosen by destiny to learn this power. In time you will become even more powerful than I ever was. If your sister, Evie, is captured by this evil mage, he will use her to get the ring from you. You must not take it to him. He will use the ring to unleash Krometh again.*

*Tanin was my student, and I sent him to the Elf lands years ago to study in the great library. I was asleep for two years and awoke to Tanin trying to kill me. I banished and trapped him in a crystal, so he could not use evil against the world again. I had no idea how far his treachery went. So, the King's daughter had twins, you and Evie. Funny how fate intertwines us. Things are even worse than I feared. Does Garren know what you are yet?"*

Jarrod shook his head no.

*"Good, the time will soon come for you to tell him. Is there anything else that has happened, strange things?"*

Jarrod relayed the events with Garren, the strange cleric, his turning into an elf, what happened today to Darrin, and then told him of the strange book he found in the desk. The old man answered with shocked worry, *"Dorgs! Book? What book?"*

Jarrod looked with surprise.

*"Dorgs, what are they?"*

Dalimar looked back at Jarrod with a serious face.

*"Those are the creatures that are hunting you. They are evil and can imitate a person in every way. You wouldn't even know they were there until they attack you."*

Jarrod trembled with fear as he asked him to wait there to go get the book. Dalimar agreed, and Jarrod was off. It wasn't long, and he returned with the book and the scroll hidden in his shirt. He pulled the two,

Dalimar's eyes opened wide, and he lit up in amazement.

*"You nor I will ever be able to read this book like it is. There is a protection spell on it that can only be broken by speaking certain words of light. This scroll was sealed?"*

Jarrod nodded, "Yes, I broke the seal, and now I have some magical power, watch."

He blew out the candle, waved his hand, and the candle relit.

Dalimar was overjoyed.

"That is wonderful. Oh, you are surely all in now."

Dalimar then became silent, thinking about what had been told to him. *"Tanin is his real father. Am I making a mistake again, by making the son of Tanin, my new apprentice?"*

Dalimar spoke out with regard.

*"I am sorry to be the bearer of bad news, but you are bound to both the ring and the book. I think that is the book I have searched for my whole life, Oracon's book of Power. The scroll is the key, the words of light are on the scroll, and there is only one way to unlock its*

*secret. That is for another time, for now, you must tie all this together."*

Dalimar pieced together Jarrod's information and told what he knew about the Elvin King Dersonyn II, and Tanin, his real father. He told him about the ring having three power parts to form a bracer, and how King Dersonyn II and Oracon forged it from the Elvin sky forge. Dalimar told Jarrod that he is being sought by evil forces and how his new-found power will grow. He talked about Sarahasyl and how he knew what wonderful woman she was, which made Jarrod feel warm inside. Dalimar looked up after spinning the events and saw that Jarrod had a much clearer understanding of things.

*"Jarrod, seriously now,"*

He took Jarrod by the shoulders and looked deep into his eyes.

*"You are a part of this, but your destiny is your own. You can walk away if you want, stay here with friends and family, and forget about all this. Give me the ring and the book, and all the danger that is coming and is already here will follow me. Or, you can take this*

*destiny by the hand and embrace what you are and what you must do.*

*I will give you until tomorrow to decide. I am staying the night at the inn. I am sorry to rush you, but we have no time left. Things are already set in motion that you cannot stop. Think about it and let me know in the morning. No shame, no pressure, it's just your decision."*

He released Jarrod who thought he already knew the answer.

*"What about Evie? Are we going to do something about her?"*

Dalimar turned back with a defiant smirk.

*"Of course, we are, and we will. Let me know in the morning. I need to know that you will follow through if you chose this, there will be no turning back, so convince me! We will discuss everything and formulate our plan then. Good night, Jarrod!"*

Dalimar left the room while Jarrod stood, staring at the wall in serious contemplation.

*"No pressure, gee, that's an understatement."*

Jarrod went back to the bar, seeing that Ms. Frieda and Garren were sending everyone out for the evening.

Garren walked up, *"What did you talk about with that old fella?"*

Jarrod's worried face showed Garren it was something important, but he really didn't want to talk about it right now.

*"We will discuss it tomorrow, Garren. Right now, we should help Ms. Frieda and go get some rest."* Just then, Dalimar walked back down the hall and into the room.

*"Here, take this, in case you get bored and want to read some."*

He handed Jarrod an old looking black leather book, which Jarrod took with no hesitation. Dalimar had a stern expression.

*"See you both in the morning."*

He turned and went back to his room.

Garren asked with curiosity.

*"So, what is it, and don't say it's A Book!"*

Jarrod laughed at that comment and shrugged, *"I am not sure. I guess I will find out tonight, and let you know in the morning. We must get up early and meet Dalimar here, and all your questions will be answered."*

Garren sighed in disgust, *"Okay, but I am not liking all this, in the dark, secret crap."*

They finished up and left together back to the house to get some rest. Neither spoke on the way, as Garren was clearly upset by all the secrecy. Jarrod thought to himself slyly.

*"Patience my brother, you will learn everything in the morning. Then you will have your own decision to make."*

# Chapter 16

Jarrod quickly told his brother, they would get up early to talk with Dalimar. He agreed that he would be up and ready to find out what all this was about, but he finally had to ask a question.

*"Does this have anything to do with Eve?"*

Garren was dead serious while Jarrod tried to come up with a quick answer.

*"Umm, the short answer is yes. For the long answer, just get some sleep brother, and I promise, all will be revealed in the morning."*

Garren seemed a bit uneasy but pleased at the thought they might be doing something for Evie. Jarrod left it there and went straight to his secret room to read the new book Dalimar gave him.

Garren cleaned up and was already in bed while Jarrod was thinking about what he was going to do in the morning. He knew that if he didn't take this task on, then Dalimar would go alone, so he had pretty much already made his decision. He closed his eyes, thinking that maybe some sign would come to him on what he should do but no ideas came to mind. Just when he was about to give up, an image started to appear. It was a dark place, and he recognized it as a vision from before. He scanned the dark room when screams of agony came forth. There was Evie, again chained to the wall.

Her back was to him with her shirt stripped away, blood was streaming down her back as a whip hit her again, and she screamed in pain, among laughter from the one slinging the long whip. Jarrod scanned to the end to see a gnarled hand holding the whip handle, and it appeared to be some creature with scaly skin and gruesome fangs.

He raised the whip to strike again, and Jarrod yelled to the creature.

*"Stop! You hit her again, and I'll kill you."*

The creature stopped and looked right at Jarrod, turning his head in confusion when another voice came, it was low and dark. The beast hit the ground on his knees as the voice spoke.

*"You think your insignificant little power can stop ME? Bring me the ring boy, or I will slowly kill her. Now, feel the wrath of true dark power!"*

Jarrod turned towards the voice and saw the black, armor-clad demon creature stand. He reached his armored clawed hand toward Jarrod and clutched his hand like he was squeezing an orange. Fear raced through him, feeling the grasp around his neck, and his air was choking off. He felt his feet rising off the ground as he kicked and fought the grip of the being. Suddenly he heard a familiar voice that was weak but defiant.

*"Let him go, you pile of filth!"* The grip released, and Jarrod fell to the ground, choking and gasping for air. He snapped awake, still gasping for air and rubbing his neck. He raised his head as he realized, *"That was Evie!"*

Jarrod gathered himself with determined courage. As he choked in the last bit of gathered strength, he knew exactly what he had to do. He walked over to his table and looked at the book Dalimar had given him. He could read the front inscription. *"Spells from a Time Lost."*

Jarrod was still rubbing his neck, wondering how the black mage could reach through a vision like that, and how he could project his voice in the same manner. He realized he had to be careful from now on because the dark mage could see into his mind now.

He turned the first page that had a list of defensive type incantations, the second page had a list of offensive spells, and the third page was a list of mind-altering spells. The fourth page touched on illusions and calling forth animations, like making a tree come alive, or calling animals for aid. The pages continued with other amazing spell types.

His mind was ablaze with wonderment and curiosity. He read down through the lists of spells and incantations that brought forth the many facets of clerics, paladins, wizards, sorcerers, illusionist, druids, necromancers, and even how the Knight of the Wind could call forth a mysterious wind and fire to slay hundreds at a time.

How all the Yshanall forces gather around a power that surrounds everything, and if used for good, it can increase the prosperity of the world. It also talked about the balance of good, neutral, or evil forces, and how there is a fine line between them. The balance must be maintained, or the land suffers as do the people. The world forces of chaos, neutrality, and good are not set in stone, and when one force outweighs the other, then they must be forced into balance by The Protector of the land.

The protector is always in touch with these forces and knows how to maintain this critical balance because he is a combination of all the forces at any given time. The book spoke about scrolls and how to write them. It also included spell lists and how they are kept, and how to cast spells either by using some component, magical item, or even calling the spell forth from deep within yourself. Jarrod read on into the early morning hours fascinated by the book and by what he was learning.

He decided to rest a bit after reading so much, he laid down on his back, and his mind wandered as he closed his eyes, to his sister, Garren, Hardin, what is going to happen with Dalimar, and finally, he rested peacefully, knowing he was going to tell Dalimar that whatever the plan was to count him in. He knew that Garren would not be left out no matter what.

*"He is still, my brother,"* Jarrod drifted into sleep with this affirmation.

He woke up hearing some rummaging around upstairs, and he scrambled to his feet and up the hatch, down the hall and into the kitchen area to see Garren already up.

*"Hey there, brother, sleeping in this morning?"* With a laugh behind the spoken words.

*"Well, I guess, I'm going to get ready and see you in a few minutes."*

Jarrod turned and left for the shower room. Garren continued making some coffee and tea when he noticed that his father was walking to the stables, with one of the horses in tow. Garren went outside and yelled from the back porch.

*"Hey, Dad. Where you been for the last...."*

Hardin interrupted, *"Shut up you overgrown stuffy hog, and where's that bratty brother of yours? I need to kick his ass for leaving a mess in the stable for me to clean up."*

Garren was stunned to the point that he couldn't speak,

*"Uhm...Uhh."*

Hardin blasted back immediately with a thrown hand and arm, *"Ahh, go back inside and stuff your face you stuttering-idiot. Leave me alone, I am busy!"*

He turned and walked into the stable, leaving a shocked and bewildered Garren. He had never heard his father talk like that before and was wondering if he hadn't hit the mead a bit from wherever he went. He didn't want to upset his father, so he went back inside and waited for Jarrod, disturbed by his father's outburst.

It wasn't long before Jarrod pranced into the kitchen dressed and ready to talk with Dalimar when Garren detailed the events from his father. Jarrod was just as shocked as Garren by the strange outburst. They talked a bit, and Jarrod decided they would stop by the stable to see why their father was in such a foul mood. He has been in foul moods before but had always apologized or at least gave an indication he was sorry.

But never had he spoke in words to that extent so this was very strange. They walked together to the stables, looked around for Hardin, and did not see him there nor the horse that was in tow. He was gone again with no explanation of where he was going or what was going on. They decided to go on up to the inn to see Dalimar and face the task of not only telling Garren everything but also informing all that he was leaving the Cove to help Dalimar in any way he could.

They walked into the place to see both Ms. Frieda and Dalimar sipping tea and chatting. *"Ahh, there you are, right on time."*

Dalimar held his hand out to the chairs at the same table for them to sit down. They sat down, and Dalimar stood up to announce himself.

*"Garren, I am Dalimar, and I have known your family for a long time. Although I have never met either of you until last night, I have learned some good things about you both and was very impressed with your performance at the trials. I must say that Master Chun-Draken was very proud of you."*

Garren blinked in surprise but managed a *"Thank you"* at the end.

*"There is much more for you to hear, and I am not sure how you will take all this, but in the end, you will have a decision to make. On that note, I will let Jarrod*

*explain what is going on and what his role in this situation is, and I am sure that he has already made his decision."*

Jarrod nodded in agreement and started with the events happening a few days ago, leading up to now. He told him that he had begun to receive these strange visions, and when he went to Ms. Frieda, she gave him a book from his real mother. How he was not really a Stromblade, and how Hardin and Garren's mother had adopted him when he was not two years old. He told him that he was really a half-elf and that he had found a power from within that he doesn't fully understand yet, but Dalimar was going to help him. His real mother was an Elf, and his father was Dalimar's apprentice.

Then he told Garren that Jarrod was not only a half-elf, but he also had a twin sister. She was left to a cleric woman who disappeared, and he found evidence that Evie was his real sister, and now she knows it too. He told him of the visions of the evil mage and that Jarrod had found a ring and possibly found the missing book of Oracon the Great. The dark mage was searching for him to obtain the ring. If he found out who Evie really was, then he would use her to get to me and the ring. He told Garren he was not sure of Evie's fate, but whatever we do, we have to find a way to help her.

Garren was solemn about the entire situation.

*"Why did you let her go if you knew this dark one would use her?"*

Jarrod spoke again, *"This all just came to light yesterday and believe me, Garren, I tried to stop her, and she wouldn't hear of it. She wanted to do anything to help her family and friends. You are still my brother to me, and I respect your decision. For me, I am going with Dalimar to try to stop this madness."*

Dalimar looked up with pride on his face. Garren was still perplexed.

*"I have so many questions that I am not sure where to start?"*

Ms. Frieda jumped in, *"Just one at a time, Garren. Think about what you want to know and just ask, we will all answer any question you have. But remember, Jarrod knew nothing of this until just a few days ago, so he was in the dark as well."*

Garren thought for a minute.

*"What is the evidence that Evie is your sister?"*

Jarrod sat back.

*"Remember, I was telling you about the book Ms. Frieda gave me?"*

Garren nodded frankly. *"Yes, I remember."*

Jarrod continued. *"That was my mother's journal, and inside was the story of how Hardin and Anida found her dying with two children. Hardin and Anida were traveling with a cleric. I was given to be your twin brother, as you know, and Evie was given to the cleric. I read the entire journal and surmised that she was my sister, but I wanted to be sure, so I gave Evie the journal before she left."*

Garren interrupted, *"Okay, but how do you know if she read it just from that?"*

Jarrod answered, *"Because the journal was in the Elvin tongue, and she could not read the cover when I gave it to her. I know she has read it now because I saw her reading it in my vision. It means her eyes are changing just like mine are, and we both can read the*

*Elvin language now. Also, I can sense what is happening to her, so we are linked only by blood."*

Garren nodded and understood what Jarrod was saying.

*"What is the plan then? I am in, you can't get rid of me that easy, Jarrod. If it involves Evie, then I want to help."*

Jarrod gave his brother a look of statement.

*"I am glad you are going with me, Brother!"*

Garren smiled! Dalimar stood up, *"Good then, it's settled. We will leave tonight. Meet me at the Restin River crossing tonight at around 5 pm! Get a good rest in and pack for a long journey. We have a lot of preparations to make, and I must talk with the elders and that cleric Rosalind today before we leave."*

Jarrod leaned forward and circled his finger round and round by the side of his head, *"She's crazy, Dalimar. Watch out for that one."*

Dalimar burst into laughter, *"Yes, you know her well. She lost her mind years ago, but she is still a good healer and is wise beyond belief. She has the gift of foresight as we do. We will discuss the book I gave you on the way. Read any yet?"*

Jarrod said, *"Oh, yes, the book is fascinating."*

Dalimar's expression turned grave, *"Careful what you wish for, son. You will have another decision to make soon."*

He turned and bid farewell, asking them to get prepared one more time.

*"Ms. Frieda?"* Garren pleaded, *"I need you to do me a huge favor."*

She was caught a bit off guard, *"sure, anything."* Garren turned gray-faced,

*"Should Evie make it back before me, could you please explain all this to her?"*

*"Oh, sure, Garren! We will fill her in on the details, and we would love to have her stay with us until you return. And you boys don't worry about the inn, Hardin, Riello, and I will handle things while you are gone."* Ms. Frieda gave them all the assurance possible.

The two boys looked at each other and back at her, *"Thank you."*

Both were still worried about Hardin and what was going on with him. Jarrod thought they better try to talk with Hardin to let him know they were leaving. The two walked on the property, looking for clues for where their father was. After an exhaustive search for most of the morning, they decided they better get packed and just leave word with Ms. Frieda and Riello to explain to him, who they were going with and hopefully be home in time for Garren to start his training as a Paladin Knight of the Realm. They packed their things on a packhorse along with each having a riding horse, weapons, clothes, bedrolls, and water rations.

Garren was packing as they used to for camping trips, but this time an extremely long one. They finished up their packing, and Garren said he was ready for an afternoon nap. The inn was going to be closed for the evening, and so there was no more work to be done. Jarrod looked over the supplies list to make sure he had everything.

He especially stuffed his new books and neatly packed them with his things in an easily accessible way. Garren was already napping, and Jarrod had his new book in tow, heading for his room to read some before they left to meet Dalimar when he thought he heard something in the living room. He ducked into the living area and saw nothing, so he went on to the secret room and started to read. Jarrod opened the book where he left off the night before and was to a place where spells were listed, how they worked, and how to cast them. They were listed in such a way that he could read and study only a few. The rest were just descriptions and the areas where the "how to cast," was blank.

He was not sure why but figured it had something to do with his knowledge level. He went back over some of the pages he skipped, and there it was, his answer. The spells will only become visible to read when the caster has enough strength and experience to draw the power. He thought about this for a moment and picked one of the offensive spells he could read and started to study it. This was the moment that he felt the pull of the ring from his pocket. He kept hearing in his mind,

*"I can help you, wear the ring, and you shall have the power."*

Jarrod resisted the urge and the strange whispers he was hearing in his mind, finding that the whispers faded as he blocked them from his thoughts. He pulled the pouch with the ring inside, looked at it, and placed it back in his pocket, dismissing the strange calls.

It was getting time to meet Dalimar when Jarrod heard some disturbance upstairs. Thinking it was Garren getting up, Jarrod got his things together and went upstairs. He saw Garren standing in the hallway looking toward the living room with a confused expression on his face. Garren saw him wondering.

*"Take a look at this,"* as he moved into the living room.

Jarrod walked in and saw the mess. The table was turned over, and things were all over the floor. Jarrod looked up on the mantle to see that the picture of Lankule had been broken.

Garren looked back at Jarrod, *"Why would my father do this?"*

Jarrod shook his head no, *"We don't have time to figure this out, Garren. Maybe he found out that we were leaving, and he is upset. We need to get on the road, if we see him on the way, we will let him know that we will be back soon."*

Garren agreed, and they went to the stables to mount up and head to the river. They left together in a slow to medium trot for the river meeting point, discussing possible plans and scenarios for what they were going to do.

They arrived just before the sun was setting and did not see Dalimar.

*"I will get a fire going, so we can at least wait in some comfort."*

Jarrod agreed and pulled his book out while Garren gathered wood and started a small fire near the river bank. They sat together, chatting lightly when they heard something coming through the woods. Both turned at the same time, sensing they were being watched. Garren put his hand on his sword and started to stand up, as both saw Hardin walk into the clearing just out of the light.

He had a sword drawn and started to talk as Garren relaxed.

*"I thought you two were in trouble, so I came to see. I heard you are waiting for the old man, and that you are bringing something to him. Give it to me and go home. I will wait for him here and give it to him."*

Jarrod hesitated and stood while Garren spoke,

*"Oh, thank goodness. I am so glad to see you finally."*

Harden shot back and took a step forward, not letting Garren finish.

*"Sit down son, I am talking to Jarrod, he is not who you think he is. He is a traitor to the world, and I need to take him to Vallenwood, where he shall be placed in the custody of the law."*

Garren looked at Jarrod, confused by what was happening.

Jarrod put his hand up to Garren, *"No, Garren. This is not true."*

Hardin moved forward again a step with the sword pointing at Jarrod.

*"You are not my son, you are a trespasser, and you shall be punished for taking my son away."* Jarrod started to think and tried to calm the situation.

*"Are you suggesting that I killed Jarrod and took his place?"*

Hardin snapped at him.

*"Shut up! You, scrawny little brat! I'm taking you in."*

Garren moved in front of Jarrod.

*"No, Dad, stop this. You are not taking him."*

Hardin raised the sword up and whistled, another strange looking man came out of the woods armed with a sword as well and moved to the other.

*"Don't make me fight you, Garren! Step aside and let us go."*

Jarrod stepped around his brother and stood beside him. He whispered to Garren, *"This is not father, Garren."*

Garren looked back, confused still, *"What?"*

They both yelled and attacked the boys. Garren blocked the swing from his father and grabbed the second man coming in and threw him while he confronted his father. Jarrod was knocked to the ground but was not hurt.

Garren pleaded with father.

*"Please stop, Father. This is not right."*

His father moved in for another swing at Garren who sidestepped the swing. Garren's training and instincts kicked into full gear. He jumped to the side of Hardin who was off balance from the missed effort and shoved him so hard that he dropped the sword on the way to the ground.

*"Okay, Garren. You asked for this."*

Hardin started to change and was growling and snarling. Just as the other man was already transformed into this giant wolf-like creature circling Garren, drooling and slobbering in-between growls and snaps. Jarrod recognized the foul odor he smelled in both the cold storage room and the cart stable. Jarrod moved to cut off Hardin, still changing into this wolf-like creature, while Garren faced the other. He made a run for the horse to get his bow as the other animal attacked Garren.

The creature leaped into the air with a snarl, and Garren caught the beast with a sword slice, as he pulled his sword and fended off the clawed and biting attack. The creature howled in pain as blueish blood spurted, but it attacked again, landing square on the sword impaling the creature inches from his face. The giant wolf snapped and snapped again, then died as Garren threw it off his sword. Jarrod saw the other wolf now attack Garren, latched on across his back and bit into his shoulder blade, scratching his back with claws that were razor sharp.

Garren wrenched in pain but managed to get the creature off him.

A third creature, larger than the other two emerged from the forest, snarling and gnashing its teeth. Jarrod realized he had no time to string up and shoot. He donned the ring from his pocket and started to speak. The smaller one turned and raced to attack Jarrod, while the bigger attacked Garren. Jarrod felt his temperature rise as he held his hands out with fingers outstretched. The wolf leaped to attack but was met with greenish-white flamed bolts from all 10 fingers that sounded like arrows shooting into the wolf's chest, neck, and face.

The creature sprawled to the ground, its tongue hanging out gasping the last breath with blueish blood leaking everywhere. Jarrod went down to his knees, just in time to see the giant wolf take Garren down with another bite to his neck and a loud scream. Garren laid motionless as the creature nudged him with his nose and snapped around toward Jarrod. He struggled to get up but could not and fell forward. The creature was moving closer and closer, starting to hiss out words.

*"Now, you die, and the ring will go back to the master."*

The giant wolf was so close, Jarrod could feel the creature's breath and smell his foul odor. From behind, there was a flash of light and an intense heat, with the beast yelling in a raged howl. He saw the wolf turn and run toward another figure, and there was another brilliant flash and intense heat. The smell of hair and flesh burning was in the air. Just before his eyes closed, he saw an image of Dalimar leaning over him.

*"Jarrod? Jarrod!"*

Jarrod awoke and gradually moved to a sitting position. Still shaking the cobwebs, he remembered Garren attacked.

*"Garren!"*

He saw him lying on the ground next to a log, with his shoulder and neck wrapped with a towel bandage. He also had a dressing around his head. Jarrod rushed to his side and shook him, but he did not open his eyes.

*"He will be alright,"* came a voice from behind.

Startled, Jarrod turned just as Dalimar dropped some more wood on the ground near the fire.

*"He was bitten, and the fangs of those creatures are poisonous. I have dressed and cleaned his wounds, and here, take this!"*

Dalimar handed a bottle to Jarrod.

*"Give him a cap full about every 2 hours."*

Jarrod looked at the bottle, *"Were those creatures, Dorgs?"*

Dalimar gravely spoke, *"Yes, those are the creatures I told you about and have not been around for centuries. They are wolf-like, intelligent creatures that can change into their victim. They look like them, walk like them, and imitate every aspect. They can even retain some memories from the victims. They are cunning and very dangerous, and they are hunting this."*

Dalimar held the pouch out, *"This is yours, I believe!"*

Jarrod took the pouch, put in in his pocket, and shook his head, yes.

*"The Dorgs are also hunting you, so you must keep a wary eye open and be ready at all times. I am sorry about Hardin. He was consumed by one of those creatures, and his body was taken over. They will never stop until they kill you and take the ring back to their master. Here, eat some of this, it will help you gain your strength back."* Dalimar continued.

Jarrod took the cracker like item and took a bite, *"Yuk, this is bitter!"*

Dalimar laughed, *"Yes, they are, but that means it is healing you."*

Jarrod took another bite and asked, *"What happened to me? I just got very weak, and all my strength was gone suddenly."*

Dalimar chuckled again, *"That is why you must practice your magic before you wield it. It is a bad side effect of having such power. It will sap your strength quite fast and leave you vulnerable as you saw clearly.*

*Good thing you sent those magic bolts because I saw them from the rise and raced here just in time."*

Jarrod thanked Dalimar as he continued.

*"Ah, no matter, I am sorry I was late, but I have been tracking those creatures heading to you all day, I am glad I arrived in time. I never made it to the elders because I stumbled on those creatures and decided it was too risky to leave you. Your mind is strong, but you are weak physically, you must gain your inner strength and constitution. Otherwise, you will not be able to wield such power."*

Jarrod curiously asked, *"How do I gain this inner strength?"*

Dalimar looked back sternly, *"You must train your inner strength, and it can only be done two ways, practice casting spells, relearn, and practice again and again. The other way is by some magical force like an amulet or piece of magically enhanced jewelry, to increase your constitutional powers. That ring you carry will not do that. That ring increases the power of a spell by tenfold, but we can discuss that another time.*

*What you need to remember about that ring is most important. That ring wants to be found, it yearns for evil, and it will try to twist your mind. You must resist this temptation, or it will gladly guide you right to your own demise and into the hands of where it really wants to be; the evil mage who is searching for you. What escapes us right now is how did he find out about the ring? Do you understand what I am saying?"*

Jarrod nodded in agreement, *"I think this is part of our plan, to find out who this evil mage is and what he is doing. I have seen that he knows me and that I have the ring."*

Dalimar looked back, *"You are close, but I have already seen what he is trying to do. He wants the ring to bring Krometh back to the world. No, what is part of our plan is to keep you and that ring as far away from him as possible. But we must also work on getting your sister back and finally thwarting his plan to bring back Krometh. Somewhere in there, we may find out who he is, but I am not so concerned with that. I am more interested in stopping him from bringing Krometh back into the world."*

Jarrod's eyes widened, *"Krometh? How would he be able to that? I thought you said Oracon killed him."*

Dalimar spoke with despair, *"No, a demon from a plane of hell cannot be killed on this plane of existence. The most you can hope for is to banish him from here and hold him at bay. The only way to truly kill him is to go there and kill him. We surely don't want to go there. The best thing is to thwart or destroy this evil mage and then close the door he is trying to open up."*

Jarrod was a bit confused, *"Uhhh, okay. How do we accomplish all that? Garren is lying there almost dead. I just found out I have no power at all, and I realize that we would probably just be a hindrance to you."*

Dalimar burst into laughter, *"I'm glad you asked, my young fella. We are going to Thane City. There, I know a master thief and assassin. Don't look at me like that, he is a good friend, and we have been on many adventures together. He is also in charge of the underground city of the Thieves Guild. His name is Nanek, and we will ask for his help. We will sneak into Idesport City, rescue your sister, and I will close the magic door with this."*

Dalimar held up a ruby looking stone, *"I will cast a magical tome on this and throw it through the door, and the door will close forever. Then we waltz out with no one even knowing we were there until we are gone."*

Dalimar looked back as if to say, *"See, how easy is that?"*

Jarrod was aghast, *"Seriously? That's our plan? That's crazy, we will all be killed!"*

Dalimar turned his eyes serious as he was putting more wood on the fire.

*"Now, now, let's not get negative. I think this is a grand plan, besides if "fate" is on our side, then it will be that simple. Oka, you are all set here, I think it will be safe for the rest of the night. I am sorry to leave you, but I must go talk with the council and convince them to ready themselves for what is on the horizon, should we fail in our task."*

Jarrod looked up with concern, *"Fail? Now, that does not sound very confident."*

Dalimar called his horse to his side, and Jarrod stared at the magnificent animal in wonder, *"I have never seen such a beautiful horse."*

The horse walked over to Jarrod and nudged him, and he cautiously reached up and stroked the neck and long hair.

Dalimar whispered, *"He likes you!"*

Dalimar continued, *"When sleepyhead wakes up over there, you two head straight to Thane City. Stay off the roads and stick to the old paths. I will meet you at the Pengrath Stables in town. Speak of this to no one and mind your thoughts, as the evil mage's power reaches across the realm, and he will be listening."*

With that said, Dalimar mounted the steed with one final warning, *"Prepare your spells tonight, you will need them on our journey."* He started to trot off and turned back, *"Practice Jarrod, learn and practice."*

He headed northeast toward the Vallenwood Council of Elders. Jarrod walked over to Garren and sarcastically mumbled to himself.

*"Oh sure, if fate is on our side? Well, fate has sure dealt us some big surprises here, recently."*

He struggled to give Garren a cap full of the liquid that Dalimar gave him and went back to the fire, as he sat within its warm distance. He thought he would practice and look after Garren until morning, hoping he would be well enough to travel. There was a strange, cool breeze in the air that night when he started to learn his spells, and the single moon rose to full strength.

He glanced at the moon and pulled his scroll out, but nothing happened. Disappointed, he put the scroll up, *"Another time, maybe!"*

He fell asleep lying on his bedroll after practicing most of the night and into the early morning hours. He woke up and checked on Garren, who appeared to be sleeping still. It was dark out there, so he stoked the fire again, getting it to a high level. He poured some more of the liquid into the cap to give to Garren who woke when he got there.

*"Here, drink this!"* Garren took the cap, *"Here I go again drinking some concoction,"* and he swigged it, *"Yuk, that is awful!"*

Jarrod smiled, remembering Dalimar's words to him.

*"Yes, it is, but that means it's working."* He grumbled but then remembered the battle.

*"Father, is he dead?"*

Jarrod sat down next to him, *"I'm afraid so."*

Garren looked down at the ground, *"I killed him."*

Jarrod replied with concern, *"No, you didn't. That thing killed him. It imitated him, and then we killed that creature."*

He answered back, *"I suppose you are right. He was not himself that is for sure."*

Jarrod told him he put his sword on the pack, set up the weapons to ready and wondered how he was feeling.

*"Tired,"* he replied in a slumber.

Jarrod commented with ease.

*"Well, go back to sleep and when you wake, let's see if you can travel."*

Garren rubbed his shoulders, neck, and stretched a yawn.

*"I think I will be able to. I don't feel that bad."*

*"Good, then. See you in a few hours."* Jarrod added.

Garren laid back down, and in just a few minutes, he was sound asleep.

# Chapter 17

Dalimar rode hard but not in too much of a hurry. He knew that he was not going to get there in time to see the Elders and would have to wait till morning. He figured he would stay at the Academy and try to decide what direction to take in their quest to stop evil from growing. He knew that he had not revealed all that he had seen to the boys, trying not to give them more than they could handle.

He knew the power of this evil mage was growing to a point where he had to stop him and could not risk this evil spreading any further. He wished he could see this man's face, but in every vision, his face is covered with a helmet or a mask. Still, there was something familiar about him, but his evil has no bounds, that much is certain.

He went over the events as he walked to the academy, where he was always welcome and had his own room. As he walked to his room, he ran into Rosalind who greeted him with a loving hug.

*"Hello, Dalimar! I have been expecting you."*

Dalimar pulled his hood back and raised a surprised eyebrow to her.

*"Hello, Ms. Rosalind, expecting me? What are you doing out here in this cold hallway?"*

She giggled and pointed to Dalimar. *"Waiting for you, my old friend. Follow me."*

Dalimar was not sure what she was up to but followed her anyway. She opened the door to her room.

*"Come in and sit comfortably while I make us some tea."*

Dalimar freely came in and sat down at the thought of some tea. Rosalind finished making tea and brought the pot and set it on the table in front of Dalimar. He poured her a cup and then himself, as she sat across from him at the little table. They sipped tea together and sat down. Dalimar was wondering why she had said nothing to him since he sat down. He decided to be patient and not push her, so he sipped his tea and smiled at her. After half a cup, she gleefully set her cup down, clasped her hands together, and finally started to talk.

*"Let's play a game, my friend. What has a "T" at the beginning and end, but also has "T" in it?"*

Dalimar thought for a minute and opened his eyes wider as the answer came to him.

*"A Teapot?"*

Rosalind laughed, *"Oh yes, you are good at this,"* as she turned serious and whispered, *"Cause this one will really test you.*

*Where there is light, is the only place I can live. But if the light shines on me I will die!*

*It has been around for millions of years but is sometimes not seen!*

*The more there is of me, the less you will ever see!*

*Three fathers have twins, but three are alone! Two fathers die, have one, and the other alive has none!"*

She sat back and reached for her teacup, while Dalimar thought and rubbed his beard. He reached for his cup and finished his tea.

*"Would you like another cup, dear?"* Rosalind asked politely.

Dalimar shook his head, *"No, thank you. I appreciate the tea, and I should go now."*

She smiled and led him to the door, *"Good night, my friend. If you figure this out, your path will be clear."*

He walked through the open door.

"Good night, Madam, and as always, I enjoyed talking to you."

Rosalind laughed with a kind of evil, sly laugh, peeking with one eye, and slowly closing the door behind him. Dalimar walked down the hall and around the corner to his room, thinking the whole time.

*"She gets more mindless, every time I see her. Still, I would like to try and figure out this riddle. She has a gift and never relays straight information. Who knows?"*

Dalimar cleaned up and wrote the riddle out on paper. Tired from the day, he laid down.

He woke up early the next morning, hoping to get an audience with the Elders. He wanted not only to warn them about the evil rising but also to seek guidance on the events unfolding. One of the maids brought breakfast to his room, and he asked her to give a message to the Elders, asking for an audience. She obliged with a quick curtsy bow and left the room.

Dalimar sat in contemplation of the riddle while sipping on tea and waiting for a reply. He opened the folded paper and set it beside the teacup and read the first line.

*Where there is light, is the only place I can live. But if light shines on me, I will die!*

*"Ah Ha, that one is easy, A Shadow! There must be a hidden meaning in each of these lines."*

He read the second line aloud.

*It has been around for millions of years but is sometimes not seen!*

*"Hmmm, there are so many meanings here. The sun, moons, stars, day, night? I will probably have to figure out the others to figure this one out."*

He read the third line. *The more there is of me, the less you will ever see!* Dalimar thought deep about this. *"There is only one meaning here. What is more but is seen less?"*

He stood up and walked around the room, looking back to where he was sitting. A big smile came on his face as he hurried to the note and read it again, *"Darkness!"*

Dalimar put the note down, trying to make sense of what the notes meant. He closed his eyes and remembered the strange, evil laugh of Rosalind as she closed the door. *"An evil shadow walks through twilight, unseen in the darkness. Well, that is part of it. What does the rest mean?"* He read the final passage.

*Three fathers have twins but three are alone! Two fathers die, have one, the other alive has none!*

*"This must have to do with Jarrod, Garren, and Evie. But what three fathers? Garren and Jarrod have two fathers, and both are dead. No, that cannot be it because Evie and Jarrod have one father..."*

Dalimar shook his head again, feeling the confusion and trying to focus. *"Okay, three fathers. Hardin, Tanin, and whoever Evie's stepfather is. Three were alone, Jarrod, Garren, and Evie. Two fathers die, Hardin and Tanin. It must be Evie's stepfather, who is the evil mage? Hmmm, I need to meditate on this, it doesn't make sense yet."*

Just then there was a knock at the door, Dalimar opened the door to see the little maid girl.

*"Mr. Dalimar, follow me, please. The Elders will see you now."* He grabbed his walking stick, put his mages robe on, and followed the girl to the audience chamber.

Dalimar walked into the audience hall where all five of the Elders were seated. Master Chun-Dracko was sitting in the highest position in the center of the semi-circle. There was a pedestal step to a standing area where Dalimar walked up and stood.

He bowed to the Elders, *"Master Chun-Dracko and esteemed counsel. I have come requesting this audience to bring you some grave news and seek your guidance."*

Master Chun-Dracko spoke. *"Ah Dalimar, it is good of you to come to see us again. I hope this is not another of your outburst warnings. The last one did not work out so well."*

Dalimar coughed a sigh and then continued.

*"Yes, well the last time it was a warning of an attack on a city, and it did happen. It just wasn't as bad as I thought it was going to be."*

The Elders laughed and then listened to Dalimar.

*"This warning is even graver. We are standing on the precipice of war. A war that will only end in the*

*destruction of Yshanall. I have dispatched a small force already to try and stop this evil from spreading, but if we fail in our task, then you should assemble the Knights from all around. This will be an evil the likes of which has never been seen, and yes, I am here to warn all who desires to live in harmony that this is fast approaching."*

Master Olvin questioned.

*"If what you say is true, then the situation is dire. But what evidence can you share that proves this?"*

*"Indeed,"* came from the others.

*"The evidence started at the trials. You saw the black knights and what happened there? The other evidence is the rise of an evil mage. He has already started his plans to bring Krometh back to the world of the living."*

Master Chun-Dracko defiantly answered.

*"We only saw a spoiled boy who did not have knightly training, and we have seen no evidence of this evil mage here. The King's realm is mighty and our Paladin, White, and Crystal Knights along with our new friends, the Bronze Knights, are more than a match*

*for anything heading south. They would not dare try to attack us. And, as for Krometh, He left this world centuries ago, never to return, so bringing him back would take powers we have never seen before. If that happens, then it is the end of this world anyway."*

Dalimar raised his voice, trying not to sound angry.

*"That is the type of power I am speaking of. We should call on all the Knights to ready themselves, dispatch messengers to the Dwarven King, and to both the Elvin lands to unite or die."*

The Elders laughed again in unison this time.

*"We have not spoken to the Dwarven Kings in over a century and visited the Elvin lands even longer. We don't even know that they still exist! Why would they help us?"*

Dalimar solemnly sighed as his voice became a whisper.

*"Because they are part of this world, and they do exist. If they do not help us, then they will suffer the same fate as us. All that we know, and love will come to an end."*

The Elders whispered amongst each other, Chun-Dracko tapped his rounded gavel on the desk in front of them.

"We have heard your words, Dalimar, and although we know you speak from the heart, we cannot move on invalidated actions and no evidence. We find that you should continue your plans, and if we see any evidence of the looming evil, then we will move on your recommendations. Until then, Dalimar, we would like to send our new Bronze Knight, Endar, with you on your journey. He is well trained and will bring back any evidence you uncover."

Dalimar spoke harshly this time, *"You fools, you do not understand what is coming, and it will be too late if you do not act now."*

The master smacked the gavel again and dismissed Dalimar with, *"We have spoken. Goodbye, Dalimar!"*

He turned and waved off Endar, *"I do not have time for you, sir knight. Best if you stay here!"* as he hurried to get his things.

Endar looked back at the Elders as if to say, *"What do I do?"* Master Chun-Dracko whispered to the knight.

*"Follow him but keep back enough, so he does not know of your presence. Take notes and report back to us what he is doing. Go now!"*

Endar nodded and scurried off to follow Dalimar.

He gathered his things and left for the stables, mumbling to himself as he went.

*"Nit-witted old fools. Too stubborn and cocky to think that anything can hurt them in this day. They have no idea what's coming, but they will soon."*

He packed his horse and jumped on with a *"HAH,"* and he was off toward Thane City, where he told the boys to meet him. They have almost a full day head start, and I should catch up with them late tomorrow afternoon should there be no more surprises.

Dalimar road most of the afternoon, stopping only for a drink and a bite to eat.

*"I wasted all day, waiting on the Elders to no avail. What a wasted day!"*

He stopped again as it was getting dark, and he moved off the road to a small clearing to camp and rest for the night. He wanted to study some spells and get some good rest before he continued.

*"Just in case, you can never be too prepared."* He said to himself.

He studied for a few hours, ate a small ration, and laid down with his horse watching over the campsite. He knew that Light-Shadow would raise the alarm if any danger was near.

He woke up early still puzzled by Rosalind's riddle but figured he would understand its meaning at some point. He packed up and was on the road, traveling for a little over half a day when an uneasy feeling came over him. He stopped the horse and looked back, feeling like he was being watched from behind but no threat. However, ahead was a sense of danger. Even Light-Shadow was a bit restless.

Dalimar rounded a curve and saw a covered cart up ahead with two men working on the cart. Sensing danger, he clutched his staff from its holding place and slowed to a walk. Once he was within a few feet of the cart, the two men leaped slinging the canvas off where four more knights jumped out. Shadow raised up on two feet, Dalimar pulled his staff and leaped off the horse, landing on his feet square in front of the now six men who were maneuvering in a semi-circle attack mode.

They tried to rush him, but Dalimar saw it coming and swirled shouting a blocking spell, which they ran into and were hurled back a considerable distance. All landing on their backs, followed by a fire burst from his staff that sent two flailing on fire, and two more were severely burned while the other two had minimal damage. One pulled a bow and fired at him, but Dalimar raised his staff that turned into a giant shield and the arrow just bounced harmlessly away.

The other two charged with weapons drawn. He thrust forth an energy bolt that caught them both in an energy field that raised them off the ground and slammed them back to the ground with a thud. The other two that were flailing on fire managed to get the fire out and bolted in fear.

Dalimar had dispatched them but now heard something coming through the woods, and he turned just in time to see a dark and tall armored man spring forth with a magical sword. Swinging at Dalimar, just in time for him to block it with his staff. He threw his other hand up and cast a beam of light that knocked the being back but only a couple of steps. The dark being held his hand out straight and shouted a spell that hit Dalimar square in the chest sliding him backward. The energy beam gained in power as the dark being yelled.

*"Die, old man. Give in to your fate."*

Dalimar resisted the beam even though it was still gaining power, and he tried to concentrate on another spell, speaking as he defended himself from the energy. Dalimar was struggling to hold the beam at bay when it stopped, and he fell to the ground on his knees with staff in the air still concentrating on his words.

The being spoke and moved forward, taking off his mask, *"And now before you die, I wanted you to see who defeated you."*

He walked into the light, and Dalimar stopped speaking, shocked in disbelief, *"Tanin!"* Dalimar closed his eyes as Tanin laughed.

*"That's right old man, and now you shall feel my revenge upon you."*

He stretched his hands out as Dalimar rose to his feet with his staff raised horizontal and shouted the spell forth.

Just then Tanin fired at him again with the pulsating magical dark energy beam, stronger than ever. Dalimar was weakening as he struggled to maintain his stance and defend against the magical energy. Suddenly, Dalimar opened his eyes, with all his strength, yelled the last of his spell. There was a massive flash of light and an explosion that sent all the men left and Tanin hurling through the air. Tanin slowly got up having the wind knocked out of him and donned his mask. He walked over, scanning the scorched ground, and his men scattered lifeless around, all except one.

Tanin kicked the ground, clutching his fist.

*"He is gone, and at last, my revenge on Dalimar is complete. With the old fool gone, there is no one left to*

*stand against me. Bring the horses up, we have a journey to intercept Mathis."*

He wryly laughed from beneath the mask.

*"We need to have a talk with our little traitor, Go, Now!"*

He glared off in the distance with both hands clenched into fists. The last man standing scrambled into the woods to get the horses and came back to where Tanin was still standing. They mounted and darted off through the woods to the north and west, leaving the dead where they laid. The two raced their horses to near death, finally catching the caravan heading to Idesport City with their cargo north and west of High Bluff and just southeast of Thane City. They were heading to the northern pass, which would take them west of Volshstein and then northeast, taking another three days' ride to Idesport City.

The dark mage shouted orders to the Knights in the camp, walking into the master tent.

*"Where is Mathis? Bring him to me."*

The knights scurried off to find Mathis, who was out scanning the area for his guards. Mathis rode into the camp and jumped off his horse, flew back the doors, and entered the great tent. He walked up towards Tanin who was now sitting at his mired throne-like chair.

He knelt on one knee then stood up.

*"You called for me, my master?"*

Tanin raised his hand.

*"Yes, Mathis, I want you to bring the traitor to me now."*

Mathis nodded.

*"It shall be done."*

Mathis stepped back out and ordered.

*"Bring the girl to the tent now!"*

The guards rushed over to the jail cart, opened the door, and stepped up inside. Mathis could hear Evie screaming at them and struggling, but they overpowered her easily. They brought Evie into the tent, and she defiantly walked in and faced Tanin. Mathis was standing beside the seated dark mage with his mask on.

Mathis pointed at her.

*"On your knees!"*

Evie just stared at him in opposition with her head held high. One of the guards came from behind and smacked her legs behind her knees with a pike, forcing her to the ground as she yelped in pain. The dark mage laughed at her as she hit the ground.

*"That is where I like a woman, on her knees."*

Hissed Tanin through the mask.

*"Your treachery has not gone unnoticed, and you shall pay for your insolence soon enough. But for now, if you just tell me where your knight boyfriend is going, then I may show some leniency."*

Evie looked up throwing her hair back in disregard.

*"I don't know, and I wouldn't tell you if I did."*

Tanin quickly stood up and pointed at her.

*"Would you rather be tortured into speaking?"*

She looked down.

*"No, but it wouldn't do you any good if you did. I don't know anything."*

She looked back up, trying to think of a way to keep herself alive.

*"I do know something important, though."*

She stood up and limped to one side then turned back, looking at Tanin.

*"I know about a ring."*

Tanin sat down.

*"Yes, his insignificant little brother has it. I will find him and get my ring back."*

Just then another Knight entered with a satchel in his hand.

*"Here is her pack, my lord."*

Tanin took the satchel and opened it. Evie broke toward Tanin, pulling her knife and screamed, startling Tanin. She leaped only to get caught by Mathis who grabbed her by the arm and slammed her to the ground, taking the knife away from her. She thudded to the ground so hard she screamed in pain and lost her breath as Mathis stood over her. She coughed, trying to regain her composure. Tanin laughed at her again.

*"Nice try little girl, I admire your tenacity, but what is so important in here that you would risk your life to try to get to me?"*

He pulled out her book Jarrod gave her.

*"Perhaps this?"*

He looked at the cover and stood up enraged.

"Sarahasyl?"

He glared at her with hatred now.

*"Take her back to her cell and lock her up. I have some reading to do."*

Evie was weak as the guards grabbed her, dragging her toward the exit, "No, No."

Tanin just stared at the cover as they hauled Evie back to the cell. They threw her back in and locked the door as if she was just a trash bag. They pulled the cover back over the cart as she laid on the floor sobbing, hoping someone would save her from this nightmare.

*** 

Endar saw the colossal explosion just over the ridge and decided to head around through the east and back, to see if he could quietly approach the area. The blast was too big to be a natural bolt of lightning. Besides, it was a clear day with no clouds in sight.

*"That had to be magic,"* thought Endar.

He tied his horse and crept around to the east of the road, staying in the shadows. He came out of the woods just in time to see the black knights, jump on their horses, and dart off to the northwest through the woods. He ran out to see a huge hole in the ground and five bodies lying around.

*"Where is Dalimar?"* He asked himself.

He lifted the dead men into the cart who was on the side of the road and looked through their things. Some had swords, but one had a nice dagger, so he took that thinking.

*"He won't be needing this."*

He grabbed some other rations and picked up coins too.

Endar mused, *"Well, this is the knightly thing to do. Stealing from the dead!"*

He rolled the cart off the road into a small clearing and left it walking back to the scorched earth. Then dug around looking for traces of Dalimar but found nothing. Just when he was about to go back and get his horse, he spotted something glimmering in the light. He moved the dirt aside, and it was an enormous ruby-like stone. He looked at it and could see through it.

*"This is interesting, I wonder if Dalimar dropped it."*

He also found a rolled-up piece of paper that was like a small scroll. He unwound it and read it aloud, it only said, "Rosalind's Riddle," and had the riddle on it with Dalimar's notes scribbled to the side, *"An evil shadow walks through twilight unseen in darkness."* Along with the entire riddle. He rolled it back up and pulled a small pouch out with pull strings. He put the note and the ruby in the pouch and tied it back to his side, heading to get his horse.

*"I must try to catch up with Dalimar or warn Garren in Thane City."*

# Chapter 18

Jarrod and Garren walked their horses into the main gates of Thane City close to dark, on their third day of travel. They made good time and were quite tired, but they were looking forward to seeing Dalimar at the Pengrass Stables to formulate the next part of their plan. They walked through the city with strange looks from the city people.

Jarrod looked around.

*"What are all these people staring at? It's not like we are the only strangers in town. This place is eaten up with strangers."*

Jarrod looked ahead down the main street and saw the outline of the city castle in the distance.

*"Garren, look at that. I had no idea this place was so beautiful."*

Garren stopped beside him.

*"Yeah, it is. I have never been here before either. I don't think this is the last wonder we will see on this journey."*

Jarrod nodded, and they turned to look for the stable area. There were plenty of stables at the outskirts of the central city, and just when they were about to give up, they saw the Pengrass Stables.

Jarrod pointed, "There it is. I hope Dalimar is here already."

Garren stared back with a hopeless expression, *"I doubt it after our last meeting. He was fashionably late."*

They both got a nice laugh out of that and moved toward the stable, hearing the pounding of a hammer on an anvil.

As they walked in, they saw the blacksmith hammering away and a young girl about their age sitting at the counter.

The master shouted, *"Leah, take care of them."*

She hopped off her chair and moved closer to them, "Hi, I'm Leah. You need a horse stay and shoed?"

Jarrod looked at Garren then back to her, *"Yes, that would be good. What other services are offered?"*

She burst into laughter as Jarrod turned red with embarrassment. Even Garren started laughing.

*"Uhh, I mean for the horses?"*

She was still laughing, *"Yes, I know. It's just the way you said that."*

She walked around Garren and took the horses' reins from Jarrod. She pulled a horse's foot up, *"Yep, this one needs some good shoes for sure. Where are you guys from?"*

She dismissed the comment, trying not to embarrass Jarrod again.

Jarrod spoke, happy to forget, *"We are from Briar's Cove Township in the south."*

She looked surprised, taking the rein from Garren and checking his horse's feet as well.

*"This one needs clipping and shoed as well. Briar's Cove? Wow, what are you doing here?"*

The master walked in and took both reins from her to lead them to the shoeing area, *"Leah, stop prying. It's their business."*

Jarrod answered immediately as Leah was feeling admonished, *"It's okay, Sir. We don't mind the questions."*

Smiling at Leah, who looked up with eyes bright and pleased, he had stood up for her. Jarrod continued, *"We are here to meet a friend and from the looks of things, wait on him to arrive. Can you point us to a good place to stay that is modestly priced?"*

She looked back to her master, walking off. *"What do you think about renting them the upstairs room for a couple of days?"*

The master looked back, *"You boys aren't in any trouble, are you?"*

Jarrod's expression turned to astonishment, *"Na no, Sir. We are just waiting for our friend to arrive, and we will be off."*

The master shrugged, *"Okay then, can you afford 3 silver a day?"*

Jarrod happily announced, *"That is a fair price, and thank you once again."*

*"You're welcome and stay out of trouble. That is the last thing I need is a bunch of trouble here. Leah, show them the rooms, and you stay out of trouble too."*

Leah gladly bounced, *"C'mon, I'll show you around! That is my Grandfather, Boream."*

Jarrod took one last look at the old blacksmith, who had a worried and puzzled expression on his face, sensing there was much more to these two than he wanted to know. Leah led them up the stairs and pulled out an old skeleton key opening the door handing it to Jarrod, *"Here it is. The place is old, but there is a small kitchen and two bedrooms. It also has a living area with a nice sitting arrangement."*

Jarrod could not help to watch her as they walked in, and she was pointing at things. She had dark shiny straight hair cut just to her shoulders and pretty, blue eyes that shined brightly when she smiled. Jarrod thought to himself while shaking his head quickly.

*"Stop it, Jarrod, we don't have time for this."*

She saw him brush her off and look away quickly, *"What's wrong, is the room, okay?"*

Jarrod glanced back quickly, "Yeah, it's great. Thank you very much."

She flashed that smile, making Jarrod a bit uncomfortable again, *"Okay, well if you need anything, just give me a shout. Hey, you wanna grab some dinner? I know a great place."*

Jarrod started to shake his head no when Garren interrupted, *"Yeah sure, Jarrod would love to go with you. I am going to stay here and get some rest. Just bring me back a sandwich."*

Jarrod looked back at Garren, who was smiling happily, ear to ear and gave him a dirty look. Jarrod whispered, leaning to Garren, *"Thanks a lot!"*

Garren laughed, *"Uh, what?"* Knowing full well, Jarrod did not want to go. Jarrod sighed and followed Leah.

She led him down the street where they ducked into an ally and into the back door of a café. She led them by the cooks and a big burly looking guy all with, *"Hey Raven, Hello Raven, and Hi Raven."*

She whispered to Jarrod flipping her dark hair, *"Everyone has called me Raven since I was little."*

Jarrod followed her to a nice room where there were four tables, *"Sit here, this is my room. I always come here to eat."*

He sat down, and Leah sat across from him. The waiter came in and brought two glasses and poured some water, *"Anything special tonight, Raven?"*

She looked back and smiled at him, *"What's the special tonight."* The waiter rattled off, *"freshly baked bread and a basil chicken pasta tonight."*

She grinned and leaned toward Jarrod, whispering, *"Do you trust me?"*

Jarrod nodded yes to her. She leaned back and in her best sexy voice, *"Good, we'll take two of those and wrap us a chicken sandwich to go, Frayerl!"*

He nodded, *"Yes, mam!"*

She started talking, and Jarrod just listened. She told him about the city and how some places were not safe to be in. Told him about her life growing up there. Talked about the King of Thane City, and how she is a distant relative of the queen. How her mother had died a few years ago, and she just stayed with her grandfather at the stables.

*"You don't talk much, do you?"* She questioned.

Jarrod took a bite of the food, *"This is very good."*

He dismissed her question, then answered, *"I'm just listening to you. Your voice is soothing."*

She gave him a big smile at that, *"Really? No one has ever said that to me, and I'm glad you like the food."*

Jarrod took another bite and leaned in, *"Yes, really! I am enjoying your company too. Thank you for looking after us. It's not always that people invite strangers into their midst."*

She giggled, *"Aww, you two looked harmless, and if I may be a little bit bold if you hadn't been so cute I would have just left."*

She sat back waiting for a response, Jarrod coughed and sat there, with a surprised look on his face.

She laughed again, *"Sorry, I didn't mean to embarrass you."*

Jarrod finally closed his mouth, *"Uhh, no it's okay,"* laughing it off. *"I was just thinking that no one had ever said that to me before!"*

They both laughed, ate, and Leah had a glass of berry wine, and so did Jarrod. They finished up, and Leah boasted when the waiter came back in, *"Put it on my tab, Frayerl!"*

He answered nonchalantly, *"As you wish, dear."* He started to pick up the plates while Jarrod starred back in amazement.

*"Wow, you have some pull around here for a tiny thing, but you didn't have to do that. I have some coins."*

She looked back a little fired up, *"Tiny thing? Hmmm, maybe I should've let you just wander around by yourself and pay up everywhere."*

Jarrod choked back his words, trying to recover. She burst out laughing at his attempt.

*"I'm just kidding you, Jarrod, you're welcome. It helps when your grandfather is one of the best blacksmiths in town. As for a tiny thing, I take that as a compliment! I don't think you disapprove?"*

She looked at him again with that smile. Jarrod was caught off guard a second time, and he laughed with her, then just laid it out there in an attempt to catch her off.

*"Well, now that you mention it, no, I do not disapprove. The fact is, I think you are absolutely gorgeous!"*

He stood up and turned while she sat for second with her mouth open.

*"Hey, wait I'm not ready to go back yet. You want to take a walk?"*

Jarrod bowed at her, halfway moving his arm forward, *"Lead on my lady, Leah. I would thoroughly enjoy a walk with you."*

She loved it, and they walked off down the back street toward the castle park. They chatted together, and then, she abruptly stopped.

*"I have some questions for you, and you can tell me to "bug off" if I am prying, but I have to know some things."*

Jarrod cautiously answered, *"There are some things I cannot tell you, but I will tell you as much as I can, and one thing you can count on, I will not lie to you."*

Her eyes melted at his gaze to her because she knew that was true.

*"I know you said you were waiting on a friend, but I was wondering who that might be?"*

Jarrod's expression became serious, *"His name is Dalimar, and as soon as he arrives, we will be leaving."*

Her voice turned to excitement, *"I know Dalimar. He has been here many times in the past. If you are waiting for him, then something is going on. What is it, maybe I can help?"*

Jarrod shook his head no, *"I cannot say what is happening but thank you for the offer. If we can think of anything, we will ask if you don't mind."*

She looked down mumbling to herself as Jarrod followed closely, *"I knew it, something is going on!"*

She dismissed it and continued questioning, *"Garren, is he a knight?"*

*"As a matter of fact, he is. He just became a White Knight of the Realm in the South."*

She was very inquisitive back to Jarrod, *"And what about you?"*

Jarrod hesitated, *"Uh no, I did not make it through. I am more of .... the scholarly type. Although I am pretty good with a bow and I am...."*

She inquisitively asked, *"And you are what?"*

Jarrod looked back at her, *"Let's just say, I have a knack for finding things out."*

She was kind of mesmerized by his mystery, thinking to herself, *"He is mysterious, and I like that about him."*

She quickly glanced back to Jarrod and only whispered, *"More!"*

Jarrod scrunched his eyes, *"More what?"*

She laughed, *"Sorry, you are just such a mystery. I see something behind those eyes of yours, and I will get it out of you sooner or later."*

She grabbed him by the hand, pulling at him, *"C'mon, I have something to show you over here in the park. I think you will like it."*

She started to run, pulling Jarrod along as he ran beside her. They came to a bridge, crossed over, and walked down a path on the other side of a flowing river to a look-out area.

Jarrod's eyes opened in amazement, *"Wow, you were right, look at that waterfall. It's beautiful, Leah."*

She moved closer, staring into his eyes, but Jarrod leaned away from her advance, placing his arms on the railing and looked out over the falls. She sighed and wished he would just kiss her. Disappointed by not getting her way, she set her arms right beside on his left side where she looked at him in almost desperation.

Softly, she whispered, *"I told you that you would like it!"*

He kept staring straight ahead, *"Yes, you did. I just want to stand here and watch awhile."*

Leah tried not to let him know that she was all for that, *"Okay Jarrod, as long as you like."*

They stood there awhile admiring the falls when Leah shivered. *"Brrr."*

Jarrod put his arm around her, *"This better?"*

She gladly snuggled in close and put her arm around his waist, *"Yes, thank you."*

She thought to herself, *"Common tactic worked again, hehe."*

She quietly chuckled to herself as Jarrod quickly noticed.

*"You okay?"*

She leaned a bit closer, *"Oh, yes, I am fine."*

They stood for a bit longer, chatting together and headed back to the stable. Jarrod was walking with his hands behind his back and chatting casually. Leah was trying her best to elicit a sensual response from Jarrod but got nowhere.

She was a bit frustrated but yearned to learn more about him, *"When do you think Dalimar will arrive?"*

Jarrod looked back with uncertainty, *"He should have been here already. I don't know, perhaps tomorrow."*

Leah stopped talking and just walked with Jarrod, knowing that she could not try to start a relationship with someone who was leaving. *"That would just suck, best I back off."*

She kept telling herself over and over to *"back off Leah,"* but her longing to learn more about him just got stronger as the night wore on.

They got back to the stable and said their goodnights. Jarrod thanked her for a lovely evening and the dinner and watched as she walked away to her room, which was on the same floor but down the hall.

She got to her door and looked back when she opened, to see Jarrod watching her, she flashed that smile.

*"I will see you in the morning. For breakfast?"*

Jarrod smiled and waved, trying to stave off the embarrassment of being caught staring at her, *"Uh. Yeah, that would be great."*

She smiled, skipping into her room and closed the door behind her. Jarrod heard a thud against her door and wondered what that was as he walked into the room to see Garren sitting at the table.

Leah put her back against the door, closing it hard with her backside as she thudded against the door. Her eyes peeled to the ceiling, blinking, and then blinking again. No one has ever kept calling me Leah after they learned that everyone else calls me Raven.

She sighed a huge sigh, *"Dammit that guy is so good-looking with those dreamy eyes, and he doesn't even know it."*

She stomped off to her bedroom to clean up.

Garren looked at Jarrod as he walked in with a sly laugh, *"Well, out a little late with her, huh? So how did the date go?"*

Jarrod looked back with a condescending face, *"Don't start on me. Here, she got you a chicken sandwich."*

Garren snatched the bag, opening and unwrapping at the same time, taking a huge bite, *"Mmmm, this is good. I was hungry."*

Jarrod smiled and walked to the window, looking out over the city, *"No Dalimar, yet?"*

Garren said, *"No, not yet,"* as he chomped another bite.

*"Okay, I am gonna clean up and hit the bed. See you in the morning."* Garren nodded, continuing to eat his sandwich.

Jarrod finished cleaning up and then laid down to rest. As soon as he closed his eyes, he saw visions of Evie in pain and wished he could just reach in there and snatch her out, feeling guilty for letting her go.

Another vision came immediately, *"So, son of Sarahasyl and brother to Evie! You are closer to me than I thought! Bring me the ring, and you will be rewarded with a dark power like you have never known. Become my apprentice, and you will know the dark powers that I have. There is no one left to help you with Dalimar dead. Yes, I killed him!"*

Jarrod tried to wake up but couldn't. *"Don't resist your fate, bring it to me now, or I shall slowly kill your, .... Sister!"* The dark mage let out this evil laugh as the vision faded.

He snapped awake, breathing hard. *"Dalimar dead? It can't be."*

Jarrod sat up thinking about the visions, *"How does he know we are brother and sister? Did he really kill Dalimar? Become his apprentice? He is evil and a liar, mixed with truth. We must wait one more day, but if he doesn't meet us tomorrow, we will move on without him. Evie needs our help and her life depends on us. Every minute we wait, she becomes closer to death. I cannot let her and Garren down, not to mention the entire world."*

Jarrod stared off into other realms, hearing a whispered voice in his head, *"Yes, the path to darkness is easy. Despair, loss, and hatred, take the easy path."* until he drifted into a deep sleep.

Jarrod and Garren both woke up at about the same time the next morning to the smell of cooking. Garren was rushing around, claiming starvation again. Telling Jarrod that it smelled like freshly baked bread and sausage.

There was a knock on the door, "Come on down, guys. I got breakfast ready."

They heard Leah scrambling back downstairs and followed shortly after. They were met with a table full of food while Leah happily set up everything, and it looked like she had been cooking all night. There were scrambled eggs, bacon and sausage, potatoes, fresh baked Thane berry bread, which is a bread with these wonderful berries, and then orange juice, coffee, and tea. They sat down and said hello to Leah's grandfather, who was sitting there with a surprised look on his face.

She sat down between Jarrod and Boream, *"Well, are you gonna stare all day? Dig In!"*

Didn't have to tell Garren twice as they all dug in and chatted about how well the stables were doing recently, how well things in the city were, and even some Dalimar stories from Boream that made everyone laugh.

He patted Garren on the back and told him, *"You should have told me you were waiting on Dalimar. It would have put my mind at ease. But I will tell you if you are waiting for him to show, he is never on time and is always late."*

They had a great laugh together, and Garren told him, *"We have found that out."* Again, they laughed with an announcement from Boream as they finished up. *"That was a wonderful breakfast, my dear. You cook just like your mama!"*

She looked sadly at him with a hug and a kiss, *"Aw Grandpa, thank you."* Jarrod agreed, *"Yes, Leah. The best meal we have had in a while, thank you."* Garren said, *"Here, Here, I don't remember a better breakfast."* Taking a big swig of juice.

She hugged Garren who almost spilled his drink, then reached over and gave Jarrod a kiss on the cheek. It surprised him, and their eyes met again. She quickly turned and started to clean up.

Boream shouted, *"I'll get that, honey. You cooked, and so I will clean up."*

The boys gathered their plates and cleaned off the table with Leah looking on. She was thoroughly enjoying their effort. An hour or so went by, and both were back up in their room when there was a knock at the door.

Garren opened the door, and it was Leah standing there, *"I thought maybe you guys would like to take a little hike today while you wait on Dalimar?"*

Garren relieved, *"Oh, thank God! Yes, take him somewhere, please! He is driving me insane, pacing back and forth like that. He has been pacing for an hour now in deep thought. I will stay here, in case Dalimar shows up."*

Jarrod looked harshly at Garren and just stared at him as he followed Leah out the door. They got out, and Garren flung the door shut as if to say happily, *"Off ya go!"* While he slapped his hands back and forth with satisfaction.

Jarrod could hear Garren quietly laughing behind the door because he thought he had set him up again. What he didn't know was that deep down, Jarrod was a bit excited about spending more time with Leah. Leah took Jarrod to the old Thane City sanctuary and museum. She told him about an underground city that was run by the guild. These are the unwanted people in the lower portion of the town, and some you wouldn't want to be around because many are just plain criminals.

Only a handful of city dwellers are welcomed. She told him of Dwarves that wander in every now and then, wanting to trade items. She took him to a trader shop where they sold items built by Dwarves, including golden tables and chairs, dishes, and items made from some material he had never seen before. The items fascinated Jarrod greatly, and Leah gladly told him anything he wanted to know.

She stopped short of the underground city, saying she only heard rumors and didn't know much about it even when Jarrod pushed, letting her know that was where Dalimar wanted to go. She just said that he might not be able to get in, but she knew someone who would. Leah led him down one of the ancient paths that went to the Library Hall. Jarrod was thrilled to see it and was anxious to go inside.

She led him into the great hall, which was lined with books everywhere. There were people there, so they whispered back and forth with Jarrod, telling her that one day he was going to visit this place and spend a full week studying. She perked up with that news, and they made some preliminary plans to spend some time together while he visited.

They left there, and it was early afternoon around lunchtime. She was having such a good time and was able to get Jarrod to open himself up, telling her about the trials, helping Garren, the trip there, and Garren's new girlfriend, Evie. He conveniently left out that she was his sister, and all that happened. Just telling her that his stepfather had died recently, and how he was Garren's stepbrother adopted by Hardin. Leah wanted more and more information and was craving for it. She told him they were going to another little dining area to sit and chat outside for lunch. He wasn't hungry at all, and neither was she, but they ordered some tea and snacks and chatted together until Leah could stand it no longer.

She had to make some kind of move to let Jarrod know what she was feeling, and if he rejected her, then she had already decided to be friends. Jarrod was talking about his home and Ms. Frieda, and how old toothless Olvin was attacked and killed by a bear or something. Jarrod paused as she was staring at him with a strange look of "Please stop talking!"

She took a bite of a cracker and chewed, never leaving his gaze and then with no warning, *"Jarrod, you have a wonderful family and the most beautiful eyes I have ever seen on a man. I just want to keep looking into them."*

She waited for his response. Jarrod was thoroughly enjoying, being with her today. Still, it took him by surprise, but he held his resolution.

*"Leah,"* he whispered to her, *"We have only just met, and I don't want this to sound like a rejection."*

She sat back with a sigh, feeling like *"here it is, rejected,"* folding her arms.

*"Go ahead, continue. It's okay."*

Jarrod thought for a moment then started again, *"As I was saying or what I meant was, you make me feel like I deserve someone as wonderful as you. We have talked closely for two days now. I just don't want to leave here without you as my friend. There is much to do, and although my heart wants to let you in, I cannot right now. Maybe when I return, we can spend much more time together. It would break my heart if we got really close then I had to leave."*

He reached and touched her face, *"Please understand Leah, I am leaving, and I don't want to hurt you by leaving you when we were so close."*

He sat back, and she responded sadly, *"I know, and I do understand, but you understand, it's too late! You are already in my heart, and I don't know why because I am not one to fall for someone."*

Her face hardened, *"You are right though, let's just be friends and leave it there. But I am holding you to your word that you will come back some day."*

Jarrod smiled, *"Yes, I promise to return one day when all this craziness is over."*

She looked back, wiping the tears that started to fall, *"Oh god, don't do that,"* as she sighed deeply and held back more tears.

Jarrod asked with honesty, *"Can we head back to the stables to see if Dalimar has come yet?"*

She got up abruptly, *"Yes, let's get this over with."*

Jarrod walked with her, silently heading back to the stables.

They got back to the stables, and Garren was helping the blacksmith Boream, *"This young fella is going to be a good forger one day."*

Garren laughed at the thought but was concerned about Jarrod who started to talk.

*"Any sign of Dalimar?"*

Garren reluctantly shook his head no.

Jarrod looked down, *"We cannot wait any longer. We must get going."*

Boream stopped what he was doing, *"Why not give it another day? He will be along directly, he always does."*

Jarrod looked back in desperation, *"Not this time. I fear we cannot wait any longer."*

He grabbed Leah, who was startled, *"You mentioned that you knew someone who could get us into the undercity, yes?"*

She batted her eyes in surprise, *"Yes, I do. I can take you to them."*

Boream interrupted brashly. *"No, Leah. I have told you time and again to stay away from there, I forbid it!"*

She pleaded with her grandfather, *"But grandad, I can help them."*

He pointed at her, *"No! Go to your room! There will be no more discussion about it."*

She hurried off up the stairs with disobedient defiance on her face, stomping and mumbling, but to her credit, she did not argue.

Jarrod looked apologetic, *"I am sorry, Boream, but we have to try to go there and see a man named, Nanek."*

Boream's eyes opened wide as he moved to his chair and slumped down into it, *"Nanek?"* Looking back to Jarrod with disgust.

*"Nanek is nothing but trouble. I have tried to keep Leah away from him as much as possible. You will not succeed in going down there. It is a hell trap for anyone foolish enough to try. If you must go, take the sanctuary road, and there is a hidden passage that will take you into the depths filled with traps and danger. If you do make it to the iron doors, there is only one way to enter. You must speak the password phrase, or the door will not open. Good luck to you, but that is all I can offer as I do not know the phrase."*

Jarrod gave him a nod, *"Thank you for your kindness and for letting Leah show us around. I have become quite fond of her, and I will miss her dearly. But our mission is dire, and we must continue on."*

Boream nodded and told them if they cannot get in to come back, and their room would be waiting.

Both the boys came up the stairs and entered their room to gather their things. Jarrod looked over at the table and sitting there with arms folded was Leah.

*"You two are going alone into the underground?"*

Jarrod looked back to her, *"How did you....?"*

Leah harshly interrupted him and stood up, *"Answer Me!"* Pounding her fist on the table.

Jarrod was a bit taken back but answered, *"Yes, we have no choice but to try."*

Leah laughed sarcastically, *"Pretty brave of you, walking into certain death."*

Jarrod was defiant, *"Perhaps so, but we have to take the risk to continue on."*

Leah stood, brushed the table with her hand, gently sweeping across it, *"No, you don't. Wait here till dark, and I know someone who can get us in. I have been there myself, and I know the way."*

Jarrod was surprised, *"But your grandfather?"*

Leah voiced her opinion, *"Yes, but in this case, I think he will forgive me. It's easier to ask for his forgiveness than ask for permission."*

Jarrod looked at Garren who was studying Leah with concern, *"We can't argue with logic like that. Okay, Leah, what's the plan?"*

Leah was glad they accepted her offer, *"I will come get you when Grandpa is asleep, and we can go then. It will be easier to get there after dark."*

Jarrod looked back with regard for her, *"Thank you, Leah, and we will be waiting for your, okay to go."*

Leah went to the door and then looked back as she opened it, *"Pack light and bring your weapons, you will need them."*

She left the room with both Garren and Jarrod, eyeing each other with disapproval. Garren walked forward, *"You know this is going to be dangerous, and I am not sure putting her in danger is the right thing to do?"*

Jarrod smiled back at him wryly, *"Your concern is surely noted, but I sense there is something more about her that she is not revealing. Yet! She is our only hope right now."*

*"I hope you are right, brother,"* Garren said with reluctance as he went to get ready.

# Chapter 19

The two waited anxiously for nightfall and was not sure what time she was coming to get them. Jarrod was reading, and Garren was thinking about Evie when finally, there was a knock at the door. Jarrod opened the door to see Leah. She just waltzed in on her own leaving Jarrod at the door with his mouth open. Garren looked up at her then eyed her up and down as he let out a surprised whistle tone.

*"Whoa, what in the world?"*

He could tell she was smiling under the half dark mask where only her eyes shown. The rest of her face was covered. She wore a dark, tight leather outfit with cat clawed gloves. The whole outfit was like a woman's tight fit, leather armor. She wore a pair of matching dark, soft leather boots and the weapons she had were crossed Sai's; three-pronged long knives that fit nicely on her back. Strapped to her side was a thin blade in a black sheath.

She spoke softly, placing her hands on her hips and standing sideways.

*"You boys ready for some real danger?"*

Jarrod walked up, regaining some of his composure. He was astonished at not only her attire but how gorgeous she looked.

*"Not really but from the looks of things, you surely are. What are you wearing?"*

She flashed her best sexy eyes and turned a bit sideways to Jarrod that just about melted him in his spot.

*"This is my night-shade armor. I am a member of the night-shade order, and I have been training for three years to be able to wear this in honor of our guild. Once I become a full member, I will have unlimited access to the underworld area. The night-shade order is also the order of Nanek. He is our leader, and it is our duty to use our skills, instead of being criminals, to help the needy and the poor."*

Jarrod looked back to Garren.

*"See, I told you there was more to her than meets the eye."*

Garren shook his head, *"You sure did, but I had no idea, we were about to be led around by a thief."*

Leah turned sharply, *"I am not a thief, as I have learned the skills so that I can use them for a good purpose one day. I don't even categorize myself with the likes of those miscreants and other scum down there. We have our own way; our own lives, and we are forbidden to associate with them."*

Garren apologized, *"Sorry, Leah, it was not my intention to insult you. The fact is, we are glad you can help us."*

She walked to the table, *"Apology accepted. Now let's go, we don't have much time. Because you are strangers, we must take the old passage through the under-crypt to get there. I have only been through there one time, and it was full of giant rats and other ilk. They say there are other things there that I hope we don't run in to. Stay behind me during the trek because we will have to sneak past some guards to get into the tomb of the ancients. Then we will enter the catacombs and the hall to the under-crypt secret passage. It is a long maze-like tunnel to the secret Iron Door where I will have to recite the passage. If we make it there, we will be safe."*

She opened the door and made sure that Boream was not around.

*"Shhh, quietly now."*

She led them out the door and down the stairs, and the boys realized that she made absolutely no sound as she walked. It was like she was walking on a sheet of air above the ground. Once outside, they made their way down the street and to the old path of the ancients she took Jarrod down once before. Jarrod was so amazed at her, she was like a shadow walking, and sometimes, he had to shift his eyes just to see her at all.

Garren was having all kinds of trouble due to his size and leather armor, as well as his weapons. Jarrod only had his bow on his back and a knife. He had something else, and as he thought about it, he slipped his ring on. He closed his eyes for a second to calm the rising temperature and overwhelming power from within. Once he opened his eyes again, he saw Garren and Leah motioning for him to hurry, waving their arms at him.

He didn't realize he had fallen behind so he caught up to Leah's chastisement, *"You have to keep up. It will get dicey in a few minutes."*

She led them forward, and Jarrod didn't want to upset her again, so he kept up easily.

Leah stopped by the mausoleum gates, *"Okay, here is where we have to get by the guards. There are three of them, two outside and one inside, so one at a time. We will have to time it; as the guards pass each other, run to the door. I will go first and pick the lock, then you,"* pointing at Garren, *"then Jarrod. Just quietly run straight into the open door. Got it? If we get caught here, we are done."*

They all nodded, and Leah started the execution. She took off just as she said, made it to the door, and began to pick the lock. She could not get it open, and Jarrod looked to see if he could see her, and she just disappeared right before their eyes.

Garren whispered, *"Where did she go?"*

Jarrod concentrated harder, and then all of a sudden, he could see her through her body heat, *"Oh, I see her just fine."*

Garren was looking harder and in despair, *"I can't see her at all."*

Jarrod quietly, *"Shhh, I will tell you when to go."*

Just as the two guards passed, Leah went back to work on the door. She got it and slipped through as the guards were coming back around. Jarrod watched as they passed each other, and he whispered.

*"Go now."*

Garren leaped into flight, and as he got close to the door, it opened, and he went through unnoticed. Jarrod easily made it to the door just at the time Leah opened it again. They were inside, breathing heavy from the excitement sighing in relief.

Garren spoke puzzled, *"How could you see Leah? I couldn't see a damn thing."*

Leah looked at Jarrod in wonderment, *"Yeah, how did you see me,"* she smiled with her best dazzle at Jarrod who could only see her eyes.

*"Uhh, just a little trick I have. Let's get going."*

Leah led the way to the hallway of the ancients, *"This will not be so easy, we will have to distract him, and maybe even knock him out."*

Jarrod looked back to her and said. *"I think I have a better way, wait here."*

They both tried to stop him, but he was too quick and walked out into the hallway, speaking quietly as he walked with his eyes peeled on the guard's back. The guard heard him coming up behind and turned to face Jarrod but could not speak or move. The guard's eyes widened as both Garren and Leah came into the hallway expecting the guard to attack. Jarrod held his hand up to them in a stop fashion which they did and watched as he touched the guard's shoulder. The guard's eyes rolled back and slumped to the ground, caught by Jarrod who set him gently down.

Leah walked up, *"Wow, how did you do that?"*

Jarrod smiled as he let the sleeping guard go, *"Just a few tricks, Leah. Lead on, my lady!"*

She responded with respect looking at the sleeping guard, *"A few tricks, uh huh? Oh, yea. On, we shall go!"*

They traversed down the great hall, Leah in the lead, hugging the wall as they moved silently to the crypt. They opened the door to the crypt, and a slight breeze hit their faces as they looked ominously into the dark and cob-webbed room.

Leah knocked the webs from the door and took a torch from one of the sconces. Staring at it with frustration, knowing they had no way to light it.

Jarrod stepped in, *"Allow me."*

He waved his hand across the top of the torch, and it lit to her surprise. She blinked, holding the torch.

*"Thanks, you didn't tell me you were a mage."*

Jarrod laughed, *"Is that what I am? I am not so sure. Dalimar is a mage, I am more of..."* He thought for a moment, *"An apprentice."*

Leah put her hand on his shoulder, *"Apprentice or mage, it's no difference. What I have seen you do so far is nothing short of what I have seen Dalimar do."*

Jarrod looked back at her as they walked through the crypt, *"You should get out more, and by the way, you didn't tell me you were a Night-Shade either."*

She laughed at that comment, *"Well, I didn't want to scare you off."*

Jarrod chuckled, *"After what we have been through, it takes a little more than that to scare me off."*

*"Oh, really?"* Leah exclaimed and in a little bit sexy voice, *"I bet I know how to scare you off."*

While she rubbed against his arm, slightly taking her hand to her mouth with a sexy side look.

Jarrod backed off, disturbed by her open behavior, *"Um, can we just continue on?"*

Leah shot him a look and just as quickly stopped, *"Okay, right up here is the secret entrance. We will have to push the crypt aside and go down the stairs."*

They continued and arrived at the huge cement crypt top. It was about four feet off the ground and looked like it weighed a ton.

Garren stepped up, cracking his fingers out, *"Allow me."*

Leah stepped aside, *"By all means. It took three of us to move it the last time I was here."*

Jarrod stepped beside Leah, *"This is what he is really good at."*

Garren leaned down and tested the strength of the block, and it didn't budge. He braced and shoved with all his might, and the top started to move. He shoved with his legs moving forward, and you could see his ripped muscles just fold into the push. The block then moved with ease, revealing a downward spiral staircase. Garren stopped and looked back with pride.

Leah said as a matter of fact, *"Well, that's done. Good job, Garren,"* surprised by his strength. Then they headed down the stairs.

Finally reaching the bottom, there was a door that was locked. Leah stepped up and pulled out her lock pick kit, *"This is what I am good at."*

Jarrod muttered under his breath, *"Except torturing me with your looks and comments."*

Leah whispered, *"What was that?"* While she was still working on the lock.

*"Nothing,"* Jarrod responded while thinking if she heard his reply.

Leah continued working on the door until finally, there was a loud click, and the door opened.

She stood up and looked at Jarrod in the eyes.

*"From here on it is not pleasant, but if we work together we can make it, I hope!"*

She pulled out both her triple blades, twirling them to the ready position, and headed in. Jarrod pulled his bow with an arrow notched, and Garren readied his sword. They headed down the vast passage, and Jarrod's eyes were entirely in Elf mode now. He could see down the passage as if it was daylight out there.

*"Hold it!"* He exclaimed, and they all stopped, *"There is something up ahead, I sense danger."*

Just then, five huge rats came around the corner snarling and headed straight for them. Before anyone could move, Jarrod fired off an arrow and then another, downing two of them before they could get a running start. The other three tripped and flailed over the fallen ones, which gave Jarrod a chance to fire again right between Leah and Garren, who made it to the giant rodents.

Garren swung with a mighty swing, lopping the fourth ones' head clean off. Leah front jumped over the pile through the air and landed on her feet, just as the last rat was attacking Garren and impaled the creature with her triple knives, pulling them and stabbing again with both, right in its neck, twisting the knives, and yanking them out. She twirled them both, catching the handle and turned for the next corner.

Leah spoke softly as they were ready to hit the turn, *"Jarrod, next time you sense danger, could we have a bit more warning?"*

Jarrod tried to answer, but Leah chuckled and was already around the corner. He sighed, thinking to himself, *"That's what I was talking about. Torture!"*

They both headed around the corner to see Leah waiting for them at a crossroads with three paths. They looked at her, wondering which way to go, and she turned determined and looked at them both, *"Left, this way."*

They looked at each other and headed that direction. They came to another two-way intersection, which was left or straight, and she ignored the left passage and went straight. They continued following Leah when a voice came from ahead.

*"Who dare disturbs my slumber?"*

The voice echoed down the passages and sent chills up Garren's spine.

Leah glanced back to Jarrod, *"Umm, that's not good."*

Garren sighed loudly, *"You think?"*

Suddenly the thing that spoke appeared in front of them and again, sent chills down Leah and Garren. Jarrod seemed to be not affected at all. It was a floating black-robed, spectral figure that was phase shifting up and down. It appeared to be holding some kind of black energy ball.

Jarrod stepped forward as Garren and Leah were somewhat weakened and were trying to regain their presence.

The phantom spoke again, *"Go back. This is a sacred place, and you cannot pass."*

Jarrod stepped forward, *"Step aside, we must pass."*

The creature made an evil hissing sound that turned to a laugh, *"Your last warning, leave or suffer the consequences of the dead."*

Jarrod looked to Leah while watching the creature, *"Is there another way?"*

Leah shook her head no.

*"Are you ready then? We are gonna have to fight our way through."* Jarrod confirmed.

Leah and Garren appeared ready. Jarrod turned, raised his bow, and fired the first shot. The arrow went straight through the apparition and did nothing.

The creature raised his energy ball, *"Then you will die."* He threw the ball, making an electrical charge-like noise as it headed for them.

Jarrod dropped the bow and raised both hands in a blocking motion just as the ball picked up speed and hit him full force. The ball discharged all around him and dissipated into nothing.

Jarrod raised his head back up to see that the creature already had another ball heading his way. He blocked that one to, but this time Jarrod rolled in front of Garren landing on one knee and fired a ball of flames that shot forward from his hands and flung outward, exploding on impact.

The creature howled in angered pain, throwing another energy ball, although this one was much smaller. Jarrod blocked that one and fired a barrage of blue, fire missiles from his hands, hitting the target again, and knocking it back. Garren leaped forward, and Lankule's sword started to glow a greenish white.

He got close to the creature, who was speaking enchanting words, but as Garren approached, the sword blinded the creature because the glow was brighter and brighter. He swung and hit the creature. The spirit's cloak slowly dropped to the ground like a feather had been dropped from the ceiling and dissipated into nothing.

Jarrod quickly turned around, *"Where's Leah?"*

Leah stepped from the shadows and behind where the creature was. *"Here."*

Jarrod sighed in relief, *"Oh, thank goodness. Garren?"*

Garren was still on one knee with his head down, *"You okay?"*

Garren raised his head, *"I think so. I just got so weak when I struck the specter."*

Leah spoke again, *"He has been drained of strength. Let's get him to the gates. We are almost there."*

Jarrod and Leah helped Garren limp to the next turn, and Jarrod looked as far ahead with his Elf eyes as he could see, *"Looks clear ahead."*

They continued to another turn and then out of the darkness, as they practically carried Garren was the massive iron door. They leaned Garren against the wall, and Leah stepped up to the door.

Another spectral image appeared on the door and asked in a woman's soft voice, *"What is the dark shade phrase of light?"*

Leah answered, *"Our dark shade mother shall guide and protect those in most need."*

The voice replied, *"Enter!"*

The Iron door creaked open, and they entered into a well-lit chamber that had an expansive staircase up to the next level and another staircase down. There was no one around, and as Jarrod stepped through, the door closed shut by itself. Jarrod looked at the door as it turned into the wall as if there was no door there at all. They set Garren down again, who laid all the way back, and Leah spoke.

*"Wait here, I will be right back,"* she sheathed her weapons and went up the staircase.

Jarrod helped Garren to his feet and walked him to the couch and chairs in the sitting area of the chamber, *"You good?"*

Garren looked up with hazy eyes, *"Yea, I'm good. Just exhausted. That thing sapped my strength good."*

Jarrod stood upright with his hand on Garren's shoulder, as Leah came down the stairs with another woman holding a tray of items.

*"This is Talia, and she will look after anything we need."* Leah introduced.

Talia bowed to Jarrod and stood back up.

*"Here is some ice water and a towel. I have taken the liberty of making some sandwiches for you, and I will bring them down in a bit. When you are ready, let me know, and I will show you to your rooms. Master Nanek will be glad for you to stay as long as you wish. Any friend of Raven is a friend of ours."*

Jarrod smiled graciously, *"Thank you, Talia, but we don't want to cause a fuss."*

Talia laughed and turned to Leah, *"You are right, my dear, he is dreamy. It is my pleasure, master Jarrod."*

She bowed and walked off.

Jarrod and Leah were both a bit embarrassed but glanced the comment off.

Leah recovered with a change of subject, *"How is he?"* Looking over to Garren.

*"Oh, he is fine. I think he will be good with some rest."*

Jarrod poured three glasses of water, as Leah took off her mask and gloves and laid them on the table. He handed Leah a glass, she thanked him and took one over to Garren, who was struggling to stay awake. He gratefully drank the water. Leah walked over and hugged Jarrod, who was startled by the gesture. She had her hands around his neck and was looking directly into his eyes, giving him another opportunity to make a move.

*"You performed very well for an apprentice. I think you are more than just an apprentice."* She put her head into his chest as he hugged her back now. She snuggled a bit closer, thinking he would give in but felt he was uncomfortable. However, he was not pushing her away, so she just hung on.

*"I am glad you reacted like you did fighting that creature, I was no help at all. You two dispatched him before I could get into position behind it."*

Jarrod squeezed her a bit tighter, causing her to let out a slight moan.

*"Oh, you were a big help. We could not have gotten here without you, and we thank you so much."*

He pulled her off him and put his hands on the front of her neck and shoulders and caressed her, which she gladly accepted.

*"Leah? Really, thank you from the bottom of my heart."* While placing his forehead on hers. She closed her eyes anxiously awaiting her prize, which she did not receive. He let her go and walked to the chair and sat down. She opened her eyes stunned, let out a huge sigh of frustration, and walked off.

Jarrod watched her leave, thinking to himself, *"God, I don't know how much longer I can resist her. She is so beautiful, and I'm afraid I am about to piss her off to the point that she just gives up. My will not to hurt her is stronger than my wanting to just give in to the passion. However, am I hurting her now by not giving in? Hmmm, I never thought of it that way. No, that is an excuse to get what I want and give her what I know she wants."*

He shook his head just as Talia came down with some food. Jarrod thanked her, *"Do you know when master Nanek will return?"*

Talia said she was not sure when, but he will be back soon, *"Shall I show you to your rooms?"*

Jarrod said yes and got Garren up who could now walk on his own but was very groggy. They dropped Garren off at his room and then she took Jarrod to his room. It was a nice room with a big inviting bed and a sitting area and a desk with a chair on the other side of the room. Each room had its own bath area with hot water and clean towels, just like at an inn. He thanked her again, and she told him if they needed anything to come and ask her.

Jarrod was not tired but wanted to get out of his leather armor and into something a bit more comfortable. He went and cleaned up, then got into his soft cloth pants and clean long-sleeved comfort shirt that just hung loose on him. He shook the loose water from his hair and thought again about Leah.

*"Perhaps I can just talk with her again tonight, let her know that I do not want to hurt her feelings or her heart."*

He convinced himself that he would see if he could talk to her, and this was the right thing to do. Jarrod walked out the door and down the hall, stopping at Leah's room. He raised his hand to knock on the door and then stopped and put his hand down, staring blindly into the door.

*"This is not going to be good. I better just go to my room and forget about it."*

He put his head down and started to go back when Leah's door flung open, and she was stepping out.

*"Oh, Goodness!"* They were startled, and both took a step back. *"Jarrod? Um, well, what are you doing?"* While she fixed her hair to the side.

Jarrod scratched his head and looked a bit confused, *"Uhh, Yeah, I was going to see if you were still up, but then figured you weren't and so, then, the door opens, and here you are, so I was going..."*

Leah interrupted with a burst of laughter with an eye roll, *"You really are bad at this. Aren't you? C'mon, let's go for a walk."*

Jarrod held his hands out, *"What?"*

Leah took him by the hand, and they walked as she gave him a tour of the facility. *"And, over here is the practice area for us. And over there is the weapons challenge area, and over there is where we are taught our thief skills."*

Jarrod stopped her, *"So, this place is like an academy for thieves and assassins?"*

*"Well, not so much the assassins. That is a master skill that only a few have. We train in hand to hand combat, acrobatics, and thievery abilities."*

Jarrod remembered he needed to study and practice as well and mentioned it to Leah, who told him there was an inner courtyard where he could practice if he wanted.

Jarrod was happy with that and let her carry on about the history of the place and how she was going through her trials to finish her acrobatic, thieving, and combat skills. She continued telling that Nanek should be back sometime tomorrow. She stopped and took Jarrod by the hands.

*"I wish you were not leaving soon, but I understand and know that I probably will never see you again."* Jarrod started, but Leah would not let him talk.

*"No, let me finish because I am going to say something that you need to understand and might shock you, but I don't care. I know what I want, and I have no regrets for wanting you, even if it is only for one night. Then at least I can say I loved more than most do in a lifetime together."*

She moved closer in again so close, her breasts were touching his chest, and he could feel her breath, as she looked into his eyes again.

Jarrod pushed back, *"Wait, Leah!"*

She dropped her arms and turned around, *"Oh my God, Jarrod. Seriously?"*

Throwing her arms up and down again, *"Okay, Fine then!"*

She started to stomp off, but Jarrod grabbed her arm and spun her back to him. He pulled her onto his lips as her eyes opened wide in shock. She closed her eyes with a quiet moan then, "mmm hmmm," as she wrapped him with both arms and melted into the most passionate kiss she had ever known.

Her heart was pounding so fast, and they held each other so tight that she could feel his heart pounding too. They only stopped for a second to touch tongues and then she opened her mouth, welcoming his with a moan of deep passionate pleasure while he held her in place, stroking her back down to her backside. Just as quickly as they started, they stopped, staring into each other's eyes right there, standing in the practice area. Jarrod whispered while he gave her a soft kiss on her neck, then to her cheek, and on the lips again as she let out soft moans and had both arms around his neck.

He started to talk, but Leah covered his mouth with hers again, so it was a muffled noise. Finally, they did three quick lip kisses, smiling at each other, locking eyes.

*"What I was going to say was that I cannot resist you anymore, and as long as you don't hate me for leaving, then I am all yours."*

She blinked at him and went flat-footed off her tiptoes being only a couple of inches shorter than Jarrod, *"Well, why didn't you just say so? Why all the coy deception?"*

Jarrod started to answer, *"I, Uh...But you..."*

She started laughing knowing instinctively Jarrod was going to try to squirm his way out of that one. She released him from his agony with a laugh and another passionate kiss up on her tiptoes again. She set down flat-footed and gently rubbed his arms to his hand, which he took hold of. They walked together up the stairs eyeing each other all the way to Jarrod's room, where they entered and gently closed the door behind.

# Chapter 20

Jarrod woke up and was on his back with sheets and blanket pulled up to his belly with Leah snuggled up close, one leg over his, and her head lying in the crook of his neck, chest, and shoulder. He listened to her sleep, trying not to move as he was enjoying her presence and her soft body touching him. His arm was under her head wrapped around, and he gently stroked her hair as she made a soft noise and snuggled closer.

The door suddenly flew open and slammed the wall with a thud. It was Garren busting in the room. Leah squealed and moved flat on her back, flinging the covers over her head, while Jarrod sat straight up and pulled to cover himself with his back against the headboard, just as Garren rounded the corner.

*"There you are. Good morning, brother,"* spying the right side of Jarrod.

Jarrod said with no concern, *"Hey there, don't you ever knock?"*

Garren walked to the end of the bed, his eyes never leaving the covered spot where Leah was lying.

*"What's this?"* Garren bolstered grinning ear to ear, slowly pulling the covers down toward the end of the bed.

*"Garren, stop it!"* Jarrod voiced just as Leah's head popped out from under the covers.

Garren laughed shockingly as Leah pulled the covers up to her chin. She blew her hair out of her eyes and quickly moved the hair back. Her hair was a mess in all directions, she flashed a quick smile.

*"Hey, Garren."*

Garren never hesitated. *"I knew it. It's about time,"* as he did a quick fist pump.

*"That crazy woman Bethel he was with, broke his heart, and he has been moping around for a year now."*

Jarrod gave Garren a harsh look, *"Okay, Garren, that's enough. Why don't you wait for us outside, and we will be out shortly?"*

Garren turned but winked at Leah, who smiled and waved her fingers at him.

*"Okay, I will just wait out here,"* as he left and shut the door behind him.

Leah sat up and kissed Jarrod as he pulled her face into his and gently rubbed her shoulder to her breast and down to her side. She eased back gently.

*"So, tell me, who was Bethel?"*

Jarrod thought for a moment and then answered, looking at her as he brought his hand slowly back to her neck. He stared right in her eyes.

*"She was the woman I was going to marry, but she left to go work in High Bluff while I was studying. Next thing you know, I got a letter from her, saying she was getting married to someone else."*

They both laid back down, facing each other on their sides, *"Wow, she broke your heart. No wonder you were so scared of me."*

Jarrod whispered softly to her, *"She means nothing to me now that you have healed my heart."*

Leah smiled at that, and gleefully pulled Jarrod on top of her, as they kissed deep into their souls. Leah tilted her head way back, as he kissed her neck and below the ear.

*"Oh, Jarrod! Mmmmm,"* wrapping her legs around him as she gently and slowly scratched his back. They

both started to chuckle because they heard a yell from Garren behind the closed door.

*"Never mind, I will see you later. Have FUN!"*

They heard him stomping off, and both started to laugh.

Garren went on down to the sitting area, and there was only Talia sitting there. She had brought out a spread of breakfast fruits and bacon sandwiches with water and juices.

*"You look like you are feeling better this morning,"* Talia boasted.

Garren looked back with a wink her way, *"Yeah, I do, and thanks for breakfast. It smells wonderful."*

She smiled, *"My pleasure. Help yourself, and I am off to the market. I will be back in a while. Please keep to these grounds until I return, the other areas are not very friendly to strangers."*

Garren grabbed a sandwich and dug in with a mouth full, *"Okay, thanks, Talia."*

She left the room, and Garren was like in heaven with all the excellent food. He had finished eating when he heard a thump and a thud from upstairs, and then some hysterical laughing, all was quiet again.

Garren looked up to the ceiling. *"Uh huh, at least someone is having fun."*

His mind shifted to Evie. He was missing her and seeing the last vision of her beautiful smiling face before he drifted off to sleep the night she left. He was thinking he may never see her again. He tried to force that thought out of his head but wished he had realized what she was doing, so he could have at least tried to stop her.

He wandered downstairs to the practice area and looked around at all the exercise devices, all the while wondering how Evie was faring. Is she all right? Is she held against her will? Are they hurting her? All these questions and more were eating him to his soul.

He sat in silence in the practice area for another hour. Finally, he stood up in defiance, pounding his fist.

*"I am not going to despair. All we can do is hope for the best and let fate decide the rest."*

He walked back upstairs to the sitting area where there was still no sign of Jarrod and Leah, but there was a strange looking fella sitting there. Garren cocked his head and realized this was a dwarf. He had long scraggly reddish-brown hair that was braided on one side. He had a Dwarven battle axe leaned against the chair and a long beard tied to a point with a lavish silver chain.

The dwarf looked up and acknowledged Garren's curious look.

*"Well now, you're a monster of a man. Never seen one of me before, eh?"* While he continued to munch on a sandwich.

Garren shook his head no while starting to speak, *"No, I haven't, but I have heard tales about your kind."*

The dwarf laughed a loud and boisterous laugh then just as quickly turned serious, *"Don't believe everything you hear. You must experience it for yourself and then pass your own judgment, that's what I say."*

Looking at Garren with a "humph" nod and a stomp of his foot.

*"Sit down with me and chat awhile. It is amusing to see someone so curious about me again. My name is*

*Fen Warfire, from the mighty Dwarven city of Kall, and you are?"*

Garren answered, sitting directly across from Fen, *"I am Garren Stromblade, from the Cove, and it is good to meet you."*

The dwarf jumped to his feet and spoke with a shock, *"Stromblade? Garren Stromblade?"*

Garren sat back and grabbed a drink, *"Yes, you can call me Garren."*

Fen plopped back down, *"Well, I'll be buggered. You wouldn't happen to be related to Clayborne Stromblade, would you?"*

Garren answered with pride, *"Yes, he is my uncle."*

The dwarf laughed, *"Well now, isn't that a coincidence. I happen to know him. How is the old fool, anyway?"*

Garren smiled, *"He passed away a few years ago."*

Fen looked saddened and a bit embarrassed, *"Uh umm, sorry Laddie, I, I didn't know."*

Garren assured him, *"Thank you, and it's okay. You couldn't possibly have known."*

They sat and chatted for an hour or so, when down the stairs came Leah and Jarrod, all dressed in their cleaned armor as yesterday. Leah was not wearing her mask but had it with her as well as her weapons. Fen jumped up with his arms stretched out.

*"Ravennnn, how is my girl,"* he said with a passionate hug.

Leah excitedly hugged Fen, *"I am great Fen, so good to see you again. What brings you here?"*

Jarrod looked on with wondered curiosity as Fen continued, *"Just came to see Nanek and get a bit of goods to trade, eh?"*

He gave her a tap on the shoulder, saw Jarrod and rolled his eyes, *"Oh goodness, another one?"*

Referring to his curiosity of never seeing a Dwarf before, *"Who do we have here?"*

Jarrod answered with a slight bow to his head, *"I am Jarrod Stromblade."*

Fen opened his mouth wide with a huge breath and held two fingers up, looking back and forth to Garren and Jarrod, *"Two Stromblades, here? Okay, would someone please tell me what is going on?"*

Jarrod and Leah went to sit down and started to eat while Fen was still standing there in shock.

Garren spoke as he had already eaten, *"Well, it's a long story, but...."*

Just then, the door opened, and a man walked in with a massive grin on his face.

Leah jumped up immediately and ran to him, giving him a hug, and he was clearly pleased to see her, *"When did you get here, my Raven sweetheart?"*

She glanced at Jarrod and back to him. The old man realized, they came with her, *"Oh, you did not go down the old passage through the crypt?"*

Leah nodded yes, seeing his displeasure as he shook his head with a slight turn sideways. *"No matter you are safe, and it is always great to see you, my child."*

She dismissed it and turned, holding his hand, lovingly looking at him, *"Everyone, this is Nanek, my Father!"*

Jaws dropped from both Jarrod and Garren, looking so shocked that they could not talk. He was a stunning looking man of lean stature, a bit taller than Jarrod but very well built. He had long dark hair that braided into a ponytail wearing a circlet with a beautiful green stone in the center. His armor was light and fit snuggly but seemed to have no hindrance to him at all. He made no sound walking into the room. You could tell he was a man of great strength, and his gray eyes had the look of wisdom.

Fen was right behind Leah. She stepped aside as they greeted each other, bending their knees with arms out and letting out a shrill yell!

*"AHHHHHhhhh!"*

They slapped each other's hands, laughing with a sweeping motion near the ground and stood up for a quick chest bump with two-handed pats on the back. They both started laughing harder.

*"How are you, Fen? Great to see you, old friend."* Nanek asked.

Fen was still laughing, *"Yes, my friend, it is great to be here and see Raven. How she has grown up fills my old heart with gladness."*

Leah kissed him on top his head on the way by to Garren, totally embarrassing the dwarf.

*"This is Garren Stromblade."*

She walked over to Jarrod and took his hand, *"And this is Jarrod Stromblade."*

Nanek narrowed his gaze and held up two fingers. He looked at Fen who nodded, one raised eyebrow with his two fingers up, *"Yep, two Stromblades!"*

He had a look of satisfaction with the same gesture as Nanek. Now both Nanek and Fen were puzzled as to why they were here.

Nanek spoke with concern, *"Well, this should be good. Next thing you are going to say is Dalimar is somewhere behind this."*

The two boys looked at each other with surprise as Nanek continued.

*"Let me go get cleaned up, and then we can sit and have a chat. Welcome to my underground sanctuary, and please make yourselves at home. Give me till noon, and we will meet back here for lunch. I'm sure Talia will have something great fixed up."*

With that, he went up-stairs leaving them to sit together for about three and a half hours.

Fen looked at Garren, excited about going to town.

*"Hey, you want to go with me to the outer underground. We can have some fun. There are dice games in an hour, and I want to see if I can win back some of my coins."*

He winked one eye at Leah who pointed at him with a warning, *"Now don't you go getting Garren into trouble. I am going to stay here with Jarrod if he doesn't mind."*

He looked at her with a big smile on his face, *"I would absolutely love your company."*

She and Jarrod walked up the stairs giggling together while Fen looked with worry.

*"Hmmm, I hope this is not what it appears."*

Looking at Garren who was grinning ear to ear, catching himself back to a serious look and changing the subject.

*"Yeah, shhhh, I like dice games too. Let's go and see what is going on."*

Fen laughed with a pat on Garren's back, *"That's my boy, follow me."*

Jarrod barely got the door closed, and Leah jumped on him. He locked the door thinking, *"I hope Nanek doesn't hear anything."* They were kissing, playing around, and Jarrod told her that he needed to study up before they left today. She bounced up and down with a pouty face, *"Oh-a-Aww."*

She folded her arms and stuck out a child-like pouty lip with her head down. He laughed and pulled her chin up, kissing her deeply, then whispering, *"We will have some time when I am done before we meet for our chat."*

She smiled, ran and jumped on the bed, rolling on her stomach with her hands under her chin and her feet bent up, *"I'll just lie here and wait then."* Rolling over on her back with her head over the edge backward, looking at Jarrod.

Jarrod looked at her and then up in the air closing his eyes and thinking to himself, *"I am so screwed if Nanek finds out. Hell, I am screwed anyway because I can't stop thinking about her."*

Jarrod went to his pack and pulled out the spell book. It was now that he realized he was still wearing the ring. No voices, no visions, nothing. He opened the book and started to study, feeling strange as he was reading his spells to memory.

*"There it is. That is the feeling I was talking about."*

He also realized that he was hardly tired at all after the battle in the crypts, Garren hurt, and Leah's antics in bed, Hmm? He shook his head fast to remove the thoughts and clear his mind. Jarrod looked up as Leah crept by to the water jug, smiling at her. He couldn't help to notice she had already taken off her boots and her leather breastplate to show her tight undershirt that was just covering her breasts.

She drank a glass of water tilting back just a bit to make sure that he saw her breasts. She didn't look over but crept back to the corner as he watched. She stopped, bent over, and teased him with a shake of her butt and a giggle before she disappeared to the bedroom.

Jarrod sighed loudly thinking, *"Oh my God, she has got to stop that!"*

He shook his head again and started to read. He was getting into the concentration mode when his vision sharpened, and spells that he could not read earlier came to life. He read and memorized them easily, looking at his hands and calling up spells to his fingertips. Leah peeked around the corner to see if Jarrod would see her. He was deep in thought and didn't notice her attempts to get his attention. She went back and pouted again, took off all her clothes and put on a loose hanging shirt while Jarrod kept reading. She waited another few minutes and hit the bed with her fist, walked to the corner again, and peaked around. This time she whined as she stepped out, so he was sure to look at her. She was standing there with one hand on the corner of the wall and the other caressing her body pulling up the loose shirt she was wearing, showing just a sneak peek of her, then letting it fall, moving her hand to her hair pushing it to one side, then slowly moving down to her lips. She moved her head and opened her eyes to see Jarrod watching her intently in all her sexiness.

He slammed the book shut and slowly stood up, never losing her gaze. He spoke a quick word and moved so fast she never even saw him move. It was like a blink of an eye, and he was right beside her as her hair moved as if the wind had just blown it. He aggressively grabbed her, which pleasantly startled her with a sweet little squeal. He pinned her against the wall and kissed her deeply. She breathed hard as they kissed again, softly moaning with pleasure, wrapping one leg around him while he gently massaged her breast. Suddenly, he picked her up like she weighed nothing and slowly carried her to the bed, never releasing the kiss, gently placing her down on the bed to her extreme enjoyment.

***

Garren was having a good time with Fen, out in the town. They even found some brew, which Fen gladly drank, and Garren had a mug with him.

*"So young fella, I haven't had this much fun in a while. You are quite enjoyable to be around. Cheers!"*

They smacked mugs and drank. Fen spilled half of it down his beard as he downed the whole mug. Garren laughed at him as he let out the loudest burp he had ever heard and then farted too. Garren about fell off the chair as Fen waved the air, *"Forgive me, Please!"*

And he busted out laughing too. *"Fill me up bartender, and another for my friend."*

Garren shook his head no, *"I have had enough already."*

Fen popped an answer, *"Well, suit yourself! Bottoms up!"* He downed another.

They headed for the dice games where Fen took a turn while Garren watched him lose roll after roll. Garren was concerned, grabbed Fen's arm, and whispered to him.

*"Fen, let's go, I think these dice are loaded against you."*

But he just *"Ahhhhed"* and brushed him off.

Fen played till it was almost time for the meeting with two and a half hours gone by already, *"Well, just the last roll, my friend."*

Just as Jarrod and Leah walked up. They had been watching for a few minutes, and Leah moved out the way as she could see Jarrod was angry.

*"Double or nothing!"* Jarrod demanded.

The rollers' eyes got big, as Fen looked at Jarrod. Jarrod prodded Fen who put up all he had left for the double or nothing, staring at him intensely. Knowing if he won this round, he would be back to even for all his loses. They handed Jarrod the dice cup, which he took. He shook the cup while asking what he needed to win.

They started laughing at him and did not tell him, but Fen knew all too well, whispering with worry.

*"Oh boy, we need a huge roll of these dice."*

Fen didn't sound too confident as he looked on with concern. Jarrod smiled wryly with his eyes closed, speaking softly while he rolled the dice. All the people around shuttered as the dice all stopped rolling.

The game handler looked up with surprise, *"All Sixes! Winner!"*

The crowd around started to cheer patting Fen and Jarrod on the back as Fen scooped up his winnings. The handler mumbling, *"Beginner's luck."*

But he was ecstatic because now there were more gamblers there than ever.

*"Come on, Fen, let's head back."*

Fen nodded, and they all walked together with Leah hugging onto Jarrod's arm.

*"That was noble of you, thank you,"* as she kissed him on the cheek.

She whispered softer and batted her eyes, quick-kissing his lips.

*"And thank you for the wonderful sex, you are an animal in the sack."*

Jarrod laughed softly embarrassed by her boldness again, looking back to see if either heard that comment!

They walked back into the meeting room, and Nanek was not down yet, so they chatted a bit with Fen speaking first.

*"Thank you, Laddie, for teaching me a valuable lesson today. I only know of one other person who could do what you did out there, Dalimar!"*

Jarrod looked over humbly, *"My intention was not to teach them nor you a lesson. I was angry because I watched seven rolls, and you won nothing. That can only mean one thing, loaded dice. Back at the Inn, I have watched men play my whole life and never did I see seven straight rolls with no win unless there were loaded dice. Getting your money back was a bonus to that, my friend."*

Fen respected that answer and knew it was true, *"Yes, well, thank you anyway."*

A voice questioned that turned everyone's head, *"Thank you for what?"*

Nanek walked over to the table that was set nicely with everyone. He sat at the head of the table with Fen and Leah seated on either side. Garren sat beside Fen, and of course, Jarrod sat beside Leah just to the left of her. She slyly reached under the table and rubbed his thigh as she was listening to Fen tell him the tale of what happened.

Jarrod shot a glance to her as she moved up his thigh towards, she chuckled and pulled her hand back, causing Nanek to look over at her.

She just flashed him that smile of "innocence."

He smiled back and continued to talk to Fen, laughing at his losing again and chastising him for gambling while Talia started to bring out lunch, which began with fresh bread and tomato soup. They started to eat quietly except for Fen, who is never quiet about anything.

Nanek seemed to enjoy his friend.

*"So, Jarrod, I expect you would like to tell me what in the world is going on?"*

Jarrod stopped eating, started slowly spinning the tale while the others listened and ate.

*"Where would you like me to start? There is so much that has happened that I am not sure where to start."*

Nanek looked at him with regard, *"How about you just start at the beginning and tell me everything. I cannot decipher codes, so you will have to just lay it all out."*

Jarrod nodded, *"Okay then, here goes! It all started a couple of weeks ago when I found out that I was not really a Stromblade, and that I was adopted."*

Leah didn't care anymore if Nanek saw her, and she reached and held Jarrod's hand, knowing how hard it was for him. Jarrod told him about the meeting of Evie through Garren, then discussed Eve's sudden departure, and the meeting of Dalimar, who wanted me to be his apprentice.

He sadly told them that Dalimar was gone, which caused Fen to gasp and drop his dinnerware. He talked about the visions of the evil mage, the visions of Evie being tortured, and how Evie was his real sister and madly in love with Garren.

He also talked about his newfound power and that being a half-elf had something to do with it. Then finally he talked about Dalimar meeting them here and was going to take us to him, Nanek, and ask for his help and wisdom. And, how lucky they were to meet Leah and her grandfather as he squeezed her hand, gently looking directly into her eyes.

*"In conclusion, Garren and I are here to do that very thing. We are here to ask you for your help and wisdom. Dalimar's plan was that you were to sneak into the dungeon and free Evie, while we waited to make a distraction if you needed it. Then throw this stone that Dalimar had into the window that Krometh is trying to break through to be released back into our world by the black mage. If we are successful, head back here before they even realize Evie is gone, and the dark gateway is closed. There is another thing, we will have to come up with a new plan because we do not have the stone. We do not know where Evie is other than I know she is not far from Thane. But I know they*

*are heading to Idesport City. My visions have been all clouded since we came down here."*

Jarrod stopped, satisfied he had told them everything. He waited for a reply from Nanek as did everyone at the table. He remained silent and continued to eat. Jarrod started his lunch as the main course came. Grilled chicken in a nice fruit glaze on top a bed of rice!

The table was solemnly quiet, and even Fen did not have any outbursts or obnoxious burping, which was odd for him. They finished their lunch in silence, and Nanek sat back in his chair, thanking Talia for another wonderful meal. He stood up, pushing the chair backward.

*"Somehow, I knew Dalimar was behind all this. I will help you, my new friends. I see in my daughter's eyes the care she has for you, Jarrod and Garren. I would be honored to help you as I know that is what my departed friend Dalimar would have wanted. Let's meet back down here in an hour, be ready to travel light but with good armor and weapons. Are your horses ready for a trip?"*

Jarrod looked at Leah, who nodded yes to him, *"Yes, they are at the stables and ready."*

Nanek spoke to Fen, *"I will not ask you to go because I already know your answer."*

Fen stood up holding a fist, *"Danger and the possibility of being killed with virtually no way to win..., sounds like my kind of gambling. I'm in!"*

Nanek smiled at Fen and then pointed to Leah.

*"Raven, I know you want to go, but I cannot allow it this time. You are to stay here."*

She sadly looked at him, *"But Dad?" "I said No, Raven! Now I will not say it again."* Nanek affirmed.

He stomped off up to his room while Leah started to choke back tears. Jarrod put his arm around her. *"He is right. This is too dangerous, and even though I want you to go, I agree with your father. Please stay here, and I promise I will return for you."*

She looked at Jarrod, and so did Fen and Garren as she spoke softly again.

*"Promise me you will live and that you will not get killed, and I will stay."* They touched foreheads at the table, *"Promise me!"* Leah shouted.

Jarrod sat back, knowing he could not answer her truthfully, *"I promise."* Jarrod choked the words out as Leah grimly nodded.

All three went upstairs to their rooms and got ready, even Leah donned her Night Shade armor with all her weapons, although knowing she was not going. They had cleaned up before they met Garren and Fen, Jarrod and Leah were just getting ready for the trip. They all met back downstairs with a few minutes to spare.

The two boys walked down together with determined looks on their faces. Fen seeing them come down stood up with his battle axe at the ready. Then Leah came down with her mask on, hiding her facial expression but not her eyes, which told all.

Nanek came out dressed in a different armor. This was dark armor, and he moved around getting used to it. He donned his dark red mask.

*"Gentlemen, are we ready? To the fate and glory of Night Shade, let's go kick some black knight ass and save Evie."*

Fen yelled and held his battle axe up, *"Yaas."*

Garren pulled his sword and held it up, Jarrod pulled his bow, and Leah pulled her dual, triple blades, twirled them, held them skyward, and they all joined in with Fen, *"YEAHHHHHHHHHH!"*

They stopped the scream at the same time and sheathed their weapons, then followed Nanek out.

# Chapter 21

There was no problem traversing the shadows of the underground city with Nanek there. They came to a dark passage with a staircase leading up to the city. Leah spoke to Jarrod as they walked silently up the stairs.

*"This staircase will lead us to the ruins of an old worship hall and from there, to the backside of the city."*

Jarrod appreciated knowing where they were located. They emerged just how Leah said, and Nanek stopped them for a moment.

*"From here, we act normal as if we are just passersby. Fen and I will go first, then Raven will lead you and Garren to the gate. Once back inside the city, we will make our way to the stables, which is about a ten-minute walk. Okay?"*

They all nodded in agreement with Nanek and Fen heading out first.

Leah looked at Jarrod with sadness as they gave them some time. Jarrod bent down and kissed her softly with Garren rolling his eyes and letting out a big sigh. Leah fiercely looked at Garren, who apologized with a *"sorry!"* They sneaked to their positions, and then each came out one by one with Leah chatting, flipping her hair, seeing guards coming their way.

*"So that was great fun today at the café, wasn't it guys? Good food and especially Mr. Folser."*

She laughed as Garren, and Jarrod had no idea what she was talking about, but both grunted an Uh huh and Yeah, as the guards passed them without incident.

Garren looked back, *"Whew, that was close!"*

Leah chuckled, *"You have to relax and just act normal."*

Jarrod spoke with sarcasm to Garren, *"Okay, I guess that was normal."*

Garren laughed as they continued to the gate, opened the door, and entered the city. People were passing by frequently, and Jarrod saw Fen and Nanek on the other side of the street. They motioned for them to come on over and together, they walked silently towards the outskirt stables in single file. The walk was more relaxed as they approached the final turn and went straight away to the stables. It was the last shop before the frontier road and the first for travelers entering the city from the north and east. Boream just stayed afloat because most business came from the southern portion, but that was what he liked. Not too much business but enough to pay the bills. They rounded the corner and looked up ahead and could now see some men standing outside in front of the stables with their horses.

As they got closer, Nanek stopped them, *"Wait!"*

Jarrod looked up ahead and concentrated on his sight. His vision shifted to closer and closer as his elf eyes took over, and he whispered in concern, *"Oh no!"*

Nanek turned to him, *"What do you see?"*

Jarrod shuddered for a second, *"They are black knights."*

Just then, two men dragged out someone and threw him into the street, kicking him.

Leah screamed, *"Grandpa!"* and took off running.

But Jarrod grabbed her as Nanek, Fen, and Garren leaped forward to help the old man drawing their weapons.

*"Leah, stay here,"* Jarrod shouted as he ran after them.

*"No way,"* she said defiantly, and she moved forward too.

Nanek dodged an arrow, and Jarrod had already caught Fen and passed him and was right on the heels of Nanek when two more arrows came through the four of them. Nanek hurled himself through the air, dodging the arrows as Garren swiped them away. There were now five Black Knights out there, and they dropped their bows and pulled their swords just as Nanek and Jarrod got there, slamming on the brakes and sliding to a halt out of weapons' swing range.

Nanek held his sword to the man holding Boream down.

*"Lower your weapons and release him."*

They laughed just as Garren slowed up, followed by Fen. Nanek quickly looked back to see Leah coming.

*"Stay back, Raven!"*

She stopped and moved off to the side, trying to see if there was a way to get in behind. Garren stared with a fury, looking at the old man limp on the ground and bleeding when he heard a familiar voice.

*"You, we have been looking for you, and your little piss ant brother too."*

Garren yelled back, *"Mathis, you ready for another ass whipping?"*

Mathis laughed, then turned and whistled. Seven more black Knights came from around the side of the building with their swords drawn.

Fen looked with serious contemplation to Garren, *"I'll take the one on the left!"*

Garren looked down at him with sarcastic concern. Mathis moved to the center of his clan.

*"You drop your weapons. Let your little brother come with us, and the rest of you may live. Do it not, and you all will die on this street. You are outnumbered. Surrender now!"*

Nanek and Garren moved to the front on either side of Jarrod.

*"We will not give him to you. We will take as many of you with us in death. You can leave now in peace, or we will die defending him."*

Mathis spat out, *"So be it then. Get them boys but leave the blonde alive!"*

They attacked with swords, and Nanek moved like a cat. Fast and agile, delivering blow after blow, and put two knights down before they swung their swords. Garren kicked one and knocked him to the ground, while sword punching another right in the face and blocking a strike with his sword. Fen attacked and was very quick blocking from one knight and punching with his axe into the belly of another.

Jarrod concentrated and flung forth a lightning bolt from his hand that struck one of the knights directly in the chest, flinging him to his back. Although the knight tried to move, he could not because of the continued electrocution.

Garren attacked again with one knight swinging madly until the knight's sword broke and with a lunge, Garren ran him clean through pulling the blade and swinging at the next as the other slumped dead to the ground. Fen was working on two blocking and dodging but not gaining when an arrow pierced the head of one, and he went straight to the ground. Jarrod had fired again hitting the next in the shoulder just as he was about to attack Fen.

Nanek had dispatched another knight they were down from a dozen to seven with two on Garren one on Fen and two more on Nanek. Garren heard another familiar sound as he sidestepped a blade thrust and did a turn swing with his arm and fist knocking one knight off balance, while dropkicking the second, sending him flailing back. Garren turned just in time to see a knight in full bronze armor leap off his horse and started fighting.

Garren yelled at the Bronze knight in action, *"Hell, Yeahhhhh!!"*

The bronzed knight yelled the knight battle cry echoed by Garren, as they stood together fighting. Mathis was sinking as he realized he was being beaten again, and he sent his last knight into battle.

*"Get in there, maggot."*

He hollered and shoved the knight who attacked the Bronze knight while Mathis snuck off around the building. Leah had made her way up and had her dual knives out, seeing Jarrod was in trouble as he was speaking again and in concentration.

One of the Knights was rushing him, Jarrod opened his eyes and spoke loudly just as the knight had his sword raised for the strike, and all the black knights in the immediate area lost their swords and stumbled, including the one who was rushing Jarrod. Jarrod sidestepped him right into Leah's triple blades, which she quickly pulled them out and stabbed him again.

He smiled at her as she rushed to his side.

Jarrod raised his hand and started to speak again. While the only two knights left in the battle scrambled to get their weapons, now fending off Garren on one and the Bronze knight on the other. Jarrod stopped speaking and turned just in time to see a crossbow release from Mathis on his horse. Leah had moved to help Garren and in an instant.

Nanek flew through the air and in front of Leah, SHhhFFFFFffffft. Nanek stepped in front just as the bolt arrived, and Leah saw the bolt hit Nanek in the center back and protruded from the front of his chest. Leah screamed and dropped her weapons.

*"Father, no!"*

Jarrod got to her side as he slumped, and he helped Nanek to his side on the ground. Glancing back over to Mathis.

*"Next time, boy!"*

Jarrod yelled his name, *"Mathis, Mathisss,"* as he turned his horse and rode off, guards were now barreling down the street.

Garren, Fen, and Endar just put down their last knights, and they rushed over to Nanek.

Fen fell to his knees beside Nanek, *"No, Nanek."*

Nanek smiled as Leah was holding his head, and she was crying. He reached up with his hand and pulled his circlet off and gave it to Leah.

*"Take this. I am so proud of you, my daughter. Don't despair as I will be with your mother soon."*

He coughed bleeding from his mouth now, and Leah tried to speak. *"Stay with me, Dad."*

She looked up and around as the guards stated, *"Help is on the way."*

Jarrod looked at Garren, who grimly and sadly shook his head no, both knowing there was nothing they could do.

Nanek looked to Fen who had his other hand.

*"Help them, Fen. I trust you, my old friend."*

Fen was blubbering now, *"I will, promise."*

He looked back to Leah, *"I love....!"*

His arm fell limp, and his head turned as the last breath came out slowly. Leah was now sobbing as she hugged his head.

Jarrod stood up and looked off at the horse, leaving a trail of dust.

*"Dammit, Curse them!"*

He walked back to Garren with profound determination in his eyes.

Garren looked at him and nodded, *"Evie?"*

Jarrod scowled and answered in anger as he heard a gleeful voice in his head, *"Yes, that's it, Anger, loathing, and hatred. Bring it to me."*

Jarrod's eyes turned to a bright hue, *"Yes, I'm going to kill them all."*

He walked around Garren, who was now looking at Jarrod with worry.

Fen was choking back tears and walked up as well as the Bronze Knight. Garren shook his hand, *"So glad you showed up, my friend. Thank you!"*

They hugged the "knight manly hug" with a pat on the back. Then looked at Fen who held his arms out to Garren. Garren looked at him strangely, sighed with eyes raised, and gave him a hug. The three went over to stand by Leah, who was still sobbing. Jarrod was leaning right at her side with his hand gently rubbing her back, consoling her sadness.

Suddenly Leah stood up with her fists clenched, startling all of them, she looked over at the limp body of Boream on the ground by the entrance.

She looked with sadness at Jarrod who was watching her, *"Not Grandpa too?"*

She made her way over wiping the tears from her eyes with Jarrod by her side, bent down to roll him over, and he moaned in pain. He was bleeding from his head, and his arm seemed broken, but he was alive.

She hugged him and helped him to a sitting position. He weakly said.

*"Hello, dear. In my younger days, I would have killed them all."*

She smiled at him and hugged him again, *"Owe, easy girl, can't you see I'm hurt?"*

She and Jarrod helped the old man up just as the physician arrived and got him into the stable's sitting area. They bandaged him up as she told him about Nanek.

*"I never liked him too much, but your mother adored him. I couldn't stop her from seeing him, so I banished him from our family. I am an old fool, and I am sorry, my dear."*

Leah hugged his neck, *"You just rest easy."*

All the rest came into the stables just as the physician had taken Boream upstairs to lie down and was getting ready to leave.

*"I will have one of my assistants check on him a couple of times a day to see if he needs anything. He is weak and very tired, but I think he will be okay. He will probably not be able to use that arm for at least a*

*couple of months. I am sorry for your loss, madam Raven."*

He smiled at her with assuring eyes and walked out. All sat around the tables when Jarrod started to speak.

*"We suffered a great loss today, losing Nanek like that. But we did not suffer defeat as he made sure of that. In his honor, we must come up with a new plan to continue this mission. I do not know what our fate is or where it may lead, but one thing is for sure, I have never been a part of something that is this important in my life, and, I have never been with such good friends like this before. I swear on my life that I will see this through with each of you if you chose to continue with us. If not, then Garren and I will part as having the best friends we have ever known, and if we succeed and survive this, I promise we will see you again."*

Fen spoke up, first pointing his nubby finger at Jarrod, *"Fine speech, Laddie, but don't be thinking you're going anywhere without me, Hmmmph!"*

Jarrod smiled at Fen, *"Thank you, Fen."*

Endar spoke next with admiration, *"To whatever end, I am in!"*

Garren patted his shoulder with a nod! They all looked to Leah, who was clearly still upset but fired her eyes up at Jarrod.

*"Don't even think about telling me to stay here. I am going, and that is final."*

Jarrod looked at her and shook his head, *"I wasn't even going to say it, but I wanted you to make your own decision."*

He walked right up to her and hugged her, then looked her in the eyes, *"I am glad you are going."*

Fen slammed the table, *"Well, it's settled then, what are we waiting for? Let's get going!"*

Jarrod still had one arm around Leah, and her head was buried in his chest, still crying a bit.

*"Fen, we need to make plans and have to make sure her grandpa is taken care of before we leave."*

Fen settled his axe down, *"Uh, yea, sorry! Just anxious to get them buggers. You are right, of course."*

They all laughed together, and even Leah choked a bit of a laugh. Garren looked at Fen.

*"Fen, you are bleeding?"*

Fen staggered a bit and wiped the blood from his head.

*"Yep, that's blood!"*

His eyes rolled over white, and he fell straight back to the ground with his arms stretched out. They rushed to him and sat him up as he shook off the dizziness.

*"Am I alive?"*

Leah wiped his head with a towel, turning his face to hers with her hand.

*"Fen, it's just a scratch!"*

They helped him to his feet, *"I knew that, I was joking with you. Got you all, didn't I?"*

As he burst into laughter. Leah went along, wiping the dust off his back, *"Yes, you did Fen."*

While everyone else knew he was lying but played along with Leah.

They were notified that Nanek's body was taken off to the undertaker, and Jarrod moved to her side, whispering.

*"I will understand if you have to go to his funeral, but we cannot stay. We must get going."*

She put her head on his arm as he held her tight, her answering back.

*"There will be no funeral, not here anyway. His body will not last the night, and he will be taken to the undercity where he will be laid to rest in the Night Shade cemetery. No procession, no people crying, and then there will be a huge party, and a new Night Shade leader will be named as well as the underground city leader."*

Jarrod sat beside her, held her, and only said, *"I'm sorry."*

Leah lifted her head and kissed him under the cheek, snuggling back down to his chest as he squeezed her tighter.

They all gathered back at the stables, and they decided right away that Jarrod was now the leader of this party. He looked serious with his eyes held small and fast.

*"First, we must gather enough money to take care of Boream until we get back or until his arm is healed."*

They accumulated coins with Fen producing a pouch, and they put all the coins they gathered together. Endar laid all he had.

*"I knew these would come in handy. I got them off the dead black knights that Dalimar dispatched."*

Jarrod snapped to Endar, *"You were there when he died?"*

Endar thought for a minute, *"Well, not exactly. I just saw the explosion. The Elders told me to follow Dalimar, as they didn't believe what he was saying but wanted to find out how much was true. I could not keep up with him because that horse he was on was the fastest horse I have ever seen. I saw a huge explosion, and when I got there, I saw a tall, dark armored man on a horse and a couple of other black knights riding off. I did find this little scroll and stone."*

He opened his pouch and pulled out the scroll and the red stone, setting them in front of Jarrod. Jarrod abounded with excitement while staring at the stone.

*"Who you saw was the Dark Mage, and this,"* picking up the stone, *"is the stone that will close Krometh's doorway forever."*

Jarrod looked deep into the stone with wonderment as did everyone else, the stone began to pulsate light red to dark red. He wryly smiled at everyone.

*"I guess our plan is back on! Now, what is this?"*

Jarrod unrolled the little scroll and read it aloud to everyone, including the passage Dalimar wrote.

*Where there is light, is the only place I can live. But if light shines on me I will die!*

*It has been around for millions of years but is sometimes not seen!*

*The more there is of me, the less you will ever see!*

Dalimar's note read, "An evil shadow walks through twilight unseen in darkness."

*Three fathers have twins but three are alone! Two fathers die, have one, the other alive has none!*

Jarrod dropped the scroll on the table as he realized what the last line meant. Leah leaned over to him, *"You okay, Jarrod?"*

Jarrod looked at her, his face was ashen. Leah put her arm over his shoulder, *"What is it?"*

Jarrod recited the lines, trying to decide whether to tell them that the final line meant, his father, Tanin.

*"The line that Dalimar wrote talks about the Dark Mage walking the lands in shadow. The final line tells us who he is, and it is for me to find out alone."*

He left it there and put the scroll in his pouch and gave the stone to Leah.

*"We are going to need your skills more than ever now."*

She put the stone in her pouch, promising to guard it with her life. Jarrod stood up from the table.

*"Leah, do you know the way to Idesport City?"*

Leah, still disturbed by Jarrod not saying who the Dark Mage was, *"Yes, there are two ways to get there. We can take the road east to the Northern Pass, and it leads straight to Idesport City. There is a hidden way that would be a rough ride and a bit dangerous, but it heads straight north through the lower Thane peaks and into the middle of the Misty Mountains. Not recommended, but it would cut a full day and a half off our ride if we make it, unimpeded by anything there. They say there are mysterious creatures that live there, and most travelers avoid those mountains altogether."*

Jarrod thought for a moment, sitting back down again.

*"Well, I don't see where we have a choice. Let's take a vote, knowing we need to cut off Mathis and his band of miscreants from Idesport City. Do we take the risky path or the easy trail?"*

Fen broke the silence, *"Aye Laddie, take the risk!"*

Garren nodded, and Endar agreed.

Leah sank back, *"What's the plan then?"*

Jarrod answered.

*"First, we take the risky passage north. Once we come out past Volshstein, we should be caught up to Mathis and hopefully Evie too, being carted to Idesport City. We slaughter them there and free her. Then we move to Idesport City. Of course, there will be guards everywhere, so we will need Leah to help us sneak into the city. Once there, we make our way to the Palace and to the Dark Mage's lair and throw the stone into the doorway, shutting it forever. Then get out of there before anyone notices us. We will have to steal some black knight uniforms. Fen will stay and guard Evie*

*because she will probably be in no condition to go with us. What do you think?"*

Leah shrugged, *"Sounds to me like we have no other options, and we can always adjust as we need to. I think we should try just to make it through the mountains first and then worry about the next step. That's just me, though."*

Jarrod smiled, *"I like it. I think you are right, but I want everyone to know what we are up against. Are we ready?"*

They all nodded except for Fen.

*"Can we stop and grab some good brew for the trip?"*

Jarrod shook his head no, *"No brew, Fen."*

Fen spoke again, *"What about some dried meat?"*

Jarrod spoke harshly, *"We have rations and water, and that is it."*

Fen grumbled the whole way as they headed to the stables for final preparations.

*"No brew, No meat, No bacon. What a lovely trip this is gonna be, hmmph."*

# Chapter 22

Garren checked the horses while Fen and Endar tended to all the supplies, including bedrolls and tents because the journey through the mountains was not only treacherous but also quite cold. Jarrod and Leah were still inside, with Jarrod speaking softly to her.

*"I am glad you are going with us, but I cannot help but worry about your safety. I just don't want to lose you."*

Leah assured him that it was not his decision, it was hers, and she wouldn't have it any other way.

*"If I die on this trek by your side, then I can say my last days were my happiest in this world."* She walked right up to him and looked him in the eyes.

*"I love you Jarrod, and I am the happiest when you are near me."*

He leaned down for a kiss. She wrapped her arms around his neck, pulled him to her face, and they kissed deeply with his hands on her waist.

They finally released, *"Why do I feel like that was our last kiss?"* She smiled and pulled him in for another kiss. She backed off and said, *"Remember that one because no matter what, I am forever kissing you like that."*

She let go of him and walked out the door into the stables with Jarrod thinking uncomfortably about that statement. He turned and walked out behind her.

They mounted up and tied the packhorse to Endar's horse. Fen's pony was carrying him, and the rest were on their own horses. They headed out the stables and saw a crowd gathering. A dull roar started as they headed out in single file. Jarrod looked at Leah, who was now riding beside him as she donned the circlet from her father and her mask while riding. She took the horse's rein and winked at Jarrod.

*"It is the entire Night Shade order to greet us, in respect of their fallen leader."*

The Night Shade started the chant low and built it but stayed low as they walked slowly down to the Northern Path.

*"Go get em, Raven,"* shouted one of the Night Shades.

The crowd shouted, *"Raven, Raven, Raven."*

All knowing that her retribution and revenge for Nanek's death was coming fast and harsh!

Raven drew her blade and raised it in salute to the crowd, Jarrod then held up a clenched fist. Garren, Fen, and Endar drew their weapons in salute to the loud roar of the crowd.

They walked their horses slowly through to emphasize their honor to Nanek. Once they cleared the crowd area, Jarrod questioned.

*"How did they know we were going?"* Leah grandly answered.

*"Nothing goes through this city without the Guild knowing."*

The pace quickened riding in twos with Endar watching the rear and holding the pack horse as they reached the old north path. It was wide enough for them to ride two by two, and that is what they did with the same order. Jarrod and Leah, Garren and Fen, and Endar with the pack horse keeping a wary eye on the path behind. They rode about seven hours up the northern path until they were clear of Thane Peaks and were now riding through the valleys.

They stopped after dark, and they came to an area where there was a clearing off to the side, *"Let's stop here for the night."* They decided.

They moved off to the side and made a small camp with fire and bedrolls. No tents this night. Fen cooked up some of the rations they had, and Raven made a huge salad that she had packed in the supplies.

Everyone enjoyed the salad, including Fen saying, *"This horse and rabbit food is not bad."* He received a laugh from Garren and Endar.

*"One day, you should come to the grand hall of my kin. The hall is filled with golden tables and chairs so lavish and comfortable, they say just sitting there makes a man fall into a deep slumber."*

He started to laugh and then went serious again, *"Which, of course, is ridiculous."*

With a wink and a low whisper, building to his usual loud self, *"It's because of the fine brew, and Dwarven maidens. Ahaaaaa haaaaa haaaa!"*

Fen continued telling stories of his home in the great Stoneforge Caverns near the great city of Kall, while Jarrod and Leah snuck off together.

They walked through the clearing and just out of the hearing distance, they discovered a small, clear stream. Leah walked down, dipping her hand into the cold water and splashed it on her face. Jarrod walked up, and Leah threw some on him.

She chuckled, *"Cool, isn't it!"*

Jarrod's eyes were closed being just splashed in the face, he opened one eye, *"Uh, Yeah. Thanks."*

She giggled a bit while Jarrod washed his face. She jumped up on a large boulder and tucked her legs under her. Jarrod jumped up there with her. Leah looked to him as he stared forward, *"Tell me about Evie. I want to know how you discovered she was your sister."*

Jarrod lowered his head and started to talk, explaining how he was given a journal by Ms. Frieda that was his real mother's. Inside the journal, it explained what happened to her, and how Evie had been given to a cleric, and how he was given to Hardin. The cleric and Evie were never seen again until the trials where Garren met her and introduced her to everyone. He told her that she had to leave because she was going to save her family and friends and how at that time he wasn't 100% sure she was his sister. But after his visions became clear and his power grew, he saw the truth. The journal was written in the Elvin language, and Evie could not read it, but he knew now that what happened to him was also happening to her, and she has read it now. That is irrefutable proof that she was his twin sister.

She leaned closer and put her arms around him, *"What about your real father?"*

Jarrod was shocked by that question but understood her inquisitive nature, *"Let's just say that he is not a real nice person. In fact, it was he who killed my mother by sending those creatures after her to get this."*

He lifted his hand and showed her the ring. Leah looked at it with concerned intensity.

*"I noticed you wearing that ring, and I was hoping that was not given to you by your last love."*

He turned to her, and they embraced for another kiss when suddenly, Jarrod had that feeling again.

A vision was forming in his mind, and he pulled away from Leah.

*"Oh no,"* Jarrod grabbed his head.

Leah was worried and threw her legs out, holding him now, *"What's wrong, Jarrod?"* While shaking him a bit.

He pushed her away and hopped off the large rock, landing on his feet, his back against it holding his arms out. Leah started to say something but was staring in disbelief as Jarrod turned almost into a glowing light.

This startled her, and she felt a tinge of fear as she watched him change right in front of her. He opened his eyes which were now a bright tan color with a strange glowing orange hue to them, like a mist. Just as quickly as it started, it stopped, and Jarrod slumped to the ground on one knee.

Leah leaped to his side with her hand on his back, *"Jarrod? Jarrod!"*

He stood up with his eyes closed, slowly opening them as he leaned his head back and then straight. He was back to normal. *"What in the blue sky was that?"* Leah asked with concern still standing beside him. He looked at her and smiled.

*"That is what I was trying to tell you. As you know, I am half-Elf, and part of my power comes from the*

*ancient Elvin lands. When I have a vision or pull forth an extreme amount of energy from within, this happens, and I change into an Elf for a short amount of time. That was a vision I just had, we are almost too late. The Dark Mage's hand reaches far across the realm, and he knows we are coming."*

Leah exclaimed, *"Should we take another route?"*

Jarrod calmly answered, *"No, it wouldn't make any difference. He welcomes this because it's me and this ring he is after. Killing all of you would only be a bonus to him. He knows my power is growing, and he wants to steal it from me. That is why he has Evie, and he now knows she is my sister. I will have to face him alone."*

Leah spoke in fear, *"No, Jarrod, you cannot face him alone! We are here, and we all can face him together."*

Jarrod looked back at her with loving eyes and gently touched her face, *"No, Leah. He will be in a place only I can go, and I might not make it out of there. The plan will have to be modified."*

She shook her head as tears started to well up. He pulled her to his lips, whispering.

*"Just remember this, I will always love you forever!"*

They kissed passionately for a couple of minutes, letting her go while never losing her gaze. Then he slowly blinked with a smile and turned to walk back to camp.

*"Jarrod, wait!"*

Leah moved quickly to be by his side and together arm in arm, they walked back to the camp.

The camp was quiet except for the loud snores from Fen. Garren and Endar were sitting quietly by the fire.

*"I was starting to get worried about you two."*

Garren nudged with a laugh. Jarrod just smiled while he helped Leah get her bedroll down and then got his out and laid it beside her.

She gazed back in wonderment, *"Really?"*

She opened hers up fully and then snatched his spreading it out on top. Looking at it with satisfaction.

*"There, now I'm happy!"* She sternly walked off to change, leaving Jarrod to stare at the makeshift bed for two.

He glanced over to Garren, who was grinning ear to ear, *"Don't even start, brother."*

Garren stopped smiling, looked down, kicking a lump of coal back into the fire. He went to get some more wood for the fire to keep it going the rest of the night, with Jarrod saying he would take the first watch, followed by Endar, and then Garren. He wanted to make sure all got a good night's rest before the arduous trip in the morning.

Leah came out with just a long nightshirt on, and Jarrod and Endar started to laugh quietly, seeing she still had her boots on. She stopped before she stepped on the bedroll with her hands on her hips.

*"What are you laughing at?"*

They both chuckled, and Endar lowered his head, shaking it no. Jarrod just stared at her for a glancing moment.

*"Nothing, we just can't get over how cute you are with your boots on."*

Endar laughed again as she "humphed" at them, kicked off one boot and stepped on the bedroll and then the other and crawled into the bed. Jarrod nonchalantly went over there and knelt, whispering to her while he stroked the hair from her eyes.

*"I will be back in a few minutes. I need to study some, and I will be right in."*

She nodded as Jarrod got up and went to his horse to retrieve his book.

Garren came back and saw Jarrod sitting off to the side reading. He went on to the bed and turned over with a thudding noise. Endar was not far behind going to his roll. Jarrod stood watch over the camp for the next four hours while studying for what he knew was going to be a hard task. Still, he felt confident that if he adequately planned, and the Dark Mage underestimates his power, he could succeed. He couldn't help but feel the fear, what if he failed? Would he at least be able to save Evie, so she could have a good life with Garren? What would it mean for the world with no mage in it as a protector?

He brushed aside all his fears and pushed them back, practicing his spells and learning more. Even more spells now were visible in the book, and he took the time to practice and learn them all. He was calling up spells solely from the power within now, and he felt stronger and stronger each time he practiced. He practiced until it was almost time to wake Endar, placing the book back in his saddle bag. Jarrod quietly eased himself over to Leah and just sat beside her, watching her sleep, taking in all of her into his memory that he could. Jarrod woke up Endar and went to bed himself. He crawled in the makeshift bed, and Leah immediately made her little sleeping happy noise as he slid one arm under her and the other over her. She snuggled close with her legs curled in the fetal position with her back to his front, and he easily drifted off to sleep.

The next morning Jarrod woke up to see that Leah was already up, changed back into her armor, and making some breakfast. He watched her move around and quietly sing to herself, as she meticulously prepared every plate. Garren, Endar, and Jarrod all got up and thanked Leah for the breakfast. She smiled back, then went over to Fen, who was still snoring and kicked his feet.

*"Get up, you old coot!"*

She brandished a huge smile. Fen farted and jumped out the bed with his arms out, and knees bent like he was ready to attack, startling all.

*"Where are they? Let me at em!! Grrrrr"*

Then realizing he was just being woke up for breakfast. The entire camp was roaring with laughter, and Garren fell off the log and was on the ground in laughter. Then all were laughing at him.

Fen relaxed and scratched his butt, pulling up his britches at the same time, *"Uh sorry Lassie, I thought you were being attacked."*

She was still in a hysterical laugh, trying to bring him a plate, *"Thank you Fen, for your concern. Here is your breakfast."*

His eyes got big with delight and proud, he was defending her, *"Well now, that's just what the old ones ordered. Thank you, Las!"*

He snatched the plate and started to devour breakfast while everyone else joined in with him, devouring theirs right alongside, acting like Fen, who thoroughly enjoyed it and took it as a huge compliment, and not a mock!

They packed camp after helping Leah clean up, all pitching in to help, including Fen who was helping her with dishes. He was quite good, tossing plates and cleaning the pot she used to make the porridge. They saddled up and were on the way.

They rode hard all morning only stopping around noon for a quick rest for the horses, a drink, and a snack. Then rode again hard till mid-afternoon when they happened upon a horse cart with a family in it, and a man working on one of the wheels. They stopped and learned that they were refugees heading to Volshstein from Idesport City. The man told them they fled because strange creatures were running around the city, and it just wasn't safe to be there anymore.

They warned them not to go there. Most of the people were leaving because Valence had become violent against the people, demanding more coins, and some were even sent to the mines to dig for gold against their will. The city is almost barren now, even the Black Knights were defecting in droves, under the boot of Valence and some Dark Mage.

Jarrod asked Garren and Endar to help them get back on the road, while Jarrod explained they were on a rescue mission.

*"Why did you bring your family this route? This is a dangerous path to travel through the Misty Mountains."*

The man stepped forward, alert of his surroundings.

*"My name is Windell, and this is my wife, Sharren, and my two children. You are right, but I am a trader, and I have traveled this path before, and I know it well. It was better to travel this way than risk being killed by the creatures Valence is sending out after the folks. When you get to the misty mountains, instead of staying on the northern path, head about an hour west. There is a huge open cavern that leads beneath the ground to a large pass. Take the pass until you see four directions, take the left fork.*

*Do not turn right, left, or the right fork. It is quicker and will take you to an underground river. Follow the river till you get to a great opening and head up. The river disappears underground, but the route will take you right back to the plains and past the Misty*

*Mountains. Not many have made it through those mountains. From there, head north to the city but be warned, I would not venture the caverns at night. There are things down there that are not of this world. Good luck to you if you must go to the city and thank you for your kind help."*

Jarrod shook the man's hand, and they mounted up, *"A stroke of luck, meeting him."*

*"Maybe a little too lucky if you ask me,"* Fen stated emphatically, *"Should we trust him?"*

Jarrod mounted his horse and leaned down to Fen, *"Yes, I sensed no dishonor in him."*

Fen looked back at Endar while he mounted with sarcasm, *"Let's hope your senses are good!"*

They headed off down the path, deciding to ride until they reached the cavern and then going through it in the morning. They rode until they saw the cavern that Windell was talking about, and it was right at dusk. Jarrod pulled his horse around to face his party.

*"We will camp here again quietly with no fire. Let's find a good resting place away from the entrance."* They searched and found a clearing off the path leading

to the cavern. Garren and Endar took care of the horses, while Fen and Leah tended to food and water. They sat quietly together, snacking on some rations and water.

Jarrod snapped his head around and stood up. Garren stood up and drew his sword instinctively, knowing that look while the others looked in the direction Jarrod was looking.

Leah quietly moved to Jarrod and whispered the question, *"What is it?"*

Jarrod whispered back, *"Something is coming!"*

He turned quickly, *"Everyone, take a defensive position and hide."*

He looked, and Fen was already up in a tree. He rolled his eyes and moved off with Leah, while Garren and Endar took positions on either side.

Just as they got into position, they saw a small column of creatures in a row of four by four with one larger to the side throwing a whip every few steps, walking toward the cavern. They were small, with fanged teeth and gnarled faces. Some were gray in color and had big humps on their backs with bones sticking out, while others were leathery faced and greenish in color. All walked in a waddle-like fashion with their fingers almost dragging the ground. All of them were armored and had spiked clubs for weapons.

They were almost past the small group when a loud noise came from the trees. It sounded like limbs snapping, and there were grunting, uhhhs, and ahhhs, and a huge thudding sound on the ground.

Fen had fallen out of the tree as the branch he was on snapped. Fen jumped up loudly, shaking his body, gathering himself, realizing he is caught. He yelled as he pulled his battle axe.

*"AHHHHHH, Slimy Goblin Buggers, Come On!"*

The goblins were caught off guard, and his faltering had startled them into chaos and fear. But one crack of the whip, and they were back in line and rushed Fen with loud snorts and chortles with high pitched clicking noises.

The big one shouted, *"Get that dwarf scum!"*

As the goblins rushed Fen, they did not see the rest of them. Endar and Garren came out of nowhere, slashing and hacking them from each side. Leah jumped into action wielding her double blades, and Jarrod was firing arrow after arrow, each finding its mark until he was empty.

The large goblin started to run toward the entrance of the cavern. Jarrod closed his eyes and spoke a word. He moved like a lightning bolt, blocking the giant goblin who slammed on the brakes and pulled a sword.

*"Going somewhere?"* Jarrod snuffed out.

The goblin smiled, licking the blade as it cut his tongue, and the creature moved toward Jarrod. Green blood came from his mouth as he raised the sword for a strike. Jarrod had already started to speak and finished as the blade was coming down. Jarrod quickly thrust his hands forward and yelled a word, the creature flew backward, being hit by an invisible force that took its breath away and slammed the creature to the ground. The four companions were standing in a row, now fending off the goblins as they tried to bum rush them.

Jarrod started to speak slowly then saying the last word that threw forth a fireball that exploded into the pack of goblins howling in fear and in rage. The giant one was now standing and moving toward Jarrod again, but did not get far as Garren rushed to the creature's backside, *"Hey, you big ugly."*

The creature turned to face Garren just as he swung lopping off his head. Green blood spurted out the neck while the creature stood there for a moment still swinging clumsily and then fell over, twitching dead.

Leah came to Jarrod, who was shaking, *"You okay?"*

Jarrod was trying to settle the power back down and shook his head yes. Fen was making noises over at the dead goblin pile, "Hah, Hah, Hah," as he was smashing them with his axe.

Garren shouted, *"Fen, they are all dead!"*

He flashed a glance and then quickly smashed another one, *"That one was still moving!"*

They all shook their heads with a smile. All understood what happened and placed no blame on Fen, although Jarrod did say.

*"Next time, be more careful, Fen. You could get us all killed."*

Fen lowered his head and walked off.

Leah snapped at Jarrod, *"You hurt his feelings, Fen? Wait!"*

As she rushed to console Fen. Jarrod just looked back at them.

*"Sorry!"*

Endar patted Jarrod's shoulder.

*"No, don't be sorry, it's true. The crazy dwarf will get us all skewered."*

He walked off just as Fen and Leah came back laughing a bit, and she hugged him and flashed another scowl at Jarrod and stomped off.

*"Wait, Leah…Okay Fen, I apologize."*

Fen looked back, *"No need, Laddie, you were right. I am just an old fool."*

Jarrod walked over to him, *"No, you aren't, and we wouldn't have got this far without you."*

Fen smiled wide, *"Well then, who's hungry?"* slapping his hands together and rubbing them with great expectations.

Jarrod asked Garren and Endar if they would pile the bodies off in the woods and hopefully, there are no more encounters tonight.

*"Fen, you called those things something. What did you say?"* Fen looked back, *"Those were goblin scouts. Probably looking for easy prey to take back to the hoard."*

Jarrod turned and faced the cavern, *"No, I bet there is a far graver purpose. Those things were out in the day time and returning at night. They were looking for something."*

Fen quietly responded, *"Yeah, us!"*

Jarrod walked through the woods to see Leah standing near the horses petting one. She turned to see Jarrod coming and rushed into his arms.

*"I'm sorry love. I was just angry because I know how sensitive Fen is."*

Jarrod kissed her gently on the lip, *"It's okay, I am sorry too. You are right, I should be more careful with him. He is a great warrior. Did you see how he didn't even flinch with that bunch charging him? He stood his ground, and that is more than noble!"*

She nodded in agreement, *"Dwarves have a special place in their hearts for goblins anyway. They attacked the Dwarven settlement many years ago, and most of*

*Fen's family were killed. They kill just to kill and especially like to kill dwarves."*

Jarrod nodded in understanding. They kissed again and walked back to the little camp together.

The same order was called, although there was no fire, and darkness settled in while they were preparing for the trip in the morning. They started hearing noises from the caverns, and all were unsettled as the noise started low and built, bang, bang, Bang, Bang, BANG.

Jarrod looked over to Fen, *"What is that banging noise from the caverns?"*

Fen's face turned sad as he started the tale, *"Those are goblin battle drums. They are gearing for war. I recognize their patterns."*

They all turned to the caverns, again listening and hearing the loud screams, snorts, and whistles from deep within, along with pounding of large drums, looking back to Fen.

*"Many double moons ago when I was just a lad, they attacked our settlement. There were thousands of Goblins, armed with their short bows, swords, and clubs. At first, it was just the dull beating of drums for*

*days, weeks on end. Each day louder than the day before. We sent word for help to the Elves, human lands, and the Stone Knights from Kall, knowing the goblins were going to attack, but no one came.*

*After enduring the raids and drums for over a month, they poured out of the mountains, raining down on us from above, but we held our ground, fending them off and battling them. They did not understand the courage of the Dwarven warriors. We drove them back time and time again for three days until we were so outnumbered, we could not survive another rush attack.*

*We stood firm, willing to die before we would be taken into slavery. Every Dwarven man, woman, and child that could swing an axe was ready to die. Then, we heard the low sound of the horns of Kall, blowing over the battlefield. We looked up, and there was the King with 1,500 Dwarven Knights on the ridge on their battle ponies. They charged, and we rallied from our side, rejuvenated by the King's presence. We killed them all, but a high price was paid at the altars of freedom that day. The battlefield was soaked with the blood of my kinfolk as far as the eye could see, but we conquered the day.*

*Our King admonished the human kind after that and the elves too until we met Dalimar. In him, we knew he would never let us down. Then I met Nanek and Raven, and I knew that these were good people immediately."*

Leah leaned over and hugged Fen.

*"We have just begun to trade a bit with the humans again but the elves, curse their souls. They never returned any invitations, and one of our emissaries never returned from Elvin lands."*

Everyone sat in silence as Fen spoke, never interrupting him. They remained that way until Jarrod stood.

*"Fen, I am very sorry about your family, and I am honored to have you with us, truly honored!"*

Jarrod patted Fen on the back, went to get his book while Leah walked with Fen to get his bedroll. She grabbed hers and Jarrod's as well and set Fen up and then theirs. The camp was solemnly quiet after Fen's story.

Jarrod came back into camp, walking by Garren, who leaned to Jarrod quietly, *"Wait till he finds out you're an Elf. Oh, boy!"*

Jarrod sighed, *"Yeah, that should be fun. Let's just try to keep that quiet as long as we can, but if he was listening to me talking to Nanek, he probably knows."*

Garren shook his head yes with a raise of his eyebrows.

They went to sleep while Jarrod practiced, learned, practiced, and learned some more. Finally, he got in his roll with Leah at his side, lying on his back. She rolled over and snuggled close on his chest. Jarrod calmly stroked her hair, kissing her gently on the head before he fell asleep.

# Chapter 23

Garren woke everyone up the next morning while getting everything ready for the trip into the caverns. Jarrod was extremely quiet, looking in the caverns to the deafening silence ahead. They mounted their steeds and headed into the darkness. Fen announced, pulling out a torch.

*"Good thing, I brought some of these."*

He was about to light one when Jarrod abruptly stopped him.

*"Don't light those, we don't want to bring undue attention to ourselves in here. I can see just fine in here."*

Fen looked dumbfounded but then, *"Uh yeah. Good idea, Laddie,"* as he put away the torch.

They headed down further and further till they could hear running water. Just ahead was the river raging wildly, fast heading even further down the mountain. The water came from above and spilled into the cavern floor, racing across the floor to form the river. As they passed it, they were soaked by the spray, but the water felt cold to the touch and not freezing, although as they walked their horses, it became quite chilly.

They walked for what seemed like hours, coming across the bones and skeletons of various creatures spewed across the cavern landscape. It was so dark that they had to watch Jarrod closely in single file, just to make sure no one was lost in the effort.

They came to a fork in the road, and Jarrod looked back, thinking, *"He didn't mention this one. However, he did say follow the river, so that is what we will do."*

The river turned to the right, and so they followed the Right Path and continued for what seemed like hours again. They finally came to the four-direction path. One turned sharply left, one turned sharply right, one veered to the left straight ahead, and the other veered slightly to the right. The river raged, turning to the right and then disappeared underground.

*"This is it. We are almost out, follow the left curve."*

Fen was happy, *"Thank the gods of thunder, we are getting out of this place, hopefully,"* as he sighed with desperation.

They moved further up the path until the road turned steep upward for about another hour, and they could see the opening of the cavern. Jarrod stopped his horse and dismounted, followed by Leah and then the others.

*"Walk slowly to let your eyes get used to the light. We have been down here in the dark for quite a while."*

They all did except for Jarrod whose eyes instantly adjusted. He walked outside, and they were standing on the edge of the Northern Misty mountains, looking out over the plains. He focused in for miles ahead and could see the Gates of Talmiris, about fifteen miles in the distance. He looked to the east and saw a long line of people heading south. He scanned in closer with his Elvin vision and could pick out wagons and carts, all heading to the Southern Pass. All except one; a caravan of carts with a Black Knight escort.

*"That's it,"* Jarrod exclaimed loudly as Leah came out into the light still shielding her eyes.

*"That's what?"*

Jarrod looked back, *"Its Evie's escort back to Idesport City."*

Leah looked as hard as she could, *"Where? I don't see anything but a trail of ants in the distance. Oh, never mind, I forget about your Elvin eyes. Can you see her?"*

Jarrod looked back, *"No, all I see are the carts that the Black Knights had at the trials, escorted by a half dozen or so guards. We must hurry to catch them before they reach the gates."*

The others came out as he finished the sentence. The others regained their sight and saw all the people that were heading down the Southern Pass, and there was no one left heading out of the city. Jarrod pointed to the north,

*"If we ride hard from here, we can lay an ambush on them a couple of miles from the gates. I was only able to salvage four arrows from the goblin encounter, but I should be able to even the odds once we spring our trap. Once they are dead, we will get Evie out of there, and Leah and I alone will enter the city while the rest stays well back. The huge iron gates are open, so it shouldn't be too hard to get in."*

They all reluctantly nodded and went along with the plan for now. They readied their horses and took off across the plains. They arrived exactly as planned, well ahead of the traveling caravan of Knights as the sun was setting across the western skyline. They waited as Jarrod watched the caravan approach in the distance.

*"At their current speed, they should be here within the hour."* Jarrod's eyes were completely elf-like now, looking like sideways diamonds.

Leah walked over to him, *"Jarrod,"* she whispered, *"I have never been more afraid than I am right now, and it is not for myself."*

She kissed him on the cheek, and he smiled at her with a reassuring smile and kissed her back, *"It will be alright. I am confident we can get this done."*

She blinked a sort of relieved quick smile and went back to her position, donning her mask and gloves.

Jarrod whispered, loud enough for all to hear him.

*"Here they come. Wait for my arrows before you attack."* He readied an arrow from an upper pile of rocks as the first cart came into view, then the second and the third. The Black Knights were riding beside the

wagons, and there were five with the three drivers. Jarrod, in an instant, decided to take out the last driver first because there were no Knights back there. Only one cart was covered, and the other two were supply carts. He released the first arrow, hitting the driver right in the head and dropping him there. The horse pulling the last cart stopped, and the Knights didn't even notice he was dead yet. He released again hitting the second driver right in the eye, killing him instantly.

This time the cart stopped, but there were two knights along each side, and they were confused and in chaos as they did not know what just happened. The third arrow released and dropped the third driver, who was standing and looking around. The fourth arrow released and dropped the lead rider off his horse to the ground.

By this time, they figured out what was going on.

*"Attack form,"* rang out as the remaining Black Knights moved to defensive positions from the hillside onslaught.

Garren and Endar charged them, Fen and Leah came from the rear, two knights moved toward Fen and Leah, and two moved to Garren and Endar. Jarrod stood on top of the rock and held his arms out speaking, while Leah and Fen were in the fight of their lives. Fen was on his pony, but he stood on the horse's back, locking his feet in the reins and swung with his battle axe knocking his Knight opponent straight to the ground. He leaped into the air with a summersault maneuver from the pony, landing directly in front of the Knight who had just regained his feet and drew his sword.

Jarrod shouted just as the Knight got to Leah, and with one wave of his hand, the horse reared straight up and threw his knight off. He started another spell as Leah ran by the fallen Black Knight, swinging one of the blades, hitting the Knight in the shoulder blade knocking him off balance. He turned to see Leah had already whipped her horse around and was on her way back. He ran toward her, leaping into the air and swinging his sword at her.

he missed her completely. She raised up, looked back, and twirled the horse for another run at him. But Jarrod had finished and fired a missile attack barrage of greenish darts that pelted the knight from his head to his midsection, causing him to drop his sword. Just as Leah got there and sliced his throat with an underhand forward swing. The Knight went to his knees, clutching his neck as blood spurted out the side. She turned just in time to see him fall forward, dead. Fen was fighting his knight blocking with his axe and punching him. The knight looked like a punching bag and could not hit Fen. Leah was on her way over when Fen suddenly got hit and went straight to the ground, rolling on his belly. Leah shouted the Night Shade scream, which stopped the knight in his tracks to see her coming straight at him. Just then, an arrow came past Leah's shoulder and right by the horse's head, hitting the knight in the upper chest toward his sword arm shoulder. The knight adjusted the sword to his other arm, barely flinching at the arrow hit and swung at Leah, who blocked it on the way by with her blades.

She jumped off her horse to see the knight turn her way. He started to lumber toward her while she readied herself. The Knight stopped and screamed in agony, throwing his arms up and out, releasing his sword to the ground. A white light in the shape of a sword came through his chest as the Knight screamed. He went down face first, and Leah could see Jarrod, who was now holding a blueish white glowing sword. It looked like the sword was made of pure light energy.

They shared a glance, and then Leah rushed to Fen, who was lying motionless on the ground. Jarrod looked for Garren who had just finished off his knight and then moved to help Endar. It looked as though Endar was just playing around with his knight. He was clearly exhausted as Endar hit his sword. It flipped into the air, and then Endar caught it as the Black Knight fell to his knees. Endar had his head in the crossed swords nook.

He screamed *"Ahhhhh,"* and pulled both swords to the side, cutting his head clean off.

*"That was for my friend!"* As he spat on the ground beside him.

Garren got there, and their eyes met, nodding at each other and together they ran back to the others, who were standing with Leah still kneeling over Fen.

*"Fen,"* she shook him, *"Fen, no,"* as she started to cry, gently hitting his chest and yelling no.

Fen's eyes suddenly popped open, and he spoke, *"If you would kindly stop hitting me Lassie, I can get up."*

Leah was ecstatic, and she immediately changed from crying to laughing tears, as Fen sat upright.

She hugged him tightly, *"I thought I lost you, Fen. You scared me!"* As they helped Fen up and all hugged them together.

Garren suddenly remembered frantically, *"Evie!"* He ran to the covered cart with Jarrod not far behind. They slung the cover back, *"Evie!"*

They looked and saw blood on the cage floor, and her pack was there, but Evie was not there. Garren was still frantic, holding his head, *"Dammit, where is she?"*

Jarrod patted him on the shoulder, *"We'll find her and bring her out of there."*

Just then they heard a groan and Garren rushed to a fallen black knight who was barely alive.

*"Where is she?"*

Garren asked harshly. The Black Knight faded, but Garren shook him again, and he awoke with a start speaking softly and slowly gasping his last breaths.

*"You are too late. My master has her now."*

He faded, and Garren shook him again.

*"Took her where? Don't you die on me yet! Where is she?"*

He yelled, shaking him.

Jarrod took Garren by the arm, *"Come on, he's gone! Let's go get her now, Garren!"*

He looked up with tears of rage in his eyes and nodded. Jarrod hugged his brother while he started to sob, looking at the others who all were tearing up too, watching Garren cry.

Leah came over as Jarrod released him, and she hugged him as she sat him down gently patting Garren, crying herself.

*"Shhh, we'll find her. We will get her out of there."*

Garren looked up to her and sniffled badly, embarrassed by his tears.

*"I'm okay, I'm good now. Thanks."*

He looked over to Fen, *"No shame, Laddie, it's called for in this case. We'll get those sorry fang bags, don't you worry."*

They gathered up what they could and went through the cage, looking for anything that would help them figure out where Evie was, but they found nothing. However, Fen found the dead black knights' coins and conveniently took all they had. They piled the bodies in the carts and led the horses to the foothills. They took off the bridles and then let the horses go just as darkness was falling.

They rested for a bit, and Jarrod knew precisely where Evie was, but he did not lead on to Garren that he knew. He formulated the final plan to try to extract Evie out of the Dark City.

*"Leah, do you have the stone?"*

She felt for her pouch, and she pulled it out, *"Yes, it is right here,"* tucking the pouch back in.

*"Alright, good."*

Here is what we do next.

*"Leah and I will sneak into the city, Endar and Garren, put on some Black Knight armor and take up positions on either side of the gates. Watch for our sign to get the hell out of here. Leah will sneak into the Palace, and once we have Evie, we will throw that stone into the window to close the gateway. That will be your sign because when we do that, there will probably*

*be an explosion, which will draw the guards toward the Palace. We will sneak out and pass with all the commotion and chaos and get out of here. We will meet Fen back here as he will be watching the horses and back to the caverns and to Thane. If we go now, there will be little to no guards as everyone will be sleeping. Does anyone have anything to add?"*

They looked around at each other and said nothing.

*"Good then,"* He put his hands to Leah's shoulders, patting them, *"You ready?"*

She lowered her head, *"Yes."*

Jarrod said with caution, *"Good, let's head that way."*

Jarrod started to leave, and Leah pulled him back, *"Wait a second,"* as she planted a kiss on him with Fen turning his head with an air-whistled pucker on his face.

They released, and she smiled, *"For luck!"*

Jarrod went over to Fen, *"If we don't make it back, Fen, just go get help. Don't try to come in there because they will capture you."*

He looked at Leah, who was admiring him lovingly.

*"Fen, you are the most important person here now. One of us has to make it back to warn the world what is coming."*

Fen wasn't happy but reluctantly agreed, *"Alright Laddie, you go now, and I will wait here. See you soon. You be careful in there, and uh…uh, Jarrod?"* Jarrod turned to face Fen who said, *"Don't go getting yerself killed in there. I've, well I,"* Fen choked up.

Jarrod patted him on the shoulders and smiled at him, *"I know Fen. Me too."*

They moved quickly toward the city on foot in twos formations. Sneaking ever closer to the gates. The gates were in sight now with two large watchtowers on either side, and one guard walking the top of the fence above. He was not really paying that much attention to what was going on around them. They ran up under the curve of the gates and under the right-hand tower, while Endar made his way to the left tower directly below it.

Garren gave his brother a pat on the shoulder, *"I will be right here if you need help. Good luck, Jarrod, and by the way, I am so proud to be your brother."*

Jarrod pressed his lips tight together and gave him a quick nod, then looked to Leah, *"Are you ready pretty lady?"*

She anxiously shook her head yes.

*"I am going to be invisible, but I will be right behind you the whole way."*

She looked with amazement in her eyes, thinking, *"I am so having his baby one day!"*

She chuckled at the thought and crept in as Jarrod turned invisible with just a few soft words, wondering what she was laughing at. They snuck down the street, moving silently and hidden from the guards, keeping to the shadows. The city was dark, ominous looking. With no candles in any windows, all the shops and stores were either boarded up or empty, and only some street sconces were lit with small fires burning inside them.

Jarrod was quite glad she was even better at this than he thought. Leah stopped and pressed up against a wall, as a horse with a Knight came around the corner.

He never saw her, and she let out a breath, whispering, *"You still with me?"*

Jarrod whispered right in her ear, *"Yep, right beside you."* She turned and gasped, *"Don't do that, you're freaking me out."*

Jarrod said, *"Uh, sorry."*

Each kept moving from one side of the street to the other side, inching closer and closer to the Palace doors. They made it to the river crossing bridge, which was a stumbling block as two guards were walking back and forth in different directions across the bridge, and then there were two guards at the gate to the entrance. The bridge was high in the middle and low at each end, so the guards would disappear heading down to the ends.

Leah scanned the area, *"I have an idea. Follow me!"*

She waited till guards were at each end and the one closest turned to head back up the bridge, facing away from her. She ran to the side of the bridge, and like an insect climbing a wall, she moved sideways up the bridge, out of sight.

Jarrod watched and thought to himself, *"Seriously? No way am I trying that!"* He just walked straight across the bridge, hugging the side of the bridge staying behind the guard. Then just walked right past them to a pile of rocks on the side of the pass to the gates. The road did a little curve to the gates, so unless all were looking closely, the guards would not be able to see each other or them.

Leah got to the rocks and was looking around for Jarrod whispering again, *"You here?"*

Jarrod sarcastically answered this time, *"Nope, I am across the road."* He could tell Leah liked that even though she didn't say anything, but mumbled the words, *"Smart ass!"*

*"Okay, how are we going to get past those assholes up there?"*

Jarrod whispered back, *"Grab a rock, and when you get over there close, throw it to the left, and see if they chase the noise."*

She shook her head yes, *"Good idea, Jarrod, I can turn you into a thief yet."*

She moved like a cat in the night slinking to a good spot to throw the rock. She didn't know it, but Jarrod had already positioned himself in front of them and was ready to open the door for Leah. She threw the rock, and it bounced loudly over around the corner. Both guards startled, *"What was?"* They looked at each other and didn't move. Jarrod whispered a word that sounded like a breeze when he uttered it, and another noise echoed from the same area. Both guards walked swiftly to the corner, looking for the sound.

Jarrod reached and snatched the door open, as Leah slinked into the Palace with Jarrod closing the door behind her.

***

Garren and Endar slumped to the ground and against the wall as they saw two Black Knights heading their way but into the gates. They rode right past them, never looking their way and into the city. They stopped inside the gates and chatted, but Garren couldn't hear what they were saying. Then they heard them go opposite ways as both Endar and Garren let their breath out with a long sigh of relief.

Garren looked over to Endar as if to say, *"What's taking them so long?"*

Endar raised his hands, slowly telling Garren he didn't know. Garren scratched under his armor because they both had donned one of the dead Black Knights armor, so they could go in if needed. The armor Garren wore was a little bit snug. They both stayed their positions waiting for their sign for entering the city.

# Chapter 24

Leah snuck into the Palace with Jarrod walking close behind. There was strangely no one around, and there were only torches burning low in the halls. They came to an entrance to a great hall. Leah peeked in and saw a throne sitting at the end in the middle. Lavish looking decorations adorned the walls. There were two guards standing at the throne on either side, but no one else was in the hall.

Leah waited for them to look in another direction and passed the doors to the hall. They continued down the hall to a set of stairs that went up and a set that went down. They decided to move down the stairs, and once they got to the bottom, there were left and right passageways and a door in front of them.

Leah whispered quietly, *"Which way?"*

Jarrod thought for a moment placing his hands on the door, *"Through this door, Leah."*

She opened the door, and there were more stairs heading down. The stairs opened into an area that had another set of stairs going down in the middle of the room, and a second door that was cracked open. Just then they heard what sounded like a whip crack and a scream from a woman, coming from the door. There was the sound of loud voices, and then it was quiet again. They knew what direction they had to go, and Jarrod's heart sank as he knew that the scream in agony was from Evie. He directed Leah down the staircase.

*"Once in, wait in the shadows for me, and I will tell you when to get Evie."*

Leah nodded, and they slowly moved to the bottom of the stairs, which opened into a huge room. Leah snuck into the room and moved off to the left, while Jarrod went on in to scan the area. The room was filled with various torture devices and a hole in the center, with a red glowing flame in the center. There was another open door at the far end, and no one was in this room.

Jarrod met Leah by the doorway, and they proceed into the room. Leah moved off to the left as this room was well lit. In the center of the room was a dead tree with gnarled branches. There was a huge chair and chains all along the far wall. Mathis was standing to the left beside the Dark Mage, seated in the lavish chair against the wall. On the right side into the wall were these two dark swirling mist portals, four or five feet in diameter. There was a massive goblin creature that was all contorted looking, with a whip in his hand waiting for instructions. Again, Jarrod's heart sank as he saw Evie in chains on the far-left wall, and her back was striped with cuts from the whip, with blood slowly streaming out from her tattered shirt.

She was slumped forward with her back toward where Jarrod came in from. Her head was lowered, and the only thing holding her up were the chains she was strapped to by her wrists, with her arms above her head. The room was not as big as the other room but was still very large. The Dark Mage looked over to where Jarrod was standing invisible, gazing at him intently from beneath the mask.

*"I feel your presence, my son. You cannot hide from me. Come forth, and let's talk."*

Leah quietly gasped, hearing the words, "My son." Mathis drew his sword, and Leah stayed pressed against the wall, slowly moving toward Evie. The giant goblin orc creature turned toward the door, looking around to see something while clutching his whip and grunting.

The Dark Mage raised a finger, and the door slammed shut, making a loud click.

*"I know you are here, in this room. Come out, or shall I have Slore strike your sister down?"*

The giant creature turned back toward Evie who groaned a bit, raising her head.

Jarrod became visible, *"No, Father. You must stop this now!"*

The Dark Mage laughed, *"There you are, Good, Goooood! You figured out who I am. I have watched your power grow to my pleasure, but I, no, we have just begun. Soon with our powers united, we can rule this world. Join me, give me the ring, and I will release her."*

He stood up, *"Stand against me, and you shall die starting with her!"* As he pointed in Evie's direction.

Jarrod shook his head no, *"No father, I will not join you, but if you release Evie, I will not fight you to the death of us both."*

The Dark Mage snapped his hand up, yelling, *"Silence, enough of this petty talk. You have made your choice. Slore, Kill that traitor!"*

Slore raised the whip to strike, but Jarrod already had the word ready and yelled.

*"Push,"* thrusting his hands at the monster orc.

The beast flew across the room, slamming headfirst against the wall, bounced off, and knocked Mathis to the ground, sprawling limply on top of him. The mage raised his hands toward Jarrod and started to speak, calling forth a black swirling ball.

*"Leah, Now! Get Evie,"* as he readied himself for the blast. Leah sprung out fast as a cheetah and got to Evie telling her, *"Shhh, I'm here, Evie. My name is Leah, and we are getting you out of here."*

She worked on the locks as Jarrod let out another blast of light toward the mage. At the same time, he released the energy bolt. The two bolts collided together and ricocheted off each other and the walls. They released again at each other, this time holding the energy. The light and dark energies blasted together, moving closer to Jarrod as he struggled to hold it back, and then he concentrated harder, causing his whole body to start to float in the air. He leaned forward, pushing it back toward the black mage. The two blasts dissipated simultaneously, and Jarrod floated back to the ground with both arms out. The black mage was surprised at the power of Jarrod.

*"My my, you have grown in strength."* Tanin laughed, *"So much the better. Think of it, son, the power together we could wield and build a stronger, better world than this place now."*

Leah was still working on the chains as Mathis got out from under the heavy limp beast. He rushed over to where Leah was as she unclasped the last chain and quickly moved Evie out of the way of his sword swing, slinging her to the floor. Mathis looked at Leah with rage, pointing his sword at her, *"Are you ready to die, little girl?"*

Leah looked at him with a defiant smirk, pulling out her triple blades, twirling them, and hissing at Mathis, *"That is why I brought these."*

She leaped to the attack, and they were battling. Leah moved so fast that Mathis could barely keep up with her attacks and movements, but still he was able to block and parry well. No matter what he tried, Mathis couldn't hit her as their struggle ranged all the way to the backside of the room.

At the same time, Jarrod shook his head, *"No, the world you want is evil and destruction. I want no part of it, Father."*

The mage was furious and yelled, *"You think I want to destroy everything? What purpose would that serve if there was no one left to rule? No one to build my cities, no one to give us all the gold and jewels in the world. We could afford to feed, clothe, and educate them to serve us, as their masters."*

Jarrod laughed, listening to the struggle behind him, knowing that Leah could hold her own against Mathis, *"That sounds like a wonderful plan, but you have forgotten one thing."*

The mage mused back with a laugh, *"What is that? Name it son, and it shall be yours."*

Jarrod thrust his hands forward again, saying, *"Freedom!"* as he threw a bolt of lightning at the Mage, who threw up his hands and blocked the bolt.

The mage slung one hand toward Jarrod, and it picked him off the ground slowly and then hurled him at high speed toward the left wall. Jarrod stopped the motion so fast, like a swift-moving horse slamming to a stop just inches from the wall. The force was so strong, it hurled back at the caster, which knocked him off his feet. He slammed the table, enraged and used it to help himself up as Jarrod floated back down to the ground.

The two faced off again, as they each stared in a fury. They both spoke at the same time, sending flames at each other. The flames collided together with an explosion that shook the walls. Jarrod brought forth another white energy bolt, hitting the mage square in the chest that flung him backward off balance. With a raged howl, the mage leaped forward, drawing his sword to attack Jarrod. He called forth his white glowing energy sword just as the Mage swung, and their blades erupted with flying sparks showering the room as they fought.

Leah dodged, blocked, and leaped over Mathis, stabbing a thrust with both triple blades into his back, sending him forward and into the wall. It was a solid armor shot that did not penetrate. He bounced off the wall to see Leah crouching at the ready with one hand overhead and the other down low, with both triple blades pointing at Mathis. Mathis was enraged and rushed flinging her backward, knocking one of the blades from her hand across the floor. She flipped the blade to her free hand and waved it at Mathis, who attacked again with an overhand swing. She dodged the swing and leaped through the air over Mathis, landing behind him. She went for the kill shot, but Mathis quickly turned, blocked the savage strike, knocking the other blade from her hand to the floor.

He grabbed her by the throat and pulled her to him, looking gleefully into her eyes while slowly raising his sword to impale her in the heart. Leah kicked and struggled, feeling the panic that her end was near. She could not speak as she was holding his arm with both hands as he was squeezing the life from her. He slowly lifted her off the ground into a position to drop her onto his sword for the gleeful kill when suddenly, he released her with his eyes opening wide, dropping his sword to the ground. Leah fell to the ground as he faltered to his knees and turned around.

Leah was regaining her breath, as she saw one of the triple blades sticking out of Mathis' back.

Mathis faintly spoke, *"Evie?"* He reached for her as she stood over him with a determined enraged look. Evie could see the evil leave his body in a dissipated mist. Their eyes met, and Evie knew it was the real Mathis, and her rage turned to instant sadness. His hand fell limp, and he crashed face-first, releasing his last breath.

*"Oh, Mathis! I am so sorry!"* Evie screeched out with tears flowing.

Leah stood, and Evie looked at her, confused, and still crying.

*"Thank you, Evie. Let's give Jarrod a hand and get out of here."*

She pulled the blade from Mathis' back and picked up her other blade as well. Evie staggered again and fell. Leah helped her to the old tree in the center of the room. She sat her up with her back against the stone wall around the tree and smiled.

*"Wait here, I will be back in a few seconds to get you."* She winked at Evie and rushed to Jarrod's side.

Leah rushed forward to move attention off Jarrod. The dark mage blocked her attempt and threw his free hand toward Jarrod, knocking him backwards flat on his back. Leah and the mage were in an acrobatic death dance as Jarrod struggled to get back up, still holding his sword.

Leah got caught with a side punch from the mage that knocked her to the ground, flinging her mask off. She immediately flipped to her feet as the mage backed up, she spat the blood out of her mouth with a quick wipe and a fearsome smile.

He took off his helmet and stared at Jarrod, who was just now back on his feet.

Jarrod stared back at his father, enraged, when the Mage's face began to change.

Jarrod's eyes opened wide, *"Valence."*

The mage laughed, *"Yes, my master Tanin imbued me with enormous power and made me invincible. You cannot kill me."*

Jarrod flashed over to Leah and back over to the Mage, who was raising both his hands, dropping his sword and his helmet to the floor. He was starting to shimmer with a black haze, and Jarrod rushed him.

Valence caught him, and they started to struggle backward as Jarrod pushed him with all his might. He pulled one arm free and spoke, the door that was slammed shut earlier flung open, and he attacked Valence again, who was still trying to get the spell out while struggling with Jarrod.

Jarrod screamed out as he shoved Valence towards the wall, *"Ahhhhh!"*

With all his strength, he pushed the mage back in between the swirling hazed portals.

*"Now, Leah. Throw the stone, now!"*

Leah struggled, dropping her blades and pulling the pouch. She saw Jarrod flash a light into Valence from his eyes that blinded the mage and stopped him from speaking.

Leah found the stone and hesitated with her hand in the air. She looked at Jarrod, who turned and smiled at her with a nod and mouthing, *"I love you."* As he struggled to hold Valence steady.

She closed her eyes and threw the stone into the portal. The portal turned light in color, and then a vast vacuum sounded, as the portal turned into a horizontal funnel into the wall. Valence's eyes opened wide as he was being sucked into the portal, trying to free himself from the powerful vacuum. He clawed and grasped at the edges to keep from entering.

Jarrod pushed him again with all his might, and Valence was sucked into the portal with an echoed scream as he went.

Jarrod managed to pull himself away but was sliding back to the hole. He looked over to Leah, who was standing there breathing hard, trying to withstand the pull from the portal herself, as it was getting smaller and smaller. Jarrod tried to free himself completely, but a hand reached out and grabbed him, pulling him closer into the portal. Leah rushed to him and grabbed his other arm with both her hands, as she was sliding toward the portal pulling with all her might.

*"No, Jarrod. No!"*

Jarrod flashed at Leah in desperation but then, calmly and without regard.

*"Let me go, Leah. It's too strong, get out of here now!"*

Leah started to cry, yelling at Jarrod, *"No, I won't let you go."*

While she held on, they were sliding closer to the entrance, and Jarrod was almost halfway in. Jarrod smiled as he reached over and pried her hands off but holding both her hands tight.

*"Go now,"* as he spoke again.

Leah flew backward, landing on her back near the tree as he released her. Jarrod flew into the portal and was gone. Leah screamed as she lowered her head into her hands and cried out loud.

*"No, Jarrod,"* just as both portals closed all the way shut, and the vacuum stopped.

Evie had made her way to Leah and was helping her up as her sobbing tears were flowing so hard she was blinded. They looked back at the wall hearing blades crash together and saw flashes of light. They could see the shadow of Jarrod, still fighting the mage on the wall.

The ground started to shake, lightly at first, and then so much that the walls and ceiling began to crack and break apart.

Evie yelled, *"Come on, we got to go."*

Leah helped Evie as she grabbed her weapons on the way out. They struggled up the stairs, dodging stones falling from the ceiling and walls, crumbling around them. They made it to the top, just as the stairs crumbled to the bottom. The girls limped down the passage, as the walls were crumbling faster like they had a fierce mission to swallow them, following quickly behind while Leah held Evie up with her arm over her shoulder, and Leah had her around the waist. They finally made it past the grand hall entrance, where two black knights saw the girls and rushed them. The ceiling fell on them and crushed them instantly.

They ran down the last passage to see two more black knights running toward them. Leah stopped with Evie's arm over her shoulder, looking back and then trying to decide what to do. The two came into the light, they were Garren and Endar. Leah was clearly relieved as Evie screamed in joy. Garren ran up to them, *"Evie!"* touching her face as she found new strength and latched on with tears of joy as they kissed each other.

He looked at Leah while holding on to Eve.

*"Where is Jarrod?"* She started to cry again, tears flowed harder when Endar came to her side, hugging her.

*"We got to get out of here,"* as walls started to crack, and the ground started to shake.

Garren picked Evie up and carried her like she was just a sack of flour cradled in his arms. Running full speed, they headed out into the street and ran to the river bridge where there were two guards. They stopped as Endar and Leah moved ahead of Garren. Endar pulled his sword, and Leah brandished her blades flipping them. Suddenly, the entire Palace started to crumble, and the two guards turned and ran.

Leah looked back at Endar, *"Well, that was easy."*

Endar laughed, *"Let's go!"*

They headed for the main gates, looking down the path to see Fen heading for the gates with the horses. It still being dark out there, they were pretty much unseen, and now with the Palace crumbling, the city was completely deserted. They got on their horses, and Evie latched on to Garren holding him tight, kissing him every chance she got as they sprinted to the clearing by the rocks to rest.

The mood in the clearing was saddened with sniffles and crying with their heads down. Garren stepped up and quietly asked Leah what happened in the castle. She started to talk but couldn't at this moment because her sobs would not let her. The others sat around her, and Garren sat beside Evie, he held her while she drank some water.

Evie looked at him with tears in her eyes, *"I didn't even get to spend time with him as my real brother, but I knew in my heart, you both would come for me, Garren."* Garren held her tighter, tearing up but choking them back.

*"I love you, Evie!"* They kissed again.

Fen was crying too, and even Endar was saddened to the point of holding back tears. Leah was sobbing, not able to hold anything back until she finally choked back the tears to start talking.

*"We made it to the room where the black mage was,"* she told them about the battle and how it raged on. Evie saved her from being killed by Mathis, and Jarrod saved them all. The black mage talked like he was Jarrod's father, but he really wasn't. It was Valence whose face was Jarrod's father, Tanin. She told them how he pushed him to the wall, she threw the stone into the hole, and it sucked Valence in. But just as Jarrod was breaking free of the pulling force, Valence reached out and pulled him in. I ran to Jarrod with both hands trying to pull him back out, but he reached and pried my hands off. He was pulled in too. I watched as the gateway closed with a flash of light. Evie and I raced out of there! She started to cry again.

*"And I killed him!"*

She fell back tears streaming down her face. Evie raced to her side and held her tight.

*"No, you didn't, I was there. He sacrificed himself to save you and me, all of us."*

Leah looked up with tears flowing, *"But if I hadn't thrown the stone, he would still be here."*

Evie spoke back with reassurance, *"If you hadn't thrown the stone, we would all be dead by now."*

They hugged and cried together for their loss.

Endar asked if he could be so bold to say something.

*"Yes, please do. Yes, yes, and yes. You are our family too, and you have the right to say what you want."*

Endar smiled and started, *"I have not known the kind of love I have seen here. I thought I was a part of something big with my comrades and friends, but now I know I was wrong, this is bigger, this is what family is. That is why we fight, and Jarrod's loss has made me become a better Knight, no, a better man. I want to thank you all for allowing me to be a part of this. I know we all mourn his loss, but this is not over yet, we need to get going soon because I want to experience the love you share with a special someone, one day."*

Garren stood up, *"Endar is right, it will be dawn soon, and we need to make our way back through the caverns and to Thane where we can help Leah get back on her feet with Boream."*

Leah looked up and sighed, *"Yes, and thank you. The amount of time I spent with Jarrod was enough to fill me with a lifetime of wonderful memories. I loved him more than anything and wish it would have been me instead, so I wouldn't have to suffer his loss. I know that sounds selfish, but I don't care because I know he loved me too, and we loved our time together. He warned me that he might not make it and even asked me when we kissed last if that was our last kiss, knowing that it was. Jarrod wouldn't want us to sit around feeling sorry for ourselves, so I say, let's get back to our lives and honor his memory with our own thoughts, our own love we have for him."*

Fen spoke with choked words, *"Well said, Lassie!"*

Evie spoke, holding Garren tight, *"I hear you girl, and I know exactly how you feel."* Garren gave her a kiss and smiled at her. They got up and packed things to be at the caverns by morning.

# Chapter 25

They were packing their horses as Leah was tending to Evie's wounds, bandaging her back and arms. Evie was feeling stronger now but was not a hundred percent.

*"Let's get you into something a little more appropriate. I am a little bit bigger than you, but this should do just fine."*

Leah went to the pack horse and pulled another leather armored suit, consisting of padded leather pants and a woman's tight leather shirt with a padded front and back leather breastplate and long leather boots. She pulled a knife and a woman's long sword with a belt and sheath.

*"Here, let's fix your hair first. You look like a mess!"*

She poured a whole leather flask of water over her head and rubbed and poured, rubbing some more to get the dried blood out. Evie combed the kinks out and looked at Leah.

*"That's better. Here, try these on."*

Evie took the leather clothes and stripped, putting everything on. Leah helped Evie with the breastplate and then turned her around, studying, holding her fingers on her chin.

*"Um, not bad. Oh here, put these on too."*

She handed her the boots and leather sleeves with little armored platelets all the way to the shoulder. Then helped her put on the leather hand and wrist straps, laced snugly around her thumb, inner hand, and up to the sleeves.

*"Now let me look at you,"* as she turned Evie around.

She whistled at Evie, *"Wow Evie, you sure fill that out much better than me. You look fantastic and fierce at the same time."*

Evie smiled at Leah, *"You think Garren will notice?"* Leah raised her eyebrow, *"If he doesn't, I will bust him in the mouth for being stupid!"*

They both laughed and headed back together. Evie told her she really liked the outfit even better than her custom fit black armor, swearing never to wear it again. They headed back to where the guys were.

*"Now, you wait here till I announce you. We will have a little fun with them."*

Evie and Leah chuckled as Leah walked into the camp alone. Leah came into the light as the sun was starting to rise from the east.

*"Guys?"*

They all stopped what they were doing and gathered around as Leah announced.

*"I want to introduce you to, Evie, The Warrior Princess!"*

Evie strutted in with her outfit as all jaws dropped open. Garren staggered, and Endar helped steady him, *"Easy, big guy!"*

Fen fell straight back with a huge clap of his hands and a laugh with a, *"How do you do,"* whistle!

Evie was smiling ear to ear, flipped her hair, and turned serious with a piercing look.

*"I'm back guys, ready for the next fight,"* as she drew her sword and flipped it into the air, catching it with her other hand and sheathing it all in the same motion.

Leah clapped her hands, *"Awesome!"*

The guys joined in the clapping as well with *"Welcome back, Eve,"* and a *"YAAASSS"* from Fen.

Garren walked up to her almost speechless as the clapping drew to a halt, *"So glad you are alright and glad to have you back in arms ready to fight. By the way, you look terrific in that outfit."*

He leaned down, and they kissed to the *"Ohhhhs Ahhhhs"* from the watching crowd. Leah looked on with quiet satisfaction with a "mission accomplished" look.

Endar spoke with haste, *"Okay, break it up, you two, we have to get going."*

Evie and Garren laughed, kissed one more quick time, and then went to the horses. Garren helped Evie up on Jarrod's horse, adjusting the fitness for her, then hopped on his horse, looking back at her with a smile.

They started walking their horses to the southern path across the plains to get to the caverns, reaching it after about a thirty-minute jog. They quickened the pace to trotting, not really in any hurry now to get back to the city, even though they all were a little anxious to get back.

They traveled at this pace for about an hour, when Fen interrupted.

*"Uh Lads, Lasses? You hear that?"*

Garren stopped the party, and they listened, far to the south was the low rumble of drums in the distance.

Fen fessed up quickly, *"Uh, that is not good. You remember those drums I was telling you about, right before them foul creatures spilled out of the mountains?"*

Everyone nodded except for Eve, who was confused but listened intently.

*"Well, there you go, they are gathering for an attack, and we are right in their way."*

Garren turned his horse to the east, *"Well, we cannot go that way. Look at that huge dust cloud marching this way."*

They all looked, and as far as they could see, it was dust.

Endar spoke up as well, *"Ummm, look to the west, the same thing to the west. Even if we rode back to the ruined city, we have no way to stop them from entering Idesport City."*

Garren looked up, *"Maybe not, but we could close the gates of Talmiris and stop up the hole with their dead when they do burst through."*

Fen shook his head, *"No Laddie, it won't work. Those critters climb stone walls like lizards. With no arrows to hold them at bay, we wouldn't last an hour."*

Garren looked back, bleakly, *"Head straight north into the mountains toward your homeland, Fen?"*

Leah spoke with solemnness, *"I don't think so, look heading south now."*

The same trek of dust storm heading their way from the north.

Garren sighed, "Well, this is a bleak turn of events."

The northern dust storm was already over the top of the largest hill, their ugly black shapes could already be seen. Garren looked to the east, west, and south with the same results. Thousands of Fen's critters from all directions were headed straight for them. Garren dismounted and drew his sword, the others did as well.

Evie was curious as she dismounted, *"Why here on these plains? How did they know we were here?"*

Fen walked over, speaking, *"Their minds are weak and easily overcome by evil voices. Something told them to come here, probably to take over Idesport City now that it is in ruins."*

Evie glanced around, *"No, Fen. I think it is because of me."*

Garren shouted back, *"What? Why are they after you?"*

Evie looked back to all, *"because Jarrod was my brother, and I am half-Elf as well. My father thinks if he can get me, he may have a way back into the Elf lands and get what he is after."*

Garren grimly paused right at Evie, *"And that is what?"*

Evie answered, *"The rest of the ring of power is somewhere in the Elvin lands."*

Fen came to her side, *"I think those buggers will have a better idea once they see me."*

Endar drew his sword, and Leah drew her blades, *"They are getting closer guys! What are we doing?"*

Garren hugged Evie, *"I am sorry, love. I wanted to save you from this, but it looks like we will all perish right here."*

Evie kissed Garren and drew her sword.

*"I would rather die beside you, my love, and I will fight till my last breath."*

Garren raised his sword, *"I am sorry, my friends, to say we come this far only to die right here, but if we must die, then I would rather do it here and now with the best friends I have ever known."*

They formed a hugging circle, and each hugged the other, and Fen pulled his battle axe.

*"Bring em to my axe. Let's show these foul beasts what this family is made of."*

They formed a small ring releasing the horses after setting up shields for an arrow attack. The creatures were in sight now, and they slowed their march to a crawl. They could start to hear them snarling, and their clicking noises as the creatures met from all sides.

There were thousands of them, too many to count as they closed within a fifty-yard circle around the five of them, now thirty yards, then, twenty, they stopped when one of them yelled out. There was the one riding a giant wolf, and he was holding something in his hand that was covered by a cloth, and he came forward and dismounted. He was a big Goblin-looking creature with fanged teeth.

The others snarled and coughed under their helmets, as the big Orc walked within twenty feet of Garren and set the covered item down. He pulled the cloth off to reveal a giant black swirling orb that floated up off the ground eye level to the Orc and Garren. The Orb started to speak.

*"Bring forth my daughter, and you shall go free."*

Evie started to move forward, but Leah stopped her shaking her head no.

*"But he will free you if I go with them."*

Leah spoke emphatically, *"No, he will not, He is a liar. He will take you and then kill us anyway, so you stay put!"*

*"We will not give her to you, Tanin. We will all die right here before we hand her over."*

The speaking orb laughed with a dark and evil tone.

*"Be reasonable, son of Hardin, you don't want to die here. I will kill all of you and take her anyway. Either way, I win. Give her to me and end this now."*

A vision of home flashed into all their minds, taking them to their homelands and loved ones. Fen smiled seeing a massive table with barrels of brew and roasted pork, Endar saw his sister and his brother playing in the grass while he chased them with a pole prodding them back to the picnic, Leah saw Broeam and the stables cooking for passers-by and enjoying meeting new friends, Garren saw his friends at the school and all those at the Inn. The visions faded, and they awoke to see the horror all around them again.

Fen growled, and Leah gritted her teeth. Endar was ready, and Garren looked over to Evie, *"You ready?"*

Evie scrunched her eyebrows and crouched low, ready to spring.

*"See how much you miss your homes and families? I can return all of that if you just give me the girl."*

Evie shouted, *"No, Father. I would rather die here with my friends than be in your evil presence."*

All looked at her and nodded her way. Garren told them in a low voice,

*"Fen and I will be up front, Endar, Evie, and Leah stay at our backs and keep them off us. Don't get separated, and we will hack our way through and run for the hills."*

Fen said sarcastically, *"Nice plan, Lad, but have you noticed how many are there?"*

They all chuckled as the orb spoke again, *"Insolent girl! I shall beat the insolence out of you. Attack! And bring me the blonde girl, alive! Kill the rest of them."*

The creatures started to close in as the big orc snatched the orb out of the air, covered it, and ran it to the wolf stuffing it in a pack.

*"Endar, protect Evie back there."*

Endar shouted back, *"I got her!"*

The front from the south creatures charged. Three hit the ground from one swing by Garren. Fen was hacking and slashing everything near. Goblins and orcs alike were falling three to four at a time. One grabbed Evie's arm as she was attacking and pulled at her. Endar cut his arm clean off and continued. Leah was moving fast, dodging, and slashing with her triple blades. In just a few short minutes of the battle, they were all covered in greenish orc and goblin goo blood.

The creatures' major disadvantage was that there were so many of them they could only close in a few at a time, and Garren's gang was hacking them to pieces, making a good show for only the five of them. The creatures backed off, stopping the slow advance of the pile through the hills, and they regrouped while the little band was watching and waiting for the next charge. The horses had already run off, so they were on foot alone on the plains, surrounded by an army of orcs and goblins.

The beasts backed off some more, and Garren stopped, *"What are they doing?"* as they heard thunderous footsteps coming from the southern section.

Fen gasped, *"Uh oh people, they have them, some Stone Orcs. They can only be killed by bashing, swords have no effect. Use the flat of your swords, or your fists or kicking."*

He finished as there was a roar from the orcs, and they were jumping up and down with glee. They came into view, and there were five 10 feet tall hulking giants, carrying stone clubs. The creatures gave them room as they moved in to attack. They swung as they moved in on them, two from the front, one on each side, and one to the rear. There was enough room to maneuver as the creatures stayed far enough back from their wild swings. The two in front attacked Garren and Fen at the same time. Garren sheathed his weapon and fought hand to hand. The beast swung at Garren, who ducked the blow, then back swung, Garren caught his arm, and he used the creature's own momentum to throw him to the ground. He was on him, pounding him with his knees on the stone chest. The beast rolled Garren off, who took the club out of his hands, smashing the creature in the head shattering it.

Fen was dodging and moving to the side with the creature missing every blow. The stone orc made a mistake and moved too close to Fen. Fen grabbed him by the head and head-butted him so hard the stone giant's head shattered. Fen picked up the club too, and both went to work on the other three with Endar dispatching his with a foot kick to the chest that crumbled the beast. The stone beasts were now all dead to the angry grunts, snarls, clicks, and whistles of the orcs.

It seemed they were banding for another attack. Garren's warriors were nearly exhausted now with hands on their knees, breathing hard. They rearmed themselves and readied for the next rushing attack. Evie and Leah were ready with Endar. Fen was growling and foaming at the mouth at the orcs and goblins. They saw long poles walking up through the crowd with blades at the ends. These were spears heading their way.

*"Watch out, they are bringing spears up."*

*"Grrreattte!"* said Leah sarcastically.

Endar voiced in the same manner, *"Yeah, thanks for the warning."*

Fen chimed in with a, *"This should be fun!"*

They brought the long spears up and lowered them within a few feet of them. The creatures were bouncing up and down with joy.

Fen calmly spoke, *"They seem to be very happy. Let's make them regret this day!"*

Evie had an idea, *"Guys, watch this."*

She moved closer, and the spears moved out of her way.

*"They can't kill me."*

Evie looked back at the group with a kind of evil looking smile. She swung her sword, chopping the tips off three spears, and they dropped to the ground with three more taking their place.

Fen glanced at Garren with shock, *"Hmm, that was a little bit dark!"*

Garren shouted, *"Start chopping all, Eve, stay between Leah and Endar."*

Fen and Garren started swinging wildly, chopping the ends off, while the beasts tried to impale them with the spears. Fen sidestepped a spear, and it hit Endar in the shoulder who screamed in pain as the orc pulled the spear out. Endar kept swinging, even though injured.

Fen was struck in the shoulder, "Uhhh" as he chopped it and pulled the spear out.

They kept swinging, and Leah got hit in the leg, but she never faltered. It was a flesh wound, but still painful. Then Garren was run through in his arm. He pulled his arm so hard that the creature went flying. Garren broke the spear and pulled it through the rest of the way, screaming till it was out with Endar and Fen guarding him, chopping the spears.

The spears lifted, and they backed away again. Goblin archers appeared in front of them as they peered in desperation.

Garren yelled out, *"Archers, bring the shields."* Just as the goblin archers released. Garren and Endar went into arrow defense mode, knocking and smashing, but there were too many. Leah screamed as she went down on one knee with an arrow in the shoulder. Evie rushed to her side and was hit in the calf, knocking her down with a scream of pain. Howls and screeches of joy came from the creatures.

Fen looked like a pin cushion, but his armor held, except for an arrow in his right chest. He stood in defiance, holding that one arrow but could barely breathe. Garren and Endar were both hit in the legs and shoulder. Garren could no longer raise his sword without extreme pain. Garren was in desperation mode, looking on as the creatures started to move toward Evie. Suddenly there was a sound from the north that sounded like thunder, and the ground was shaking.

The band of five were just about finished with all of them wounded, including Evie. The spears raised, archers lowered, and the creatures backed off to gather themselves again, looking to the North. Fen stood up, and Evie limped to help Garren. Endar and Leah stood over them on their guard, breathing in huge breaths of air.

Fen looked to the North and gasped with glee. He pointed.

*"Look, on top of the ridge."*

It was a lone rider on a white horse. He raised his weapon sideways, and it shined like the bright spot of the sun, just as another shorter rider showed up. *"King Wargton!"*

Fen yelled with glee, *"Dalimar!"*

Just then the entire Dwarven Knight kingdom was on the ridge. Fen held his battle axe in the air, *"Ahhhhhhhh"* The others rose as the southern side of the creatures broke in a run to the western flank, not even paying them any mind. Some got too close running, but Endar and Fen dispatched them as they passed.

The low sound of the Horns of Kall sounded with Fen jumping up and down. The Dwarven knights were still badly outnumbered by at least five to one.

Leah saw a flash and looked to the west.

*"What is that heading this way?"*

There was a dot in the sky moving at high speed. They all looked as Garren rose uncertainly.

They squinted to see better, as the figure started to emerge, Garren shuttered with despair.

*"I think that it is a dragon. We got to move folks."*

Fen spoke with regard, *"Now there's a sight you don't see every day."*

They started to move, limping, and helping each other as the dragon was gaining on them. Leah's leg was hurt more than she thought, and she hit the ground.

Garren couldn't even move one arm anymore, and Endar was in the same boat with his arm, leg, and shoulder.

Fen could move, but he was starting to bleed internally as he coughed up blood.

The figure was now fully visible, and there was a rider on top of the dragon. The rider screamed down at them as he passed over, Leah jumped up because it was the Night Shade battle cry. She screamed it back, and they all yelled as the Dragon roared overhead with a loud dragon growl. Garren gasped,

*"Knight of the Wind!"*

Then they saw him, Jarrod held up his sword and leaned over the slowing dragon, yelling, *"Leah! All to the glory."*

Evie and Leah broke into tears of joy hugging each other, Leah screamed, *"He's alive, he is alive!"* with tears rolling down her face.

The Dragon turned sharply with another thunderous roar and dusted one whole side with a cone of frost that froze the creatures in their tracks. Jarrod called forth a stream of fire at the same time, blasting into the orcs on the western side.

Goblins shot arrows at the dragon and its rider, but they just bounced off as another blast of fireballs from the north smashed into the center of the creatures, right when the Stone Knights from Kall got there. The five wounded warriors could only watch the carnage as the dragon blasted another freezing cone into the far western section, freezing them so fast that some exploded in their places. Many started to flee south for the mountains, while the dragon stopped in midair with its tail hanging to the ground and beat his wings with such a wind force that everything in hundreds of yards rolled across the land. The dust cloud from the wind blast was choking to the Orcs as they were sent fleeing, making them easy targets.

Just then, the white horse, Light-Shadow ran up to them and stopped raising in the air with its rider. He jumped off and moved over to them.

Fen gasped again, *"Dalimar. We thought you were dead."*

Dalimar smiled ear to ear as Fen coughed up more blood. *"You just stay quiet, my old friend. We will have you back in a jiffy. Everyone else okay? The Dwarven physicians will be here in a minute!"*

He stood up and greeted Garren.

*"I think so, Dalimar. So glad you could make it to the party."*

Fen sat up, *"Late as usual, but better late than never."*

He laughed and coughed some more, making everyone laugh.

*"And you must be Evie?"*

She gladly said, *"Yes, and so happy to meet you,"* Evie continued with a hug for Dalimar.

*"This is Leah,"* who had her hand over her mouth and was still crying tears of joy, watching Jarrod and the Dragon attack again and again.

*"Nice to see you again, Raven,"* Dalimar said softly reaching to hug her.

*"Sorry about Nanek. He was a dear friend!"*

She smiled and still couldn't speak but buried herself in the hug.

*"I am Endar, Master Dalimar. Great to see you again."* Endar introduced himself.

*"I know who you are, and so glad you could join us."*

Dalimar turned and shook his hand with arm clutched together, just in time to see the dragon start to land. Jarrod hopped down, petting the dragon.

He saw Leah and immediately ran toward her while she limped a run toward him. Catching her, he lifted her off the ground with a kiss, squeezing her tight as she just kept saying in between kisses, *"I love you, I love you,"* over and over again, *"I thought I had lost you!"*

All he could keep saying was, *"I love you, and never!"*

Jarrod finally set her down, and they touched foreheads, looking into each other's eyes.

*"No more last kisses, eh? You okay?"* Leah nodded with sheer happiness.

Leah smiled as they embraced again. He released her and walked to the group holding Leah's hand, who were all hurting and in pain. The Dwarven physicians were working on the group as he greeted each one until he got to Evie. She beamed at him.

*"Brother?"* as she latched a hold with a hug and kiss on the cheek. He looked at her, deeply straight in the eyes.

*"You alright, Evie?"*

With her nodding yes.

*"Nice to see you, my sister, for real, instead of just in my visions. I was not sure this day would come, but I am glad it did."*

Evie was so happy to see him.

*"Jarrod, we thought you were gone, and when we saw you flying on that dragon, we just fell in relief. Thank you for rescuing me. I would have died if you and the group had not come."*

Jarrod smiled at her as he turned back to Leah. With a wink and flashing a smile, he let her go and walked over to Dalimar, pointing at him.

*"You, Mr., I saw you die."*

Dalimar laughed uncontrollably.

*"You saw exactly what I wanted you to see. I knew that Tanin was after you and that ring, so I had to*

*remove all doubt. Also, I got ambushed and was losing strength, so I went to the only place I knew where I could regain my strength. To my friends in Kall and the King. I told them of the peril, and they nursed me back to health. We marched forward to help in any way we could at the City, and that's when we saw all these beasts and followed them right to you. Ahh, Jarrod, my young friend, you have the control of the ring, and you have grown your power well. How did you find the dragon? He was a quite a surprise, sir knight! You have learned more than I even thought that you would."*

Dalimar stopped and turned serious.

*"But I just need to ask you something. Did you really have to blow up an entire city?"*

The others burst into laughter as Dalimar smiled and so did Jarrod, as they embraced a hug.

*"Now, what about this Dragon, that was impressive?"*

Jarrod looked back at the dragon with pride, *"I will explain that another day,"* and he went over to Leah to look after her wounds and helped the others.

Just then, King Wargdon walked up.

*"Where's Fen?"*

Fen saw him coming toward him and tried to get up, *"No stay put, stay put. Good to see you Fen. Here, drink this, made it me-self."*

Fen took the leather flask and slammed a sip down.

*"Ahhh, that is just what I needed. Wine from the mountain home."*

Wargdon laughed, watching Fen.

*"That was quite a show you put on here, I must say. The most blanket sets of courage I have ever witnessed. Five against five thousand, now that's a tale to remember."*

They all smiled and joked as Evie sat by Garren, kissing him on the cheek. They kissed each other.

Jarrod and Leah walked over to the dragon, who was sitting up. The dragon bowed to her,

*"Hello, Madam Leah, I have heard a lot about you from my new friend here. All he could think of was getting to you and your friends."*

Leah was amazed and laughed.

*"He talks. Oh, how wonderful!"*

The dragon shook his head proudly and lowered so she could pet his neck. He moved his head and turned so she could scratch his head.

*"Ahh, that feels good. Thank you, I can never reach there,"* the dragon proclaimed with relief.

Leah laughed, *"He is magnificent, Jarrod."*

Jarrod answered, *"Yes, he is, and he saved my life."*

The dragon boasted back, *"And you set me free."*

Leah leaned to Jarrod, *"How?"*

*"I will tell you about it sometime, but let's get back to the others for now. I just wanted you to meet Shianthor, the Silver Dragon. We have to help him get home later."* Jarrod informed.

They walked back to the others as some dwarves brought up the horses and even found their packhorse, the physicians were still caring for all in the group. The sun was low in the sky, and Dalimar stood on the ridge with the six new family members arm in arm; Endar, Leah, Jarrod, Evie, Garren, and Fen with the King next to Dalimar, with Yshanall's double moons, starting to rise from the east.

*"Look to the north. See the dark clouds looming north of the city, like a slow crawling dark monster in the skyscape? That is Tanin, still trying to bring Krometh back from Ovesgard. This is just the beginning, he will not stop that easy, and now he is angry, he will retaliate swiftly. But with his apprentice gone, he will be more desperate to find a replacement."*

He quickly glanced to Jarrod and back to the dark clouds. No one saw his glance except for Jarrod himself as they all stared wondering about the future.

Dalimar turned to the group, *"We must prepare the world for what is coming!"*

## The End

# KNIGHTS OF THE WIND

www.ingramcontent.com/pod-product-compliance
Lightning Source LLC
Chambersburg PA
CBHW031020030726

47497CB00004B/936